ADVANCE PRAISE FOR

# BLACK RAIN

"*Black Rain* sizzles with tension and twists that both entertain and magnetize. The plot envelops the reader into a brilliantly conceived world, full of strange and amazing things. Graham Brown is an exciting new talent, a writer we're going to be hearing a lot from in the years ahead. I can't wait."

—Steve Berry, *New York Times* bestselling author of *The Paris Vendetta*

"*Black Rain* is an adventure that's not only a terrific read but is smart, intelligent, and poised to shake up the whole thriller community. Every copy should come with a bucket of popcorn and a John Williams soundtrack to play in the background. I loved it."

—Linwood Barclay, #1 internationally bestselling author of *Fear the Worst*

# BLACK RAIN

a thriller

## GRAHAM BROWN

A DELL BOOK

NEW YORK

A Dell Mass Market Original

Copyright © 2010 by Graham Brown

Published in the United States by Dell, an imprint of
The Random House Publishing Group, a division of
Random House, Inc., New York.

DELL is a registered trademark of Random House, Inc.,
and the colophon is a trademark of Random House, Inc.

978-0-553-59241-2

*Cover art and design by Carlos Beltran*
*Book design by Diane Hobbing*

Printed in the United States of America

www.bantamdell.com

2 4 6 8 9 7 5 3 1

## ACKNOWLEDGMENTS

Only the writer knows how instrumental others are in the work that he gets to call his own. In my case, at least, those brief moments of intervention often seemed far more important to the final outcome than all the months of furious typing.

And so, first I must thank my wife, Tracey—both for putting up with me to begin with and for all the things I've learned from you. Without you, this book would still be a poorly written first draft, gathering dust in a drawer somewhere. Also, thanks go out to all the friends and family who read those early drafts, particularly Larry and Shelly Fox (*gracias,* los Zorros); to Christopher Gangi, who is like a brother; to my actual brothers; and, of course, to my parents, who never stopped me from trying anything, even if it was dangerous or just a little crazy.

And, of course, a writer never feels like a writer until they're published. None of which would have been remotely possible without my agent, the fantastic and amazing Barbara Poelle; how I was lucky enough to sit at your table, I'll never know. The same goes for Irene Goodman, Danny Baror and the crew at Bantam Dell, beginning with my editor, Danielle Perez, whose suggestions and thoughts are so on point it seems she knows the characters better than I do. Thanks as well to Marisa Vigilante for her input and assistance, Carlos Beltran for the fantastic cover and everyone else whose efforts went into making this happen.

There came one called Destroyer, who gouged out their eyes, and another called Jaguar, who devoured their flesh. They raced for the trees and they raced for the caves. But the trees could not bear them and the caves were now shut.
And then came the torrent; a rain of black resin that poured from the sky. Rain through the day and all through the night and the earth was blackened beneath it.

—*The demise of the wooden people, from the Mayan text* Popul Vuh

## PROLOGUE:
### THE RAINFOREST

The darkness of the jungle loomed above, its dense, tangled layers spreading like a circus tent from the towering pillars of massive trees. Gorged on the rain, it grew impenetrable and unyielding, a home to thousands of species, most of which never left the confines of its elevated embrace. Life was lived up there, high in the canopy; the ground was for shadows and crawling things and for that which had died.

Jack Dixon allowed his gaze to fall from the lush world above him to the soil beneath his feet. He crouched, examining a set of tracks. The tread of the heavy boots was easy to discern, but subtly different from those he'd found earlier. These were deeper at the toe, pressed down into the earth and spaced farther apart.

*So the targets were running now. But why?*

He looked around, wondering if he'd come up too quickly and given himself away. It seemed unlikely. Knotted undergrowth blocked most of the sight lines, and where one could see, the vaporous fog grayed the distance to infinity. It was as if nothing else existed, no world beyond, only endless trees, clinging moss and vines hanging limp in the mist like ropes from an empty gallows.

*Besides, if they had seen him, he'd already be dead.*

Dixon motioned to a man trailing him. He pointed to the tracks. "Something spooked them," he said.

The second man, whose name was McCrea, studied the print for a second. "But not us."

Dixon shook his head. "No. Not us."

As cicadas buzzed in the distance, a subtle tic fluttered across McCrea's face. But nothing more was said and the two men moved on, holding their assault rifles in front of them and creeping even more slowly than before.

A few minutes later they came upon what Dixon had begun to expect. Another kill. A fresh kill with no stench, though the birds had found it already. As Dixon brushed past the last of the blocking undergrowth, the carrion flock scattered in alarm, flapping to safety in the trees.

Exposed by their departure was the mangled body of a man in the same jungle fatigues as Dixon and McCrea. He lay facedown on a swath of crimson mud with a native spear broken off in his back. Chunks of flesh had been gouged from his legs, and his right arm and shoulder were gone, not cut clean but torn away, leaving only tattered strips of flesh and sinew draped over bloody spits of protruding bone.

"What the hell," McCrea said, turning at the sight.

Dixon stared, disturbed but pragmatic. He addressed the dead man. "That's what you get for trying to leave me behind."

Beside him McCrea fought to hold it together. "The bastards did a number on him."

*The bastards* were a native group known as the Chollokwan, a tribe that had been harassing them ever since they came west of the river. In a pair of skirmishes weeks before, Dixon and his men had gunned down a handful of the charging natives. But it seemed one lesson was not enough.

"Saved us the trouble," Dixon said. "Now search him."

McCrea dropped to the ground and rifled through the man's pockets. Finding nothing, he pulled out a small device and switched it on. It began clicking slowly, accelerating into a rapid buzz as he zeroed in on the right spot.

"I told you he had them," Dixon said.

McCrea put the Geiger counter away and dug into the man's pack. He froze in place as a shrill cry rang out from the depths of the jungle.

Silence followed in its wake.

"It's just another bird," Dixon said.

"It sounds like . . ."

Dixon glared at McCrea. "It's a long way off," he growled. "Now just find the damn stones and we'll get out of here."

Under the weight of Dixon's gaze, McCrea went back to work, soon plucking a greasy rag from the litter. Unfolded, it revealed a group of small stones, slightly larger than sugar cubes but twelve-sided and shimmering with a dull metallic gloss. Beside them lay a scratched, colorless crystal.

Dixon eyed the stones, the crystal and then the tortured face of his former charge. "Thief," he said finally: a last pronouncement on the dead man, an epitaph for a traitor who would never see a proper grave.

McCrea rewrapped the bundle and Dixon took it.

"His papers too," Dixon said.

Reluctantly, McCrea held out the man's passport.

As Dixon took the ID packet, the shrill cry sounded in the distance once again. And this time a second call answered it, louder than the first, closer; a wailing screech that seemed to bypass the ears and pierce the brain directly.

"That's not a goddamned bird," McCrea said.

Dixon did not reply, but silently he agreed. They'd heard that call before, back at the temple, just before everything went to hell. He was not happy to be in its presence once again.

He shoved the stone-filled rag into a pocket and tightened his grip on the rifle, the veins on his massive forearms bulging. His eyes darted around as he strove to see through the mist and the trees and the same blocked sight lines that had hidden his own approach.

His thoughts turned to his dead former comrade. This was not good ground to be stalked upon.

Beside him, McCrea mumbled something unintelligible and then added, "We stayed too long."

Dixon ignored him, drawing a machete from the scabbard at his hip and stepping forward, rifle in one hand, long metal blade held high in the other. He pushed through the fronds and then stopped.

On the jungle floor, beside another trail of dark, coagulating blood, he spotted a new set of tracks, long two-pronged depressions, like someone had shoved a tuning fork into the earth and then bent it forward. Try as he might, Dixon could think of nothing that left such a mark.

As he crouched to study them, he smelled a familiar odor. Pungent, almost ammonialike. And then the piercing call echoed through the forest once again, rolling over them like a wave and on into the distance.

"We need to get out of here," McCrea said.

"Quiet," Dixon replied as he studied the tracks.

"Man, don't you see? It's happening again."

"Shut up!" Dixon ordered. He struggled to concentrate. Running would get them killed, but staying . . . There was something wrong with this place, a truth he hadn't recognized until it was too late. Men were not the hunters here but the hunted.

From somewhere far ahead of him, Dixon heard movement, soft, like the flutter of owl's wings, but at ground level. He put the rifle to his shoulder.

"Dixon," McCrea begged.

The sound was coming toward them, faster now, racing through the forest but treading lightly.

"Dixon, please!"

Dixon rose up, preparing to fire, but the sound dodged to his left, passing him. He spun, pulling the trigger even as a dark blur exploded through the trees.

McCrea screamed. Gunfire boomed through the forest and a spray of red mist fanned out over the leaves, but there was nothing left to hit; no target, no enemy, no McCrea, just the low-lying fronds, swaying from the impact and covered in a sheen of human blood.

Dixon stared at the blood dripping from the leaves. "McCrea!" he shouted.

He listened for sounds of struggle but heard none. McCrea was gone, dead and gone just like all the others. Only this time it had happened right in front of him.

Dixon began to back away. Not a man given to fear, he could feel his heart beginning to pound, the flight reflex growing uncontrollably within him. He looked in one direction and then another. He began with measured steps, but soon found his pace quickening. His heart was pounding, his mind spinning. And when the echoing screams rang through the forest once again, he took off running with all he had.

Unbalanced and panicked, Dixon charged forward, crashing through the undergrowth like a bull, stumbling as the vines clutched at his feet. He twisted at the sound of hidden movement, turning one way then the other, shouting angrily and firing into the trees.

"Get away from me!" he screamed.

As he ran, he heard movement, crunching foliage and native voices, chasing him, closing on him.

He tripped, landed on his hands and knees and came up firing. The flash of a dark shape hit him anyway and sent him flying. Tumbling through the air, he caught a brief glimpse of his attacker before it disappeared into the forest. Eight men dead and this was the first sight he'd had of their killer, its hide like polished, blackened bone.

He hit the ground with a jarring crash, aware enough to hold on to his rifle even as a stabbing pain shot up through his leg.

With his breath coming in spurts, he rolled over and

forced himself to look. The lower bones of one leg were broken, the tibia sticking through the skin. Running was no longer an option; he probably couldn't walk.

In agony, he propped himself up. He used his good leg to scoot backward until he reached the base of a wide, gray trunk. With shaking hands, he checked his rifle, then lodged it in the crook of one arm and braced himself for the inevitable and painful end.

In a few moments, he was shivering and growing weak. His head wavered and tilted backward until it rested on the fallen trunk. Far above him the tangled web of branches moved on a breath of wind that did not reach the ground. Pinpoints of light made their way through gaps in the foliage, painful to look at with eyes grown accustomed to the shadows. As he watched, the light seemed to be fading, though perhaps it was his vision.

A minute went by without incident, and then another. The silence surrounded him, broken only by his labored breathing. As the seconds ticked away Jack Dixon prayed that he might be left to die on his own, to fade and fall into an endless, peaceful sleep. After another minute or two he even began to feel hope.

And then that bitter shriek rang out again, freezing his heart, piercing his skull and echoing across the depths of the Amazon.

# CHAPTER 1

*Manaus, Brazil*

Danielle Laidlaw sat alone on the terrace of a small café overlooking the great river. In the heat-induced calm of a sweltering afternoon she watched the sun paint traces of gold on the river's surface. It was a mesmerizing and hypnotic sight, and one she'd gazed at for too long.

She turned her attention to the café, looking past the tables and their bright yellow umbrellas to what she could see of the café's interior. In the heat of the afternoon the place was all but empty. Certainly there was no sign of the man she was waiting on, a man who was running atypically late.

With quick hands, she retrieved her BlackBerry, checked for any messages and then typed a none-too-subtle text. It read: Where the hell are you?

Before she could press *send,* she caught sight of him, speaking to a waiter in the café's foyer.

She spotted his silver hair first, and then his craggy face as he turned in her direction. He walked toward her, as nattily dressed as always, today in dark slacks, a button-down shirt and a navy blue dinner jacket. She wondered how he could wear such clothes in the heat of central Brazil, but then Arnold Moore didn't do compromise very well, not even with the vagaries of nature.

"You're late," she said. "Did you have trouble finding this place?"

He pursed his lips as if the suggestion itself was ludicrous. "Of course not," he said. "I simply asked where one might find a brooding, dark-haired woman angrily checking her BlackBerry a hundred times a minute. Surprisingly, only seven different people pointed me in your direction."

As she smiled at his barb, Danielle sensed the eyes of the waitstaff upon them. It happened more often than not. She was thirty-one, tall and fit with high cheekbones and glossy chestnut hair, and he was twice her age, gray and refined, almost continental in his bearing. People who saw them together commonly gawked, assuming her to be his mistress or trophy wife or perhaps, less cynically, a niece or daughter. The truth would have surprised them: she was his partner, his protégé and one of the few people in the world he actually trusted.

As ranking field operatives for an American organization known as the National Research Institute, Danielle Laidlaw and Arnold Moore had traveled much of the globe together. In just the prior year they'd spent time in eleven countries, studying everything from oil field resuscitation in the Baltics to nano-tube production in Tokyo. They'd even been to Venice as the NRI partnered with the Italian government on a plan to protect the island with a band of giant sea gates.

Their stock-in-trade was to examine cutting-edge projects and determine what technologies, if any, could be valuable to the United States. Then, through a combination of relationship building, bribes, or even outright theft, they were to secure for their country what might be of interest.

To that end, she and Moore spent their days in cutting-edge labs or at illustrious seminars. Their nights resembled those of the jet set, attending state functions and elaborate parties thrown by corporations and wealthy entrepreneurs. It was often as glamorous as it was rewarding. So far, however, the mission to Brazil was proving to be an exception.

The NRI's interest in the country was unrelated to anything being designed, developed or produced there. In fact, it concerned the past as much as the future, beginning with a group of artifacts recovered from the Amazon by an American explorer named Blackjack Martin.

A fortune hunter more than anything else, Martin launched his expedition in 1926, in search of anything that might bring him fame. He returned a year later having mostly failed. The stories he told were laughed off as fanciful exaggerations or outright lies. And the few artifacts he did bring back raised little more than passing interest and were soon consigned to the dusty backrooms of various museums, forgotten if not lost. At least, that is, until a chance encounter with one of them, and an examination with modern tools, had drawn the NRI's substantial interest.

Since then, Danielle and Arnold Moore had been in Brazil, trying without success to pick up on Blackjack Martin's trail. After months of fruitless effort, Danielle believed she'd finally found something that would help.

"I have good news," she said. "And something to show you."

Moore grabbed a cloth napkin and snapped it open. "And I have bad news," he said, "straight from the mouth of our director."

The words were spoken in a tone that Moore reserved for moments of disgust. She sensed a hint of resignation on Moore's face, the bitterness of another argument lost or some new and bizarre order being implemented over his objection, something that had become a pattern on this particular assignment.

"What's happened now?" she asked.

Moore shook his head. "You first. Perhaps something positive will take the sting out of what I have to tell you."

"Fine," she said, reaching into a small leather bag at the foot of the table. She pulled out a flat gray stone and placed it in front of Moore. "Take a look at that."

About two inches thick, the stone was roughly rectangular in shape, with jagged edges on three sides and a face slightly larger than a postcard. It tapered at one end and was covered with weathered symbols, including one that resembled a skull and others that appeared to represent animals.

Moore took the stone from her, holding it out at arm's length. He squinted hard before giving in to necessity and pulling a pair of bifocals from his pocket. With great precision he placed them in their proper spot at the end of his nose.

"Hieroglyphic," he noted.

"And clearly Mayan," she said.

He nodded, angling the piece for a better view. As he

did, the edges of the glyphs caught the sun. "My, my," he whispered to himself. "Now, this is a sight."

"Take a look at the top right corner," she said. "Recognize that one?"

Moore studied the glyph, a grin creeping onto his face. "The same mark we saw on Blackjack Martin's cradle," he said. "Xibalba: the underworld."

Her eyebrows went up in triumph. If they were right, this was the first real proof they'd found supporting what Martin had described in his wild journals. "Hard to believe, isn't it?"

"Yes," he said. "Very hard." He looked at her suspiciously. "Where did you get this?"

"I bought it from a logger who'd taken his crew upriver for contraband hardwoods. Mahogany, for the most part."

Mahogany was an important cash crop in the Amazon, but the trees grew slowly and most of those in accessible areas had been felled long ago. Others were protected. As a result, increasing amounts of illegal logging took place far upriver, where the loggers went in search of untouched lands to harvest. As time went by, this trade took them deeper and deeper into the watershed, to places where few others journeyed.

"How far in was he?" Moore asked with renewed enthusiasm.

"Eight days from here, a trip we could make in four or five."

As Moore examined the stone, Danielle felt a new surge of energy. A reverberation of the jolt she'd felt when first viewing the stone herself—and something sorely needed by both of them.

"Did he know what he was selling you?" Moore asked, flipping the stone over.

"Not the specifics," she said. "But he knows where it came from and he claimed to have seen a much larger stone nearby, one with similar markings. Too heavy to carry, apparently, so he took this one instead."

She watched as Moore ran his fingers across the sharp edges on the back of the stone; the rest was relatively smooth and weathered.

"Recent break," he said. "I wonder if he chipped this piece off of the bigger one."

"My thoughts exactly," she said.

Moore looked up. "What else did he tell you?"

"He said they hired some members of the Nuree tribe to act as guides upriver. One of the tribesmen pointed out the larger stone as they were hiking along the banks of a small tributary. They treat it as a marker of some kind, denoting the border of a land they consider to be cursed. Beyond it lie terrible things, apparently: shadows darker than the night, a tribe that converses with the spirits and controls wild animals . . . and a wall," she said, "made with the bones of human beings."

It was local folklore—more often outright false than even partly reliable—but in this case they had reason to trust it, at least enough to hope. One of the few landmarks Blackjack Martin had used in his journal was a place he called the Wall of Skulls. If they could find it, they might be able to trace the rest of his movements and locate the source of the items he'd brought back. And if they could do that . . .

"A wall made of bones," Moore repeated.

She nodded.

"Big step," he said, "if you could find that."

He placed the stone back on the table.

"And when I say *you*," Moore continued, "I mean you alone."

Danielle glared at him, not certain that she'd heard him right. "What are you talking about?"

He elaborated. "There are changes afoot. Gibbs is calling me back to Washington, and, despite my best efforts, I haven't been able to talk him out of it."

Gibbs was the NRI's director of operations. The man who'd sent them here in the first place. Gibbs seemed to have a strong personal interest in what he called the Brazil project—unfortunately, he also had a strong personal dislike for Arnold Moore. And the two men had been clashing since the word go.

"Tell me you're joking," she said.

Moore shook his head. "Afraid not. I'm going back, and you're staying on. It's going to be your show from here on out. Your team to run, when all the players get here."

She stared at him, eyes wide with shock. Moore had been her mentor almost since she'd first joined the NRI. He was also one of the few people she trusted in the strange and perilous world in which the NRI operated. The thought of being suddenly denied his assistance in the middle of a critical operation infuriated her.

"Why?" she asked. "Of all times, why now? I mean, we're finally making progress here."

Moore took a deep breath and pulled the reading glasses from his face. "I'm sixty-three," he reminded her. "Too damn old to go traipsing around the jungle in search of lost cities. That's a job for the young—and the foolish, I might add—and you seem to fit at least one of those categories," he said. "I'll let you decide which. Besides, Gibbs is well aware of my aversion to snakes, mosquitoes and poisonous frogs. I expect he's just trying to save me from all that."

"That's a crock of shit," she said. "You've been begging Gibbs to send us out there with the snakes and frogs since the day we got here." Her eyes tightened their focus, as if to prevent him from hiding something. "Give me the real reason."

Moore faked a smile. "Two reasons," he said. "First, Gibbs thinks you're ready, and he's right—you are. You have been for some time. I've just been selfishly holding you back. And second, he's worried. He thinks we're getting close, but he fears someone else may be closer. He's afraid they may already have people in the field."

She was sick of hearing about Gibbs and his paranoia. The operation was being run so quietly that they had no staff, a shoestring budget and nonstandard channels for basic communications. "Impossible," she said. "The only people who even know the whole story are you, him and me."

"Yes," Moore replied quietly. "The only three."

As she worked out what he was suggesting, what Gibbs had suggested without speaking the words, her face betrayed her once again. "I'm not going to listen to this. If he thinks—"

Moore interrupted her. "He didn't say it, of course, but he wonders. He's not sure about me anymore. We argue too much. Besides, he thinks you're the stronger

horse now. You're young and full of ambition. He figures you'll do almost anything to make this work. I, on
the other hand, am not so young and might not be as
willing to risk my neck—or other, more vital body
parts—on what could very well be a fool's errand. He's
afraid I might even look at this as a chance to retire with
something more than a measly pension. And he surely
can't afford that."

"This is ridiculous," she said.

"It's not all bad," Moore insisted. "He's got one big
carrot to dangle in front of you—one I wouldn't care
about either—promotion. You pull this off and he'll give
you a full director's position, with a group of regionals
working under you."

As he paused, she looked away—unwilling to answer.

"I know this isn't how you want it to happen but you
should look at this for what it is—a chance to prove
yourself."

"What this is," she said emphatically, "is more bull-
shit. No one else would have to do something like this
for a promotion."

Moore's face turned serious but still kindly. "You're
younger than the other field reps, and you're the only
one at your level who didn't come directly from the
Agency. Those are two disadvantages. The fact that
you're close to me is another. With that kind of background, you'll always have to do more. You have to beat
the others just to draw even with them."

She didn't want to listen. Despite her rapid ascent in
the NRI, she continued to feel like an outsider. And why
not—Gibbs ran the organization like a private club:
there were those who could do no wrong, "Gibbs'

Boys," and those who were looked on as perhaps problems in waiting, staff with loyalties that ran to the organization itself rather than directly to Gibbs. Chief among them was Moore—and by extension, Danielle. Outsiders.

"You have a choice here," Moore added, not allowing any time for self-pity. "You can take this task and see it through, or you can quit, fly back to the States and confirm everything Gibbs thinks about you in the first place: that you're a good second but not a first."

She ground her teeth, the suggestion infuriating her. The project was a long shot at best, setting her up for failure. They had no real budget, no backup and no middle ground. Either they would find what they were looking for or they wouldn't. And no amount of effort or explanation could make the second outcome acceptable.

She exhaled, visibly frustrated. And yet, as angry as she was at the circumstances surrounding the change, she couldn't deny feeling a thrill at the prospect of finally being put in charge. For the past few years, she and Moore had worked as almost equal partners. Through no fault of his own, Moore received the lion's share of the credit, with others seeing her as mostly a beneficiary of his expertise. One thing about a long shot—if she could somehow pull it off, she would prove everyone wrong, prove to Director Gibbs and the rest of them that she was more than a good second, that she was a force to be reckoned with.

"You know damn well I won't quit," she said. "But I'll promise you this, when I get back to Washington with this thing in my hand, I'm going to march into Gibbs' office and shove it down his damn throat."

He smiled. "Just make sure I'm sitting ringside."

Moore played the good soldier to the best of his abilities, but Danielle could sense his anger and frustration. He clearly hated being moved aside. Not too far down the road, a bigger move was coming: forced retirement. At that point she'd be his legacy. It made her even more determined not to let him down.

As she steeled herself for the work ahead, Moore's face grew serious. "You must know," he said, "things have gotten more dangerous. And not just because you'll be leading on your own. There's another party involved now, an outside player."

She listened intently.

"We lost our transportation this morning," he said. "The guy took another charter. I offered to beat whatever they were paying, but he didn't want anything to do with us. That makes our porters and our transportation all in one week."

Danielle thought about the men who'd backed out. At least one of the porters they'd hired had been assaulted and badly beaten, while the rest of the group had just disappeared.

"Not a coincidence," she said.

"No, it's not," Moore said, sliding his glasses into a jacket pocket. "It doesn't really matter anyway. Gibbs was going to replace them. He's got a hand-picked crew coming in, and they're not locals either."

"Who?" she asked.

"Private security first, led by a man named Verhoven, a South African mercenary. Well thought of, from what I hear. He'll be arriving the day after tomorrow, along with his crew. Then there's a pilot Gibbs wants you to meet: an American who goes by the name of Hawker. He's known in Manaus but he spends much of the year crop-dusting for the owners of a coffee plantation a few hours drive from here."

"What's he doing down here?"

"Ex-CIA," he said. "Black-flagged, apparently."

"Then why are we using him?" she asked.

Moore smiled like a jackal but he didn't reply. He didn't need to.

"Has it really come to that?"

"Gibbs doesn't trust anyone now. He's convinced we have a leak and he wants people with no connection to the Institute. He thinks that should make them clean— and he's right, at least to begin with. It doesn't mean someone can't get to them later, but it gives you some insulation."

As Moore took a sip of water, Danielle realized he'd slipped back into the role of mentor. This was it, she guessed, the last words of advice she'd receive for a while.

"What's their cover?"

"No cover," he said. "Hawker's already here and Verhoven and his group are coming over the fence, not through it."

"And their clearance?"

Moore shook his head. "No one's cleared to know what you know," he said. "Not them or the civilians. They can know about the stones, the ruins, the city you're looking for. Everything that's obvious. But beyond that they stay in the dark."

And that was the rub—the burden of leadership on

this particular expedition. They were ostensibly planning to follow Blackjack Martin's tracks into the rainforest in search of what would be an astounding discovery, a branch of the Mayan race living in the Amazon, thousands of miles from the rest of Mayan civilization; but there was more to it than that, a goal that coincided with the search, one that the others would never be informed of.

"And if I run into trouble?" she asked.

"You're not to contact the Brazilian authorities under any circumstances," he said bluntly. "In the case of abduction, coercion or other scenarios which might force your hand, the loss of the entire team is considered preferable to any disclosure." That was the order in writing. Moore added his own clarification: "If something happens, do what you can. But if there's no other choice, then you get the hell out of there and leave them behind."

She listened to the directive, one she'd known was coming ever since Gibbs started jamming the civilians down their throats. She had little doubt that Moore shared her revulsion at the order, but they had a job to do.

As if sensing her hesitation, he said, "I don't have to remind you how important this thing is."

"How important Gibbs *thinks* it is," she corrected. "If he's right."

"He is," Moore said, bluntly. "One way or another, he's right about this. You've been asked to take it on faith so far, but since you're now in charge . . . The test results on the Martin crystals were unequivocal. They confirmed the presence of tritium gas sequestered in the quartz lattice."

Tritium was a radioactive by-product, one that could only form during a nuclear reaction of some kind. Its presence could mean only one thing.

Moore explained. "Somewhere along the line, those crystals were involved in a low-level nuclear reaction. Cold fusion, almost certainly."

"And the source of that reaction?" she asked. "Do we have any new thoughts on that?"

Moore squinted into the distance, his blue eyes lit up by the setting sun. "I've come to believe that what we're looking for is out there," he said finally. "I couldn't explain how or why, but I believe it exists. And if we can find it—if *you* can find it—then we have a chance to literally change the world."

## CHAPTER 2

The rusting aircraft hangar stood at the end of a seldom-used airfield just outside the small mountain town of Marejo. Weeds grew unchecked around its edges and pigeons nested in the roof, giving it the appearance of an abandoned hulk, but the structure, and the concrete airstrip it served, still had a few sporadic users.

One of those was a dark-haired, forty-year-old American, owner and operator of a weather-beaten, olive-drab helicopter—a Bell UH-1, commonly called a Huey, a craft that currently absorbed both his admiration and scorn.

Three hours of work in the sweltering hangar had left him concerned about the Huey's state of airworthiness. In truth, he marveled that it was still operating at all. And as his eyes flashed from one section of the craft to the next, he wondered just how many things he could patch together and still continue to fly. Grimly amused at the thought, he guessed he'd find out soon enough.

As he moved to put away a case of tools, the open mouth of the hangar doors caught the sound of an approaching vehicle, a well-tuned, expensive engine, completely out of place in a town like Marejo.

Glad for any excuse to move toward the fresh air, he walked to the entrance, wiping the grease from his hands with a tattered rag. Across the tarmac, a dust-covered Land Rover approached, moving slowly down the access road. He guessed this would be a follow-up to the call he'd taken the night before, an offer he had turned down without hesitation.

*So they'd come to talk in person now. They must really want something this time.*

The black SUV swung toward him and parked at the edge of the tarmac. The door opened. To his surprise, a woman stepped out. Attractive and fashionably dressed, she slammed the door with more than a little edge and strode toward the hangar, her eyes hidden beneath tortoiseshell sunglasses. There was something confrontational in her gait, like a tiger spoiling for a fight.

As she approached, Hawker considered his own grubby appearance, covered in grease and sweat and three days of unshaven stubble. "Great," he mumbled to himself, then stepped back inside, where he could at least splash some water on his face.

Leaning over the sink, he heard the soles of her boots clicking on the concrete floor.

"*Com licença,*" she said in Portuguese. "Excuse me; I'm looking for a pilot named Hawker. I was told I could find him here."

He shut off the water, dried his face with a towel and looked in the tarnished mirror; a marginal improvement. He turned. "You speak Portuguese," he said.

"And you speak English," she replied. "American

English. You must be Hawker." She put out her hand. "My name's Danielle Laidlaw, I'm with the NRI—the National Research Institute—from the States."

He shook her hand cautiously. "The NRI?"

"We're a federally funded research house," she said. "We do a lot of high-tech work in partnership with universities and corporations. Though that's not exactly why I'm here."

He'd heard rumors about the NRI in the past. And however unreliable those sources might have been, there was more to the Institute than her little sound bite let on. "You people are persistent. I'll give you that."

"You should be flattered," she said, smiling.

"'Flattered' is not quite the word," he said, though he couldn't help but smile back. "I turned your friend down on the phone. Apparently you didn't get *that* word."

She removed her sunglasses. "I did, actually. But from what I heard, our men didn't get a chance to make an offer."

He threw the towel in the sink. "There was a reason for that."

"Look," she said, "I'm not exactly thrilled to be out here myself. Four hours on a dirt road is not my way of enjoying an afternoon. But I've come a long way to see you. The least you could do is hear me out. How much could that hurt?"

He stared at her. She was a bold, attractive woman, working for a questionable branch of the U.S. government and about to offer him a contract that would undoubtedly involve some type of covert, illegal or otherwise dangerous activity. And she wanted to know how much it could hurt?

Still, he didn't want to send her away. "You thirsty?" he asked. "Because I am."

She nodded and Hawker led her to the side of the hangar, where a dingy refrigerator stood beside a table with a coffeepot. He scooped some ice from the freezer and poured a cup of black coffee over it. "This or water?"

She looked suspiciously at the scratched glass and the dark liquid within it. "I'll take the coffee."

"You're brave," he said, placing the glass in front of her and pouring himself a drink of water. "And you have come a long way," he added, taking a seat across from her. "Up from Manaus, I'm guessing, since that's where your friend wanted me to go. Apparently you have gainful employment to offer. So let's hear it, tell me about this job."

She took a sip and her expression did not change. He was impressed; the coffee was absurdly bitter.

"The NRI is funding an expedition into a remote area of the western Amazon," she said. "The final site hasn't been determined yet, but we're pretty certain it'll be accessible only by river or air. We're looking for a pilot and helicopter for up to twenty weeks, with an option for next season as well. You'll be paid for flying, local knowledge and any other duties that would be mutually agreed upon."

His eyebrows went up. "Mutually agreed upon," he said. "I like the sound of that."

"I thought you would."

"What's the cargo?"

"Standard field supplies," she said. "Staff from our Research Division and some university-level experts."

He had to stop himself from laughing. "Doesn't sound so bad. What are you leaving out?"

"Nothing of importance."

"Then what are you doing here?"

A perfect pause, practiced. "I don't follow you."

He felt certain that she did, in fact, follow him. "What are you doing all the way up here when you could have hired someone in Manaus? Why the long journey to see me? Why the midnight phone call from the man with no name?"

The response was deliberate, with gravity in her voice that he recognized from his past. "We're interested in maintaining a low profile, a vision local hires don't always seem to embrace. We're looking for someone who won't ask questions and won't answer them if they come his way." She shrugged. "As for the phone call. Well, we needed to make sure that you were in fact *you*."

The call had included a lot of questions, questions he'd chosen not to answer. That had probably been enough.

Calls like that, or inquiries by other means, had been common over the past ten years, especially during his exile in Africa, after his separation from the CIA. They came from rebel elements, foreign governments and from corporations and proxies of the same Western interests he'd supposedly been excommunicated from. When a man is listed as a threat by his own country, he is presumed to be open to offers from all sides.

Depending on who was asking, the questions took different forms. The dictators, generals and warlords were refreshingly, if disturbingly, direct. The agents of the various Western governments were far less clear, their words always couched in the hypothetical. *If this individual were to disappear, then the killing in this region might stop. If this man were to fall into our hands . . . if this party were to receive these weapons . . . then funds might be placed into this numbered account.* For years he'd listened to these proposals, picking and choosing from a litany of offers up and down the West African coast and into parts of Asia.

He told himself that he'd rejected all those that might be patently evil, but in places that reeked of madness it was often hard to tell the difference. Guns begat guns; one dead warlord was replaced by two with a blood feud between them; an oil terminal that gave money to a mad dictator also gave jobs and food to people who worked on and around it—was it moral or immoral to blow such a thing up? Finally, he couldn't tell anymore. He'd left Africa and arrived in Brazil, ready to vanish forever. It seemed for a while that he had, but the call had come anyway. Apparently some people were not allowed to disappear.

Hawker stared at the woman across from him, realizing, at least, that her offer had not been phrased in the hypothetical. "You have security issues."

"Anonymous threats and a break-in at our hotel. Items were taken, others destroyed. Things of little value, but the message was clear: someone doesn't want us going out there."

"Any candidates?"

"Plenty of them," she said. "From radical environmentalists who think we're out to destroy the rainforest, to mining and logging concerns who think we're trying to stop them from destroying the rainforest." She paused. "But we have reason to believe it goes deeper than that."

He understood what she was saying: there was more at stake than she could or would tell him. But she needed him to know it in general. It made him wonder how much she knew. She seemed a little young to be in such a position and making such a request. No, he decided, "young" wasn't the right word. More like "keen" or "zealous." Perhaps that's what people looked like when they still believed in what they did. He couldn't remember.

"No questions asked?" he guessed.

"Not many that I can answer."

He'd try another tack, one she'd be able to confirm, at least to some extent. "And what do you know about me?"

"Enough," she said.

"Enough?"

"Enough to wonder what someone with your reputation is doing in the middle of nowhere."

"People who trusted me died," he said, thinking that if she didn't know that, she didn't know *enough*. "You still want to hire me?"

She appeared unfazed. "The people I work for do. You were the only name on a short list. Chosen personally, it seems."

"By whom?"

She took another sip of the coffee, maneuvering the glass carefully and examining the chips in the rim as she placed it down. For a second he thought she wasn't going to answer, but then her eyes flashed at him again. Apparently she'd made him wait long enough. "Stuart Gibbs," she said. "The NRI's director of operations."

The name rattled around in his head. Hawker didn't know the man, but he'd heard of him. Gibbs had been fairly high up in the Agency when Hawker had left, a rising star with a reputation for arrogance and ruthlessness. And now he ran the NRI, or part of it anyway. Such a nice little organization.

As he considered the offer, every instinct in his body shouted at him to turn it down, to tell this zealous young woman that Director Gibbs could go to hell and take his offer with him. After all, the only right that those in exile retained was the privilege to remain that way. But another thought had begun to form in his mind: the possibility of a door opening, one that he'd expected to stay forever closed. It began with Director Gibbs and his personal interest in the operation.

"How long have you been with them?" he asked.

"Seven years."

"Almost from the start," he said, showing her that he knew a little something about the organization. "And Gibbs?"

"From day one," she replied, annoyed by his probing. "As you've probably guessed."

Hawker had guessed exactly that and it only reinforced his intention to say no, but she didn't give him the chance.

Suddenly, the tiger was tired of playing. "Look," she said, "I can see this is going nowhere. I didn't come out here to waste your time. We just want an American pilot for what is essentially an American expedition. Obviously, you'd prefer to remain here." She looked around. "And why not? I mean, who'd want to give up all this."

She handed him a business card. "My problem is time—I don't have a lot of it. Here's my number. Call me before noon tomorrow if you change your mind. Wait any longer and I'll have someone else."

Hawker watched in detached amusement as she stood and turned to leave. He stole a quick glance at the battered old Huey. Whatever the other considerations were, the job would pay well. More than he could make in a year or two in a place like Marejo. Not to mention the half-dozen things on the Huey that he could repair or replace and bill to the NRI, things that weren't likely to get fixed any other way. Simple choice, simple compromise—that's how it always started.

"Relax," he said. "I'm interested. But you have to understand: I don't take checks."

She halted her departure and looked him in the eye. "Somehow, we didn't think you would."

The next thirty minutes involved negotiations over timing, charter fees and operating costs. Formalities really, and for the most part quickly out of the way. When they were done, Hawker stood and walked her back to the waiting Land Rover.

"I should be in Manaus by tomorrow night," he said, holding the door as she climbed in.

"That works," she replied, her lips curving upward into a perfect smile. "I'll see you then."

Hawker slammed the door, just as the engine roared to life. As she drove off, his mind replayed the conversation and the decision he'd just made. There would undoubtedly be more to the journey than archaeology, but how much more was difficult to determine. The presence of civilians made it unlikely that anything too outlandish was in store, but the personal attention of NRI's director suggested just the opposite. The contradiction bothered him; it left him wondering which direction the danger would come from, a sickly familiar feeling.

As he watched the Rover take the main road, another thought occurred to him, the kind that flashes into one's head and then pretends to disappear, only to lurk in some dark corner of the mind and whisper incessantly at the consciousness.

He could understand why the NRI didn't want a Brazilian pilot. Having someone like himself enhanced security no matter what type of operation they had in mind. But the NRI was a big organization, with people all over the world. They had to have their own pilots; probably had them in spades, and *nothing* could be more discreet than using an insider for the job. So why go through all the trouble and expense of hiring him when it would have been easier and even more secure to bring in one of their own? The thought nagged at him as the Land Rover vanished into the setting sun. It was a question, he decided, that could not have a healthy answer.

## CHAPTER 3

The man in the black jacket stared down the alleyway that ran out before him, a street made of dust and sand and cobblestones held together by what appeared to be dried and hardened mud. Most of Manaus was modern, even thriving in a way not seen since the rubber boom of the 1920s, but every city had its barrios, and Manaus was no different. The nameless jumbled street lay in one of them, and as he started walking down it, the man in black could feel the eyes of its inhabitants upon him.

His name was Vogel, and he had a business meeting to attend in such auspicious surroundings. He followed the street back, walking between faded buildings that sagged with age. Halfway down, where the road bent slightly to the right, two chickens pecked at something in the corner and a scrawny, lazy dog panted quietly in the shade. Just beyond, a man wearing a narrow fedora sat on an overturned five-gallon bucket, smoking a cigarette in the afternoon sun. The man seemed to notice his approach, but did little more than stare.

"Are you Remo?" Vogel asked, walking up to the man and failing to hide a German accent.

The man looked up, revealing a gap in his teeth. "Depends," he said, "on who you are."

Vogel recognized the voice; to this point they'd only spoken on the phone. "You know who I am," he said. "So tell me what happened."

Remo stood up, flicked his cigarette into the cobbles and pushed his hat back. "I did what you wanted," he said. "That captain, he ain't gonna be taking any charters from them for a while. No matter how much they pay."

"Good. What else?"

Remo shrugged. "Not much. They met with another trader. Bought some more junk. Those two are like tourists with their souvenirs. And then yesterday the girl drove up to the mountains . . . alone."

Vogel knew that. In fact, there wasn't much the NRI agents did that he didn't know about beforehand. "Moore is going back to America," he said. "We don't want that. We want you to take the girl out, so that he has to stay behind."

Remo looked at Vogel as if he had said something crazy. "We could have done that yesterday. Why the hell didn't you tell us? It would have been easy."

Vogel understood that. In fact, it would have been a perfect chance to take her, but the people he worked for had continued to hesitate, preferring to stall the NRI instead of confronting them head-on. The reasons were not revealed to him.

"We didn't want that yesterday," he explained. "Today we do. Are you up for it?" As he finished, Vogel reached inside his jacket, grabbed an envelope filled with cash and tossed it to Remo, who snatched it out of the air.

Opening it and guessing at the proceeds, Remo looked disappointed. "For kidnapping someone? For killing them? You need more than this."

"She's going to book another charter," Vogel said, ignoring Remo's complaints. "We know who it's with. She'll need to inspect the boat just like last time. You can do it then. Easy work. That should cover the cost."

Remo leaned back against the wall. "No," he said. "I don't think it will."

He rapped his knuckles against the window and two men, both larger than Remo or Vogel, appeared in the doorway. One rested a shotgun on his shoulder; the other held a machete in one hand and displayed a pistol tucked in his belt.

Vogel's eyes went back to Remo, who had produced a black 9mm from his own belt, racking the slide once to load it. He held it toward the ground but the intention was obvious.

With a smug grin Remo put his foot on the overturned bucket and leaned forward. "I think it's time to renegotiate, no?"

Vogel's stare went from one man to the next and then finally back to Remo. He broke into his own smile, which seemed to crack his wooden face. "No."

At that instant the bucket was blasted out from beneath Remo's foot by a rifle shot. He fell forward, regained his balance and looked up in a panic. Bright red dots were dancing around him, zeroing in on his chest and the torsos of the other two men. The man with the shotgun ducked back into the building but the other froze. Remo did likewise, straining to look past Vogel for the source of those laser sights, afraid to move.

"*Isso bom,*" he said, holding up his hands. "It's cool. It's cool."

*Locals,* Vogel thought. *Sometimes they needed to be reminded who they were.* "Good," he said finally. "Good to know we are all in agreement."

## CHAPTER 4

For Professor Michael McCarter the day had begun fifteen hours earlier in the darkness of a cold New York winter morning. From there he'd crossed two continents and an ocean, traveling in everything from a blue Super-Shuttle with a dysfunctional heater to a first-class seat on a shiny new Boeing. He'd changed planes three times, consumed several helpings of what the airlines euphemistically called food and traveled nearly nine thousand miles in all. Now, only minutes from his destination, he'd finally begun to wonder if it was all a terrible mistake.

McCarter sat in the rear section of Hawker's helicopter on a narrow strip of tan canvas that passed for a seat. Above his head, the engine whined in a furious pitch while the rotors bludgeoned the air with a sound that shook his body like the thumping from a pair of massive bass speakers. Tropical air poured in through the gaping cargo door across from him, while beyond it dark green shapes, which he assumed to be trees, flicked by in sudden, violent blurs. Inside the cabin, everything rattled and jostled and vibrated on its own particular frequency, no doubt contributing to the ominous hair-line cracks he saw near many of the joints and rivets.

"What the hell am I doing here?" he said aloud.

For fifteen years, Michael McCarter had been the senior professor of archaeology at a prestigious university in New York City. An African American in his late fifties, McCarter stood tall and distinguished, with a touch of gray at his temples and wire-rimmed glasses on his face. Early in his career he'd published extensively; more recently he'd become a media favorite, appearing on several PBS specials and as a star speaker at various conferences and symposiums, something his deep, resonant voice lent itself to perfectly.

The NRI had been after him for the better part of six months. He'd politely turned them down twice and had ignored all the letters and e-mails that followed. Then, in what he could only describe as a moment of weakness, he'd taken a call from Danielle Laidlaw and she had convinced him, despite all his intentions to the contrary, that this was an opportunity he could not afford to miss.

Now, staring through the open cargo door at objects that were far too close and moving entirely too quickly, he was certain that he'd made the wrong choice.

He turned toward the cockpit and pressed the *talk* switch on his intercom. "Shouldn't we be a little higher?" he said.

The pilot turned and studied McCarter from behind dark sunglasses. His reply was unsettling. "Sorry, Doc. These things drop like a rock if the engine fails. I'd just as soon be closer to the ground, if it's all the same with you."

It was a lie, of course. Helicopters had their own way of gliding, called auto rotation, and additional altitude only helped, but the one thing pilots liked better than telling stories to one another was lying to those who didn't fly.

McCarter looked around him. "What if it's not all the same with me?"

This time Hawker just laughed. The helicopter continued to skim the trees.

McCarter leaned back in his seat and began to look around the cabin, examining the interior, making eye contact with the others who were there, glancing anywhere but out that open door. Three other passengers accompanied him, two of them NRI regulars: Mark Polaski, a communications tech, and William Devers, a linguist who spoke various native languages. The third passenger was a student named Susan Briggs, whom McCarter had agreed to take along at the insistence of the university dean.

She was only twenty-one years old and about to enter the masters program in Archaeological Studies; McCarter had taught her in two classes and found her to be an excellent student, if something of an introvert. She had a tomboyish quality about her, wearing little or no makeup, preferring jeans and T-shirts to more stylish clothes. When she did speak there was a nervous tone to her voice, and despite her intelligence she often spoke in superlatives and other words that seemed to mean very different things to her and the rest of the young people than they did to him.

McCarter knew little of her outside the classroom.

Except that she'd been raised by wealthy, absentee parents who were very close to the dean, and that if the young woman didn't return in the exact condition she'd left in, there would be hell to pay. On the flight over, she'd explained that her parents had wanted her to spend the spring in Europe, beginning in Paris. They couldn't understand why she'd go on a trip like this instead. As usual, permission had finally been granted with her mother's passive-aggressive parting shot: they would keep the Paris ticket on hold, in case she got out in the jungle and didn't feel that it was right for her. In other words, they figured she wouldn't last a week.

For now, at least, Susan's face was beaming. She sat closest to the open door, gazing out at the terrain flying past.

McCarter tapped her on the shoulder. "You look like you're actually enjoying this."

"Aren't you?" she said, her eyes round and innocent. He shook his head.

"Well, maybe you should check out the view." She waved him over.

As Susan spoke, the man to her right turned toward them: Mark Polaski, somewhere around fifty, sporting a five o'clock shadow since early morning and in the midst of a losing battle with male pattern baldness. He took one glance out the door and then looked at McCarter. "I wouldn't if I were you," he said.

"You see," McCarter said, triumphantly. "I'm not alone in this." He looked Polaski's way. "Don't you think we should be a little bit higher?"

Polaski nodded. "Or in a bus, on the ground, like normal people."

McCarter and Susan both laughed. And across from them, William Devers did the same. Though he'd just turned thirty-five, Devers was a fairly accomplished young man, full of pride; piss and vinegar, as McCarter's dad used to say. He claimed to be an expert in the native languages of Central and South America. As he'd informed everyone, he also spoke Russian, French, German, Spanish and Latin and had authored a pair of books on what he called language mutation. Though exactly what that was McCarter had pointedly avoided asking.

Devers leaned in closer. "This is the NRI," he said, shouting to be heard above the noise. "We don't do things like normal people. We have to show off—especially when we're overseas." He examined their surroundings. "To be honest with you, this chopper is a piece of crap compared to the last one I was in: a brand-new Sikorsky or something. That thing had leather seats, air-conditioning and a fully stocked wet bar." His eyebrows went up and down for emphasis and he looked directly at McCarter. "NRI, it stands for *Nice Rides Incorporated*." He turned to Polaski. "You should know that."

Polaski shook his head. "This is my first time in the field."

Devers' face wrinkled with suspicion. "I thought you had five years with us?"

"I do," Polaski said. "But I'm with STI. We don't get out much."

As the concern grew on Devers' face, McCarter and Susan exchanged glances. McCarter asked the obvious. "What's STI?"

"Systems Testing and Implementation," Devers said, beating Polaski to the punch, and then looking at him disgustedly. "What the hell are you doing here?"

"We're running a field test on a new satellite transmission protocol."

"I knew it," Devers said. "You're a damn section five!"

McCarter looked at Susan, who shrugged. "What's a section five?" he asked.

"Last page of the logistics manifest," Devers said. "And the place where we stick untested prototypes when we want to burden another project with them. It's supposed to hold research costs down, but all it usually does is screw up the main operation."

"It's not that bad," Polaski insisted.

"Don't tell me that," Devers said. "I spent last summer in Siberia on a pipeline project. Instead of good old four-by-fours we got stuck with something called a Surface Effect Vehicle." He turned to McCarter. "It's a type of hovercraft that's supposed to replace good old box trucks in places with bad terrain or no roads. Like Siberia in the middle of summer, after the permafrost melts."

"Permafrost doesn't melt," Polaski said. "That's why they call it *perma*frost."

"Well, something damn well did," Devers replied. "And whatever the hell it was, we were supposed to ride over the top of it. Only that piece of crap kept breaking down and crashing face-first into the mud. Nine times in three months we ended up sitting on the roof, praying we wouldn't sink and waiting on a truck from the Khrushchev era to come bail us out. Let me tell you, it impressed the hell out of the Russians. They kept calling it the Yugo—as in, you go and we'll come get you later."

Polaski scratched his balding pate. "Yeah, I heard about that one. Things didn't go exactly as planned out there."

"Hell no, they didn't. Tell me we have some type of backup to your satellite protocol."

"Standard shortwave," Polaski said.

Devers settled back a bit. "Well, that's better. Even I can work an old-fashioned radio." He turned to Susan and McCarter. "What about you two?"

McCarter nodded. Susan said proudly, "I built a ham radio when I was fourteen."

Devers scrunched his face. "I bet that made you popular with the boys."

For an instant she shrunk back, but then replied, "It did. With the boys in Australia."

All of them laughed at that, as Devers turned back to Polaski. "Don't take this the wrong way. But who'd you piss off to get stuck on this deal anyway? I mean, a beta test in the middle of the jungle?"

"I volunteered," he said proudly. "It sounded like an adventure. My youngest daughter just left for college in the fall and she made me promise to have more fun in my life."

"Fun?" Devers asked. "You call this fun?" He turned to McCarter. "What do you think, Professor, you having any fun yet?"

McCarter's face was grim. The helicopter had started a steep turn to the right, tilting him toward the open cargo door. He gripped the rails of the seat with both hands, fearing that his belt might give way at any moment and send him tumbling out the hatch. "This flight's only a short one," he managed. "I'm sure things will be a lot more enjoyable once we get in the field."

"Right," Devers said. "Sweating our balls off in a hundred degrees of heat and humidity—that's when the fun starts."

Devers leaned back in his seat, laughing even harder at his own comment.

"Don't listen to him," McCarter said. "It's probably no more than ninety-five degrees out there. Ninety-six, ninety-seven, tops."

As another wave of laughter moved through the group, McCarter thought of his own reasons for joining the expedition. For a moment he felt the grip of sadness creeping in, but then the helicopter began to slow and the treetops gave way to acres of manicured grass and sculptured botanical gardens. A leisurely turn to the left revealed the main buildings of the Hotel San Cristo, and a moment later they were touching down on the helipad.

McCarter climbed out, thankful to be stretching his legs. He saw a young woman in black slacks and a sleeveless khaki shirt walking toward them from the hotel.

"Welcome to Brazil," she said. "I'm Danielle Laidlaw."

## CHAPTER 5

That night, Danielle brought the team together for dinner in one of the hotel's private dining rooms. The atmosphere was pleasant, the food outstanding and the camaraderie genuine. As far as she could tell, everyone seemed to be enjoying themselves . . . everyone except for Professor McCarter.

She watched him as he grew progressively more introspective, and when he left the table before dessert, stating he wanted to get to bed early, she excused herself and followed him, trailing him to the hotel's main bar.

A drink before going to bed, she thought. Not a bad idea.

She walked up behind him as the soft music swirled around them and the bartender rushed off to grab a new bottle of whatever McCarter had ordered.

"Can I pay for that?" she asked. "The prices at this place are outrageous and the dollar's not what it used to be."

He turned, leaning against the polished mahogany and looking at her with a glint in his eye. "I should be ashamed to ask," he said, smiling. "But what's a nice girl like you doing in a place like this?"

She laughed lightly at the cliché. It was something Bogart might have said, something her own father might have thought would pass for the height of cool. At least it made for easy conversation. "Who says I'm a nice girl?" she replied.

"Vicious rumor," he said.

"I see," she said, thinking, *If he only knew her better.* "I'll have to do something about that. I'm here for a nightcap, actually. Sometimes it's the only way for me to sleep. Something tells me you feel the same."

McCarter sighed. "Just getting used to being alone," he admitted.

She nodded. The NRI background check on McCarter had revealed many things, most important of which was the crisis he'd been through for much of the last five years. His wife had been in and out of hospitals, battling cancer, eventually losing to it. She could sense in him the emptiness that such a loss brought on, the questioning.

Upon learning this, Moore had suggested they find someone else, but Danielle knew a little bit about what McCarter was going through. She believed that once he reengaged with life he would throw himself into the project more fully than another scholar might. She thought that would be to his benefit and was certain it would be to theirs. And so even though McCarter had turned them down initially, Danielle had convinced Moore that they needed to go after him again. Now here he was.

"I know about your wife," she said, finally. "For what it's worth, I know how you feel."

"Do you," he said, giving her that look, the one that

said he'd heard those words from so many people and most of them had no idea.

"My father died when I was twenty," she explained. "Lung cancer from smoking two packs a day. He was sick for a year and a half before he passed and my mother didn't deal with it very well, so I left school to come home and help."

McCarter's face softened. "I'm sorry. I didn't mean to . . . Were you close?"

That was a question, she thought. One she'd asked herself a thousand times. "Yes and no. More so when I was younger. I think he wanted boys, but instead he got stuck with just me. By the time I was ten, I knew how to throw a spiral and hit a fastball. On my twelfth birthday we changed the oil in the family car. But once I hit fifteen he kind of couldn't pretend anymore. I was wearing makeup and dying my hair . . . and dating. We didn't do too much after that. At least until I came back to take care of him."

McCarter nodded. "I'm sure he appreciated that."

She shook her head. "Actually, he considered me a quitter for letting his sickness affect me. For walking away from a scholarship, missing out on a year of academics. It made him furious, especially as he was too weak to force me to go back."

As she spoke, the sting of that day hit her again. To her father, *quitter* was the worst thing you could call someone. Failing was one thing, quitting was a disgrace. It had always been his most bitter attack.

"He probably just—"

She put a hand on his arm to stop him. "He had a lot of misplaced anger," she explained. "But he had a right to be angry, even if it was directed in the wrong way. And you and I have a right to be sad . . . and also to go on."

McCarter took a sip of his drink. "You know, one counselor told me to accept it. Accept aging, accept dying, even embrace it, he said. That seemed like a bunch of defeatist crap to me. So I said, to hell with that, but I still have this sense of purposelessness. You're young, you have different goals and drives. But when you get to be my age you'll realize you do everything in life for the people you love. For your spouse and kids. Now the kids are grown, they don't need you anymore, they kind of pat you on the head when you offer advice or try to help. And your partner is gone and you . . ."

He looked more directly at her. "And you can do anything you want to. *Anything*. But there doesn't seem to be any point to it. You're suddenly afraid to die and at the same time acutely aware of your own mortality. But instead of prodding you to live, it just sucks the joy out of life and you're not really living anymore anyway."

Danielle nodded. She remembered going back to school and finishing a double major in two and a half years just to prove she wasn't a quitter, charging forward on autopilot, keeping herself so busy that she couldn't think about her loss. And then, after graduating, she'd gone in a different direction, entering a profession totally unrelated to all that she'd learned. "You just have to keep looking," she said. "You'll find something. And in the meantime you can help me."

McCarter laughed and then looked at her with a sort of astonishment in his eyes at what she'd said. "How old are you again?"

"Older than I look," she replied. "And younger than I feel."

Laughing lightly, McCarter agreed. "I know how that goes."

As the bartender returned with her drink, McCarter held up his glass. "To the expedition," he offered. "May we *go on* and find the truth."

They clinked glasses and Danielle thought to herself, *he will never know the truth, but perhaps he will find what he needed.* "And anything else that might be out there," she added.

McCarter placed his tumbler back on the bar. "Speaking of that, what exactly will we be looking for anyway?"

She hadn't given out details yet. She didn't want any leaks. "You're not going to wait for the offical briefing, are you?"

"Not if I can help it."

She pursed her lips and then relented. "I suppose a little sneak preview wouldn't hurt."

She took another sip of her drink. "As I told you before, we've discovered evidence suggesting the existence of an organized tool-using culture in the Amazon over two thousand years ago. Unlike the current native groups, this culture seemed to use stone as a medium and may have even smelted metals such as gold. What I left out was that we believe they were a branch of the Mayan race."

"The Maya in the Amazon?" He shook his head. "I don't think so."

"I realize the thought is contrary to what most Maya scholars believe. One guy I talked to called it silly science. But we have some concrete evidence and some local folklore that I think you'll find interesting in regards to what we're looking for."

He furrowed his brow. "Which is?"

"A very old place," she said. "Ancient even in comparison to the classic sites of the Maya. You would know it as the Citadel, or by the name Tulan Zuyua."

McCarter's eyes grew wider. Tulan Zuyua was a name out of Mayan mythology. It was the mythical birthplace of the Mayan people; their version of the Garden of Eden, a legendary city once shared by the different Mayan tribes before they went off on their own.

"Well," he said, almost dumbfounded. "You don't think small."

"Never," she said. Certainly, there was nothing small about the goal. And that was only the half of it.

"What evidence do you have suggesting Tulan Zuyua actually exists—let alone down here?"

"We have a chain of artifacts, none conclusive but all suggestive. We believe they show evidence of Mayan writing in a more ancient hieroglyphic style than found at the classic sites in Central America. An older culture with a single starting point, and we intend to find it."

She noticed McCarter lean a little closer as she spoke. His interest seemed piqued.

"I'd share the details with you tonight," she added, "but I don't want to spoil the surprise."

He frowned and leaned back. "Well, then," he said, as if making some tough decision, "I choose not to pry, though I must say I'd like to."

"A gentleman," she said. "As I'd been told to expect."

"I admit, it does sound interesting," he said. "At least to someone like me. But what's your interest in all this? I thought NRI was a big lab of some kind, a research house working with all the high-tech companies."

She nodded. "We are. We do industrial design and tech research, for the most part. But we also grant endowments to other sciences. And we do a lot of PR work, things that all our member corporations can claim to be part of." The words slid from her mouth with ease, unforced and completely believable. She'd said them before in different forms, different places. Neither McCarter or the others would ever know where the money really came from, or what it was for.

"So this is a PR job?" he asked. "I suppose that means we'll end up with Nike logos on our equipment and a Budweiser sign over our camp."

"Nothing that drastic," she said. "Though you may have to dress up as a giant cheeseburger for a series of interviews with the BBC."

He laughed.

"Honestly," she said, "there are no strings attached. Except that you do the best you can. And in that vein, I'll tell you all that I know tomorrow. It'll be up to you to take us from there."


McCarter promised not to be late and Danielle said good night before walking off toward the elevators.

As he watched her go, McCarter had to admit that she'd somehow brought out the optimist in him—a quality he wasn't sure he still possessed. He turned back to the bar and put his hand on the tumbler, tilting it toward him until the ice swirled to the low point. He was fairly certain that the NRI's crazy theory would be nothing but a gigantic bust, but what the hell, even proving that could be a great deal of fun.

After leaving McCarter, Danielle returned to her hotel room, where the message light on her phone blinked silently in the darkness. A man named Medina had called; another name from Arnold Moore's inexhaustible supply of contacts. Medina captained a small riverboat and it had been Moore's intention to meet with him and secure the charter prior to leaving for Washington. But Medina had been delayed and Moore had left without getting the chance.

Danielle dialed and a voice answered on the first ring. "Hello, Medina speaking."

"Señor Medina, this is Danielle Laidlaw. I work with Mr. Moore."

"Yes, hello," Medina said. His English was heavily accented. "I was told to contact you. Señor Moore has gone back to the States, then?"

"Yes," she replied. "I'll be your contact now."

"Okay, no problem," the man said. "Señor Moore wanted to inspect the boat before we go out. Will you be wanting to see it?"

"Yes, of course. When would be a good time to look it over?"

"Tonight is okay," he said.

Danielle almost laughed; it was nearly midnight. "Tonight is not okay," she said. "How about tomorrow, around noon?"

"No good," Medina said. "We go back out very early. Best to do it now."

Danielle had no desire to make a late-night trip to the waterfront, especially after what had been a long and grueling day. Before she answered, Medina made another suggestion. "Or we could do it in three days, when we return."

That wasn't going to work. If the boat proved to be inadequate, she would be delayed further while they found a replacement. "It'll have to be tonight, then."

"Okay," he said. "Fine. We're on the west side of the harbor, in the old section, beyond the Puerta Flutante. There are no numbers out there, but we are closest to the *dezenove:* pier nineteen. If you meet me there, I take you to the boat."

"I can be there in forty-five minutes," she said. "Is that soon enough?"

"Yes," he said. "We'll still be unloading then, so I'll wait for you."

"Forty-five minutes," she repeated. "I'll see you then."

*"Buena,"* he said. *"Ciao."*

The dial tone returned.

*"Ciao,"* Danielle muttered, unhappy at the options ahead of her.

She walked to the balcony and looked out over the city. Manaus was gorgeous at night, with the city lights blazing. But the danger remained, lying out there hidden in the shadows. This trip to the waterfront would expose her to it. She thought of calling Medina back and canceling, but it would quickly reach Gibbs, and that

would just give additional ammunition to her detrac-
tors.

The hell with it, she was going. But proving yourself
and being foolish were two different things; she would
bring help. Verhoven or one of his men seemed a natural
choice, but they were bunked down on the north side of
the city near the airstrip they'd flown into, too far away
to reach her in time. Besides, she'd barely met them and
didn't feel any level of trust there yet. Another face came
to mind.

She grabbed her cell phone and dialed. An American
voice answered.

"Hawker, this is Danielle. How fast can you be at the
hotel?"

"Ten minutes," he said. "Why? Is something wrong?"

"Not yet," she said, hoping that the status quo
wouldn't change. "But I have to meet with someone and
I'm not interested in doing it alone."

"All right," he said. "I'll see you in the lobby."

Danielle hung up, took a last look at the city lights
and walked back into her room. She changed into dark
slacks and a black sweater, then opened the safe in her
closet. From beneath some papers she retrieved a Smith
& Wesson revolver. Out of habit, she opened the chamber to make sure it was loaded, then snapped it shut and
slid it into a trim holster strapped around her right
ankle. If trouble came, whoever brought it would find
out just how nice a girl she was.

## CHAPTER 6

Hawker arrived in the lobby dressed in black from head to toe, just as she was. "I assumed this would be something formal," he joked.

She glanced at him for a moment and then signaled for the valet, trying not to appreciate how well he cleaned up. For certain he looked a damn sight better than he had in the sweaty hangar in Marejo.

As they drove off together Danielle thought about the meeting. *A friend of a friend of someone who owes me a favor.* That's how Moore had described Medina. The thought made her smile; in all their travels, she couldn't recall a place they'd ever been to where Moore didn't have a friend of a friend of someone who owed him a favor.

She turned to Hawker. "How well do you know the waterfront?"

"Is that where we're headed?"

"We're going to see a man about a boat. Our charter, actually."

"And you're expecting trouble?" he said.

"Just being cautious. The guy is docked at one of the smaller jetties, out near the old harbor somewhere, but we're meeting him at pier nineteen and following him back."

Hawker grew quiet for a moment. "Nineteen's one of the big commercial docks at the west end. It's a cargo pier, pretty wide open, but just up from there everything gets cluttered. Narrow alleys and blind corners. A lot of small buildings. The locals tie up over there, fishermen mostly, and some of the ferries. If this guy's a local, that's where he'd be."

Danielle had expected as much.

It took twenty minutes to get from the hotel to the harbor, and another five to find their way to pier nineteen. But even so, they arrived on site ten minutes earlier than Danielle had promised. She pulled up against the wall of a massive warehouse that ran along the waterfront.

At this hour of the night there was little activity. A few slips down, a Liberian-flagged tanker was offloading a shipment of crude, while out in the channel, a blue-hulled cargo vessel sat idle but making steam, its decks stacked high with multi-colored containers, its crew waiting patiently for a river pilot to come aboard.

Hawker eyed the empty pier. "Don't take this the wrong way, but couldn't you meet this guy during normal business hours?"

"It's all part of that low-profile thing."

A few minutes went by with no sign of Medina.

Hawker adjusted his mirror to see behind him and then tilted his seat back a bit.

He seemed calm, relaxed enough to take a nap. She fiddled with a pen, clicking it repeatedly. Something didn't feel right to her. "Are you armed?" she asked.

"No," he said, quietly. "But you are."

"Good of you to notice."

He laughed softly. "You either need a smaller gun or bell-bottoms."

She smiled in the darkness, half angry, half amused. "This guy isn't my contact. He's my old partner's. I'm not sure what to make of him yet."

Hawker nodded and the interior of the Rover grew quiet as the two of them scanned the surroundings for any sign of the contact or trouble. Several minutes later, headlights appeared in the distance, moving toward them along the wide frontage at the water's edge.

Hawker straightened up.

The sedan slowed as it approached them, stopping under a streetlight ninety feet away. A man stepped out of the car, squinted in their direction and then waved. When they didn't respond fast enough, he reached through the driver's window, flashed the headlights and leaned on the horn for a couple of long blasts.

"So much for the low profile," Hawker said.

Danielle smiled and flashed her lights. As the man walked over, she put her window down.

"Señora Laidlaw?" the man said. "I am Medina, at your service."

Danielle introduced herself and then pointed to Hawker. "He's our transportation specialist. He'll be doing the inspection."

Medina seemed unconcerned. "*Isso bom,*" he said. "That's cool." He waved his hand toward his sedan. "Ride with me. I'll take you over."

"Just show us the way," Danielle said. "We'll follow."

"Okay," Medina said. "No problem. Stay close, then—there are many streets but not enough signs, you know? Easy to get lost."

Danielle assured him that she would stay close and Medina began walking back to his sedan.

"When did I become the transportation specialist?" Hawker asked.

"Just now," she said. "You've been promoted. I hope you know something about boats."

"They go in the water, right?"

She smiled and started the engine while Hawker watched Medina.

As the man climbed back into his car, Hawker scowled. "He's not alone."

Danielle had scanned the car earlier, but there was no way to see through the darkened windows. "Are you sure?"

"He looked into the back when he opened the door. A brief pause as he made eye contact with someone."

The headlights of Medina's car came on and it began to move, making a wide circle, swinging close to them and then heading back the way it had come.

"Do you think that's a problem?" she asked.

"I don't think it's good. Then again, you didn't come alone either. Maybe he's afraid of you."

She took her foot off the brake. "He wouldn't be the first."

Hawker glanced at her. "Or the last, I'll bet."

Danielle followed Medina through the narrow maze of streets. In a few minutes they had passed by the Puerto Flutante, the floating harbor built by the British in 1902, with its amazing system of docks and jetties that rose and fell with the level of the river. From their vantage point the docks appeared low, near the limit of their downward travel, the result of a rainy season now a month overdue.

Farther on, they reached the oldest section of the waterfront. Here the jetties were little more than a tangle of crooked, wooden fingers. The small boats crowded them from all directions, like worker bees surrounding their queen. Two, three, even four rows deep, so many boats that some could not even find space on the dock for a rope and had to tie off to other vessels. Danielle imagined the congestion in the morning, the chaos of an aquatic rush hour that she and her team would slip away in.

Medina made a right turn, away from the crowded edge and down a patchy, uneven road that led inland. A half mile later, he stopped beside a black steel gate, waiting as it slid backward along a greased metal track. When it had retracted far enough Medina drove through.

Danielle moved the Rover up to the track.

She looked around. The area was cluttered with vehicles and pieces of construction equipment. Stacks of oil drums vied with containers and other bits of junk for space. "A lot more commercial than I'd have guessed."

Down at the waterline, a group of men worked beside a small boat, beneath the glare of two floodlights. "I guess that's your boat," Hawker said.

"And if we want it, we have to go inside." She took her foot off the brake and, with two bumps, they eased across the track and the steel gate began to close behind them.

Medina, now out of his car, directed them across the lot to park near an old white pickup truck. Danielle pulled in next to the truck. She turned toward Hawker to speak, but didn't get the chance.

With his left arm Hawker reached out and slammed her back against her seat. His right hand came up, a heavy black pistol in his grasp, swinging toward her face. She turned away and shut her eyes. In that split second of darkness she heard an explosion and felt a flash of heat across the side of her face.

She opened her eyes to see a man falling away from the Rover, an Uzi machine pistol in his hand, a fedora hat falling to the ground behind him. Stunned and immobile, she heard Hawker shouting at her through the fog. He fired at another target and she grabbed the gearshift, threw it into reverse and stomped on the gas pedal. The wheels spun and the Rover shot backward.

"Go!" Hawker yelled, firing again.

Looking over her shoulder, Danielle aimed straight for the closed gate and continued to accelerate. With the engine roaring, she slammed it dead center. The heavy gate shuddered, bending backward at a thirty degree angle. Chunks of concrete flew out from the retaining wall and the gate's wheels ripped clear of the tracks, but, somehow, the mangled hunk of iron held them in.

She put the transmission in drive but the engine had stalled. She threw it into neutral and twisted the key. Just as the big V-8 turned over, the windshield shattered from a hail of bullets.

As the glass rained down, she and Hawker ducked for cover. Hawker raised his arm above the dashboard and fired back, five shots sent out blindly. In the restricted cockpit of the Rover the sound was tremendous, but the incoming bullets stopped and Danielle had enough time to shift into drive and hit the gas once again.

The Rover lunged forward for thirty feet before Danielle stomped on the brake and slammed the transmission into reverse. By now Hawker had his bearings, snapping off shots into the darkness. One man went down and then another, while the other assailants dove for cover.

The Rover thundered backward, hammering the gate a second time, blasting it from its moorings and sending it flying across the road in a shower of sparks. Danielle turned the wheel and the nose of the vehicle swung to the left, pointing in the direction of safety.

She jammed it into drive and hit the gas, accelerating away as renewed gunfire poured from the gated area. Flying lead tore into the vehicle, punching holes in the sheet metal and shattering the side and rear windows, even as Medina's car, now driven by someone else, accelerated hard in an effort to cut them off.

Hawker targeted the driver's area of the oncoming vehicle. As his shots hit the windshield, the sedan swerved, crashing into what remained of the gate's retaining wall. Whether the driver was dead, injured or had just turned wildly to avoid being hit, they would never know, as the Rover accelerated away and the scene passed quickly out of view.

With the throttle wide open the big vehicle gathered speed at a surprising rate, barreling down the same road they'd come up only minutes before. At the first corner, Danielle turned hard and the big SUV leaned over, threatening to tip then straightening out and roaring off down a long, unfamiliar street.

They sped through a dark canyon now, a narrow street running between the connected buildings on the left and the great slab walls of the warehouses on the right. The alley was unlit, except for pale swaths where other streets crossed it. Danielle watched the intersections ahead, expecting a car to block their way at any moment. It didn't matter, she wasn't stopping.

Behind them the headlights of two cars swung into the alleyway. "Here they come," Hawker yelled, shouting to be heard above the noise pouring into the cabin where the windshield had been.

Danielle heard but didn't reply. The same airflow that made it hard to hear was wreaking havoc on her eyes. She squinted against the wind, blinking away the tears. She spotted a marker: Ave de Setembro—the main road out of the harbor. She cranked the wheel over and the tires bit into the street, squealing and sliding. A moment later, they shot out onto the open road.

Danielle floored the accelerator again, but this time the Rover picked up only a little extra speed and then the engine started to labor. The needle touched a hundred twenty kph and then began an ominous slide backward.

"Fuel or air," Hawker yelled.

"I'm thinking air," she shouted. "Mainly because we're not on fire."

"Not yet anyway," he said.

The Rover had begun chugging like an old steam

train, gaining speed for a few seconds and then faltering further. In the mirror, Danielle saw the two cars swerve onto the road a mile behind. She coaxed more speed from the vehicle by pumping the throttle, but the cars were clearly gaining. "Any thoughts?"

"Head into town," Hawker said. "We have to find a crowd."

Danielle took the first turn that would bring them into the heart of the city, and three blocks later turned again.

The turns had two effects: they reduced the Rover's speed, which made it run more smoothly, and they reduced the rate at which their pursuers were gaining, as they had to slow down for the same turns.

In another minute, they were nearing the center of town, weaving in and out of calmer traffic.

"We need to ditch this thing," Hawker said.

Danielle looked for a spot that might offer some cover. She passed two streets and an empty lot and then swerved down a narrow alleyway populated by trash cans, Dumpsters and uneven stacks of wooden pallets. She drove halfway down the alley, turned the vehicle sideways and slammed on the brakes, bringing it to a skidding halt.

Hawker bolted out the door before they'd even fully stopped, shouting at her to follow.

She jumped from the car, making her way around the vehicle as their pursuers came barreling down the road. The noise of their engines filled the alleyway and the light from their high beams climbed the walls like a specter, but the sound of screeching tires came next as the two cars skidded to a halt. They could not fit past the Rover. They'd have to move it, back out, or follow on foot. And with the keys in Danielle's pocket, the first choice was not really an option. She raced around the corner without looking back.

"This way," Hawker said.

They were out on the main drag, moving along the sidewalk, mixing with the pedestrians. It was Friday night and the bars and cafés were jammed to capacity, the sidewalks teeming with the overflow. But Hawker and Danielle were dressed differently than the clubgoers in their bright, revealing outfits. After all, it was summer in Brazil. "We have to get off the street," she said.

"I know," Hawker replied, pressing forward, his eyes searching for something. "Keep moving. I know a place."

Hawker pushed through the crowd with Danielle right behind him, leading her to a nightclub at the center of the district with a line of people waiting for a chance to enter. A doorman stood at the entrance, flanked by two muscular bouncers. The doorman greeted Hawker with a smile and one of the bouncers shook his hand.

In a moment, Hawker and Danielle were upstairs, seated at a private table on the club's open-air balcony, a spot that gave them some respite from the pounding music inside and, more important, offered an excellent view of the main entrance and the crowded street below.

Danielle watched in silence for several minutes, waiting for cars filled with armed men to come flying up to the front doors. She put her hand casually to her ankle to make sure her weapon was accessible and then slid her leg under the table and out of view.

Hawker exhaled deeply and looked right at her. "You want to tell me again about this *archaeological expedition?*"

## CHAPTER 7

Danielle ignored his question. She looked around. The club was not that crowded, not yet. It was certainly not as busy as the street below, but the movement was still chaotic enough that there would be little chance to spot a threat until it was right on top of them. "Why did you bring me here?"

"These guys are friends of mine," he said.

She waited for a better explanation.

"I did a favor for the owner once," he added grudgingly, as if that explained everything.

"What kind of favor?"

"His daughter was taken from him. I brought her back."

Danielle went quiet, imagining the scenario and guessing that such an act would buy a good measure of loyalty. "And the men who took her?"

Hawker shook his head slowly.

"Some favor."

"Trust me," he said, "no one's getting to us unannounced."

She gazed out over the balcony once again, guessing that their attackers were not about to shoot their way into a crowded club, even if they knew where she and Hawker had gone. She dialed the hotel on her cell phone, making sure they increased security on the NRI's private floor, and made a mental note to move Verhoven and his people there in the morning. She turned her attention back to Hawker, realizing he had lied to her. "You said you were unarmed."

"I did," he admitted.

She reached for a glass of water. "Apparently, that wasn't entirely true."

He smiled. "You all right?"

"Deaf in one ear, but I'll live."

Hawker's face grew serious. "Someone set you up. Your old partner, maybe?"

There was no way Arnold Moore would have put her in danger. They'd been too close for too long. "I don't think so. I'm not saying it was an accident, but it wasn't a setup from our end."

"What, then?"

"A shakedown maybe, or a kidnapping attempt. Well-connected American disappears and gets held for ransom. Like your friend. It happens more often than you'd think down here."

"I know all about 'down here,'" he said. "And you're right, it could have been anything. But it wasn't. It was connected with this expedition."

She didn't want to go down this road. But if they were going to do so, she preferred for it to happen quickly. "What's your point?" she said.

He hesitated, appearing to be put off by her directness. "I still know a few people," he said. "And I've done some checking. I know your responsibilities and your reputation. You've been all over the world, but that was prior to becoming a regional director."

The words lingered. It was the promotion that had come through as part of this assignment, but in reality she was still Moore's lieutenant. The promotion would take effect only upon successful completion of the mission. "You're half right," she said.

"That's more than usual," he replied. "And it's enough to make me wonder what the hell is really going on here. In the Agency, big shots ride desks and read reports; they tell other people where to go and what to do."

He sat back, looking very pleased with himself. "But then here you are," he added. "And until your partner left a few days ago, here you both were, two high-ranking directors working the ground floor like a couple of stiff necks, dragging around a bunch of civilians who have no idea what they're getting into."

She glared at him. "Not my choice."

"And yet, I'm guessing it would cause problems if I told them we'd been shot at."

"Mostly for you," she said coldly.

He studied her, seeming to agree. "Funny thing is, I rode shotgun on an operation like this once. We had a Chinese defector coming in through Hong Kong with a list of operatives and part of a cipher code. The only face he trusted was a pretty bank teller's from Macau, so we brought her in, covered her seven ways from Sunday and prayed that no one got killed. Security was so tight that the Asian director of field ops met with the guy himself. No regulars around, no station involvement or paper trail. Just a couple of guys who don't exist, a DFO who was never there and a young woman who went back to her normal life, a little wealthier and none the wiser."

She listened, hoping that her own team would fare as well and contemplating the concept of a man who doesn't exist. At the very least the China operation did not appear in his file.

"Look," he said, "I have no idea what you're after down here, and to be honest, I really don't care. But whatever it is, it's big and it has to be kept quiet. Otherwise you wouldn't be here. Your partner wouldn't have been here. And you sure as hell wouldn't have come looking for me. Not with my situation."

His "status," she thought. "By situation, you mean the fact that you're wanted."

He seemed offended. "I'm not 'wanted,' like some common criminal."

"Really?" she said. "The State Department has a warrant out for you. Interpol does as well. NSA, CIA, FBI, they'd all like to have a few words with you, preferably in a locked room somewhere. How much more wanted could a man be?"

"Right," he said. "Well, where the hell are they? Don't you think they could find me if they tried? You did." He shook his head. "They don't want to find me. They just want to make sure they don't lose track of me."

This much she knew, though it was unclear as to why.

"Besides," he said. "That just proves my point. You say I'm wanted, but you hired me anyway. You made a four-hour drive to the middle of nowhere to do it, when a single phone call could have brought in one of your

BLACK RAIN                    69

own. And that can mean only one thing: this operation goes beyond quiet; it has to be invisible, even to your own people. To make sure that's the case, you hire a guy who can't talk to anyone, a guy no one would listen to even if he did."

"I see," she said. "Apparently, we're smarter than I thought."

"I hope you are, because they've left you in a bad spot. They sent you to fight a war without any bullets and told you failure's not an option." He leaned back. "And that's the catch, isn't it? You don't mind the task; you just want the equipment to get the job done. But security requires that you go it alone."

He backed off a bit. "Okay, maybe tonight did take you by surprise. Or maybe you've been waiting for this since you came down here. Either way, now you know for sure: the word's out and whatever the hell you're after, someone else wants it too. Bad enough to kill you for it."

That fact hadn't escaped her. They'd begun this task secure in the knowledge that they were alone, but somewhere along the line, despite a maniacal focus on security, word had slipped.

"I'm not your enemy," he added. "I know the position you're in. I know it all too well. And I'm not pressing you. I'm offering to help. To *mutually agree* upon some additional responsibilities."

Perhaps it was his new tone or the realization that there was no point in further denials, but as he used her own words from their conversation in the hangar, she couldn't help but brighten a fraction. "What kind of responsibilities?"

"I can talk to people who would run from your shadow. I can get things done that would be impossible in your official capacity. And most important of all, I can give you cover from a direction no one would expect, because as far as anyone knows, I'm just the guy who flies the plane."

Danielle weighed Hawker's words carefully. He was right, of course; Gibbs' ever-increasing paranoia had led him to call Arnold Moore back to D.C. And for what? It had only made things worse. In Moore's absence she was vulnerable and exposed—out on an island, exactly as Hawker had described. She peered across the table. Perhaps he was right, perhaps he could be of assistance. "So you'd like to help me?"

Hawker nodded, leaing forward in his chair as if he were bowing. "I offer my services. Meager as they may be."

The edge of her lip curled almost imperceptibly. "Your services," she repeated, interested now. She leaned forward, stirring her glass of water with a straw. "And in exchange for such services, you would require . . . what?"

"A ticket home."

"A pardon," she guessed.

"Pardons require charges, conviction actually. Nothing like that exists in my case."

"What, then?"

"Simple clarity." He motioned toward her with his hand. "You guys have friends in high places. Over at State, with the NSC, and whether you admit it or not, everywhere in the Agency. They're the ones who have it out for me. The right words are said, specific assurances are given and the problems disappear. Then I can go home again. Start living a normal life."

It was hard to look at him and think of a person living a normal life. It didn't suit him, or really even seem possible that he could have relatives, family and friends somewhere. His file was blacked out, partially to protect the innocent, of course, but it gave the impression of a person with no past, as if he'd just come into existence out of the ether, fully formed as the man she saw in front of her.

"So you help me see this thing through," she said, "and I get them to forget your past. So you can go back to Kansas with Toto and Dorothy and Auntie Em? Am I understanding this right?"

He laughed. "More likely somewhere with a beach, and if Dorothy is there, she'd better be wearing a blue and white plaid bikini and sharing a cold beer with me, but yeah, that's the general idea."

It didn't cost her a thing to promise, but she wasn't sure she could deliver, and in a strange onset of conscience found she didn't want to lie. "What makes you think I can do all that? I can't even find out what you did to get yourself into this mess."

"If this thing's as important as I think it is, you'll have carte blanche. You probably do now. You just don't know it yet."

She thought about that. Gibbs' obsession with the project suggested he was right.

Hawker elaborated. "Somewhere back in Washington there's a file you'll never see, with the letters R.O.C. stamped in one corner. Those are mission attainment parameters. R.O.C., depending on who you ask, means

*Regardless of Cost* or *Regardless of Consequences*. It means this thing is the express train and everything else gets out of the way. You want to pay someone off, done. You want someone to disappear, done. You want to cut a deal with a tragically misunderstood, ruggedly handsome fugitive, fine, just bring us what we want and don't ask why."

"Handsome?"

He glared at her in mock disappointment. "You could do worse."

She nodded. "I suppose."

"The point is, they don't tell you about things like that when you're in the field, but after a while you start to know. I'll bet your old partner knew."

Silently, she agreed. Gibbs had given them everything they'd asked for without batting an eye, everything except allowing Moore to stay on. Perhaps Moore *had* known too much. "You'll be in the dark," she said.

"I do my best work that way," he said. "Just tell me what you think I should know. You can start by giving me some info on the guy we met with tonight. I'll find out who he associates with. Maybe we can figure out who paid him off, or who the payment came through. He seemed like a nervous type, probably not doing this by pure choice. Beyond that, I can arrange a new charter, with someone I know and trust."

"And how do I know I can trust you?" she asked.

"You can't," he said. "Not the way I trust these guys." He nodded toward the center of the club, indicating the friends who worked and owned the club, providers of their temporary refuge. "But you can trust people to act in their own self-interest. And at this point you have something to offer me that no one else can match."

"And assuming that's true, what makes you think you can trust me?"

Hawker leaned back in his chair and smiled at her. It was the look of a rogue and a cheat, the look of a man who knew just what the next card would bring and had been waiting forever to see it played. Somehow it was charming just the same.

"My options are more limited," he said. "I can walk away and keep scratching out a life down here or I can take a chance on you. So there it is," he finished. "Time to roll the bones."

Danielle failed to suppress a grin. It made sense to her. It fact, it actually seemed fair. The bargain itself would probably infuriate Gibbs, but that almost made it more appealing. "All right," she said. "I'll take your offer. I can't promise anything until I have it cleared, so I won't. But I'll talk to the people I know and if there's a deal to be had, I'll give it to you. Fair enough?"

"Fair enough for me."

As Hawker finished, a broad-shouldered man with a thick moustache and deep tan approached. With his impeccably moussed hair and a spotless white dinner jacket, he looked like a movie star from a bygone era. He carried two glasses in one hand and an expensive bottle of Chilean wine in the other. He introduced himself as Eduardo, owner of the club and sometime benefactor of young Mr. Hawker. The two friends shook hands and then Eduardo turned his full attention to Danielle.

"Who is this lovely vision?" he asked. "And what

great misfortune has her spending the evening in such company?"

Hawker feigned distress at Eduardo's comment even as Danielle held out her hand. "Pleased to meet you," she said. "My name is Danielle."

Eduardo smiled, kissed her hand, then turned back to Hawker. "An American," he noted. "Like you."

"An American," Hawker said. "But not like me."

Eduardo raised an eyebrow. "A good thing for her, no doubt."

"No doubt," Hawker said.

Eduardo turned serious. "You ran into a problem."

"I can't tell you what they look like," Hawker said. "Or even what they're wearing. But I'd guess they're still searching for us."

"Don't worry," Eduardo said. "I'll send you home in my car. In the meantime I've put some extra men on, friends from the *policia*. They like big paychecks and hassling troublemakers. And I told Diego no one else crosses the ropes tonight."

Hawker looked pained. "This is your biggest night, that's going to cost you."

Eduardo laughed softly and then turned to Danielle. "Our friend Hawker, he's okay, but not too bright when it comes to business. I know of no better way to attract a crowd than to tell them they can't get in. I'll do this again tomorrow night and all through the week and by next Friday, I can double the prices and still fill the place three times over." Eduardo shook his head softly. "Already I'm asking myself, why didn't I think of this years ago?"

"I owe you for this," Hawker said.

"No," Eduardo said. "Not you."

His attention returned to Danielle. "I'm afraid I must leave you for a while." He placed the bottle of wine on the table. "But please, cheer him up while I'm gone. He's far too serious for one sitting with such a beautiful woman."

Danielle smiled at Hawker, and then back at Eduardo. "I'll do my best."

With that Eduardo bowed and stepped away.

"Your friend is charming."

"Yeah," Hawker said, rolling his eyes. "I think he likes you too." He picked up the bottle of wine, examined the label and then uncorked it and let it breathe. "Looks like we're going to be here for a while," he said. "Might as well make the best of it."

She agreed and pushed her glass across the table toward him.

## CHAPTER 8

Arnold Moore had returned to Washington, his residence in absentia for three decades spent traipsing the world. In all that time, he'd spent less than a thousand days in Washington, and never longer than two months at a stretch. After so much time away, returning felt awkward, like being a stranger in his own land, a guest in his own empty home.

Still, this time it would be different. He'd come back to a career winding down and a superior who appeared to be growing tired of their endless clashes. This time, Moore reckoned, he'd come home for good.

Stuart Gibbs, director of operations, was a fairly paranoid man—paranoid and grossly ambitious, a combination that had led to many a metaphorical beheading of former colleagues and confidants. Based on the deteriorating tone of their last few conversations, Moore guessed he was next on the chopping block.

As if to reinforce the point, Stuart Gibbs had spoken to him only once since his arrival. No explanations had been offered and Moore's repeated calls since had been blatantly ignored. Now, after a week of such treatment, he'd been summoned to a meeting. If it was to be his end, then he intended to air his grievances.

To meet with Gibbs, Moore traveled to the NRI's main office, a sprawling campus known as the Virginia Industrial Complex, or more affectionately the VIC. The VIC consisted of five sleek buildings nestled among rolling hills, winding paths and rustic stone walls. The glass-walled structures were modern and attractive, the paths around them lit and manicured like those at an expensive resort. Even with the trees and lawns dormant for the winter, the complex felt more like a university mall or suburban office park than anything governmental in nature. Only the presence of armed guards in the parking lot, with their bomb-sniffing dogs and long mirrored poles, suggested otherwise.

Looking forward to the meeting, Moore arrived at the lot early and began a determined march through the crisp January air. Because of a quirk in the topography of the land, the five buildings that made up the complex lay spaced at odd intervals, with four clustered on the eastern side of the property and the fifth, housing the Operations Division and its director, Stuart Gibbs, alone on the western edge, separated from the others by a low-lying ridge and a row of seventy-foot oaks. As a result, Building Five wasn't visible from the street or the main gate or even from the other structures, and one had to make a lengthy winding trek to reach it. It was supposedly a random occurrence, one Moore had his doubts about, but either way it had always struck him as both ironic and perfectly symbolic of the NRI's dual and conflicting nature.

The NRI had come into existence in the late '90s, a

Frankenstein's monster of an organization, divided and charged with two completely separate tasks. The Research Division, its main component, worked with corporate America, universities and leading entrepreneurs. Under that umbrella, corporate members gained access to advanced facilities, specialist personnel and reams of declassified data from NASA and the military. Its purpose was to boost the fortunes of American industry, to counter the subsidies and government assistance that corporations in Europe and Japan enjoyed.

But Research Division was only part of the organization, sometimes referred to as the civilian side. There was another side to the NRI, a darker side, and that was the Operations Division.

Six months after NRI's creation—and well before the first shovel of dirt had turned at the VIC—a rider was attached to a last-minute spending bill being rushed through Congress. The rider amended the NRI's charter, effectively dividing the organization in two, or more accurately adding a new division to the NRI's existing structure. That new entity was called Operations Division, or OpD.

OpD was tasked with a more sinister mission—the active gathering of industrial secrets, including those belonging to foreign powers and entities. In other words, industrial espionage. Appropriately, OpD had been run from its very inception by former members of the CIA, beginning with its director, Stuart Gibbs.

To the outside world the change was invisible. OpD appeared to be almost irrelevant, little more than the support apparatus for Research Division, a handmaiden to its charming and successful big sister. It was Research

Division that garnered all the press, Research Division that senators and CEOs enjoyed being linked to, that articles in *Time* and *BusinessWeek* focused on. To the adoring public, Research Division *was* the NRI; it claimed eighty percent of the budget, ninety percent of the staff and four of the five buildings at the Virginia Industrial Complex. But to the few people who knew the truth, OpD was considered the more important entity.

As Moore walked past the other buildings he couldn't help but smile. In all his years with the NRI he'd yet to set foot in any of them—a fact that wasn't going to change today. Whatever the future held, it waited for him on the other side of the hill, with Stuart Gibbs, in Building Five.

At the end of his half-mile trek, Moore felt energized. He bounded up the steps and into the lobby, flashed his ID badge and placed his thumb on the infrared scanner. He cleared a second checkpoint on the fourth floor and a minute later stood in the director's waiting room.

Gibbs' secretary barely looked up. "He's ready for you now."

Moore set his jaw and stepped inside.

The director's office was a windowless inside room, well lit and large, but surprisingly spartan for a man who carried such a big stick. As Moore entered, Stuart Gibbs stepped forward, extending a hand. "Welcome, Arnold," he said, "early as always."

The greeting was odd and hollow; the smile was uneven, like the jagged teeth of some rabid predator. Moore felt anything but welcome.

"Have yourself a seat," Gibbs said, steering Moore

toward the visitors' chairs in front of his desk, one of which was already occupied.

"I've asked Matt Blundin to join us," Gibbs explained. "He has some information that might interest you."

Matt Blundin was chief of security for the NRI, a huge apple of a man whose sheer volume could not be contained within the arms of the leather vistors' chair. He was a smoker and known to be a heavy drinker who preferred late nights to early days. At eight in the morning he reeked of nicotine, and his greasy hair and wrinkled suit did nothing to belie the assumption that he'd been out all night.

Still, Blundin was one of the best in the business, consulted at times by the FBI, the SEC and the Congressional Budget Office, and if he ever left the NRI, a long list of companies waited to make him a wealthy man.

Moore took a seat next to Blundin and wondered if he should have an attorney present.

Gibbs began the conversation. "How long has it been since we spoke face-to-face? Nine months? Maybe a year?" He shrugged. "Too damned long, either way."

Thin, angular-faced and eight years Moore's junior, Gibbs stood rigidly straight. His sandy blond hair was turning grayer by the year but remained swept back and gelled with utter precision; his designer suit was impeccable but hanging a little loose. Gibbs had always been gaunt, but he'd lost a few pounds since the last time Moore saw him. It left him looking almost ferretlike. Gibbs the Rodent, Moore thought. Gibbs the Rat.

Moore fired first. "All right, Stuart, enlighten me

with your reasons for bringing me here. If you have any."

"I'm not sure I like your tone," Gibbs said.

"I'm quite certain that you don't," Moore replied. "But that's what happens when you pull the rug out from under someone and then ignore them for a week. They get a little off-key."

Gibbs glared at Moore. "The *three* of us are here for several reasons. Beginning with an incident involving Danielle Laidlaw and the man you sent her to meet last night, a Mr. Duarte Medina."

Moore felt his face go flush. "What type of incident?"

"She was attacked at the meeting," Gibbs replied. "Her vehicle was shot up badly and she was almost killed."

"Damn it," Moore said. "I knew something like this would happen. I warned you not to pull me out. I could have protected her."

Almost imperceptibly, Gibbs nodded. "Perhaps," he said, glancing at Blundin, "or perhaps not. I find it interesting that you didn't choose this particular contact until after I informed you of the change."

"Meaning what?"

Gibbs shrugged, as if it were obvious. "If she'd been killed, we'd have had no choice but to send you back."

Moore ground his teeth. "You can't actually believe what you're suggesting."

"Medina was your contact," Gibbs said. "Supposedly secure, supposedly trustworthy. Yet the meeting turns out to be an excuse for a hit. Who do you think we're going to look at? In our position you'd do the same."

Moore turned to Blundin and then back to Gibbs. He could have throttled the director. "If you think—"

Gibbs cut him off. "You argued with me for weeks about putting her in charge. You've been calling for updates every day since you returned despite the fact that you're no longer a part of the project and were told to forget it. It almost seemed like you were expecting something."

Moore snapped, "You listen to me, you son of a bitch. Danielle is a friend and a partner. You knew what that meant once. I know, because I know people who worked with you. Maybe you've been in this office for too damned long, because it seems you've forgotten." Moore shook his head, realizing midstream that he'd taken the bait. This was just Gibbs' way of pushing him, of screwing with him and setting him off balance.

"You know goddamned well that I would never endanger her, so cut out this fucking charade and tell me what the hell you really brought me here for."

Gibbs was silent for a moment, as if he was mulling over what Moore had said. He tilted his chair back. "It's taken some effort," he said finally, "but I believe we've managed to clear you."

Moore sat back. The words were spoken too precisely. They were a setup to something else, though he could not guess what.

"Show him the photos," Gibbs said to Blundin.

Blundin opened a file folder that rested on the desk in front of him. He pulled out a black and white surveillance shot. "Is this your man Duarte?"

Moore studied the photo. It looked like Medina. "I think so."

"Well, this guy's dead. Been in the morgue since the day before the attack."

Moore winced. Medina was the nephew of a man who had helped him before. A man he considered a friend. "Are you sure?"

Blundin nodded.

"Do we know who killed Medina?"

"Not yet. The police down there don't have much to go on."

The director took it from there. "But we have a plan to lure them out, and that's where you actually become useful once again."

"So now we come to it."

Gibbs smiled wickedly, and as he spoke there was a certain amount of glee in his voice. "We're going to make it look as if you've fallen into disfavor here. This meeting is the first step. I'm sure the tongues are already wagging out there. In a day or two it'll be all over the office. Then you'll be put on administrative leave, pending an investigation. All expectations will point to an early, forced retirement. But don't worry, it won't be for disloyalty—that would be too obvious. The write-ups will be for incompetence, misuse of funds and our mutual inability to get along with each other."

"At least the last part's true."

"It makes for a better lie," Gibbs assured him.

Beside him, Blundin remained quiet, and Moore wondered if he was involved in the scheme or just along for the ride. His jowly face didn't give much away. Blundin was a good man, but he was one of Gibbs' boys. Gibbs protected them and they protected him. Moore couldn't blame Blundin for that; he directed his anger at Gibbs. "And to what end am I to be treated with such scorn?"

"Matt thinks they'll attempt to buy you off—or rent you, at least. I forgot to tell you, we've ruined your credit as well, made it look like you're in over your head. Big gambling problem. Came on strong when you were in Macau last year."

Moore grimaced in disbelief. "You can't actually be serious. The head of the operation suddenly pulled from the front line and put out to pasture? It's too obvious."

"These bastards are bold," Blundin grumbled. "They lured your partner to a meeting connected with the operation and tried to gun her down in plain sight, making no attempt to disguise it. That's unusual," he said. "Unprofessional, really. My guess: they're either disconnected from their controls, or just a bunch of desperate amateurs."

"Amateurs?" Moore said. "Desperate and disconnected?" His eyes darted from the security chief to the director. "Are you talking about them or us? Because this plan smacks of all three traits, if you ask me."

"We've been planning this for a while," Gibbs said. "If they want info, and we're betting they do, they're going to go after the best target available—and that will be you, a disgruntled, phased-out window-sitter with a lot of information rattling around in his brain."

Moore shook his head, doubting anyone would be so foolish.

Gibbs showed little sign of being moved, but when he

spoke again his tone had become more genuine, no doubt by design. "Arnold, we don't get along. Never have, right? If we asked the company shrink, she'd say that you resent me for taking what should have been your post and that I'm threatened by your ability. After all, given the chance, you could probably do my job at least as well as I do it, maybe better. Why do you think I send you running all over the damn world? To keep you out of Washington, where you're the one person who might be willing and able to usurp me. That, and the fact that you're the best at what you do. But this is the way it is: I run the show. I'm the one who says jump, not you. And right now you're going to do what I tell you for the greater good of the organization."

Moore smirked in disgust. The hard sell and the soft sell all wrapped up in one. "I wouldn't do your job," he said. "Not the way you do it, at least. So don't give me that line of crap. What you sense from me is not that I want your title, but that I'd rather you didn't have it either. Your judgment is poor and you're reckless, too damned reckless for my taste." He shook his head again. "This plan is absurd. It's ludicrous. As ludicrous as everything else you've asked us to do. Splitting us up at the last minute, concocting this ridiculous story and throwing me out there as some kind of bait. *This* is amateur work and it's going to get people killed. It almost did already."

"You presume too much, Arnold." Gibbs' voice had become a warning; lines were close to being crossed.

"And you think too little," Moore said. "Do you actually still intend to send her into the jungle with a bunch of civilians and some loan-outs from the Research Department? Even after all this?"

"She has protection."

"So did Dixon," Moore shouted. "Where the hell is he now? Did his team suddenly reappear, all tanned and rested and carrying souvenirs from a holiday somewhere? No, they're missing and probably dead. Cut to shreds by those natives you're so worried about, or ambushed by the same sons of bitches that shot at Danielle. And now you intend to send her out on the same path. A road people keep going down and not coming back. You're all but throwing her life away." Moore pointed an accusing finger at Gibbs. "There are better ways to do this," he said, "smarter ways. The sooner you admit—"

"Enough!" Gibbs slammed his hand on the desk, his face red with frustration. "There's no other way. We need this. Your country needs this."

The room was silent. Moore watched Gibbs rubbing his fingers together while he got ahold of himself.

"You know what we do?" Gibbs said finally. "The greatest country on earth? We borrow money from China to pay the Arabs for their oil. That's what we do. One day the Chinese are going to stop loaning it to us, or the Arabs are going to stop accepting paper for their hard assets."

He pushed a folder aside and leaned in toward Moore. "If this thing is out there, then it's the key to a whole new world, beginning with energy independence and leading the world in power generation for the next hundred years or so. Cold fusion means unlimited clean energy. It means a nation filled with clean, cheap power plants pumping out electricity for cars, trucks, trains and homes without creating carbon-based pollution, global warming or unstorable nuclear waste. And in *our* possession, it means the end of being a debtor to one possible enemy and a beggar in the eyes of another. You want that to fall into someone else's hands?"

Moore had heard this speech before. And while he agreed with Gibbs' assessment as to the magnitude of the changes that a working cold-fusion system would bring to the world, he continued to disagree with the man about the effort needed to get those results.

At Moore's silence, Gibbs exhaled in frustration. "This is what we pay you for. To run around and gather things up that will keep the country ahead of the competition. This one just happens to be in a hole in the ground somewhere instead of in a lab or on a database. And it also happens to be the big one, the Manhattan Project of our time. I'm not giving that up, but we damn well can't have an army running around down there, now, can we?"

"No," Moore said. "But you can send me back before anything else goes wrong."

Gibbs' mind was not one to be changed by argument or persuasion; he would only dig in further out of pride. Moore knew this, but had been unable to check himself. He watched as Gibbs took the folder back from Blundin and closed it. The discussion was over.

"You don't want to do this for me?" Gibbs said. "Fine, don't." He leaned forward, the sunken eyes and hollow cheeks suddenly menacing and evil. The Rodent possessed. "But you're not going back and your partner is still out there. And she *will* be in danger until we find out who's shadowing us."

Moore refused to look away, but he could say nothing. He stared at the director in a dead silence and watched as the jagged smile returned—the deal was done.

## CHAPTER 9

Professor McCarter stepped out of the service elevator with Susan Briggs and William Devers at his side. They entered a narrow, angled hallway that ran beneath the hotel toward the chosen meeting room. Bundled pipes and electrical conduits ran overhead and the floor was solid, unadorned concrete. Odd surroundings that left McCarter quietly surprised. His surprise changed to concern when they passed a stocky man with a radio bug in his ear and the bulge of a weapon clearly visible under a dark windbreaker.

The man waved them around a corner, toward their destination.

"Security," Devers said. "We always have them when we're overseas. Remember that Russian job I told you about? We had a bunch of ex-paratroopers following us; strangely enough, most of them had no teeth."

Susan laughed. "Gross."

"Good people, though," Devers said. "Very willing to share their vodka. Just didn't have the best dental plan." He turned around and studied the man behind them. "We'll have to see how these guys turn out."

McCarter glanced over his shoulder. "At least this one has his teeth."

The hallway dead-ended at Parlor A, and the group entered to find Danielle standing with Mark Polaski.

McCarter chose a spot both front and center, like all his best students. The roll reversal amused him.

As they settled in, Danielle walked to the entrance, signaled the man at the end of the hall and shut the door. "Sorry about the accommodations," she said, turning back to the group. "I didn't want to do this in a big hall and this was the only small room available—now I can see why."

Danielle dimmed the lights and clicked a remote. A picture of a Mayan temple appeared on the screen at the front of the room. "We're about to embark on a great adventure," she began. "As some of you already know, we'll be searching for a branch of the Mayan culture that certain scholars believe may have existed in the Amazon. But to say only that is to sell ourselves short. Our goal is far more ambitious. We're looking for a place that the Maya considered the land of their own genesis, their Garden of Eden—a city called Tulan Zuyua."

Susan Briggs turned to McCarter as she realized what Danielle was suggesting. "Are they serious?' she asked.

McCarter nodded. "I think so," he said.

Danielle clicked the remote and a photograph of a colorful mural came up. The mural depicted four men in native garb walking fearfully under a midnight sky.

She addressed Professor McCarter. "Feel free to correct me if I get any of this wrong."

He nodded, expecting to be busy.

"According to Mayan legend, there was an age before the first sunrise, a time when the world was dark, lit only by a gray twilight that lingered on the edge of the horizon. Into the darkness of this pre-dawn world, the Mayan gods created the first humans and then called them to a place named Tulan Zuyua, where they presented each tribe with a patron god. The Quiche Maya, from whom the story comes, received the god Tohil, the creator of fire. And in a world of darkness, this gift set them apart, as they alone now possessed the power to create light and heat.

"Secure in this knowledge, the forefathers of the Quiche tribe set out from Tulan Zuyua in search of a place to call their own. As the legend goes, they left the city transporting their patron deity with them, his spirit contained in a special stone. After a trek across both land and sea they settled in Central America, in areas that became Guatemala, Belize and Mexico, never to return to Tulan Zuyua."

She clicked the remote and brought up a new photo, a Mayan ruin somewhere in Central America. "Many in the academic world consider Tulan Zuyua to be a myth," she explained. "And that we're as likely to find it as we are to locate Atlantis or the Garden of Eden itself. And if it is real, most experts believe it will be found buried under some other Mayan site, the way old San Francisco is buried under the present-day city.

"We, on the other hand, expect to find the great city here in the Amazon, thousands of miles from where anyone would have even thought to look."

Danielle clicked to the next slide. It displayed a weathered stone with raised markings on it, fronted by a tape measure for scale. "This artifact came to the NRI several months ago, though it was recovered from somewhere in the Amazon some time before that."

Another click, another photo: a picture of the stone from a different angle. McCarter found himself squinting to make out any details.

"As you can see," Danielle said. "The surface of the stone is extremely weathered and most of the markings are almost invisible. But through a type of computer-assisted analysis called a micro-density relief, we were able to reconstruct some of the patterns, and the results were surprising."

The next slide displayed the same stone, this time with a computer-generated outline overlaying it. "These patterns are consistent with only one known writing system: Mayan hieroglyphics. And these two glyphs are well known. One is the name of a person, Jaguar Quitze, one of the original Mayan humans. The other, which was only partially reconstructed, is believed to represent Venus, the morning star."

McCarter studied the pattern formed by the computer-drawn outline. Clearly Mayan in style, but the underlying rock was so worn down he wondered how they could derive anything from it at all. Well-meaning guesswork perhaps.

While McCarter considered this, Danielle explained more of the NRI's theory. "Eight months of work has put us in possession of several other items that seem to confirm the existence of the Mayan writing system within the Amazon, but none of them offered proof quite so dramatically as the one stone we do not possess."

The next image was different from the others, a scanned copy of an old, sepia-toned glossy, complete with a crease running diagonally through one corner and brown discolorations along the edges.

The photo showed two men beside a large rectangular stone. One man had his arms folded across his chest and a foot up on the block. The other man crouched beside it, pointing to something on its face. The image brought to mind a pair of fishermen posing beside a prize catch.

"This photo was taken in 1926 on Blackjack Henry Martin's first expedition into the Amazon. He left from Manaus in April of that year and did not return until March of 1927, when he was finally chased out of the jungle not by native tribes, wild animals or swarming insects, but by two months of torrential, seasonal downpours.

"Martin, as you may know, was something of a minor celebrity at the time. A wealthy adventurer and a self-described fortune hunter who scoured the globe in search of rare and valuable items, preferably those worthy of a little newsreel footage.

"While he was untrained in any formal way, Martin did record his adventures in a marginally professional manner, and before leaving the stone behind, its dimensions were recorded and this photograph taken."

She clicked the slide show forward.

"By using another type of computer modeling, one that examines light-source angles and shading density, we were able to enhance the photo, especially this section." She used a laser pointer to indicate specific parts of the photo and then advanced to the next image—a cropped and magnified view of the large stone with the outline of a new glyph written over it.

As he studied it, recognition hit McCarter in a flash. He'd seen the glyph many times before. During a two-year stint in Yucatan he'd seen it and touched it and traced its outline over and over again. "Seven Caves," he whispered aloud. "Seven Canyons."

Danielle smiled. For a moment she was in awe. She looked at the others. "Seven Caves and Seven Canyons are other names the Mayan people use for Tulan Zuyua."

Susan Briggs opened a notebook and began writing something. "You don't have to take notes," McCarter said.

"I know," she said. "I like to."

McCarter nodded politely.

"According to Martin he discovered this stone on November 17, 1926, on the side of a prominent rise, a mile from the banks of a secondary tributary they were exploring. The exact location is unknown; the only geographic reference Martin offered was its distance from another landmark he discovered, a place he called the Wall of Skulls."

The name lingered in the quiet of the room and McCarter glanced at Susan. Her eyes were wide, her face alight with interest. *Good for her,* he thought.

Danielle continued. "Martin's notes recall his feelings upon first sighting the wall." She read from a tattered copy of his autobiography.

*"A sight of prominence and order this day, after so many in a land of chaos, disorder and nature in its endlessly tangled forms. The Wall is horrible and yet it is grand. A thousand skulls at least must be part of it.*

*Enemy or friend, it remains unknown, for we were prevented from examining them by the foot soldiers of the tribe known as Chollokwa. Four of whom stood upon its crest when we arrived. Spears they held at the ready and adornment of headdress upon their brow, proud men, all of them with the bearing of Rome's finest legions."*

"They welcomed him," she added. "In fact, according to Martin, they insisted that they'd been foretold of his arrival. And they took him to their village in the forest, a few days' hike from the river."

She finished up. "By using this information, along with the help of a local trader who claims to have been told of the wall and taken near it, we think we can find it rather quickly. In a week, or perhaps two at the most."

*A week or two.* McCarter almost laughed at the timetable. He wondered if she knew how absurdly hard it was to locate anything within the jungle. But then again, that was the least of their problems.

"My interest is piqued," he said. "Especially by what Martin apparently found out there. But all you've really shown us are grainy pictures, a man's self-serving writings and computer-generated guesses that, with all due respect, might as well be Rorschach inkblot tests. In other words you're seeing what you want to see. I'm afraid it'll take more than that to convince me."

Curt but polite, Danielle replied, "I would expect no less. But then, I'm not finished yet." She brought up another image, a photo displaying a group of four clear hexagonal crystals.

"These are the Martin's crystals. A group of quartz objects our intrepid explorer claimed to see during a

Chollokwan rain-calling ceremony. The crystals themselves are unremarkable, made of simple quartz with various inclusions. What turned out to be quite remarkable was another object related to them. An object Martin called the cradle."

Danielle brought up the next image: a golden tray with slots in it, one for each of the crystals, with a fifth slot that went unexplained. "This is the cradle. It's made of a gold/brass alloy similar to today's eighteen karat blend. The crystals from the earlier photograph were stored in it—hence the name. That connection was of great interest to Martin, but our research focused on something he largely ignored."

She switched to a new photo, which showed a design carved into the gold; it almost looked like Braille.

"This is a close-up of the underside of the cradle," she explained. "It is in fact a highly detailed star pattern. A representation of the night sky as viewed from the southern hemisphere. It is consistent with Mayan art at other ceremonial centers."

McCarter stared at the picture. It did look like a view of the night sky. He saw a horizon line and what he thought was the Southern Cross. He also realized that the photo had been taken so closely that it showed only a small portion of the underside of the cradle.

Before he could ask why, Danielle clicked to the next photograph. And as he stared at the new image, McCarter forgot about his previous question and found himself struck silent. This time the symbols appeared clearly, perfectly preserved in the surface of the noncorrosive metal. No guesswork was involved, no highlight or computer enhancement needed. The symbols were easy to read in the unretouched photograph, and he knew them well.

Danielle explained to the rest of the group. "This glyph represents a place the Mayan people called Xibalba—the equivalent of Hades or Perdition, sometimes described as a dwelling place of the punished and at other times as the dominion house of the Lords of Darkness. Like Dante's inferno, it was considered to be an underground realm. There's even a famous relief depicting Xibalba as a mirror world of the earth, with the Xibalbans and the Lords of Darkness walking inverted on the ceiling of their world, their feet directly beneath those of the humans standing around on the earth's surface above."

Still staring at the screen, at evidence he could not refute or explain, McCarter realized that Danielle was looking toward him. "Remarkable," he said quietly, still in utter astonishment.

"We think so," she said with a grin.

"And you're sure Martin found this tray in the Amazon?"

"Apparently," Danielle said, returning to her spot beside the podium. "It seems the Chollokwan showed it to him before a ritual performance designed to bring forth the season's rains. Not a rain dance, per se, but roughly the same concept."

"And they just gave it to him?" he asked.

Danielle rolled her eyes slightly. "Well, that's a matter of some debate—not just in this case, but in many of Martin's recoveries. According to his log, the crystals and the cradle were traded to him for a telescope, a kerosene lantern and a compass."

McCarter sat back, crossing one leg over the other. "I find that a little hard to believe."

"Count me in on that," Devers added. "To begin with, the Chollokwan are an extremely violent tribe. When I was here ten years ago they'd just been involved in an attack on a BrazCo mining party. Five team members were killed, a lot of others badly wounded. It wasn't the first time either."

McCarter nodded. "Makes it doubtful that things went as Martin suggests. More than likely the negotiations were conducted at gunpoint."

Danielle took the conversation back. "I would tend to agree. One assumes he didn't get the name Blackjack for nothing. But we're not here to pass judgment on the man, just to try and determine what he found out there. And it's our belief that the cradle and the crystals came from a Mayan ruin that the Chollokwan ransacked in their wanderings. Perhaps even this Wall of Skulls itself, which certainly sounds like a place the Xibalbans might make their presence known."

McCarter turned back to Danielle with excitement in his voice. "Where's the cradle now? Can we see it?"

"Unfortunately, no," Danielle said. "The Martin's crystals and the golden cradle were housed until recently at the Museum of Natural History, back in your home port of New York."

"Until recently," McCarter repeated. That didn't sound promising.

"They were stolen over a year ago," Danielle explained, "along with five additional crates of Central and South American antiquities. In a theft that made the headlines."

McCarter recalled seeing a news clipping, but he did not recall any headlines. "It was a backroom theft," he said, cautiously. "Wasn't it?"

Danielle nodded. "None of the items had been on display for quite some time. In Martin's case, never. The prevailing theory was an inside job from someone who picked and grabbed from an unmonitored area. Security was so lax that the authorities couldn't even determine when it happened. The items may have been missing for several months before the theft was even discovered."

"Did they catch anyone?" McCarter asked.

Danielle shook her head. "No one was ever charged. Two boxes of items were recovered at Miami International just prior to being shipped out of the country, but neither the cradle nor the crystals were among them. It's feared that the cradle may have been melted down for its rather marginal value as a precious metal and the crystals were probably sold for pennies or simply thrown away."

McCarter sighed. Strangely enough he'd seen it before. Discoveries made and then lost, artifacts recovered after a thousand years only to be misplaced or destroyed by accidents. "At times, some hidden things seem to posses an almost sentient desire to remain that way," he said.

Danielle smiled at him and put down the remote. "I couldn't agree more."

Susan closed her notebook. "I can't believe no one saw this before. It's so obvious, it's crazy."

McCarter stroked his chin, wondering if she meant *crazy good* or *crazy bad*. The only thing he knew for sure was that it no longer seemed *crazy foolish*. In fact, as he thought about it, he found himself genuinely excited, almost giddy at the possibility that they might be right. Stones with the names of the first humans in Mayan mythology, others with Tulan Zuyua's descriptive name: Seven Caves. It certainly pointed toward something early in the Mayan culture. And even if the stones had been inaccurately morphed by the NRI's computer program, the untouched golden cradle proved that Mayan writing was being performed in the Amazon. As Danielle had told him the night before, something was out there.

He allowed his gaze to return to the screen. The symbols carved in gold stared back at him and he thought of the contrast: Tulan Zuyua and Xibalba, a form of paradise and the very gates of hell. He couldn't help but wonder which one they would find.

# CHAPTER 10

Pale light from the risen moon filtered through gaps in the trees, illuminating the uneven ground. It wasn't much, but it was enough to see by, enough for the young man, a member of the Nuree tribe, to track his prey.

He cut through the forest silently, following the scuffed trail of the animal he hunted—a large brown tapir, two hundred and fifty pounds. He trod cautiously, not willing to lose the chance that lay before him. It had been a long hunt and this animal was the first major game he'd seen in weeks. If it heard him it would race back to the river, where tapirs spent their days hiding and waiting for nightfall, when they foraged for food.

He moved carefully, pausing as he detected a new scent: smoke. Not the pleasant, woody scent of a good fire, but the stale, acrid smell of soot from a dead, burned-out blaze.

A minute later he came upon the source of that smell. In a small space between the trees, what looked like a compost heap smoldered; piles of leaves and branches and the fired remnants of dried fronds lay blackened and spent. A wisp of gray smoke lingered around it, hugging the mound like an apparition.

He stepped closer to the pile. The burned mess had been compromised, one side had fallen away and the top layer had slid off. Included in that layer was the body of a human being, burned beyond recognition. He looked over the blackened bones.

"*Chokawa,*" he mumbled in disgust, the Nuree word for the Chollokwan people, the strange tribe that bordered them at times, attacking anyone who entered their territory. His uncle feared these people—the Shadow Men, he called them—claiming they did evil things and begging him not to go this way.

The young man was less afraid, but at this strange site he paused. For a moment he thought about turning back, but his eyes fell upon the tapir's trail once again and he chose to push on.

Minutes later, he came within earshot of the foraging creature. He stopped, seeing it for the first time, rooting through the undergrowth for a particular type of vegetation. He tensed his body, raised his spear and flung it forward.

The weapon flew straight, hitting the animal in the side. It squealed with pain and bolted into the forest. The hunter raced after it, trees and brush whipping by on either side of him. He tracked the fleeing creature by the sounds it made, the labored breathing, the grunting and the crunching foliage.

Up ahead he heard a sharp, sudden squeal. He assumed the tapir had fallen, but he arrived at the spot to find only his spear lying on the ground, soaked with blood and surrounded by tufts of dark fur. The animal was nowhere to be seen.

He wondered if it had shaken the spear loose and escaped, but its tracks simply ended. As if it had disappeared in midstride.

He picked up his fallen weapon, examining the tip to make sure it was intact. As he did, his ears caught a slight rustle coming from the bushes ahead of him. He was still, listening. In the quiet, he heard the sound of shallow breathing. He crept toward the shrubs, raised the spear above his head and drove it down with all his weight.

The tip hit something solid and glanced off. The shaft cracked, ringing his hands as a black shape launched itself at him from the thicket. He saw the flash of jaws and knife-edged teeth, smelled the stench of rotting meat.

He flew backward at the impact, with twin gashes across his chest in diagonal cuts. He slammed into the ground, twisted and tried to scramble away. But daggers pierced his calves and he screamed.

He slid across the ground as the thing dragged him backward. Shouting in pain, he managed to grab an exposed tree root. He wrapped his hands around it, halting his slide for the moment and wrenching in anguish as his attacker pulled on him and his body drew up into the air like a rope stretched taut.

His face hit the dirt and he realized he'd been released. He pulled himself forward. But the reprieve lasted only a second, and he howled in anguish and arched his back as the teeth plunged into his legs once again, this time into thick muscles on the backs of his thighs.

Suddenly his body wrenched and his hands ripped free. He flew backward, scraping across the ground and shrieking in fear as he disappeared into the tangled brush.

## CHAPTER 11

Darkness filled the lab's interior, broken only by the pinpoints of colored LEDs and the glow of several rows of computer monitors. The room's precise, symmetrical organization brought to mind a top-level government facility, like NASA's Johnson Space Center or the darkened rooms of Air Traffic Control. But the lab was not a government facility, and the two men who occupied it were unaffiliated with the federal bureaucracy. That is, aside from the fact that they were studying information hacked from the database of the National Research Institute.

As the data ticked in and the numbers on the screen slowly changed, the two men reacted with opposite expressions. The first man—tall, charcoal-haired and in his midfifties—broke into a satisfied grin; a smug, confident look accentuated by his relaxed, commanding posture and an expensive, custom-tailored suit.

His name was Richard Alexander Kaufman. The lab belonged to him, as did the twenty-story building surrounding it, with its rakish, angled lines and a facade of sapphire blue glass.

Kaufman was CEO and principal owner of Futrex

Systems Inc., one of the largest privately held defense contractors in the world. And while Futrex raked in a fortune from the yearly defense budget, it made neither missiles nor bombs. Instead, Futrex created power through the virtual world of zeros and ones; it designed computer systems, data networks and hyper-fast programs that relied on a type of architecture called massive parallel processing.

Futrex programs were used in the design and testing of weapons platforms; they linked AWACS aircraft and satellites to ships, tanks and men on the ground. It was said that battles were not won or lost with weapons but with information, and Futrex Systems enabled American soldiers on the street to see the same information their counterparts in the air and back at headquarters had access to. The military considered this particular data-stream so vital to national security that its contracts included a healthy premium paid specifically to prevent Futrex from adapting the technology for any other purpose. Because of this Futrex had no presence in the civilian world and, as they were privately held, no ticker on any stock market. The result was an oddity in the modern industrial world: a twenty-billion-dollar corporation that almost no one had heard of.

Two decades of such success would have been enough for most people, but not for Richard Kaufman. He wanted more. Kaufman wanted the next wave: an unconditional chance at success, a chance to change the world and, perhaps more important, to tell everyone that he'd done just that.

He was a man accustomed to getting what he wanted. He had friends in high places and low places, he had the money, power and expertise to do anything. All he needed was the right vehicle, something he'd spent the better part of a decade searching for.

Kaufman looked to his left. "What do you think?"

The man beside him appeared exasperated. Norman Lang was close to forty but he dressed in the wrinkled casual way of a college student: corduroys and an untucked flannel shirt, now covered by a lab coat. His thin hair was buzzed and his goatee neatly trimmed.

Lang was Kaufman's chief scientist in areas of unusual interest—the head skunk in the skunk-works, as it were. A brilliant scientist, Lang had fallen into disgrace when he'd been caught falsifying the data on some experiments, ending up in the academic world's version of purgatory, until Kaufman had hired him.

To some extent, Kaufman admired a man with a little larceny in his heart, and at the very least, Lang's record gave him nowhere else to go, something Kaufman knew would make him extremely loyal. And so he'd brought Lang on board, given him an almost unlimited budget and sent him to work on the long shots, to swing for the fences. Lang's marching orders were simple: to find Kaufman's next wave, to bridge the gap between the theoretical and feasible. So far Lang had struggled.

The scientist scratched his head and then pulled the black plastic–framed glasses from his face, rubbing at the indentions they left behind on the bridge of his nose. As was his habit, he answered a question with a question.

"Why are there no abstracts or explanations attached to any of this?" he asked. "Why all this raw data?"

Kaufman had wondered about that himself, but in

truth he liked the raw data approach—it forced Lang to reach his own conclusions. "I don't know," he said. "Is it a problem for you?"

Lang put his glasses back on. "I can run it. The problem is, a lot of it seems . . ."

"Fabricated?" Kaufman asked.

"Beyond the realm of current theory," Lang replied.

Kaufman exhaled. He had always been an expert at reading people and knowing which buttons to push. With some he used kindness, on others force; with Lang it was constant reminders of his failure to spur him on, to push him into taking steps he would otherwise avoid.

"As a research scientist," he said, "you are without peer, but your thinking is shallow. The NRI stole these crystals from the Museum of Natural History and created a fake story to cover the theft. Spent millions of dollars testing them and then encrypted the results in the highest level of code. They then dispatched two separate teams to the depths of the Amazon to find the source of these crystals. Now, what does the scientific method tell you about that?"

Lang held his tongue.

"I'll answer for you," Kaufman said. "They think they've discovered a new source of power—a clean, unlimited source of power, nuclear energy without that annoying little problem known as nuclear waste."

Lang nodded. "Fusion."

"Exactly," Kaufman said.

Nuclear fusion was considered by many to be the energy source of the twenty-first century—the solution to a world choking on fumes, sweating under global warming and allegedly running short of fossil fuels. After all, nuclear fusion had already given us the hydrogen bomb, and a similar type of reaction powers the sun. As the theory went, if such a process could be harnessed without incinerating entire cities, fusion could power the world. And as a result, nations around the world were studying it, and almost universally they were focused on a particular type of fusion: hot fusion.

To be a player in the hot fusion game required a massive entrance fee. The effort cost billions, took years, and so far had led only to monstrous machines that actually used more energy than they produced, the equivalent of burning two barrels of oil to pump one more up to the surface.

Despite that fact, billions more were going into the next step, a sprawling project in the south of France called the ITER, an acronym which in Latin meant "the passage" or "the way." Whether that moniker would prove true or false was anyone's guess, but certainly it would take a long time to find out. The latest estimates had construction of the ITER lasting through 2018. And even if all went as planned, it would only lead to bigger, more expensive prototypes before any working reactors were produced.

Estimates on the debut of a viable system ranged from fifty to a hundred years. And in all likelihood, the energy source of the twenty-first century wouldn't actually arrive until sometime in the twenty-second. A date that was too far off for Richard Kaufman.

Instead, he pursued a different goal, a smaller, more controversial form, one forever tainted by the scandal of its birth: cold fusion.

"Now," Kaufman began, "assuming they're not the village idiots, are they or are they not onto something?"

Lang hedged. "*If* their measurements are accurate, then yes, they may be on to something."

"Explain."

"Based on their descriptions, it appears that they studied four crystals, two of which contained inclusions, filaments of palladium. And yes, almost every successful cold fusion experiment that's been run has used palladium. Even Fleishman and Pons used palladium before they were burned at the stake as heretics."

Fleishman and Pons were the researchers who'd first discovered cold fusion. They were hailed for a while, before the hot fusion community, fearing for their grants and endowments, attacked and savaged both them and their experiments. Very quickly Fleishman and Pons found their reputations destroyed, their concept shunned and treated as a hoax. In the aftermath, scientific journals followed suit, refusing to publish papers on cold fusion, while mainstream universities barred their fellows from working the field. To even express an interest in the subject was considered the death knell for a career.

"Palladium," Kaufman repeated, one eyebrow raised. "Interesting. What else?"

Lang plucked one of the printouts from the stack and handed it to Kaufman. "If the NRI is correct, the crystals show the following: a background level of radiation consistent with a low energy reaction, indications of metallic transmutation on the inclusion, primarily streaks of silver and copper at the tip. A high concentration of sulfur in the quartz. And a measurable residue of trapped, gaseous tritium."

Kaufman studied the printout, moved by the magnitude of the moment. Tritium was the one element they'd been looking for, a radioactive waste product that could only form during a nuclear reaction of some kind. The inclusion's other properties were rare and extremely odd, and they could almost be explained, except for the presence of the tritium. It proved that the crystal had been used in a reaction that released nuclear energy. Its continued existence could only mean that the reaction had been a type of cold fusion.

"If their data are correct," Lang repeated.

Kaufman had no doubt that the NRI had gotten its data correct. "What else does the data describe?"

Lang acquiesced. "First of all, the crystals are primarily quartz. But they're also filled with microscopic lines running in geometrically precise patterns—almost molecular in size. I'm talking several angstroms, here. I don't know how they were made or what they're for, but they act like fiber-optic channels, directing specific wavelengths of light through the crystal while screening others out. The effect is only visible under a polarized light."

"What wavelengths are we talking about?"

"High-energy spectrum: violet, ultraviolet and beyond. According to the report, the tunnels are present in all four crystals, and they're similar on the crystals containing the inclusions. But the pattern on the other two is far less complex." Lang paused. "The NRI report tentatively labeled them as blanks. You know, like a hunk of metal that hasn't been drilled and lathed into whatever it was supposed to become yet."

"What about the last data transfer?" Kaufman asked. "Were you able to make sense of that?"

Lang reached over and clicked open a new program on the monitor. "There you go," he said smugly.

Kaufman saw a bunch of dots spread randomly about the computer screen—dots of various sizes—along with a few streaks and arcs on a black background. The screen was divided into four by a pair of lines that crossed in the center. It meant nothing to him.

"What am I looking at?" Kaufman said.

"This is the data displayed in a graphical form," Lang replied.

"Is this some kind of distribution?"

"No," Lang said. "Of all things, they're star charts—four separate panels of them."

"Star charts?"

"Like the kind old sailors used to navigate with," Lang said. "I've done a little work on the first one. It's a sky pattern viewed from the southern hemisphere."

Kaufman grew deeply interested. The NRI had their people in Brazil, looking for the source of the crystals. "Assuming the chart is accurate, does it correspond to a particular longitude and latitude?"

"Not sure yet," Lang said. "The best I can tell you: Western Hemisphere, south of the equator."

Before Kaufman could reply, his cell phone rang. He stepped away. "What is it?" he asked.

"We've been checking the hospitals, like you asked," the German-accented voice reported. "And we've found a man who might interest you. He's a John Doe, resting up in a small hospital on the outskirts of Manaus. He was brought in ten days ago, after spending some time at a clinic upriver. Apparently, he was pretty bad off when he first arrived: delirious, suffering from exposure, dehydration and first-stage malnutrition, along with a compound fracture of the right leg. But the fact is, he's alive, and he's still here. And I think you're going to want to meet him."

"Why?"

"Because he says he works for Helios."

Very rarely was Richard Kaufman at a loss for words, but for a moment, he was struck silent. Kaufman had acquired two contacts in the NRI, frustrated parties who were willing to sell out the organization for a fair price. One had been part of the first mission into the rainforest, a group that had stopped signaling and disappeared. He'd given that man a code word to be transmitted over the radio when he needed to be extracted from the jungle, after he'd stolen what the NRI group recovered. That code word was "Helios": the Greek god of the sun. It had seemed appropriate.

"Worked for Helios?" Kaufman repeated. The right word but the wrong statement. "Are you sure those were his words?"

"Absolutely. He wanted to know who we worked for and when we didn't tell him, he said he worked for Helios and we should know what that meant. He says he has something that might interest Helios. Something he'll only give up in person."

"Have you tried to persuade him otherwise?"

"As much as we could. But he is in a hospital."

Kaufman appreciated their finesse. "All right. Keep

an eye on him, and make sure he's not an NRI plant designed to draw us out. Once you're certain, I'll meet with you, and then, when I'm ready, I'll meet with him. But he goes nowhere without our approval, got it?"

Kaufman switched off the phone and glanced over at Lang, who'd turned a subtle shade of green.

"What the hell was that all about?" Lang asked.

Kaufman smiled. "Our next stop. Western Hemisphere, south of the equator."

Lang did not look pleased, but Kaufman knew his man, he knew that Lang would follow along, chasing the carrot of his own greed as much as taking orders. All Kaufman had to do was avoid bombarding him with too much truth at once.

## CHAPTER 12

Seventy-two hours after the briefing at the hotel, Danielle and the new NRI team were five hundred miles upriver, traveling aboard a diesel-powered boat called the *Ocana,* which was captained by a friend of Hawker's. Known by the locals as a milk boat, because it delivered goods to the smaller settlements up and down the river, the *Ocana* had a wide deck, a pointed bow and plenty of fuel for the journey there and back. What it didn't have were cabins or other accommodations, and the group stopped each night to camp along the riverside, as much to get off the claustrophobic boat as anything else.

During the day, however, they chugged upriver, spread out on the boat as best they could. The group numbered fourteen, including Pik Verhoven, his four South African mercenaries and a trio of Brazilian porters to help with supplies and equipment.

With snow white hair, a ruddy, tanned face and a scar that twisted across it like a broken strand of barbed wire, Pik Verhoven was a menacing sight. Six foot one and two hundred and forty pounds, he didn't walk as much as lumber, allowing others ample time to clear his path. Those who stood too close might end up with a none-too-subtle glare, an awkward bump or at least tobacco juice stains on their boots as well-aimed spittle was fired from the ever-present chaw in his mouth.

Aside from Danielle, no one seemed eager to interact with either Verhoven or his men any more than necessary. Even Hawker, who knew Verhoven from his days in Africa, did little but glare at the man.

Danielle had been told Hawker and Verhoven had worked together before Hawker's fallout with the CIA, and that bad blood lingered between them. All she could get from Verhoven on the matter was a grunt of dismissal and a statement alleging that she and the NRI must have been "scraping the bottom of the barrel" to hire Hawker.

Hawker's response was more verbal, if no less hostile. "The man is a son of a bitch," Hawker had explained, "and he's sure as hell no friend of mine. But then, that's not what you hired him for, is it?"

Her sense of Hawker's response was that woe would befall anyone foolish enough to get in Verhoven's way, possibly including him, but especially anyone that might attack her team. It was a fact she took comfort in, even as the unease between the two men lingered.

With this divided dynamic in place, the *Ocana* traveled to the northwest, branching off the Amazon and tracking the dark tannin-stained waters of the Negro, following the path that Blackjack Martin had once taken. As they moved farther into the rainforest, Danielle felt herself growing more focused. She spoke less and became suspicious of everything around her: a strange glance from one of Verhoven's men, an aircraft that crossed almost directly above them and seemed to linger for a bit too long.

She told herself to relax; it was important that she rein in her emotions, or risk telegraphing the stress to the others. It was an effort that had worked for most of the morning, but one that was suddenly tested by a strange object floating in the river ahead of them.

There was nothing overtly dangerous about what she saw, but something struck her as odd about the shape and the way the leaves and other debris had gathered around it. Try as she might, Danielle was unable to shake the feeling that it was an ill omen of some kind.

"Cut the throttle," she called back. "There's something in the water."

Her shout brought the others to attention. Verhoven caught her eye and began to move to the forward section of the boat.

"You see it?"

He nodded. "Yeah."

"Block it before it passes."

As Verhoven grabbed one of the boat's long oars, a crowd gathered beside them.

Behind her, the boat's captain cut the throttle and turned the *Ocana* sideways. As the vessel settled, the floating object bumped softly against the port side. Verhoven trapped it.

First glimpses surprised them all. "Oh, that's disgusting," Susan said.

For those who couldn't see, Danielle spoke. "It's a body."

It was the body of a native man, facedown in the water, surrounded by a tangle of branches, leaves and other flotsam. The lower half of his torso and his legs disappeared beneath the surface, leaving only the back of his head and his shoulders visible.

"Can you clear him?" Danielle said, her tone calm but concerned.

Verhoven used the the oar to scrape off some debris, pushing away a tangle of sticks that had hooked onto the man and then turning his attention to a three-foot log that floated near the man's head. He shoved it with the oar and it moved away, but the body jerked along behind it and the man's hands floated to the surface. A thin length of twine connected each wrist to the branch.

Verhoven fired a shot of tobacco juice over the side. "He's tied to the damn thing."

Danielle could see the lengths of crude native rope that ran to each wrist. It was not a good sign and truthfully not something she would have wanted any of the others to see.

But they did see, and like onlookers at a car crash, they rubbernecked for a better view, watching as Verhoven used the oar to try to maneuver the log further. As Verhoven worked, the body twisted and rolled, eventually turning faceup. The onlookers stared in silence. The brown face, with a frame of wet, black hair, appeared relatively untouched by whatever had killed him, but the torso carried scars from a variety of assaults: two great holes in the chest, a pair of long slashes that ran from his left shoulder down across his stomach, and a group of bulbous swellings—spherical blackened blisters the size and shape of half a grapefruit.

Polaski asked the question on everyone's mind. "What on earth happened to him?"

Danielle stared at the holes in the chest. They were large and circular. "Are those bullet wounds?"

Verhoven shook his head. "Too big. Can't make a hole like that without blasting a train tunnel out the back side. And I didn't see any exit wounds."

Verhoven offered a guess. "Looks like he was impaled on something. A couple of blows from a sharpened stave, maybe."

Danielle needed a better opinion. She crouched at the edge of the *Ocana*'s deck and studied the holes in the chest herself. There was damage to the man's skin that indicated movement both ways. "Something went in and then came back out," she whispered. "It didn't go through."

Behind her the deck became crowded as the others moved in for a better view.

"What about those?" Devers asked, pointing to the blackened swellings. "I mean, please tell us it's not Ebola or anything."

Some of the blisters displayed ragged tears, as if they had exploded. Others showed a cleaner cut, as if they'd been lanced on purpose, perhaps to keep them from breaking. At that moment she wished they had brought a doctor along, but another civilian was one too many. The limited medical training the NRI had given her and a degree in biology would have to suffice. "There's no discharge," she said, moving in closer and sniffing the air. "No smell of infection either."

In fact, there wasn't much odor at all, which led her to believe the man died quite recently, probably within the last twenty-four hours.

"It looks more like a reaction to something," she told them. "Like a chemical burn or a raised welt from being struck." She wondered if the skin and tissue had swelled from being in the water. She turned to Devers. "And, besides, Ebola is only in Africa."

Devers nodded, moving closer. "Good to know. Ebola, permafrost—I'm learning all kinds of things on this trip."

Uncomfortable with Devers' crowding presence and his babbling, Danielle stood up, put a hand on him and pushed him back with the rest of the crowd. "Stay," she said, glaring at him, then turned to Verhoven. "Can I see his legs, please?"

The request was easier asked than answered. Verhoven was using his pole to keep the body from floating away, and each time he released the pressure, the slipstream that had formed on the side of the boat began to move it. He turned to one of his men. "Get another pole."

Verhoven's lieutenant grabbed an oar and worked to leverage the dead native's legs to the surface, but it was a struggle, and it took a minute before they realized why: his legs were tied to a small net full of flat stones.

"Hell of a way to treat a man," Verhoven said, spitting to emphasize the point. "A buoy to keep him afloat and a weight to keep his legs down. Boy must've pissed in the wrong chief's pot."

Verhoven's lieutenant appeared disgusted. "Goddamned natives," he mumbled.

By this time McCarter had moved up beside Danielle, careful not to invade her space. "That's right. Civilized men never do anything like this."

The man started to respond, but a stern glance from Verhoven stopped him, and McCarter knelt beside Danielle to help her examine the body. They studied the twine where it wrapped the wrists; there was some discoloration but little indication of rubbing or friction. "I think he was tied up after death," he said. "He doesn't seem to have struggled against the rope."

"Killed first, then tied up," Verhoven said. "Seems an odd way of doing things."

"Well, it looks like he's been clawed too," Polaski added, pointing to the long parallel slashes. "Perhaps he was killed and tied up for the animals as some kind of offering."

McCarter shook his head. "Never heard of anything like that from an Amazonian tribe. Besides, if an animal got to him I'm guessing he'd have been eaten."

Danielle stayed out of the discussion, trying to think. The traders she and Moore had spoken with often told stories about the different tribes, many too outlandish and absurd to believe. Spice for the foreigners to buy perhaps, but most genuinely feared the Chollokwan. And the stories about them always seemed to involve strange mutilations like this one—bodies burned, impaled and hacked up; men who hunted men in conjunction with the animals of the forest: *the Shadow Men of the pestilence.*

As she stared at the round face, she thought of Dixon and his missing squad. They were well trained and heavily armed but still missing. She wondered if they'd find those men floating and mutilated farther upriver somewhere. She hoped not, for every reason under the sun.

Even as Danielle considered this, the others were overcoming the initial shock of the discovery and giving way to a morbid curiosity. Various theories began flying back and forth. After several minutes even Hawker came forward. He appraised the body for only a moment.

"Wonderful," he said sarcastically, and then turned to Devers. "Can you tell what tribe he's from?"

The dead man was naked, with no identifying marks or jewelry of any kind. "No," Devers said. "Why?"

Hawker nodded into the distance ahead of them. "Because they seem to be as interested in him as we are."

Danielle looked up to see a trio of native canoes being rowed frantically toward them. There were two men in each boat, paddling furiously and shouting as they approached. Their pace was almost panicked and their voices were filled with a mad fury, every ounce of it directed toward the *Ocana* and its spellbound passengers.

## CHAPTER 13

Danielle watched the approaching canoes. Six men in small boats were not much of a threat. But they were incensed, and caution dictated that she be prepared. "Start the engine," she said.

"Should I get us away?" the boat captain asked.

"No. I want to talk to them, but be ready." She looked to Verhoven, who was still holding the body to the side of the *Ocana*. "Let it go."

Verhoven gave the body a shove and it carried slowly out behind the stern of the boat and then on downstream with the peaceful flow of the current. Ahead of them, the canoes were closing in, and neither the intensity of the shouting nor their paddling had diminished.

"Make sure your weapons are handy," Danielle said.

Verhoven grinned. "They're always handy."

She turned to Devers. "Are they Chollokwan?"

Devers hesitated for only a moment. "I don't think so," he said. "Some of the words are Portuguese. The Chollokwan only speak Chokawa. Plus, this is Nuree territory."

Danielle relaxed a bit. The Nuree were not a threat

like the Chollokwan could be. They were a tribe in transition, caught halfway between the old world and the new. They still hunted with blow guns and spears, yet at times they would paddle downriver to trade, selling pelts and buying clothing, fish hooks and cigarettes. They weren't known to be violent. And with the right form of persuasion they might even be helpful.

The canoes slowed as they approached and the shouting ceased, perhaps because the floating body had been released, or more likely because the natives had spotted Verhoven and his men holding rifles.

"Find out what they want," Danielle said.

Devers stepped to the prow of the boat and addressed the men in the Nuree language. They shouted back, a menagerie of voices.

"They ask why we touch the dead," Devers translated. "They say this one is cursed, and he is to be left alone."

"Ask them who he is." Danielle said. "Why was he killed?"

Devers translated the question, and as one of the Nuree men responded, he explained the answer. "He says they did not kill him."

"Why is he in the river, then?" Danielle asked. "Why is he tied up like that?"

This time a different tribesman spoke.

"The man is a relative of some kind," Devers said, translating, "a nephew, I think. They went upriver ten days ago on a hunt. He says they found no game, so they continued until they reached the place they should not have gone. A forbidden place. The uncle warned his nephew, but the boy wouldn't listen and he continued on while the uncle came back."

Another of the tribesmen spoke.

"It is the forsaken place," Devers said. "Forsaken by life. To go there is to invite death. Most who are foolish in such a way do not return. Some have come back like this—floating in the river, their spirits ripped out." The native man clutched his chest where the two great holes had been seen in the dead man. "They drag the stones to keep them from the shore. They hold the reed to show their punishment. We have even seen animals this way. It is the spirits that send them back. Cursed and abhorred. Even the birds and piranha will not eat them."

As she listened to the translation, it occurred to Danielle that the body had not been touched by the scavengers of the forest or river. A strange thought, because there was so much competition for food in the rainforest. Odder still, because if the man was telling the truth the body had been in the water for several days, not less than twenty-four hours as she'd guessed.

Beside her, Verhoven laughed. "Right, then. The spirits are using twine these days, ay?"

Danielle ignored him. "What else?"

Devers replied, "He says only the Shadow Men go to this land. I think he might mean the Chollokwan. He says that they kill all who go there, or that they make the animals do it for them. Something like that. Either way, he says, once they parted, he knew his nephew would not come back alive. He went looking for him every day. This morning, one of the boys from the village spotted the body floating down the river. No one is to touch it."

Danielle considered the situation. They had to be

close to the right area. She took a chance. "Ask him if he can take us to where he left his nephew. Tell him we are looking for the place of these spirits."

Through Devers' translation, the tribesmen continued to speak. "Death lingers there," one of them insisted. "Accursed things come out from the shadows of that place. They should be left undisturbed."

Another, older tribesman added, "If you go there you will be taken. You will not return, except as a warning, punished like this one. This is why the body appears today," he added, pointing accusingly at the NRI group. "It is a warning. Sent for you. To choose another way."

With that the natives began talking among themselves. Excited words flashing back and forth between the small canoes, all of it too quick and overlapping for Devers to intercept, but after a moment the result was clear: the Nuree were moving on. They dug in with their paddles, powerful strokes that swirled the water into deep eddies. They moved around the *Ocana* and headed downstream in the direction of the floating body.

Danielle asked for an explanation.

"It seems that we're already cursed," Devers said. "Or maybe just too foolish to waste any more time on."

Behind them one of the porters laughed. He'd heard it all before. "To the Nuree, everything is cursed," he said. "The trees, the foam on the water, a log that floats with the wrong end down—all deadly, all cursed."

Danielle turned back to her interpreter. "What do you think really happened?"

Devers shrugged. "The place we're looking for is somewhere upriver from here. That's where Blackjack Martin ran into the Chollokwan. I told you they were violent. It's probably their territory that these guys are afraid of. Truth be told, I'd think the place was cursed too, if every time one of my people went up there they came back looking like this."

"The Chollokwan," Danielle repeated. She looked upriver. Somewhere ahead they would enter their territory.

"As the man said, it's a warning," Devers added. "And as strange as it sounds, I think we should take it that way."

"I didn't come here to worry about native superstitions." She gave the order, "Let's get moving."

A moment later, as the engine began to rumble beneath the deck, McCarter came up beside her. "It seems like the day for warnings, apparently."

"What do you mean?"

"Susan and I have been studying the stone you gave us, the one that the logger brought back from out here. And we think we know what the other glyph represents. It's a one-legged owl, a great deformed bird that struck terror into the Mayan hearts."

"Why would they be afraid of an owl?" Danielle asked. "What does it mean?"

"It's the herald of the underworld," McCarter said. "The messenger of destruction."

## CHAPTER 14

Two hours later, they came to an area where the character of the river began to change. The larger trees receded from the banks, replaced by a rocky shoreline of great smooth-sided boulders, the first they had seen in hundreds of miles. It was as if they'd suddenly been transported to a different place and, geologically speaking, they had, for the heavy granite they saw was rare in the Amazon, except in the far north near the Guyana Shield, the well-worn remnants of an ancient mountain range. Farther on they began to hear a sound that was as foreign to their ears as the stones were to their eyes: the tumbling chorus of white water, where a smaller stream joined up with the Negro.

"The rapids," Danielle noted. Blackjack Martin's notes described these rapids, as did the logger who'd sold her the stone. This was the marker. If the information was correct, they would come to a small tributary in just over a mile, where they would exit the main river and travel due north.

Danielle turned to the captain. "Take the next stream on the starboard side."

A mile later the stream appeared just as promised,

joining the Negro at a wide intersection with a small island in the middle. An island that the logger had described as a sandbar.

As Hawker joined her at the bow she said, "The water's low here." She looked around, thinking about the wide sandy beaches they'd camped on downriver. "Low everywhere right now."

"The rainy season's late," Hawker said.

Danielle nodded. Even out over the western Amazon where they were headed, there had been less precipitation in the supposedly wet month of January than in the months of the drier season. Everywhere the beaches were wide, the sandbars high and the water low.

The captain agreed. "El Niño," he explained. "Few clouds but nothing more. In Matto Grasso there is no rain at all. El Niño."

For South America, El Niño meant the dry winds of the Patagonian plateau, high desert air that swept down across the Amazon and stole the moisture away, reeking havoc with the normal weather pattern of daily and weekly rains. It meant dying fish in lakes and ponds and failing crops on the plains. For a month, forecasters had been suggesting an El Niño was forming, but as yet no official announcement had been made. Looking around, Danielle realized she wouldn't need one.

"Can you get us through?"

The captain nodded. "Slowly."

Slowly meant three or four knots, with Hawker at the bow watching for trouble. Fortunately the wide-bottomed *Ocana* only drew a foot or two of water and progress was adequate. Twenty miles upriver lay the spot that the logger claimed to have seen the stone. They would make that in just over five hours. With a little luck, they would find the Wall soon after.

As it turned out, *a little luck* had not been forthcoming, and the NRI group searched the banks of the river for a week after passing the rapids.

McCarter knew the problem. "The jungle swallows things," he said. "A hundred years ago cities like Palenque, Copán and Tikal were so covered in vegetation that the monuments looked like rugged green hills. Dirt piles up and the weeds and trees grow out of it. Eventually the place is covered from head to toe. Left alone, the jungle creeps in and simply takes the land back."

He explained how they should proceed. "One thing you have to avoid looking for is the finished product, a monument or a temple of some kind. You won't find that out here. It'll be something subtle—a small hill that doesn't flow with the land the way it should, or a bit of rock sticking out where it shouldn't."

These had been McCarter's instructions five days before. Since then, they'd split into teams, scouring different sections of the river's bank on foot, hiking and slashing their way through the tangled foliage, moving slowly upriver in a systematic search. It was all to no avail, until Polaski discovered a squared-off stone at the edge of the river. McCarter and Susan stared at it with approval.

McCarter smiled as he inspected it, then turned to

Susan. "The two of us experts out here, and he finds the first clue."

"Beginner's luck," she said, smiling. "And thank God for it."

McCarter looked around. "Luck" was the word. A month earlier the stone would have been submerged in ten feet of water.

"Not bad for a systems nerd," Polaski proclaimed.

"No," McCarter said. "Not bad at all." He looked skyward. Dusk was approaching fast. He considered calling the others but they were spread out along the river's edge, and in the fifteen minutes it would take them to gather he would lose the remaining light.

McCarter gazed up the sloping bank. It was quite steep. "It probably tumbled down in a deluge at some point." He looked at Susan and Polaski. "We have to go up," he said. "Straight up."

Susan went first. Younger, lighter and more athletic, she outclimbed both McCarter and Polaski as they struggled to scale the steep, tangled embankment. She paused on a flattish section, pointing to something.

As McCarter reached her he was gasping but energized, especially as Susan directed his attention to another jumble of stones. A few feet away they found a second pile, uneven and dislodged, but it seemed as if they might have once been a flight of stairs. With his hands on his hips, McCarter took a deep breath and then began to climb again. "Up," he said.

This time he led the assault, pushing forward, tripping and stumbling on the steep ascent, almost causing a minor avalanche at one point. Near the top, he arrived at a tangled spread of vines that hung over the bluff like falling water. With the light fading around them, Mc-Carter swung his machete and the vines fell. In their place, two empty eye sockets stared back at him from the mottled brown countenance of an ancient human skull. He stepped back.

"Well, this is something," Polaski said, wide-eyed.

"Isn't it?" Susan said. "Can you believe *we* found it?"

McCarter looked at her. He had begun to think it was all just a waste of time. "And to think, you could have been in Paris instead."

"Listening to my mother go on about clothes," she said. "No thanks. Much better here."

McCarter turned back to the vines and hacked through another section. Next to the first skull, they saw another, this one with a broken cheekbone and a missing jaw, and beside that another. The skulls were set into a wall of stone—placed into sections that had been left open, cemented and braced into position somehow.

Susan and Polaski stepped back as McCarter swung the machete again and again, hacking at the brush and revealing more skulls or the remnants of them with each slash. He stopped as his shoulder began to hurt, wondering when he'd gotten so out of shape.

Breathing hard, he said, "Now that we've staked our claim," he said, "someone call the others."

## CHAPTER 15

That night, after a celebration that included repeated toasts and a bottle of champagne, the camp was quiet. Pik Verhoven stood watch, covering the north side of the camp, while one of his men stood seventy yards downstream, covering the south end.

If and when they decided on a permanent site, Danielle had promised all kinds of equipment to help—motion detectors, heat sensors and other electronic devices, the type of equipment that often failed at precisely the wrong moment in places like the rainforest. Verhoven insisted he'd put more faith in a pack of trained dogs, and so Danielle had promised that as well, but until then Verhoven and his men would guard the camp the old-fashioned way—watching the forest day and night, easy money for a group more accustomed to hard fighting in close combat.

Verhoven and his men were mercenaries in the truest, hardest sense of the word. All five were former South African Special Forces members who had drifted abroad in the years after apartheid. Under Verhoven's leadership they'd become a sought-after group. Their résumé included places like Somalia, Angola and the Congo.

They'd stormed their way into the Rwandan carnage of the mid-'90s to rescue members of the TransAfrican mining corporation. A decade later they'd fought in Liberia, pointedly searching for Charles Taylor, the nation's faltering, maniacal leader, first on a contract to aid his escape, and then, after being stiffed on the payment, attempting to catch him and collect the million-dollar bounty that had been placed on his head.

Verhoven smiled as he remembered that particular dustup. *So close, too bad it hadn't worked out.* Still, he figured they'd get their chance again someday, and when they did, he'd leave the world with one less madman, and he'd do it for free.

In the meantime, he and his men would go where the money led them, and if it meant a fight, so be it, the bloodier the better. For the right price, they would storm the gates of hell.

As Verhoven scanned the quiet jungle around him, he saw nothing that would force him to do that tonight. He'd seen no sign of danger since the body in the river; not the natives on the warpath or the competing parties that Danielle had warned him about, not even any wildlife to speak of.

Only the last part struck him as odd.

With a dearth of rainfall over the interior, the animals should have been plentiful near the streams that still flowed. This wasn't Africa, where the herds crowded water holes until the monsoons arrived, but the principle was the same: lack of rain brought animals to the water, concentrating them in a restricted area. They should have found tracks and droppings and heard them day and night at the riverbanks and in the areas of forest around them. But the jungle had been strangely vacant and muted. Plenty of birds, along with fish in the streams and reptiles on the banks, but the animals seemed to be missing, the mammals in particular. Verhoven had seen nothing much larger than a rat. *Maybe the rainforest was dying, like all the tree-huggers said. A shame if it was, but not really his problem.*

Verhoven put a thermal scope to his eye and scanned the broad swath of jungle that lay ahead of him. Little blips of heat could be seen here and there in the undergrowth, phosphorescent flares in the red tint of the eyepiece; more rodents and other tiny mammals. He panned along a wide arc and saw nothing more. As he lowered the device something rustled the trees.

He brought the scope back up. Deeper in the forest, almost at eye level, he saw a spread of branches swaying in a vertical recoil, the way they did when a monkey launched itself from them. He scanned across an arc, looking up into the trees and then back down. Nothing. No sign of anything that might have bent the branches in such a manner.

He heard a sound to the right and swung in that direction, bringing his rifle up as he turned.

A figure held out a hand in warning: Hawker.

Verhoven lowered the rifle slightly, staring at his old acquaintance. He spat a shot of tobacco juice onto the dirt an inch from Hawker's feet. "You're supposed to be dead."

Hawker stared back at him for a long moment. "I was once."

Verhoven lowered the rifle the rest of the way. "Walk up on me like that again and you'll be dead for good."

Hawker stopped a few feet from Verhoven and searched the forest himself. "Any particular reason that you're so jumpy?"

Verhoven didn't like the question, nor did he like the fact that Hawker was armed, carrying a black pistol: a PA-45—a big gun, forty-five caliber, fourteen shots. "What the hell are you doing out here?"

Hawker nodded toward the trees. "Something didn't feel right."

Verhoven turned back to the forest. Hawker had always been slightly paranoid, but that sixth sense had saved him more than once. Verhoven remembered a time when he and Hawker had been targeted for a mortar round that ended up hitting the spot they'd been standing in only a minute before, a spot they'd left because of Hawker's paranoia. "You're hearing things again, mate. There's nothing out there."

"You sure about that?"

In all honesty, Verhoven wasn't sure, but he didn't like the question, or having Hawker poking around. He held out the scope. "Take the watch, if you want. I'll go catch some rest."

Hawker declined the offer and Verhoven began to wonder what Hawker was really doing out there, both in the immediate sense and in general. "So you're with the NRI now."

Hawker shook his head. "Hired hand, just like you."

"Odd coincidence, that."

"Very odd," Hawker said. "Almost like fate."

Verhoven believed in fate, but he knew Hawker didn't. *Do everything right and you can live forever,* Hawker had once said. Verhoven disagreed. *When your number's up, it's up.* Maybe one of their numbers was about to be up, a long-standing debt about to be paid. Maybe Hawker had even recommended him for the mission in order to draw him out, to finally settle the old score. He laughed at the thought. *Who sounded paranoid now?*

He checked the trees and then looked back at Hawker. "So why'd you take the job, then? Find the Queen's shilling in the bottom of your flask?"

"Something like that," Hawker said.

Verhoven moved the ever-present tobacco wad around in his mouth, forcing it back into place and spitting out some of the excess. He looked over at Hawker. They hadn't spoken on the boat or in the jungle for the past week, doing their jobs and ignoring each other, and it was a strange, almost surreal feeling to be holding a conversation with him now. Old friends and old enemies who'd spent two years working together in Angola a decade ago, when Hawker was with the CIA and Verhoven was still with the SASF.

The alliance had worked well, until new orders came down from the CIA, orders that Hawker had chosen not to follow. That decision divided them, setting Hawker on a collision course with everyone he knew, making enemies out of friends. Verhoven had even played a small part in Hawker's capture, but then things had spiraled out of control, leading everyone to anguish, and eventually to what had seemed like Hawker's death.

Not long after, he'd learned that Hawker was alive, and seeking some manner of revenge against those who had betrayed him. Quite sure his name was on that list, Verhoven never expected to see Hawker and have the moment pass without one of them ending up dead. And yet here they were, standing in the middle of the Amazon, half a world away from where they'd fought, talking and not shooting.

"Well, you couldn't hide forever," Verhoven said finally. "Not from what you fear."

Hawker looked at him strangely. "And just what might that be?"

"You fear yourself, Hawk. You want to talk about destiny, you know what yours is. You can hide from it all you want, but it still comes to find you. Why else would the two of us be here?"

Hawker glared at him, as close to a look of hatred as Verhoven had ever seen in the man's eyes. The truth did that to people.

"Our time is going to come," Hawker said. "But not here, not now."

So that was it, Verhoven thought. Hawker had come out to set the ground rules; fine by him. He stared at the pilot. "It's all clear out here, Hawk. Go back to your tent."

Hawker cut his eyes at Verhoven and then nodded out toward the trees. "Keep your eyes open," he said. "I'm telling you, we're not alone."

Hawker turned to head back to the camp, but stopped as a pair of night birds whipped by, cawing as they flew overhead. The sound masked a second noise, a rustling in the trees, but both he and Verhoven sensed it.

Hawker dropped to one knee.

Verhoven scanned the jungle with the scope. He saw

nothing, but again the branches were swaying. "Something moving to higher ground," he said, trying in vain to track it.

A second later the sound of gunfire jolted the night. Shots fired to the south.

"Who's down there?" Hawker asked.

"Bosch," Verhoven replied. One of his men.

From that direction something was racing through the forest, coming toward them. Verhoven raised his rifle.

Two natives burst through the undergrowth, eyes wide with shock at running into Verhoven and Hawker.

Verhoven went to fire, but as he did Hawker shoved the barrel of his rifle aside. The shells tore into the loose earth.

The natives dashed off.

"Damn you," Verhoven shouted.

Hawker was up and running, giving chase.

Furious, Verhoven followed, charging through the forest. "Where the hell are you going?"

"We need to talk to them," Hawker shouted back.

Ducking around a tree, barely keeping Hawker in sight, Verhoven yelled, "What the hell for?"

Hawker again shouted to him but didn't slow, and Verhoven couldn't make out the words. He heard the natives ahead, crashing through the branches. He caught sight of Hawker for a second. And then he was gone.

Before he could stop, Verhoven met the same fate; the ground suddenly gone from underneath his feet, he fell through the darkness. He slammed into a musty wall of earth and then crashed backward with a splash, landing in three feet of mud and water.

He looked around but could see nothing; the blackness was complete. The only light he saw came from thirty feet above, a thin veil of a lighter black in the shape of a rectangle.

He'd fallen into a pit of some kind: a trap. He stood awkwardly, the mud squishing under his feet, the cold muck dripping off him. The fetid water stank, but it had probably saved his life.

"Hawk!" he shouted. "Are you down here?"

Sounding as if he was in a certain amount of pain, Hawker replied, "Unfortunately."

Verhoven turned toward the sound of Hawker's voice, the water swirling just above knees. "Better hope it stays dark, mate. Because if I see you I'm gonna kill you."

"For what?"

"For bringing me down here."

He heard the sound of water sloshing as Hawker moved around in the darkness. "If you hadn't tried to shoot the son of bitch, we might have been able to talk to him."

"A bloke charges you like that, you shoot first, ask questions later."

"He wasn't charging," Hawker replied. "He was looking up in the trees, hunting something. He just found us by accident."

Verhoven paused, realizing that Hawker was right. He moved to his right, bumping against something. He touched it with his hand, and realized it was the carcass of a dead animal. He pulled back. "Looks like we're not the only ones to fall in this . . ."

The words died on Verhoven's lips and he went still.

He thought he'd heard something moving around in the pit, in the opposite direction from where Hawker's voice came. He turned slightly, stirring the water.

"Don't move," he whispered. "There's something else down here."

Verhoven crouched, his nose close to the stinking muck, straining to see. The pit was clearly designed as a trap, and any animal that might have fallen down there with them could be dangerous. He moved slowly to one side, feeling for the wall of the pit, bumping against it.

A low, almost inaudible growl reached toward him, drifting out of the darkness, like the guttural rumble that comes from the back of a crocodile's throat. The sound was labored, a deep heavy groan, a warning almost below the range of human hearing.

What made that sound? A caiman, a large snake, maybe—pythons were rumored to make low rumbles in their guts—or even a jaguar, wounded and weak in the bottom of a pit, it could still kill with a single claw.

Verhoven backed away from the sound, moving along the length of the trench.

"I have a flare," Hawker said, his voice a whisper.

Verhoven paused, making sure his hands were ready. "Light it."

Behind him the flare snapped and with the sizzle of the phosphorous it lit, flashing in the darkness. For an instant, Verhoven went blind. When his eyes adjusted, he saw nothing in front of him except filthy water and the muddy walls at the closed end of the rectangular pit. Something moved on his left, clinging to the wall. It lunged toward his face, hissing, with its jaws open.

Verhoven jumped backward, firing. He crashed into

Hawker, knocking the flare into the muck. The light vanished as murky water swallowed the burning stick.

Scampering sounds came toward him. Verhoven fired from his fallen position.

Something clawed him and then pushed off, using him as a stepping stone to launch itself up the wall. The flare bobbed to the surface and Verhoven caught a glimpse of a shape clambering up the side of the pit. He fired as it went over the top, blasting it forward as its momentum carried it out into the jungle night. The thing shrieked in agony.

As Hawker plucked the flare from the water, the light improved. Verhoven dropped his gaze, checking the rest of the pit, side to side, up and down.

They were alone.

Hawker fell back, racked with laughter.

"What's so damn funny?"

"Keystone Cops," Hawker said, barely able to get the words out.

"You're the chief, then."

Hawker couldn't stop chuckling. "And you're having monkey for dinner."

Verhoven hadn't gotten a good enough look at the scrambling thing to know what it was, but the size was about right—thirty to forty pounds—and there was little else he could think of that could climb like that. For a moment he was almost embarrassed, blasting a little monkey with an AK-47. Then again, a starving, cornered monkey could have made a mess of them, even if it wasn't a life-threatening situation.

"Better than him having us," he replied.

As Hawker continued laughing, Verhoven fished out

his radio. Fortunately, like everything else electronic they had brought along, it was waterproof. He clicked the switch, told one of his men what had happened and ordered him to bring a rescue party and some rope.

As Verhoven finished the conversation, Hawker tapped him on the shoulder and pointed to one of the walls, holding the flare up to give him more light.

The central part of the left wall appeared to be made of stone. It was covered in lumpy chunks of mud, but even in the flickering light, a large face could be seen beneath that mud. A face carved in the stone. Around it were other marks, hieroglyphics that looked remarkably similar to those Danielle had showed him.

As they studied it, the rescue party arrived and dropped down a rope. Hawker and Verhoven climbed out and the group shined their lights into the pit. Danielle nodded her approval. "We'll show McCarter in the morning," she said.

Weary and covered in muck, Verhoven began his walk back to the camp, ignoring the questions about what had happened and glad that the ridiculous situation was over.

Before he'd gone ten paces Hawker spoke, stopping him in his tracks.

"Where is it?" Hawker asked.

"Where's what?" Danielle replied.

Hawker's voice rang with suspicion. "Verhoven's monkey."

Danielle, and the men who'd helped with the rescue, only seemed more confused, but Verhoven understood. He looked around. There was no monkey carcass, no blood on the ground or a trail to indicate that something else had dragged it off into the woods. No sign of the thing he'd blasted.

"There was a monkey in the pit," Verhoven explained. "I shot at the bugger as he went over the top of the wall. Looks like I missed."

The others seemed to accept that and appeared unworried, but Hawker's stare was unrelenting, his suspicious nature locked on to the latest small thing that seemed out of order. Verhoven met his eyes and then scanned the forest around them again.

Both of them knew he didn't miss.

## CHAPTER 16

Richard Kaufman glanced around the confines of the small hospital room. The walls were covered in a muted green. A pair of ancient beds, complete with rusting iron frames and tall IV stands, sat opposite and parallel each other, while a wilting, forgotten plant spread its thin arms in a corner near the window.

He waited there as a nurse helped the room's sole patient return from a trip to the communal rest room. The man entered, struggling with a crutch under each arm.

Stooped but still over six feet tall, the man was broad-shouldered, thin and bony, appearing almost emaciated. A ragged nest of tangled dark hair sat on his head, while dark circles hung from his eyes and his skin looked a sickly color. He reminded Kaufman of a house that had caught fire but remained standing: hollowed out, discolored and lifeless.

A look of surprise appeared on his face as he studied Kaufman. "You're not a doctor," he guessed.

"I would have thought you'd seen enough of doctors." Kaufman replied.

The man nodded slowly, then hobbled to a new position with a smile covering his ragged face. "Yeah, I have," he said. "Which means you must be Helios."

"That's right," Kaufman replied, sarcastically. "I'm the Greek god of the sun, and I spend my time visiting patients in small hospital rooms." He stood. "The real question is who you are and how you came to know about Helios, considering that you can't remember your own name."

The man tried to smile, but it seemed to cause him pain and he quickly gave up. "Give me a second. I'll explain."

He crossed the room, struggling with the crutches in the narrow space. He reached one of the beds and leaned the crutches against the wall. When they started to slide, he grabbed them and slammed them back into place. Anger and bitterness, Kaufman thought. Here was a man who hated his current predicament. Then again, who wouldn't?

The patient looked up at Kaufman, his legs sticking out beyond the hem of the gown; one leg was white, the other a dark tan color.

Noticing Kaufman's gaze, the man explained. "They took it off," he said. "Didn't even ask me. Just took it off and gave me this one to replace it." He glanced down at the dark prosthetic. "I guess there aren't too many light-skinned Caucasians in these parts, so the legs all look like this, and in the end, they just give you what fits."

"You were going to explain some things," Kaufman said. "Let's start with Helios."

"Right," the man replied. "But first I have something

you might want to see." With great effort he retrieved a small backpack from beside the bed, rummaged through it and then tossed something to Kaufman.

Kaufman studied it: a hexagonal crystal resembling those the NRI had been examining; the erstwhile Martin's crystals. The meeting's importance grew.

"Interested in talking?" the patient asked.

Kaufman closed the door. "Who are you?"

"I'm Jack Dixon," the man replied.

Kaufman had seen photos of the NRI's team, including Dixon, and he now recognized the man, a shell of his former self, perhaps fifty pounds lighter, not including the leg.

"The NRI is looking for you," Kaufman noted. "Not interested in getting in touch with them, for some reason?"

"Not particularly," Dixon said. "Not if I can do better."

"What makes you think I can help you with that?" Kaufman asked.

"Because a two-faced son of a bitch stole something from me," Dixon said. "Stole what we were fucking dying for out there." The burst of anger seemed to come from nowhere. "My guess is he did it for you."

As Dixon paused to calm himself, Kaufman considered what he'd said. Futrex had two moles within the NRI. Out of prudence, he'd tried to split them up, and as luck had taken its course, one had ended up on the current field team while the other had joined Dixon on the first effort.

When the NRI had stopped receiving reports from Dixon's field team, Kaufman had taken it as a good sign, thinking his man had made some type of move. From Dixon's comment, it was apparent that he'd done so, only something had gone wrong. There had been no radio call requesting extraction, no communication of any kind, and for several weeks no sign of either Kaufman's mole or the NRI team.

"You caught him," Kaufman guessed.

"No," Dixon said bluntly. "But something else did. The natives skewered that son of a bitch and then let some animal feed on him. When I found him he was missing half his body, but he still had his pack. He had that crystal and some other items. He also had a piece of paper tucked into his ID packet with a list of frequencies on it, and the word 'Helios' circled a few times."

Dixon paused to scratch carefully at one of the sores on his face. "The thing is, no one in my unit touched the radio except me. And Helios . . . not our code word. Sounded more like a buyer or a corporation. Some big shot waiting for delivery. Maybe a Greek god among men." He nodded toward Kaufman. "So what do you think, big shot? You still want to buy?"

Kaufman listened to the man's words, their abrasive quality seemed false, a forced effort as the man's voice wavered ever so slightly. Kaufman wondered what he was hiding.

"Maybe," Kaufman said. "First I need to know a few things, beginning with what happened out there."

Dixon went quiet for a moment. He gazed at the floor before looking back at Kaufman. "I took eight men out into the jungle," he said finally. "And I left all eight of them behind, dead," he said. "Most of them ripped to shreds by some animal we never saw."

"What are you talking about?"

"We were the rover party, our job was to cover a lot of ground, talk to the locals and categorize what we found. Sinkholes, caves, anything that might have once been a stone structure. For the first three months we didn't find anything that wasn't just shit. But then we hired on these two native guides, and after jerking us around for a week, they got all liquored up and told us about this place no one was supposed to go. To go there was death, they said, but for enough whiskey and the promise of a couple of rifles, they told us how to find it. And so we did. A big-ass temple, just sitting there out in the middle of nowhere. We cracked it open and I found that crystal in there, along with some metallic-looking stones, the kind that set off a Geiger counter, if you get my drift. And just then everything started going straight to hell."

"In what way?" Kaufman asked.

"The first night we heard sounds in the forest. Weird little scuffling noises and bird calls. The next day we found some poor bastard covered in dried-up mud and all slashed and cut. Looked like they tried to burn him but it only caught on his arm and his neck and part of his head. You should have seen his face, frozen in agony. He might have been alive when they burned him, I don't know."

"What do you mean some poor bastard?" Kaufman asked, concerned.

"Not one of us," Dixon replied. "Don't know who he was. But the next night we heard these screeching calls, like a carrion bird, only a hundred times louder. And then one of my men disappeared. Went out to take a piss and never came back. We looked for him, but we never found him." Dixon shrugged, as if he was still baffled by the disappearance. "No sign of struggle or anything. Then we started hearing the natives, a different tribe from the guys who led us there. I think they called them Chollokwan or something. They started hounding us at night.

"We planned to break out the next day, but by dawn two more of my men were gone. I found a trail this time. Me and a guy named McCrea followed it, while the others held tight." He looked up at Kaufman. "You don't want to know what we found."

"Dead?"

"Torn apart," he said unevenly, "and stuck up in the trees."

Kaufman listened, concerned with the man's state of mind. Dixon's voice had begun wavering, changing pitch and cadence.

"That was it," Dixon said. "Time to fucking go. Only your little friend had already made that decision and by the time we got back to that clearing he'd bugged out with the last of my people. So we got on his trail and hauled ass until we caught up to him. Seems we interrupted something making a meal out of him, and then . . . well, then it came after us."

Kaufman had heard from the doctors that this patient was unstable. They'd warned him not to ask too many questions, but he needed more information.

"What the hell are you talking about? What came after you?"

Dixon looked out the window, the light filtering through the leaves seemed to calm him. It was a strange sight, a man of Dixon's background and reputation, gulping at a lump in his throat, trying to fight off what seemed like waves of fear.

"I don't know what it was," he said finally, turning back to Kaufman. "We heard those calls in the mist and I stepped forward to take the point. There was something moving out there. I couldn't see it, but I heard it, sensed it. I moved forward to take a shot, but it went for McCrea. It moved so fast. Like a barracuda in the water, or that spider that jumps out of its hole to get you. Bang!" He slammed his hand against the wall. "Now you're dead.

"I took off running, but one of them caught me. I blasted the damn thing dead center. But it didn't fall, it just changed direction a bit, snapped my leg and left me there for the natives to finish off."

"And yet you're still alive."

"I couldn't tell you why," he said. "A squall line came through a little while later and I crawled out of there in the downpour. Maybe they couldn't follow my trail. Maybe they figured I was as good as dead, why not let me suffer."

"Interesting story," Kaufman said, leaning back. "Sounds a little strange, don't you think?"

"I didn't say it made sense."

Kaufman shook his head. He decided to be direct. Either the patient would crack or he might be jolted back into reality. "What really happened to you out there, Mr. Dixon?"

"I told you."

"You've told me gibberish. Animals and natives killed eight armed men? Ex–Green Berets like yourself?"

"It's the truth," Dixon said.

"Is it?" Kaufman asked. "The doctors don't think so. They think you cut your own leg. That the gash was so clean it was done with a blade."

Dixon shook his head. Looking at the ground he mumbled, "It was one of them."

"Them what?"

"I don't know!" he shouted. "I don't know what they were. Why the hell does it matter? Why the hell do you care?"

The man was bordering on a nervous breakdown. If he went over the edge he might never return. "Maybe you don't know," Kaufman offered. "I've seen your toxicology report—your body's chemical levels were so far off you were hallucinating when they brought you in. Your temperature was one hundred and six degrees, high enough to cause brain damage. You had a massive infection where your leg had become septic and you'd lost a lot of blood."

Dixon looked away.

"You screamed at the doctors," Kaufman added. "Do you remember that? Do you remember calling the nurses demons, threatening to kill them if they put you under?"

Dixon shrank back slightly. "I didn't . . . I didn't want to sleep."

"Terrors," Kaufman guessed.

Dixon turned slowly toward Kaufman and when he spoke this time, his eyes were flat, unblinking, his voice gravelly and low. "My men," he said. "I see them when I sleep. Their faces, their bodies."

Kaufman paused. Whatever had happened, Dixon

seemed to believe it. And for certain the NRI had taken preparations against the possibility of a native attack. Perhaps he could turn Dixon's fear to his advantage. "Then maybe you want revenge?"

Dixon looked up at Kaufman. "What?"

"Take me back there," Kaufman said. "I'll bring an army with us. And we'll wipe those natives from the face of the earth."

Dixon blinked a few times but remained silent. "I'm not going back," he said finally.

"If you want a big check, you will," Kaufman said.

"No. I'm not going back," Dixon repeated, sounding more like a man admitting to a newly discovered reality than one making a conscious decision.

"You'll be safe. I promise you. We'll all be well protected."

Dixon started to laugh, but it was a sad laugh, a nod to the irony of life. He looked Kaufman in the eye and shook his head: the shipwreck survivor, unwilling to reenter the sea.

"I hope you understand what you're throwing away," Kaufman said.

The emotion drained from Dixon's face and when he spoke again his voice had dropped. "Most people are born afraid," he said. "But some of us only learn how to fear along the way. I spent half my life spitting on the weak and gutless. But now . . . it's worse for me than it is for any of them, because I remember what it was like to be different, I remember a time when I didn't know what it was like to be afraid."

He choked back the lump in his throat once again. "I don't eat much and I never sleep. And sometimes, even when I'm wide awake, I hear those things calling to one another, stalking us." He shook his head emphatically. "I'll sell you what I have, the crystals and the rest of the artifacts. But it don't matter how much money you got. It ain't enough to get me back out there."

Frustrated, Kaufman glared at the man. "Then you can give me the location," Kaufman said. "The spot on the map. That might be good enough for a partial payment."

Dixon hesitated for a moment and then turned his gaze to the floor and Kaufman began to realize the truth. "You don't know," he said. "Do you?"

"It's not clear," Dixon whispered. "The natives took us there. The GPS went out."

As Dixon answered, he seemed like a different man from the one who'd greeted Kaufman so glibly from the doorway. Kaufman sensed overwhelming disappointment from him, directed mostly at himself, at what he'd become: fearful, weak.

"I can give you the general area," he offered.

"How general are we talking about?"

Dixon did not quickly reply and Kaufman knew it would be all but worthless. Perhaps it was the fever, the blood loss and the trauma; and if not the physical pain, then perhaps the mental damage he'd incurred had done the trick. But it seemed as if the facts had been erased from the man's brain.

Kaufman pitied him, but also focused on his own concerns. He felt the opportunity slipping away. Despite all his efforts, despite having two moles in the NRI's operation, despite hacking into their database and now grilling one of their former employees who had actually been there, the temple's location still eluded him.

Time was running out. If the new NRI field team was on the right track they would soon find the temple and the prize, if it existed. And in that case all of Kaufman's efforts would be for naught.

He stared at Dixon and realized there was only one option left to try, one that would be far more dangerous than any move he'd made yet.

## CHAPTER 17

The NRI discovery of the Wall of Skulls had been the result of information combined with hard work. The discovery of the pit had been pure luck, a result of Hawker and Verhoven chasing the natives through the jungle. Both proved fruitful.

The Wall appeared to be a natural stone embankment with shelves carved out for the skulls and other bones that had been wedged and cemented into place. Glyphs and decorative markings populated its base and capstone.

And while it was true that the Wall matched Blackjack Martin's description aesthetically, his calculations of its dimensions left something to be desired. At ninety feet in length and seven feet tall, the Wall was almost exactly one fifth of Martin's boast. It made McCarter laugh. In Martin's business, in the early twentieth century, a little exaggeration went a long way.

As he dangled over the gaping pit, suspended in a harness, McCarter wondered what Martin would have written about it. It was almost thirty feet from the ground level to the surface of the muck at the bottom, but McCarter guessed that Blackjack would have claimed a depth of at least fifty feet, or a hundred, or perhaps even called it bottomless.

Twisting on the rope and looking down, he decided it didn't matter, thirty feet was enough.

"Lower me down," he said, "before I change my mind."

The porters released some of the tension on the rope and McCarter began to drop. This was his fifth trip to the bottom. In fact, he'd spent more time down there than anyone, but he had yet to get used to the voyage in or out.

As the pulley creaked and he dropped below ground level, McCarter's attention was drawn to the stone slab that made up a large portion of the pit's eastern wall. A great face, five feet across, dominated the slab. It had sad, round eyes from which stone tears ran, highlighted by dripping condensation. Its thin lips were closed tight and a spiked barb passed through each ear, drawing rivers of blood. Stylized torches burned on either side of the face, while beneath it, what appeared to be a massive crocodile head had been carved, complete with something bloody lying in its open jaws.

Danielle and Susan waited beneath it, looking silly in their oversized fishing waders.

McCarter touched down in the cloying muck, his feet stretching for the bottom. Never a fisherman himself, he hadn't gotten used to the odd feeling of cold mud and water pressing against him through the thin rubber skin of the waders.

He released the harness, sloshed his way over to Danielle and Susan and pulled two printed photographs from his breast pocket, handing one to each.

"It's a match," he said to Susan.

The photos contained an image from the database of Mayan glyphs. The image was a representation of a name.

Danielle and Susan examined the photo, comparing the image to the glyph on the stone wall above them.

"I think you're right," Susan said.

"I'm not sure what I'm looking at," Danielle said. "How about a little help?"

McCarter pointed out the matching sections. "This is Seven Macaw," he said. "The name of an exalted being from Mayan prehistory. From a time even before Tulan Zuyua."

"Before?" Danielle asked. "I thought Tulan Zuyua was their Garden of Eden."

"It is," McCarter said. "In a manner of speaking. But their version of Genesis runs differently than ours."

She gave him a sideways glance, which he took as a request for more information.

"Let me put it this way," he said, "in the Judeo-Christian version of Genesis, we begin with God creating the heaven and the earth. The second and third verses tell us that the earth was in darkness and then God created the light. By verse twenty-six, we're on the sixth day and God creates man. But there was nothing before this, nothing before these six days.

"Now," he said, "in the Mayan version, history stretches back from the creation of man as well as forward. It goes back to a time before Tulan Zuyua, before mankind even existed, to a race that preceded us, a race the Maya called the wooden people."

Danielle's eyes narrowed. "I've heard the name. How do they relate to this?"

"In the Mayan view of creation, it took the gods four tries to successfully create the human race. On the first attempt they ended up with things that squawked and stuttered but didn't speak. Seeing some value in these things the gods kept them around, letting them become the animals of the forest and going back to the drawing board once again. The second time, they used mud as the medium and it was more or less a complete failure. The creation kept dissolving into sludge and muck. So they let it die and tried again. On their third try, they used wood to create with and they brought forth the wooden people: a sort of a prototype for mankind."

McCarter paused to make sure she was with him. "Now, the wooden people looked something like humans," he explained. "They were intelligent, ambitious, they could count and talk and reason, but they were odd in many ways. The Mayan manuscript *Popul Vuh* describes them as having no muscle in their arms or legs, no fat on their bodies. They were said to be able to speak but had stiff, masklike faces and ungainly deformed shapes—like stick people, I suppose."

Susan chimed in. "Basically they needed a good makeover, some time in the gym and about ten thousand collagen injections."

"Right," McCarter said, smiling. "But even in this somewhat decrepit state, they were viable, and according to the legend they grew prosperous and even powerful."

"And this Seven Macaw," Danielle said, pointing to

the glyph on the slab. "He was one of the wooden people?"

"Absolutely," McCarter said. "Their leader, in a sense. He was described as having eyes and teeth that shined like jewels. He had a throne or a nest made of metal, and the power to create light in the darkness. He boasted that he could light up the whole earth. But the Mayan writings also tell us he was a fraud, and though he could create brilliant light, it didn't reach out into the great distance of the whole world, but only lit up his immediate surroundings. Despite this, Seven Macaw exalted himself, holding himself out as a god, forcing the others to worship him as if he were both the sun and the moon."

Danielle seemed to understand. "I'm thinking the gods didn't like that much," she said.

"Not good to anger the gods," McCarter replied. "Not in any culture. The outcome is predictable."

"The wooden people were destroyed," she guessed.

McCarter nodded. "The gods sent vicious beasts to attack them and even turned their own animals against them. And as if that weren't enough, the sky god, Hurricane, sent a massive rainstorm to drown them like the sinners in Noah's day. *'Rain through the day and rain through the night. A rain of black resin that poured from the sky,'*" McCarter said, quoting the Mayan text. "*'And the Earth was blackened beneath it.'*"

"Burning rain?" Danielle asked.

"I've heard it described as a rain of fire," McCarter said, "like hot oil or ash or napalm. And because the earth was blackened some think it might represent a volcanic event, with hot ash and fire falling from the sky, but the *Popul Vuh* definitely describes it as rain."

"And Seven Macaw died in this rain?"

"Actually, he disappeared prior to the Black Rain," McCarter said. "But the mythology of the work seems to suggest it was necessary to get rid of him to allow the rain to fall, as if his power could challenge the gods and prevent it."

"I see," Danielle said. "So what happened to him?"

"Two demigods were sent for him. They shot Seven Macaw with a blow dart when he was up in a tree, and after he fell to the ground, they removed the metal from his eyes and his teeth and took all his jewelry—the things he used to light up the night. Without these items he lost the power to light up anything, even the immediate surroundings. He went into hiding and never bothered anyone again. And then, with Seven Macaw vanquished, the gods sent the rain."

She understood. "So the heroes killed Seven Macaw and then the rain came to destroy the rest of the wooden people. Take out the leader and then finish off the troops."

"That's one way of putting it, yes."

She was gleeful. "This is good news. The slab certainly proves the Mayan connection," she said. "No computer inkblots required."

McCarter chuckled. "It does more than that," he insisted. "It proves that these people were intimate with the particular mythology of the Mayan creation, a fact that not only connects them with all the other Mayan tribes, but suggests they were very early in the Mayan cycle." He raised his eyebrows. "You may just be right," he added. "Tulan Zuyua may be down here after all."

Danielle smiled confidently and then turned back to the slab embedded in the wall. She looked at the other symbols—the big sad face, the dashes and swirls of the glyphs around it and the angry crocodilelike head with its bloody meal. "What about that one?" she asked.

McCarter's eyes crinkled as he smiled. It was an important discovery. "That one is Zipacna," he said. "The Destroyer."

Later that night, sitting beside a flickering Coleman lantern, Danielle was pressing McCarter and Susan for more details. Hawker had joined them.

McCarter began by explaining the obstacles. "One problem we face is the condition of the find." The glyphs on the Wall are in terrible shape, for the most part unreadable. The ones found on the great stone in the pit are better off, perhaps because they've been buried and protected from the elements for much of their life. The exposed tree roots and steep incline of the vertical walls suggest the pit to be quite a recent excavation."

This response concerned her. She wondered if their adversary had somehow gotten here before them. McCarter, unknowingly, assuaged that fear.

"For whatever reason, the natives seem to be using it as a trap."

"With all the bones we had to fish out of there, you wonder if they ever came back to check it," Hawker said.

"Apparently, we're not the only ones that can be wasteful," McCarter said. "But from the look of things, it seems to have been dug with fairly primitive tools. And almost without regard for the relics it uncovered. In many places we see chips and scratches from their digging that have damaged the wall. My guess is that they knew of the slab and chose to excavate there to make specific use of having one solid, steep wall."

Hawker rubbed his sore shoulder. "The sheer face makes for a better trap," he said, ruefully. "You don't see the drop coming."

"And the glyphs in the pit," Danielle asked, bringing the conversation back on track. "You were going to tell me something good."

McCarter got down to business, opening an aged, leather-bound folder stuffed with drawings and notes. He pointed to a group of sketches he'd made. "Remember what I told you about the wooden people and Seven Macaw—that they were a mythological race the Maya believe existed before man?"

"And how the gods destroyed them with a burning rain," she said. "Yes, I remember all of it."

"Remember the other glyph you pointed out?"

"Zipacna," she said. "The Destroyer."

"Well, much of the writing on this slab concerns the two of them. Seven Macaw, the father, and Zipacna, his son."

Danielle was surprised. "Zipacna looked like some type of reptile to me."

"I know," McCarter said. "He was, sort of. But you have to remember, it's mythology. Like the Minotaur and the Kraken in Greek mythology, much of it is mysterious and nonlinear. So even though Seven Macaw was a proto-human, so to speak, his son was this beast, this destroyer, who was usually described as resembling a hideous crocodile, though he walked and lived on the land."

Danielle listened as McCarter spoke, unsure where this was heading.

McCarter looked over at Susan. "You recognized it before me," he said. "Why don't you tell the story."

She spoke up. "The glyphs on the stone slab describe Zipacna doing the work of his father, terrorizing the peasants and anyone who might challenge Seven Macaw."

"Everybody needs a henchman once in a while," Hawker said.

Susan laughed. "In a lot of ways that's what Zipacna was. In fact, the main story here depicts a group that wanted to topple Seven Macaw, deciding they must first get rid of Zipacna. Tricking him into digging a pit for them and then trying to kill him by dropping a huge log into the hole while he was down there."

"A pit," Hawker said. "Like ours?"

"Possibly," McCarter said. "I believe that the stone in the pit was once on the surface. The land probably built up around it like sand blowing against the side of a house. Even now the top sticks out a bit. And in the story it is more of a narrow well."

"So what happened to them?" Danielle asked, keeping things on track.

Susan finished the story. "After thinking they'd crushed Zipacna, the group began to celebrate by throwing a big party. While they were getting drunk in their victory celebration, Zipacna climbed out of the hole and destroyed them all by bringing their house down on them."

McCarter smiled. "Some think it's an ancient morality tale, a warning against the dangers of drink."

"I can understand that," Hawker said. "I've had a few houses come down on me because of the dangers of drink."

Laughter made its way around the group, then Danielle asked another question. "So that pit may represent the one they dug for Zipacna and perhaps this wall is supposed to be the resting place of the people he killed?"

"I think you're right about this being a monument to them," McCarter added. "Some kind of a monument anyway. The place seems to have religious significance but was not a population center."

Danielle considered his words. They confirmed what she'd feared. They'd found a monument, but no evidence anyone had lived there. And in their search of the surrounding area they'd found no sign of other structures.

"Someone had to build it," she said. "Can you tell me who, or where they came from? Or are we going to have to work on your definition of 'good news'?"

McCarter smiled. "Do not despair," he said. "All is not lost in our quest to make a legitimate hero out of old Blackjack Martin. There are glyphs on the base of the slab that refer to another place, perhaps even a city. A place with stone buildings and great fires."

She perked up.

He raised a cautioning hand. "Don't get too excited. It isn't named, just described."

"Where? Close to us?"

"If we're reading the glyphs correctly, it should be two days' travel from here."

"Which way?"

"The glyphs define the direction as that of the setting sun on a date, a date the Maya called 8 Imix, 14 Mak, ruled by the Ninth Lord of the Night."

Hawker shook his head. "I think I have a dentist appointment that day."

Danielle smacked him on the arm, though she couldn't contain a brief snicker at the comment. She turned back to McCarter. "Please tell me we know what day that is on our calendar."

"Well . . ." he said, "not exactly."

She exhaled in frustration. "You're torturing me, Professor. Just give me an answer. Can we get there or not?"

Susan laughed. "This is what he does," she said. "We call it McCarter Syndrome. It's like the Socratic Method, only worse. He can take three lectures to answer one question, and by that time you've forgotten what you asked."

McCarter smiled and obliged. "Sorry," he said. "Old school tradition. The thing is, we've been looking for dates on the ruin to place it in the time line with the other Mayan sites. We could only do that if we found one of their Long Count dates."

The Long Count was the Mayan supercalendar, a cycle of interlocking names and numbers that gave each day a multipart name and number in a sequence that would not be repeated for over five thousand years. A date in that format could be matched to an exact Gregorian calendar date: day, month and year. It would also allow them to place the ruin exactly where it belonged in the time line and to prove beyond all doubt if the sight predated other Mayan structures.

"Only, we haven't found any of those," McCarter said. "But there is another glyph connected with the date glyph on the slab, and this other marking indicates a special occurrence happening on the date. It calls this date the day of the yellow sun. But they're not using yellow to describe the color; rather, it corresponds to a direction. In the Mayan scheme, each cardinal direction has a color: red for east, black for west, white for north and yellow for south. The day of the yellow sun means the day of the southernmost sun: the Solstice; down here, it's the longest day of the year. So whatever year it actually was, 8 Imix, 14 Mak occurred on December 21 or December 22."

Danielle was beaming; finally she had something to grasp. "So we just need a little astronomy work to tell us where the sun would settle on that date."

"I suppose we'll need it for accuracy," he said. "But as luck would have it, it's only January and we're so close to the Solstice that I can point us in the rough direction." He extended his arm toward the western horizon, his palm flat and vertical like a blade. The line of sight ran down his arm and over his thumb to indicate the course. "Right about there," he said. "Just south of where the sun went down."

As she looked in that direction, Danielle could feel her heart racing. She had to believe they would find what they were looking for there. It made sense in every way. A large population center would be more important than an outlying relic. Items of stature would be brought there, or kept there: gold, silver, jewels and possibly crystals like the ones Blackjack Martin had found. One step closer, she thought. "We leave at first light."

"We should do some cleanup and weather-proofing here first," McCarter said. "It's only right."

"Twenty-four hours," she granted. "No more."

He nodded and she turned to Hawker, who seemed less enthused. In fact, he seemed disappointed. "What's wrong with you?" she asked. "Aren't you impressed?"

"Absolutely," he said. "This is incredible. It's just . . . I wanted to hear the rest of the story. What happened to Zipacna? I mean, it couldn't end like that. Surely someone paid Zipacna back for what he did, right?"

Danielle laughed. "Revenge?"

"Justice," Hawker said, smiling.

Susan spoke up. "Actually, someone did take care of Zipacna. The same demi-gods who destroyed Seven Macaw."

"How?" Hawker asked.

This time McCarter replied. "They used a crab to bait him, luring him into a cave. Once he was inside they trapped him underneath it. Sealing him there for all eternity, beneath a mountain of stone."

## CHAPTER 18

While the rest of the team packed up and readied themselves for the journey across land, Danielle sat on the deck of the *Ocana*, using the satlink to report their progress.

To her great joy, Gibbs was unavailable and she'd been connected with the only other person cleared for communication with her: Arnold Moore.

She explained their discovery to him and made a request. "I want to send the rest of the team home. I'll go on with Verhoven's group, but we need to get the civilians out of here."

"Professor McCarter and Ms. Briggs?"

"Yes," she said. "Along with the porters and Devers and Polaski," she said, reminding him that they were part of Research Division, not Operations, and didn't really belong out in the field on an operation of this magnitude.

"Why now?" Moore asked. "Has something happened?"

"I don't think we need them anymore," she said. "And yes, there was a small incident the other night with a pair of natives," she said, referring to the incursion that had led Hawker and Verhoven into the pit.

"Anyone hurt?"

"No," she said. "But I have a bad feeling that it won't be the last we see of them. Besides, we have our trail now. We can follow it and get assistance remotely if we need it for translation or interpretation."

"Gibbs will never go for that," he said, telling her something she already knew. "You can't imagine the paranoia back here. He wants you to stop reporting completely now. Only verbal communication with him or me from here on out. No record."

They'd been sending bogus "filler" reports for the past month, but now Gibbs didn't even want that. He seemed to be coming unglued.

"Why?" she asked.

"He's become convinced that someone took out Dixon's team and he's on a mole hunt to find out how the info got out. He's worried that any type of disclosure could endanger you."

"All the more reason to get these people out of here," she said, exasperated.

Silence followed for a moment.

"You know I agree with you," Moore said finally. "But it's not going to happen, so we have to stop talking about it."

Danielle listened to the meaning behind the words. Even in the somewhat distorted pitch that the satellite and the encryption technology caused, Moore's point was clear: Worry about what you can control, not what you can't.

"I know this is difficult," he added. "But the best

thing you can do for them is to keep moving at top speed. The sooner you have a confirmed location, the sooner Gibbs will let you pull them."

In her heart she knew that. She'd hoped the trail would be enough, but things often worked backward in Gibbs' mind. The closer they got to success, the more he would push the boundaries, and the more he would risk to close the deal. She would go forward and one of two things would happen. They would find something strong enough to make Gibbs pull the civilians. Or the overdue rains would finally come back to the Amazon and the whole group would have to leave as torrential downpours flooded the forest.

"Fine," she said. "Then tell him we're moving. I'll contact you in twenty-four hours."

"Affirmed," he said, then added, "And Danielle, watch your back. And your front and both sides. Gibbs is paranoid, but it doesn't mean he's wrong. So be careful. I don't want you disappearing on me."

She smiled at his concern, and out of the corner of her eye she saw Hawker approaching. "Don't worry," she said. "I'll be fine."

She terminated the link and began to shut down and pack up the system as Hawker walked up.

"Everyone's ready," he said.

They'd come to a temporary parting of the ways. Hawker would reboard the *Ocana* and sail downriver back to Manaus, while the rest of the group moved westward on foot in the direction indicated by the glyphs they'd found. Upon discovering any sign of the expected Mayan outpost, they would contact Hawker and cut a landing zone out of the forest so that he could fly in the heavier equipment and bulk supplies that were too cumbersome to carry.

"Good."

He studied her. "You seem a little upset. You're going to miss me, aren't you?"

She laughed. "That's debatable," she said. "But I *am* worried about being extended this far out. You're our only link back now. So don't fall in a hole or anything."

As he laughed, she broke into a broad grin. She couldn't remember the last time she'd joked with someone so easily. "I'll contact you as soon as we've found the site. Be ready to bring in the equipment I listed."

"Your defense system," he said.

"And the dogs Verhoven wants," she replied, pulling her pack on.

"Right," he said. "I'm really looking forward to a helicopter filled with barking mutts."

Behind them the *Ocana*'s big diesel rumbled to life. The captain whistled to Hawker, who nodded and then turned back to Danielle. He reached out and straightened her pack, adjusting one of the straps like a parent sending a child off to school. She slapped his hand away and then stepped down the makeshift gangplank to join the rest of the group.

Ten minutes later the *Ocana* was out of sight and Danielle and her people were moving deeper into the forest. As they left the river behind, any semblance of a fresh breeze vanished and the air took on the feeling of a sauna, stifling and motionless and growing hotter with each passing hour.

The rains had held off so far, with the weather pattern influenced by the forming El Niño. For the most part that had been a blessing, but after two weeks without a hint of shade, a quick, cool shower would have been welcome relief.

Despite the conditions, the group made good time, traveling through the twilight beneath the canopy, surrounded by towering shapes of impossibly large trees. McCarter in particular seemed to have a new spring in his step, and Danielle watched as he pointed out things on the way, particular plants and bright orchids, and trees dying in the twisted embrace of the strangler fig.

Danielle tried to ignore him. She was thinking of the bigger picture, prodded on by Moore's faith in her, the desire to prove herself to Gibbs and her own need to finish what she started. But there was more to it than that. If she was right, they were closing in on the source of the crystals Martin had found years ago, crystals that seemed to be capable of creating energy from cold fusion.

It was bigger than her, she knew that, bigger than them all, but she was the one carrying the knowledge and it left her feeling very alone, isolated, back out on that island that Hawker had so accurately described. And though Hawker was still in the dark, he had a sense of what she was going through and in some way had begun to share that weight. It had given them a bond and she had even begun to trust him.

She hated to admit it but she missed his presence,

even his bad jokes. She found herself looking forward to his return, to a degree she would not have expected.

At the moment though, her attention returned to the march and the latest delay in their progress. McCarter had stopped the procession for another Discovery Channel moment, showing the others a huge rubber tree with its smooth, plasterlike wood and a trunk that spread apart like a group of massive vertical blades. A thin black line of ants were crawling along the bark, hundreds of them in single file with little leaves in their mouths.

*Ants! He'd stopped the hike to watch some ants!*

"Look at them," he said. "Don't they remind you of us, carrying their little packs?"

She shook her head. "Not unless you can show me one who keeps stopping the group and holding everyone up."

His face wrinkled, he'd been as giddy as a schoolboy since the discovery of the Wall, with a demeanor to match. "No," he said. "But see this little one over here bossing the others around. He reminds me of—"

She gave him *the look* and he stopped midsentence. With a smile he turned from the ants and reengaged in the trek, launching into a whistling chorus of "High Hopes" as he went. This time she couldn't help but laugh.

By the fifth day, they came across evidence of a small structure. It wasn't much more than a loose pile of stone covered with plant growth and moss, but it was enough to tell them they were in the right area. A few hours later they stumbled upon a sight Danielle could not explain, even as she gazed at it in wonder.

She stepped from the shadows of the rainforest into a large, circular clearing populated by nothing more than scrubby weeds and pale, dry grasses. The darkness they'd hiked through for the past five days cowered behind her, while the blinding sunlight poured in unchallenged. Here, the forest surrendered a dominion that held sway for hundreds of miles in every direction. But that was the smaller surprise.

Danielle squinted against the sudden brightness, using a hand to shield her eyes. At the center of the clearing a gray stone pyramid towered above the flat, open ground. Its steep walls were smooth and unmarked on three sides, while a single stairway ran up its face to a small, square roof, fifteen stories above the forest floor.

A structure of unmistakably Mayan design, as perfect as could be—and yet, for reasons Danielle, and later McCarter, found hard to explain, it seemed out of place and foreign. Not only shouldn't it have been there in the greater sense of all they knew about the Mayan race, but it shouldn't have appeared as it did. It should have been buried in a tangled web of living trees, vines and soil, just as McCarter had been telling the group since day one. It should have been crumbling under the weight of its own stonework, failing and dilapidated as it drowned in the thickening rainforest and its ever-constricting grip.

But it was none of these things. It stood unencumbered and menacing, defiantly unbowed. It unnerved her in a way she could not explain.

At the mere sight of it, the other members of the team began shouting, whooping and hollering in celebration and congratulating one another. Several of them began running toward the pyramid, racing to the foot of the temple as if the first to touch it would win some unspoken prize.

They sprinted past, pausing briefly to congratulate her, before corralling McCarter and dragging him off with them, victorious.

Danielle let them go, preferring to savor the moment. As she walked farther into the clearing and its blissful daylight, she felt a great sense of accomplishment. At long last, she had something concrete to point to. The temple could not disappear like the other leads had. It could not turn out to be a sham or a hoax or a mistake in translation. It was tangible, concrete and irrefutable. She *would* find what they were looking for and she *would* return to Washington a hero.

## CHAPTER 19

M att Blundin sat in Stuart Gibbs' office, aggravated and exhausted at the end of a seventeen-hour day. The director sat across from him, leaning back in his chair, head tilted upward, eyes staring blankly at the ceiling.

At 2:00 A.M. in Washington, Blundin had just finished explaining the nuances of a developing situation: a security breach and data theft that he'd only recently discovered.

Gibbs brought himself forward and exhaled loudly. "What else do you have?"

"That's it," Blundin said. "All we know right now is what happened."

"I don't give a shit about *what happened*," Gibbs cursed. "I want to know how it happened, why it happened and who the fuck made it happen." With the last phrase, Gibbs threw the report across the desk, where it fanned out and crashed into Blundin's prominent gut.

Blundin rubbed his neck. He was sweaty and grimy after such a long day and ready to lash out. But that would just make for a longer night. He plucked the report from his lap and placed it back on the desk, out of

Gibbs' reach, then pulled a dented pack of Marlboros from his breast pocket.

He drew one out and stuck it between his lips. Two flicks of the lighter and the tip was glowing red. Only after a long drag on the cigarette did he begin to reply.

"Look," he said, white smoke billowing from his mouth. "I can tell you *how* it was probably done. I can even tell you *when* it was probably done, but that doesn't help us with the who, because it could have been anybody on the network, either inside this building or out."

Gibbs leaned back, looking pleased for the first time all night. "Let's start with how."

"Fine," Blundin said. "We can start there, but we're going to end up right back where we are now." He exhaled another cloud of carcinogens and reached for an ashtray to lay the cigarette on. "It all starts with the codes. Our system uses a matrix code generated from a set of prime numbers and then exercised through a complex algorithm."

Gibbs seemed lost already, which came as no surprise to Blundin. Maybe this was why he hadn't listened in the first place.

Blundin leaned forward, demonstrating with his hands. "Just think of it like a combination lock. If you don't know the combination you can eventually figure it out by checking every number against every other possible combination of numbers. You know, one, one, one, then one, one, two, then one, one, three—until eventually you get to thirty-six, twenty-six, thirty-six and it finally opens. Only in our case, we're not talking about forty numbers or whatever you have on one of those locks, we're talking about a massive set of possibilities."

"How massive?"

"Try a one with seventeen zeroes after it," Blundin said. "So many numbers that if you counted a thousand a second it would take you a hundred years just to count that high."

Blundin eased back in his chair. "And that's just to count them. To crack the code, each number would have to be checked against every other number, and then tested to see if it worked."

By the look on his face, Gibbs seemed to understand. "What about the vendor, the manufacturer who sold us this encryption?"

"No," Blundin said. "The illegal entries were made using an inactive master code reserved by the computer in case the system locks up."

"What about an ex-employee?" Gibbs asked. "Someone who might know the system, but quit or got fired."

"I already checked. No one higher than a receptionist has left Atlantic Safecom since we installed the system."

"And here?"

"Every time one of our employees leaves, their code and profile are scrubbed from the system—and like I already said, it wasn't an employee code, it was a master code."

Gibbs pounded a fist on the desk. "Well, goddamnit, how the hell did they get the master code? That's what I'm asking you. I mean, they didn't fucking guess it, did they?"

"Actually," Blundin said, "in a way, they did."

Gibbs' eyes narrowed, which Blundin took as a veiled

threat that if he didn't become more forthright, there would be repercussions.

"They made a lot of guesses," Blundin said. "Over three hundred and fifty quadrillion."

Gibbs' face went blank. "That doesn't even sound like a real fucking number."

"It is," Blundin assured him. "That's what it takes to crack the code. That's what I've been warning you about for the past year."

Gibbs was silent, no doubt recalling Blundin's requests to de-link from Research Division and his claims that the code could be vulnerable to a special type of computer-assisted probing. "The hacker problem," Gibbs said finally. "Using a supercomputer or something. Is that how this was done?"

Blundin shifted in his chair. "Under normal circumstances, I would say no. Because even a supercomputer basically does things in series, checking one number against another, raising them by a single exponent and running them through a single algorithm. Even at the speed of your average Cray or Big Blue you're still talking too many numbers and too much time." Blundin paused and did some calculations in his head. "Might take a year or two of continuous, uninterrupted operation."

Gibbs tapped his pen on the desktop. "You said 'under normal circumstances.' Am I to assume we're firmly in the *abnormal* realm now?"

Blundin wiped his brow. "There's a different type of programming out there," he said. "In some cases, entering its third and fourth generation. It's called massive parallel processing. It's used to link computers together, everything from regular PCs to servers and mainframes. And it can turn those units into the equivalent of a supercomputer . . . or ten. Aside from NASA and the Defense Department, not too many people even use it, because no one needs that kind of power. But it's out there and it's faster than anything you can imagine."

"How fast are we talking about?"

"Exponentially faster. In other words, four linked units aren't four times faster, they're sixteen times faster. A hundred linked processors can be ten thousand times faster. Instead of a one-lane highway for your information to roll down, you now have a fifty-lane highway, or a thousand-lane highway or even a million-lane highway. The numbers get checked in parallel, instead of series. A sophisticated program could run a hundred teraflops per second. That is a hundred trillion calculations every second. And like I've been trying to tell you, this type of programming makes systems like ours vulnerable."

The director appeared shocked. "Our system is the same one used by the FBI, even the CIA. You're telling me their files are unsecured?"

Blundin shook his head. "Aside from a few criminals, nobody gives a shit what the FBI has in its files. You can't make any money off what the FBI has in its files. And the Agency system is a pure standalone. Unless you drill a hole in the wall and plug in, there is no way to link up. But we're attached to Research Department and they're hooked up all over the fucking place— universities, member corporations, affiliates. It's like Grand fucking Central. And if you steal one of their

projects—or one of ours—you've saved years of research for your company, and hundreds of millions in R
and D. What the hell do you think we're all about? It's
the same thing we do to the other side."

Gibbs looked ill and Blundin thought, *If he's sick
now he's going to puke when I tell him the rest.* "It gets
worse," he said.

A look of disbelief covered Gibbs' face. "Really?" he
said. "Well, please tell me. Because I can't fucking imagine how."

Blundin hesitated. This time when he spoke, the
words came reluctantly. This was the part he hated, the
slap in the face that made it so much harder to bear. "I
told you they couldn't do this from the outside. Well,
that leaves only one possibility. The actual grunt work
of going through the numbers happened on the inside."

"Our own computers?"

"We have mainframes, stacks of blade servers, and
two hundred and seventy-one linked PCs in this building alone. Add in the Research Department and the total
network is five times larger, including a pair of brand-
new Crays in a climate-controlled room over in Building
Three. Link all these units together and you have one
unbelievable number-crunching machine."

"Some kind of virus," Gibbs guessed.

Blundin nodded. "I have no proof yet, but I suspect
when we're done we'll find that someone introduced a
massive parallel program to our system which instructed
our machines to work on breaking our own code."

Gibbs' bloodshot eyes looked like they might bug out
of his head. "That's just absurd," he said. "I mean, I'm
waiting for you to tell me that you're kidding."

Blundin pulled at his shirt collar. The button was already open but it still felt tight around the bulge of his neck. "I'm not."

Gibbs leaned back in his chair, mumbling a string of expletives, as if enough swearing could purge him of the feeling welling up inside him. Finally, he focused on Blundin once again. "All right," he said. "I find it hard to believe this shit, but I guess I don't really have a choice. So now what? How do we find these bastards?"

Blundin had already begun a counterattack. "Since they probably tapped us from Research's side, we should start there. Go into Research Division's back door ourselves. I'm already looking at the programs they were running, to identify candidates for this Trojan. Once we have our list, we investigate the companies that own those programs."

The director approved with a nod. "Okay, but I want you to do it personally, and then bring the information directly to me." He clarified. "Only to me."

"What about the boys at the Bureau?"

Gibbs was adamant. "No one from the outside. Not even anyone in your department. Not until I tell you."

That was fine with Blundin. Better to solve the problem before telling the world about it anyway.

"What else do we know?"

"Not much," Blundin said. "They accessed information all over the place, like they didn't know exactly what they were looking for at first. Their queries covered at least a dozen projects, maybe more. I'm still checking. Their last entry was three weeks ago, on . . ." He leafed through his copy of the report until he found the right page. "January 4." He said, "Nothing since then."

"Did we change the codes that week?"

"No, they haven't been changed yet."

Gibbs' face went red again. "You might want to get around to that."

"Actually, I don't," Blundin said. "Our best chance of catching them is to have the idiots make another entry. I've put a tracer on the system, a slick little runner that they'll never see coming. If they tap the system again, we'll follow them home."

Gibbs held up a hand, relenting. "All right. It's your area of expertise, you run the investigation. Do whatever the hell you have to do, but keep it to yourself. I don't want another soul involved until I know what happened. Do you understand?"

"Yeah, I get it," Blundin said. "I pretty much got it the first time." He reached for his cigarette, and saw that it had burned down to a stub. He looked at it sadly, wondering if he could get one more drag off the thing, before giving up and crushing it out. He reached into his pocket for a new one, only to find the pack empty. *Another aggravation.* "I'm too tired for any more of this shit tonight," he said, standing up and grabbing his jacket off the back of the chair. "We can have another bitch session in the morning, if you want. But I'm going home."

Gibbs looked at the clock, then nodded his permission.

Blundin walked toward the exit, stopping in the doorway and turning around, remembering another discrepancy. "There is one other thing," he said.

"What's that?" Gibbs asked, looking down at the report again.

"We don't know for sure," Blundin began, "but we're pretty much assuming this has something to do with the Brazil project, right? So I took the liberty to check those files. Sure enough, they were all accessed. Every single one of them." Gibbs looked up, and Blundin pulled on his coat as he continued speaking. "The thing is, in checking them, I noticed the file sets didn't have any project codes attached. And the funding codes belonged to a completely different project."

Gibbs looked surprised. "Whose entries were they?"

"Your junior achiever down there in Brazil, Laidlaw."

Gibbs waited. "And . . ."

"Well, does she know what the fuck she's doing?"

Gibbs' face relaxed a bit. "Don't worry about that," he said. "It's accounting's fault. They've screwed that up before, because she's outside of her sector. Let me guess: the funding codes belonged to one of her other projects."

"Yep."

"See," Gibbs said, "accounting. I'll chew their asses for it tomorrow. You just find the son of a bitch who hacked us."

"All right," Blundin said. "I figured it was something like that. I'll give you the file numbers in the morning."

Gibbs nodded and Blundin gave a half-assed wave as he ducked out through the door.

With Blundin gone, Gibbs was left alone to ponder the situation. He sat quietly for several minutes, silently rejoicing at the limits he'd placed on Moore and Laidlaw, limits that had saved him from dumping the most important information into the database, including the location of the recently discovered temple. That was good news, and it eased his mind considerably, but other news was less pleasant. He stared hard at the doorway through which Blundin had just departed, his eyes burning from anger and lack of sleep. In some ways, things had just gone from bad to worse.

## CHAPTER 20

Danielle stood atop the roof of the newly discovered Mayan temple, gazing out over the clearing around her. She could see the remnants of a procession of small buildings aligned directly with the temple's stairs and a causeway that ran between them and off into the jungle to the west. She could see outcroppings of stone and sunken areas that had once been buildings and plazas. The clearing covered at least ten acres, but the temple was the center. In her heart she believed the source of the crystals would be found here, but they needed to hurry.

There were many reasons to push; openly, she worried about the rains. They would only hold off for so long, and when they did come, work would have to cease for several months. But the real problem was their as yet unknown competitor.

Gibbs' latest satellite call had informed her of the computer breach, and though he insisted that the temple's location remained secret, Danielle could not shake the feeling of an enemy growing closer with each passing moment.

She glanced over at Professor McCarter, who was working with Susan and the porters. Their lives were in danger, and they didn't know it in the least. Certainly, they watched Verhoven and his men patrol, listened as Hawker flew in with a load of defensive equipment, including motion sensors, computerized tracking devices, lights, flares and boxes of ammunition—and the pack of trained dogs Verhoven had insisted upon—and in all likelihood they considered it only a precaution. A little bit of the government's heavy hand when a lighter touch would have been fine.

Danielle knew better. Somewhere out there an enemy sought them, and despite the time they'd bought by racing up the river, eventually that enemy would find them. She wanted the civilians long gone when it happened. To make sure that happened, she had to keep pushing.

She looked to Professor McCarter, crouched on the rooftop, running his finger down a seam in the stonework and explaining to the group what he'd found.

"Tell me again what this means," she said.

"You see how precise the fit is?" he said, pointing. He waved the others closer and then used his knife to scrape at the moss. The stonework was so tight that the moss hadn't grown into it, just covered it over like a tarp. "You couldn't get cigarette paper between these stones. All the great sites that have stood the test of time show this type of craftsmanship. In the Yucatan, in Egypt, in Mongolia.

"This structure must be remarkably stable to look like this, perhaps built onto some bedrock like the skyscrapers of Midtown Manhattan. I have seen some damage on the north side," he admitted. "But the foundation itself can't have subsided too much or these seams would be loose and jumbled. I'm quite excited about that."

"You said you might have found a way inside," she reminded him. "Can we skip ahead to that part? That's what *I'm* excited about."

"You're not one for slow cooking," McCarter replied, only slightly bothered.

"Microwave," she replied. "Or faster."

He smiled and moved to another section of the roof, waving the group over. "This stone tells us another story. The connection here is less precise, the workmanship less exacting." He dug at the moss, pulling it loose where it had burrowed into the cracks, clearing the seam all the way to its corner. The exposed edge was gouged and chipped, dozens of hairline fractures revealing damage yet to come. He looked up. "Of all the stones on this roof, only this one appears in such condition. That can mean only one thing—this stone has been moved . . . repeatedly."

*At last.* "You think this is the way in," she guessed.

"If there is one," he said. "Most Mayan temples have nothing inside except an earlier temple."

Puzzled looks came his way.

"The kings and Ahau of Maya wanted monuments to themselves like all the other leaders of the ancient world. But in a surprisingly pragmatic twist, they would often commission a new structure to be built over the existing ones, a sort of pre-Colombian municipal rehabilitation project, one that enabled them to leave behind a greater temple than their predecessor. The result is something like those Russian nesting dolls, where each larger doll covers the smaller one. At places in the Yucatan some temples have half a dozen underlying layers."

He returned to his original thought. "But other Mayan temples are stand-alone structures, some of which contain inner chambers, rooms for the kings and the priests to meditate and communicate with their long-passed ancestors. A process usually accompanied by the letting of blood, as they passed barbed ropes and stingray spines through their lips and their earlobes and, um . . . through other parts considered more sensitive."

Hawker winced. "Kind of puts a damper on that whole being a king thing."

Danielle laughed and looked back at McCarter. "So you think this is one of the latter types?"

"It looks that way," he said. "And that could help us determine if this place is Tulan Zuyua or not."

"How?" she asked.

"Remember how Tulan Zuyua had other names," he said. "The stone Blackjack Martin found contained one of those names. Seven Caves. Other Mayan writings refer to it as the Place of Bitter Water."

"Seven Caves," she said, running the scenario through her mind. "So you think there might be a cave under here or a group of them?"

"Possibly," McCarter said. "But I'm thinking on a less dramatic level. Other Mayan sites linked to the word 'cave' have been found to contain inner chambers. And why not? After all, what is a cave? A dark place with walls of stone. It's only semantics that differentiate a stone-walled chamber from an actual stone cave. Spelunkers even call the open chambers of a cave a room. The Mayan description probably follows a similar line of thought. And if this temple was to have a set of inner chambers, seven of them, then that would support our theory that it is Tulan Zuyua."

"Our theory?" Danielle said.

"I'm co-opting it," McCarter said, smiling. "Besides, there's another reason to go inside as well, a more important one perhaps. Anything that's inside will have been protected from the sun and rain for all these years. The walls out here have been worn smooth by the environment, but in there, we might find writings, murals or pottery. Even ritual objects with information on them. The best and quickest way to gather information is to get inside, and that means we start here."

It would take the better part of four hours, a rash of strained muscles and one broken pulley, but eventually the slab was dislodged and forced upward by the leverage of the pry bars. A nylon rope was passed beneath it, and with a jerry-rigged tripod they managed to raise the stone and move it backward an inch at a time. It had traveled almost two feet before the contraption collapsed and the stone ground to a halt.

As McCarter got down on his stomach to peer through the slot, he began coughing and then turned away. Danielle could smell acrid fumes in the air escaping from the temple's innards. A sulfurous and wretched stench.

McCarter looked up, his eyes watering. "That'll clear your head."

As he moved back toward the entrance, Danielle took a deep breath and got down beside him, the beams of their flashlights playing across a flight of wide steps that dropped into the darkness beyond.

"Let's get in there," she said.

McCarter caught her eye and seemed to realize there would be no point in arguing. He took a fluorescent lantern from her hand.

"Anyone else?" he asked.

As a few of the others backed away to *unvolunteer,* Hawker stepped up. "What the hell, another hole in the ground. At least this one has stairs."

McCarter nodded then looked at his student. "Susan?"

Susan had backed away from the entrance, coughing and wheezing from the sulfur smell. "I can't," she said. "I won't be able to breathe."

McCarter nodded. "I'll give you a full report." He turned to Danielle. "Okay, boss, let's go." With that McCarter squeezed through the gap, disappearing from view. Danielle followed, with Hawker right behind her.

Once inside, they were soon able to stand, descending a flight of stairs while pungent sulfur fumes assaulted them, stinging their eyes and burning their throats. The thick stone walls deadened the place to outside noise and distorted their voices with strange reverberating echoes. When the others spoke too loudly or too quickly, Danielle noticed that their words became unintelligible.

She stopped next to McCarter at the bottom of the stairs, pointing her flashlight in various directions. Despite their lights it was hard to see any details. The sulfur in the air had condensed into a yellowish fog and was scattering the light from their torches.

Hawker spoke. "Twenty steps. Mean anything to you, Doc?"

"Not particularly," McCarter replied. "But there are twenty named days in the Mayan Short Calendar. Then again, that might have been how many stairs they needed to reach the top."

Danielle shined her light along the floor. It was made of the same gray stone as the exterior, cut and laid in precise blocks. "Amazing," she said. As she stepped past McCarter and into the darkness beyond, her foot hit something and sent it rolling across the floor. The object came to a stop near the far wall and one of the flashlight beams soon found it: a skull, weathered and discolored with time, now laying beside a large pile of similar skulls. There were dozens of them, perhaps fifty or more, some intact, others smashed and broken.

McCarter walked up to the jumbled pile, set his lantern down and picked up one of the skulls. He examined the damage then placed it down, exchanging it for another.

"What do you think?" she asked.

"Trauma on all of them," he said. "Damage from heavy blows and edged blades." He held up another skull and shined his light on it. "I could be wrong but these look like teeth marks to me. Makes me wonder just what kind of rituals were being practiced here."

"Let's not dwell on that thought," she said.

McCarter stood and the three of them continued on through a wide doorway and into an apparently empty room. The new room wasn't entirely dark, however. A thin ray of light filtered in from somewhere up above. Danielle strained to see the source of the light but it was hard to make out. In the dust the beam of light resembled a curtain.

"Crack in the structure," McCarter guessed.

"We're on the north side now," Hawker said.

They proceeded through the curtain of light and back into the darkness. Another doorway took them to the left through a small foyer to a much larger rectangular room. The shafts of their flashlights cut through the haze and darkness and touched on a platform centered at the far end. It appeared to have markings on its face.

Danielle crossed the room to the platform and bent to inspect it. Impact marks from some heavy object were visible all along the platform's face, repeated strikes that had destroyed and distorted much of what had once been carved there. Crumbled bits of stone rested in a pile of sloping dust at the base of the platform.

"It looks like vandalism," McCarter said. "I wonder if grave robbers have been in here."

She scooped up a handful of dust and fragments and let them slide off her hand and back onto the pile. As McCarter continued to examine the ruined markings, Danielle stood up and studied the platform: ten feet wide with a shallow depth, it seemed to be an altar of some kind. Its front edge and sides were straight, but the back line curved inward where it formed part of the circular rim at the edge of a deep well.

She placed her torch on the platform, scaled it and gazed into the pit beyond. "Look at this," she said.

McCarter climbed up beside her.

They directed their flashlights into the well and the beams were partially reflected.

"Water."

Hawker peered over the edge. "Why would they have a well down here?"

McCarter spoke reluctantly. "More sacrifices, I'm afraid. The ancient Maya had a nasty habit of drowning people too."

"I hate to say this," Hawker replied, "but I'm kind of glad they're gone."

In the darkness it was hard to judge the depth of the well. At least a hundred feet to the water's surface, Danielle guessed. She picked up a small stone and released it over the edge.

"One thousand one, one thousand two, one thous—"

The splash interrupted her, but it was the next occurrence that surprised them. A moment after the impact, bright, phosphorous foam began to bubble up and the odor of sulfur became instantly more pungent.

"It looks like . . ." Danielle began.

"Acid," McCarter said, finishing the sentence.

"Acid?" Hawker asked.

McCarter turned to him. "The sulfur in the air had to come from somewhere. Looks like it's coming from down there. The gasses are bubbling up through the water like the carbonation in a soda can. Sulfuric acid."

Hawker's face wrinkled. "Do I even want to know what they used that for?"

"Probably," McCarter said, "to get rid of the bones."

As Hawker looked into the pit, Danielle turned to McCarter.

He spoke her thoughts aloud. "Bitter water," he said. "Bitter water, indeed."

## CHAPTER 21

That night, a wailing call echoed across the clearing, a human voice, rising and falling in a wavering chant. It was a hollow and haunting sound. And one Pik Verhoven had been expecting.

Danielle turned to her left where Verhoven sat, his coffee mug on hold in front of his mouth. He'd told her earlier that something would happen, he'd told her it would happen tonight. Movement in the trees had given it away. *Voorloopers,* he said: scouts.

In the hours since, he and his men had made a sweep into the trees looking for the natives, hoping to chase them off. They'd found only footprints, strange gouges in the trees—like some kind of territorial markings—and tracks with only two claws. Nearby, they'd found the remnants of two animals, butchered horribly, covered in mud and the same open blisters they'd seen on the body in the river. "More warnings," he'd told her.

In response, Danielle had chosen not to sleep. She ran a battery of tests on the ring of motion sensors they'd placed around the clearing and made sure the laptop on which their inputs displayed was close at hand.

For his part Verhoven had positioned his men at various points in the clearing and had brought one of the German shepherds to sit beside him at the table. As the eerie chanting wafted through the air, the canine stiffened and put itself between Verhoven and the source of the call.

Danielle watched as Verhoven patted the dog proudly and glanced her way. She turned back to the laptop. The motion sensors had yet to register an alarm.

When a wailing cry drifted in on the night air, Verhoven put his mug down and grabbed a walkie-talkie. "What do you see?"

*"Nothing out here,"* came one reply.

*"Clear on this side,"* came a second report.

"Well, open your damn eyes," he said, "because you're missing something."

Danielle had heard enough. "I'm waking the camp."

There was no need. Stirred by the chanting, the other members of the team were already in motion, peering out of their tents or making their way to spots beside the fire, near her and Verhoven.

Polaski was one of the first to reach her. "What is that?"

"Sounds like a cat in heat," Devers said.

The porters gathered together. McCarter and Susan arrived by the fire with Hawker right behind them.

Danielle stepped nearer to Devers. "Is that the Chollokwan?"

He did not reply immediately, seeming startled by the echoing voice.

"Of course it is," Verhoven replied.

She wanted confirmation. "Come on, yes or no?"

"I think it is," Devers said. "It sounds like their language but . . ."

As Devers strained to listen, Hawker stepped past, taking a seat on a wooden crate. "Time to see if this plan of yours works."

The plan was simple: they'd create a secure area at the center of the camp in case of attack. The area was ringed with smoke canisters and a group of tripods holding metal halide flood lamps, like those used in the Olympic stadiums.

If they faced a daylight raid, the smoke canisters would pump out thick volumes of dark smoke, obscuring the group in seconds from any onrushing attackers. But the smoke would not interfere with the infrared scopes attached to Verhoven's rifles and they could fire at will from this hidden spot.

If the attack came at night, like the one that seemed imminent, the floodlights would do the same thing, blinding anyone and anything that came at them, while the NRI team disappeared into the dark void at the center, firing out of it if necessary.

Danielle scanned the clearing. For now they were alone.

"Anything on the screen?" Verhoven asked.

Danielle looked at the laptop. "Not yet," she said. "They must be too far out."

"*I see them now,*" said one of Verhoven's men over the radio. "*A few in the trees to the south.*"

As he spoke, the laptop began to beep softly. Targets popped up on the screen: little red dots on a field of gray, some to the south and a few more on the west side.

Verhoven picked up his radio. "Fall back. No need

getting all strung out if we're going to have ourselves a
tussle."

Verhoven calmly unslung the rifle on his shoulder.
"It's going to be an interesting night," he said. He
sounded more aggravated than concerned, like a man
being forced to perform a chore he'd put off far too
long.

Danielle looked his way. "We'd better get out the
extra rifles," she said.

Verhoven tossed a key to one of the porters. "Move
quick, now."

The rifles were in a long crate near Verhoven's tent,
but as a precaution the box was locked. It would take
the man a minute to reach it and retrieve the rifles inside.

As he dashed off, the voices came around again,
louder this time, a chant of several joined together.
"This isn't good," Polaski said. "I really don't see how
this can be good."

"What are they saying?" Danielle asked.

"It's hard to tell," Devers said. The voices rose, then
fell away, then rose again. "It's almost a song of some
kind, not really a—"

A second native voice interrupted Devers, breaking in
over the top of the chorus with a shout from the western
edge. It was quickly answered by one from the east and
then one from the north and finally the south.

Danielle turned in each direction, looking for the
source of the cries even as they died away, replaced once
again by the low, rhythmic chanting.

Polaski mumbled something unintelligible at this latest development and McCarter put his hand on Susan's
shoulder, glancing around.

"What do they want?" she asked.

"I don't know," he said.

Civilians in danger, exactly the situation Danielle had hoped to avoid. She turned to Devers. "What the hell are they saying?"

"It's hard to make out."

"Come on," she snapped. "You're useless right now."

"It's not that easy," Devers insisted. "Their language isn't like ours, it's not completely linear." He strained to hear. "They're calling on the spirits," he said. "Asking them to wipe the forest clean of the plague and infestation that we've brought to it. Or maybe *we* are the plague and infestation. Either way, we seem to be the problem."

Verhoven laughed. "Of course we are." He racked the slide on his rifle and stepped forward. "Well, they'd better bring more than spirits if they want to get rid of us."

As the wave of chanting grew again, Danielle had the distinct impression of a situation spinning out of control. She was afraid the Chollokwan would attack en masse, and almost as afraid that Verhoven wanted them to, just to prove what he could do.

She glanced at Hawker. He seemed unconcerned, almost amused. He shook his head calmly, his eyes suggesting there wouldn't be trouble, that it was all bravado, just Verhoven and the natives puffing themselves up in some kind of pissing contest.

She turned back to the trees, hoping he was right, and just then, the chanting stopped.

As the silence lingered she turned to Devers. "Now what?"

He shook his head.

A moment later Verhoven's men rejoined the group and he directed them to cover the points on the compass with the expedition's members gathered between them.

Danielle feared that four armed men would not be enough. She stared into the darkness searching for the burly porter who'd gone to get the extra rifles. She couldn't see him and she wondered what could be taking him so long. "Should we hit the lights?"

"Not yet," Verhoven said.

New shouts issued from the trees as the gathering of red dots on the computer screen grew and the chirping alarm continued unabated.

"Look out!" Polaski shouted.

Everyone ducked as an object trailing flames hurtled through the dark sky toward them. It fell short, bouncing and skipping oddly across the ground, some type of bololike device burning at both ends. The dry grasses lit around it, just as more flames arced into the sky.

"Everybody down," Verhoven said.

The trails of fire swung through the air in strange wobbling paths, two balls of flame orbiting each other on a piece of twine. They crashed and sparked. Ten, then twenty, then more, one after another in bunches, hailing down from all directions.

Susan began kicking sand toward the licks of fire that came closest. McCarter joined her, but the thin weedy grasses quickly burned to embers and there was no real danger.

Just then, the porter returned, awkwardly carrying four rifles and a box of loaded clips.

Verhoven grabbed them.

"Pass them out," Danielle ordered. The chanting voices around them had taken on a different sound, darker and more ominous, curling around the clearing as one voice after another repeated a single word.

From the look on his face, Devers recognized the word, but this time he didn't translate it. That was a bad sign.

Danielle checked the computer screen—there were targets all around them, too many to count. She turned to Devers.

"White Faces," he said, catching her glare.

"What does it mean?"

"The White Face is a spirit. The ghost. The bringer of death."

Before long, the shouting voices began to seem like a roll call. One after another the Chollokwan were announcing themselves. Bellowing at the top of their lungs, working themselves into a frenzy. Danielle guessed their number in the fifties, and then the seventies, and then more.

Beside her, Hawker stood up. He stepped forward to where Verhoven was about to hand over the last rifle. "Better give that one to me," he said.

Verhoven held back for a second and then slapped the rifle into Hawker's outstretched hand.

Danielle gazed at Hawker once again, but this time she found no comfort in his eyes. They were cold and grim. He was amused no more.

One of Verhoven's men spoke. "There's a hell of a lot of them out there. A hundred at least, maybe more."

Verhoven disagreed. He glanced at the screen and its multiple flashing dots. "Less by far. Certainly less than they want us to believe." He glared at the man.

"Maybe," Devers said, "but this sounds like a war party, these guys consider themselves the spirits of death. They cover themselves in white paint and they go out on raids. They believe the paint makes them invincible like the White Face, the one they consider already dead. They believe it protects them, because if they're already dead then they can't be killed."

As if in response to what Devers had said, the voices stopped cold. Danielle looked around: no one had charged yet. The bolos still burned where they'd fallen and thin wisps of smoke drifted across the camp. But the air was still.

Danielle saw the movement on the screen and looked up. She saw a shape in the tree line, silhouetted by small fires. In seconds, a dozen or more were burning, blazing up into the trees, with new fires being lit all along the perimeter. The end result was like a fuse running slowly around the edge of the clearing, tracking along the trees in a clockwise motion, down to the south and up along the east.

The undergrowth crackled and burned as the fires merged and the flames tracked up the eastern perimeter. With the naked eye, she could see the silhouette of runners with torches in their hands, sprinting past the fires, the flames trailing out behind them. Before long, the clearing was encircled in a rapidly growing conflagration.

"My God, they're going to burn us," Polaski whispered.

Hawker tried to calm him. "There's nothing to burn in here."

Danielle took a breath. That was true. The clearing was barren of any major source of fuel, but smoke was another problem. The fires surrounding them were oily and the smoke hung thick and heavily. It quickly became difficult to breathe. With one eye on the perimeter, she broke into the first-aid kit, pulling out a stack of thin paper respirators. With only a half dozen, she gave one each to Susan, Polaski, McCarter and the porters.

One of Verhoven's men dropped his night-vision goggles. "We're blind now. They've made the scopes useless."

"They don't know that," Hawker said.

Aside from Verhoven and Hawker, everyone had become jumpy. She sensed it even in herself. She needed information and turned to Devers. "Come on. What the hell do they want?"

"I don't think they *want* anything," Devers said.

"What do you mean?"

"They just keep repeating the same words over and over again. Fire for fire, fire for the plague." He shouted to be heard above the crackling flames now surrounding them. "They're either telling us something or telling themselves. Winding each other up."

In places, the merging tongues of flame had reached an inferno stage, climbing up into the trees, creating their own wind, spinning in wicked little vortexes like whirling genies unleashed from their bottles.

"That's it," Danielle said. She glanced at Verhoven.

"Turn on the damn lights and hit them with a few flares. We're not waiting anymore."

Verhoven smiled and pressed the switch. The lights blazed instantly and the generator cranked to life. A blinding glare reflected back at them as the swirls of white and gray smoke lit up like a fog of overlapping ghosts. In truth, the visibility got worse.

Verhoven pressed another key and began firing flares from the canisters pre-positioned in the forest. Two flares went off to the north and then two more in the west; he fired more in the south and the east, flares from canisters that were behind the Chollokwan warriors.

Danielle hoped the sound of the flares launching would startle the natives. And as she looked to the computer screen, she saw holes in the Chollokwan lines where groups of them backed off, but they weren't leaving en masse, and in a moment the lines began to reform. She turned back to Verhoven, eyes burning from the smoke. "Now what?"

Verhoven was silent for a moment; he turned to one of his men and then looked past him to Hawker. "What do you think? Are they coming in?"

Hawker shook his head. He pointed the rifle toward the towering fires around the edge of the clearing. "If they come in now, they're silhouettes against the flames; a good way to die, even if you are a White Face."

Verhoven turned back to Danielle. "You see, they know better. We watch for now. But they're not coming in. Not tonight."

Danielle sighed, more convinced because Hawker and Verhoven had actually agreed. "So this is a warning, then. I suppose we won't get another."

Devers coughed. "They're not known for giving one in the first place."

For the rest of the night, the group watched the flames burn in the circle around them. Occasionally there were new waves of chanting, especially when the higher branches burst into flame, but at no point did the Chollokwan attempt to enter the clearing. As dawn approached, they drifted back into the forest and disappeared.

The jungle around the clearing continued to burn. But though the forest was dry by Amazonian standards, it wasn't the type of parched brush that lent itself to an inferno. The flames could not reach the critical temperature required to become self-sustaining, especially as it reached the wetter foliage back from the clearing's edge.

With the cool mists of the dawning hours, the fires began to die. The layer of ash and smoke thinned throughout the morning, and by late afternoon all that remained were the smoldering hunks of burnt and blackened trees and the trepidation of what the next encounter might hold.

## CHAPTER 22

A bitterly cold morning arrived in Washington, D.C., a morning of cloudless blue skies and plumes of steam on the horizon. The glaring sun lingered, low and bright, but for all its piercing brilliance, it remained a harsh and distant companion, a mere candle on the mantel of the world.

No warmth could be felt on this day, not in the sunlight or in the air. To Stuart Gibbs it seemed appropriate for a day on which the NRI was burying one of its own.

Gibbs had stood in the frigid air, giving the eulogy, keeping it short for the sake of those who had gathered. He'd offered his personal condolences and then moved respectfully away, watching as others stepped forward to console the widow of Matthew Blundin.

He watched as they spoke to her, hugged her and held her hand. He guessed at their words—kind words, no doubt, words of sorrow for her loss and praise for the job her husband had always done. No one would mention that he'd been found on the wrong side of town, shot and robbed on a street known for its drug dealers and prostitutes. No one would ask if his penchant for alcohol or late nights had led to their separation and

pending divorce, or if either vice might have had a hand
in his demise. They would think these things of course,
but such thoughts would not be spoken, for death was
not only the great equalizer but also the great eraser of
misdeeds. In its wake, Blundin's errors and habits would
be forgotten, his wit and wisdom raised into legend.

Gibbs watched the procession, feeling uneasy and
distracted, the rolled-up newspaper in his gloved hand
crushed subconsciously in a tightening grip. There was
trouble everywhere for him, the team in the rainforest
had been attacked by natives, the computer system had
been hijacked and made to hack into itself—and his security chief, the one man Gibbs could have trusted to
find the culprit, was now dead and buried.

A pang of remorse stabbed at Gibbs. *The man deserved better.*

To most of those attending, the security chief's death
marked a small footnote in their own particular stories.
Even the soon-to-be ex–Mrs. Blundin would move on,
as she had already begun to. But for Stuart Gibbs and
the NRI, the event was a massive occurrence—existence
changing, in scale—and Gibbs couldn't shake the thought
of changed destiny any easier than he could ward off the
chilled winter air.

Before long, the crowd began to thin. Soon, even
Blundin's widow and her party turned to go, moving
slowly up the path toward the parking lot.

Gibbs lingered for twenty minutes, standing alone,
thinking about Blundin, the rainforest project and the
various scenarios that now presented themselves. Only
as the bitter air began to seep through his coat did he
move toward the parking lot himself.

By the time he arrived, his car was alone. But as he reached for his key, another vehicle turned in toward him, a silver Mercedes with tinted windows.

He eyed the car, waiting for it to pass. But it stopped beside him and the rear window descended smoothly into the door.

"Stuart Gibbs?"

Gibbs hesitated. He couldn't see much inside the car, but there was no reason to deny who he was. "What can I do for you?"

A man with thick, gray hair and wearing a muted, charcoal-colored suit leaned toward the open window. "I noticed your tire was flat," he said. "I thought you might need a lift."

Gibbs glanced at the tire. The right rear was indeed flat, though it was a brand-new Michelin and had been fine when he drove in. "That's all right," he said. "I'll have someone come out."

"We need to talk," the man insisted. "I was at the funeral today with Senator Metzger from the Oversight Committee. I have some information about Mr. Blundin's death that I think you should be aware of."

"What kind of information?"

"The type that can't be given to the police until it's properly sifted and filtered."

Gibbs stared.

"It's extremely time sensitive," the man said, "so if you don't want to listen I'll have to deliver it to the good senator instead."

Gibbs stared at the man in the car. He looked familiar, but whether Gibbs had seen him earlier at the funeral or knew him from somewhere else, he couldn't be sure. "Who are you?"

The door opened, and the man in the gray suit slid to the other side. "My name is Kaufman," he said. "My company is one of your charter members."

*Of course. Kaufman was the head of Futrex, one of the NRI's charter affiliates. And one of the companies Blundin had been investigating.*

Without a word Gibbs climbed into the car. It began to move and the tinted rear window rose smoothly back into place.

He looked around. Aside from Kaufman there was only a driver.

"Quite a shame about a man like that," Kaufman said.

"Blundin was one of my best people," Gibbs explained. "And a good friend as well. But he had his own issues. I guess they caught up with him."

Kaufman nodded somberly. "They always seem to."

The tone in Kaufman's voice bothered Gibbs; it seemed smug and condescending. "It would be of great satisfaction to me if we could catch the person who did this. Even if it's just some punk off the street."

"Not likely to be some punk off the street," Kaufman replied. "Not when the man was killed because of your Brazil project."

Gibbs froze. Even Senator Metzger didn't know about the Brazil project. "I'm not sure what you're talking about."

"You have a group of operatives working in the Amazon at this very moment. They're down there— somewhere—without the knowledge or consent of the

American Consulate or the Brazilian government. Care to tell me why?"

"We have people in fifty countries," Gibbs replied, fighting to maintain his composure. "I don't keep track of them all. As far as the consulate and the Brazilian government are concerned, I'm sure you're mistaken. But more importantly, what does this have to do with Matt's death?"

"It's simple," the man replied. "He was killed because of what he knew. He was investigating your data loss, making certain people nervous. But then, you know that, don't you?"

Gibbs glared at the man beside him, his sense of restraint failing. The man was vile. "Whatever the hell you're getting at, say it."

Kaufman exhaled. "Let's start with the project," he said. "Your people are down there looking for the ruins of an ancient Mayan city. A city that may be the source of some very special items. Items that create power, all but unlimited power."

The man stared into Gibbs' eyes and then continued. "Eight weeks ago, you lost another party attempting the very same thing. In fact, you're still wondering what happened to them at this point. Another answer I can give you, if you care to listen."

"You're the son of a bitch who hacked us," Gibbs said.

"We ran a program with your Research Division's permission," Kaufman said, proudly. "Something to do with weather simulation, I think. Seems to have caused a little storm on your end, though."

Gibbs glared at the man. Just as Blundin had predicted, the chink in the armor of Research Division had cost them. "It makes sense," he said angrily. "A big tech company like yours would have the expertise. My question is, why? Do you have any idea what kind of hell you're about to bring on yourself?"

Kaufman leaned back, showing little concern at Gibbs' aggressiveness. "Under different circumstances," Kaufman said, "you might be right. But not here. Not now. I'm offering you a way out. The best—and last—chance you'll ever get to put this thing behind you."

"The NRI doesn't need your help."

"Not the Institute, my friend, *you*. It's my intention to help you."

"Help me do what?"

"To survive, for one thing," Kaufman said. "It took me a while to figure it out. But it's become apparent to me that you've run this thing privately. You've used NRI assets and proxies, but it's your operation."

Only at this moment did Gibbs feel the true weight of his actions. They hammered him in rapid succession; decisions made, steps taken to hide his tracks, lines crossed from which there was no going back.

Kaufman appeared impressed. "I have to admit—that's a bold play. But it puts you in a bad position now that you've run into problems. The simple recovery you planned for has become tangled up with all kinds of issues and delays. You're running out of money, or close to it. You're just about out of time too, because people are starting to ask questions—questions you can't answer."

Gibbs' jaw was clenched. He tried to relax.

"Maybe you'll get lucky," Kaufman said, offering him a line. "Maybe you'll find what you're after and disappear with it before the walls come crashing down. But then what? You can't take it back to the NRI—or any other American organization, for that matter. Not only will they wonder where it came from but they'll want to know what the hell you're doing with it in the first place.

"Develop it yourself, then? With what? You can't possibly have the resources to make a play like that or you wouldn't have tapped the NRI accounts to begin with. So you have to sell it. The only question is: to whom?"

Gibbs remained silent, his proverbial right.

"National governments are your best bet, but which ones?" Kaufman said. "You can't turn it over to your own; we've already established that. So where do you go? The Japanese? Sure. Why not? They import virtually all of their energy, they're technologically advanced and they spend millions on this kind of research every year. But in your world they're your chief rival, the economic equivalent of the Russians in the Cold War, and while you may be a thief, you're not a traitor. So the EU, the Russians and the Chinese are probably out as well, at least until you've exhausted all the other options. And that leaves mostly the destroyers."

"The destroyers?"

Kaufman elaborated. "Those who stand to profit most, if this revolution *never* comes to pass: the nuclear industry, big oil, the OPEC countries."

Kaufman's tone became pragmatic. "If I were you, the nuclear industry would be my first choice, although they're not exactly a monolithic group. They might even use it one day, when their trillion dollars of capital investments run out of useful life. But more than likely they'd prefer to keep building big, expensive, dirty power plants, instead of small, cheap, clean ones—there's more responsibility to it, more prestige and of course, more money. They'd pay you handsomely for it, though. So would big oil, OPEC and the Seven Sisters, or what's left of them. They'd bury you in petrodollars to keep this thing on the shelf, or they might bury you for real—maybe both. At the very least it's something you'd have to worry about for the rest of your life, because as long as you live, they have exposure." He paused, looking Gibbs in the eye. "A terrible thing," he said, "to live with exposure."

Gibbs listened to Kaufman's line of reasoning with a strange sense of déjà vu. He'd run through the same process a hundred times in his own mind. He had a plan, and it involved his disappearance, something his CIA background would assist him in, but there would always be danger. He counted on being able to handle it. "Why tell me all this?" he asked, bitterly. "In other words—what the hell is your point?"

Kaufman obliged him at last. "Because what you hoped to find out there—what we both hope to find out there—is the beginning of a revolution, one that will render the industrial and computer revolutions mere blips on the time line.

"The industrial revolution improved the lives of twenty percent of the world's population, mostly those in Europe and North America. In other areas, it condemned vast swaths of previously happy people to lives of abject misery. Virtual slaves who toil in the ground for natural resources while their own lands are left polluted and spoiled.

"The information revolution has done the same thing on a smaller scale. The lives of twenty percent are improved, while others are rendered jobless, destitute and excess to society's needs. Poor countries fall into the information divide and their populations lag ever further behind as they squander all their measly income just trying to keep the lights on."

"I'm not really in this for the poor," Gibbs said.

Kaufman sat back. "So sell it to the destroyers, then. The world will go on just as it has: pumping oil, shoveling coal and piling up nuclear waste by the ton. The wars will go on. We'll have more debacles like Iraq. Iran will be next, and the whole Arabian peninsula when the House of Saud collapses. America will bankrupt itself fighting wars in the desert while Europe and Asia watch and reap the rewards. The poverty and pollution of the oil age will go on, and you'll spend the rest of your days wondering just when that stray bullet will find you."

Gibbs took his eyes off Kaufman, glancing out the window at the world flying past. Too quickly, he thought, much like the conversation he found himself trapped into. It left him dizzy, unbalanced—a terrible feeling for a man unused to anything but complete control. "You paint a rosy picture of my future," he said.

"That's just one possible future," Kaufman explained. "On the other hand you can look at this meeting for what it is—your way out. You can turn this find over to me and see it brought to its full potential. I have billions set aside to develop this technology, and access to billions more if I need it. I have armies of engineers, powerful friends on Capitol Hill and in the military. And I have time, a luxury you no longer possess."

Kaufman leaned toward him. "What lies out there is the key to equalizing things, to resetting the vast imbalance between the first and third worlds, to stabilizing what has become a dangerously unstable world."

"My God," Gibbs said. "You're some kind of crusader. You intend to give this away?"

"No," Kaufman said. "I intend to build a fortune with it. One that will make Mr. Gates and Mr. Buffett look like welfare cases. And once I've done that I'll build power plants all over the world. I'll provide cheaper energy than anyone could have dreamed of—cheaper than coal and oil, cheaper than solar or wind or even hydrothermal power and with none of the environmental drawbacks. In twenty years I'll control all the electrical power generated in the Western Hemisphere, and even though I will sell it cheap, I'll produce it for almost nothing. With the profits and influence, I'll light up the world of the poor. And when the whole planet has equal access to such power, a sense of equilibrium will come to this place that has never existed. No longer will there be three *have nots* for every one who *has*."

As Kaufman spoke, Gibbs wondered just where the man's greed and nobility intersected, or if he was lying or simply mad. A combination of all four, he decided. "You're insane, you realize that."

The charcoal-haired CEO's eyebrows went up. "Insane is embezzling from your own agency. It's hiring a group of burned-out mercenaries to search a river bed and following up their disappearance with a group of civilians who will likely meet the same fate. Insane is your place in the world, my friend, not mine."

Gibbs stewed. Kaufman had hit the mark dead-on; he'd gotten every fear and every angle just about right. Gibbs was greedy but he wasn't a traitor, and he didn't fancy himself a sellout or a politician either. Giving up the future wasn't his big concern; it would come some-day regardless of what he did, but the destroyers, as Kaufman had called them, were not forces to be trifled with. Perhaps Kaufman *was* offering him something bet-ter. He chose to bite, at least enough to taste the dish. "And what would such an offer look like?"

Kaufman obliged him. "First, you'll receive immedi-ate repayment of all the funds that you or your backers have laid out. That should get the investors off your back and allow you to replace any NRI funds that might have gone missing. Second, you'll receive a one million dollar payment upon recovery and authentication of the artifacts. And finally, you'll have a position within Futrex, a six-figure salary and a small residual from all net profits." Kaufman shrugged. "Your cut will be a rounding error somewhere on the bottom line, but in a few years, you'll make more than you could in ten life-times with the NRI. The more we make, the more you'll make. That ought to guarantee your full cooperation."

Stuart Gibbs listened in silence, mulling the offer over. "And if I decline?"

"Then one of two things will happen. Either your group in the rainforest will be eliminated before they have a chance to bring you what you want, or the proper authorities will be informed of your activities."

Gibbs laughed. Kaufman wouldn't bring the authorities into this, whatever happened. "My people are well protected."

"Yes," Kaufman said. "I know who protects them, and how. I promise you, I have all the firepower I need to take them out. The only thing I don't have is their location, but sooner or later I will. And once I do, your ability to bargain will have expired."

Gibbs mulled over the offer: ten million dollars or so, when all was said and done. The buyers he'd contacted had deep pockets but they were skeptical. If he could prove what he had, they might pay ten times what Kaufman had offered. Up front and in cash, not spread out over decades. And even that would be a bargain. The technology itself would be worth an unfathomable amount in that time, more than all the oil in Alaska or all the gold in South Africa, and he was being asked to give it up for a pittance.

He glared at Kaufman, galled by the man's arrogance. And yet, even as he fumed, his black mood began to fade. He could see the offer for what it was: a thieves' bargain, even if the division of spoils was mostly one-sided. *This was the way of things,* he thought. *The rich take from the poor. They pay only a penny and sell for a dollar, but the poor are always grateful for the pennies.*

He threw out a counteroffer. "Why not let my people finish the recovery? Whatever we bring out, I'll give you the first bid."

"Why?" Kaufman said. "So you can charge me more?"

Gibbs had expected that. He ground his teeth anyway. "And what about my people?"

Kaufman pursed his lips. "They won't be coming home again, if that's what you mean."

Gibbs was silent.

"I've seen your roster," Kaufman added. "At first I couldn't understand why you chose this particular mix of individuals. But then it hit me; for the most part, they won't be missed."

As Gibbs listened to the last point, his face grew stern, almost angry, but not out of sadness. In fact, he had never planned to bring the team home in the first place, not without an accident somewhere along the way—a plane crash or an explosion. *But now, and because of Kaufman, no less, one of them was already here: Arnold Moore.*

"More deaths," he noted.

"Yes," Kaufman said, respectfully. "But none as shocking as Matt Blundin's. Then again, I suppose he left you no choice."

Gibbs' face went blank, an emotionless slate. He hadn't wanted to kill Blundin, but the security chief had, indeed, left him no choice. In his zeal to find the party responsible for the data theft, Blundin had dug into areas that he'd been ordered to ignore. In doing so he'd uncovered the loose threads in Gibbs' setup. And though they were irrelevant to the investigation, Blundin couldn't help but pull on them.

Sooner, rather than later, he would have realized that only Gibbs could change the funding codes, not Danielle, or the accounting clerks or anyone else in the organization. That would have led him to the missing money, to the funding requests for projects that existed only on paper and to the bland reports and unlogged transactions that had moved the project forward. And before long, Matt Blundin would have realized what it all meant. Maybe he'd realized it already and was allowing Gibbs time to fix things. After all, he had been a friend.

Kaufman broke the silence. "I'll give you twenty-four hours. Have an answer ready."

Gibbs focused his attention on the world outside. They were in the business district now; he could catch a cab from here. He looked at the driver. "Pull over."

With a nod from Kaufman, the driver acquiesced and the Mercedes pulled to the curb.

One last warning came from Kaufman. "Don't be a fool," he said. "There's no other choice for you now."

Gibbs stepped out of the car, slammed the door and watched the shimmering vehicle drive off. He knew his enemy now, and he knew what he had to do. The only question was how to do it without destroying himself in the process.

## CHAPTER 23

The backseat of the old yellow cab had seen its fair share of life. The ripped vinyl with its frayed cords of fabric and stray pen marks, the graffiti and the stains, all of it testified to a long and turbulent existence. From that royal throne, Arnold Moore surveyed the snow-covered streets of Washington as he slowly passed them by.

In a year of strange weather, another storm had reached the nation's capital, the fourth in six weeks, but the least troublesome so far, as it had arrived on a Friday and would be gone by Sunday night.

On Saturday morning, however, the snow was still falling, covering the lawns and trees in a pristine blanket of white and leaving the streets awash in a layer of gray slush. It was enough to keep the masses at home and the District as vacant as Moore could remember.

The taxi brought him in from the Virginia side, rolling along the Jefferson Davis Parkway and then up onto the Arlington Memorial Bridge and across the Potomac. The Lincoln Memorial loomed in the distance, its great columned shape half-shrouded in the falling snow.

The city was a different place in weather like this, the monuments more grand and worthy in their isolation, the reflecting pools more majestic in their silence and emptiness, more dignified for the lack of tourists, vendors and vagrants.

Moore preferred the city in this dress on any occasion, but especially this one. He was on his way to a meeting, having finally been contacted by someone interested in the Brazil project. The city's emptiness would make it easier to confer in the open, easier to spot trouble if it came.

The cab dropped Moore off in front of the monument and he took to the sidewalk, the snow crunching and squeaking underfoot.

Feeling the chill of the air, he pulled the lapels of his heavy wool coat tight and thrust his hands into its deep, warm pockets—the same pockets in which he'd found the note, just two days prior. At the door of his apartment, when reaching for his keys, his hand had made contact with a folded piece of paper bearing writing that was not his own. The text began simply "Call" and provided a number. Beneath the number were the words "we can help you." Nothing else, no mention of the Brazil project or the NRI, but the connection was unmistakable.

Moore had gazed trancelike at the little scrap of paper for a good, long while. It bothered him that he hadn't detected its placement; as he stood in line at the coffee shop perhaps, or on the crowded Metro platform itself. No one had bumped him, rushed by or lingered too long at his side, no clumsy pickpocket's distraction had been attempted. After boarding the Metro, Moore had sat by himself and gotten off at his regular station with very few others. And yet, somehow the little slip of paper had come into his possession. It made him feel old and slow, as if his senses were dulling with age. Perhaps the calendar was right, perhaps it was time for retirement.

Back in the present, Moore noticed a car approaching and did his best to banish the thought. The tan vehicle slowed marginally, but rounded the curve and drove on, spitting a small wake of slush as it went.

Moore looked beyond the departing car to the white horizon. Somewhere out there Gibbs was listening. In addition, there were people watching him, at least three groups of backup. Two cars, and a third group on foot, though Moore did not know exactly who or where. It was entirely possible that the passing car contained one of Gibbs' teams.

He tried not to think about that either. It was a distraction and his current task demanded his full attention. He was about to meet with one of the enemy, the same enemy who had attempted to kill Danielle. His job was to find out who they were. To do that he'd have to convince them that he was ready and willing to betray the NRI, not an easy task, considering his reputation. It was a trap laid for a party who must undoubtedly expect a trap; a hard sell in any book. But with Matt Blundin's untimely death several days before, it was the only chance they had left.

Another car came down the road. A white Lexus with yellow fog lamps blazing in the grill. It pulled up next to him and stopped. An open window revealed a man seemingly in his midtwenties, with a neatly trimmed goatee.

"Arnold Moore?"

Moore nodded.

"Why don't you get in," the man suggested. "We can talk while we drive."

Moore shook his head. "I don't think so." He pointed to the lot. "Go park down there. There's plenty of space. Then come back here and we'll take a walk through this glorious winter wonderland."

The driver's face wrinkled at the thought, but he hit the gas and did as Moore said. A moment later he returned on foot, making his way in a casual saunter.

Moore studied the man. He was young and good-looking, with blond highlights in his hair and a glowing tan in the middle of winter. He wore sharply creased slacks and a cashmere turtleneck. "Dear God," Moore whispered, "they've sent me a ski instructor."

As the man reached Moore, he said, "Which way?"

"Does it matter?" Moore asked gruffly. He took a quick look in both directions and began to walk away from the monument and out toward the bridge. He needed to stay in the open.

The blond man rolled his eyes and followed. For a minute they just walked—no words or gestures, just two men walking on the slope that led up to the bridge.

"What's your name?" Moore asked, finally.

The blond man laughed.

"No names, then," Moore said. "Fine. I'll call you Sven. You look like a Sven to me."

Sven didn't seem to object and the two continued walking—Moore in his heavy boots, orange scarf and bulky layers of cotton and wool; Sven in his cashmere and expensive Italian shoes, now getting ruined in the snow.

"You're the guy on the phone the other night," Moore guessed.

"Very observant," Sven replied.

"Are you also a dry cleaner?"

"What?"

"I'm wondering how you got that note in my pocket," Moore said. "I never felt it placed there, so I thought it might have come back from the dry cleaners like that."

Sven kept walking.

Moore read his face. "Not your doing."

"I just took the call."

"Somehow it figures," Moore said, the tone of a disgusted veteran in his voice.

With that, he picked up the pace, heading out onto the bridge deck, out over the river, where it would be colder and Sven's thin clothes would be less adequate than they already appeared to be.

Sven seemed aware of that fact. "Where the hell are we going?" he whined.

"We're not going *anywhere*," Moore said, looking down at the Potomac, dark and ominous against the white snowbanks. "We're just walking. Staying out in the open, out in public, where I'm less likely to perceive you as a threat and have to kill you because of it."

Sven laughed. "Am I supposed to take that seriously?"

"Take it however you want," Moore said, continuing the walk. "Not like they would miss you anyway."

Sven seemed to clench his jaw, and Moore guessed the remark had hit the target.

"I don't think you understand the situation," Sven told him. "You're the one who needs us. I'm just here to find out if you're worth the time."

"Really?" Moore said. "Important errand they've sent you on. You must be so proud."

Moore turned away from him, but Sven grabbed his shoulder to spin him back around. "Listen to me, old man—"

Moore knocked the hand away and bore into Sven with fury in his eyes. "No, you listen to me, you worthless little fuck. I don't deal with pawns or messengers. Forty years in this business—that's what I've got. So if the people who sent you have anything to say, they'd better have the balls to come see me themselves. Or at least send someone who matters."

Sven began to say something but Moore cut him off.

"You're a fucking nobody and you don't know jack shit about this operation. You don't even know how your people contacted me."

Sven's face was red with anger.

Moore's eyebrows went up in mockery of his opponent. "Come on, then. Let's hear it. Tell me I'm wrong. Tell me how important you are and just what it is that you know."

"I know enough," Sven said finally. "I know they pulled you off an important job and you don't like that. I know that your career is pretty much done and you don't like that either. Forty years you've got. I say forty years they used you, now you're getting kicked to the curb, and that must burn you up pretty bad or you wouldn't be here in the first place, would you?"

Moore stared at Sven and the anger, both real and pretend, seeped away. When he spoke again his voice was like gravel. "As a matter of fact, it does," he said truthfully. "But coming here was a mistake."

He looked at Sven with a trace of pity in his eyes. "Go home," he said. "Go home before you get yourself killed. You think this is going to happen? You really think so? If people switched sides every time they got pissed off, then where the hell would we be?"

Sven didn't answer and Moore shook his head in disgust. "Go home and tell your people that I'm not interested. You tell them that money is not enough to get me. And the next time they want to offer me something, they better not send some punk kid who's wet behind the ears and worried about his lips chafing in the cold." Moore shook his head even more dejectedly than before. "I've got files older than you."

With that he turned his back on Sven and looked out over the stone railing of the bridge. With a gloved hand, he brushed the snow from the section in front of him and rested his forearms on it, gazing out at the black water rippling gently beneath the gray-white sky. "Forty years," he mumbled, "and this is how it ends. What a joke. What a fucking joke."


In a heated room far from the bridge, Gibbs listened to every word, and for the first time he began to understand why Moore was held in such high regard. He'd played it masterfully. Sven was furious, angry enough to tell Moore volumes just to prove that he mattered, or to run back to his superiors and insist that Moore had balked and would need more prodding to come aboard. A sure sign that Moore was legit as opposed to being bait for a trap.

It was almost enough to make Gibbs wish the drama were real. But the situation was not as Moore had been led to believe, and despite his work, Moore was involved in a game he couldn't win.

Back at the bridge Sven smiled for the first time. "Why don't you come with me?" he said. "You can tell them yourself."

Moore turned to face Sven, his back to the railing. He was tempted. He and Gibbs had planned for this eventuality. The two cars would be able to track him, follow him to whatever site Sven had in mind, but it felt rushed. Moore declined. "Not until I know who I'm dealing with."

Sven shook his head and looked down the road. Moore realized it was vacant. "Wrong answer," Sven said, pulling a slim pistol from his coat.

Before Moore could react, Sven fired twice into his chest. Moore fell back against the railing and then stumbled forward. Sven caught him as his knees buckled, holding him up and shoving him backward against the railing and then forcing him up and over the top.

Moore tumbled toward the river, his coat fluttering like a cape, until he plunged into the icy, black water and disappeared beneath the surface.

Back up on the bridge, Sven watched for several seconds. The foam of the impact receded, smoothed over by the flow of the river. Only Moore's orange scarf reappeared, floating to the surface and twirling in the current before passing out of sight underneath the bridge.

Satisfied, Sven turned back to the street. A shiny black Audi pulled up and the rear door opened. He jumped in and the car sped off.

Farther away, Stuart Gibbs listened through headphones that issued nothing but static now. He turned to the control panel, found the switch for Moore's wire and flicked it off.

Moore was gone. Blundin was gone. And within twenty-four hours the entire team in the Amazon would be gone. Vanishing with them would be the last evidence of the NRI's Brazil project.

## CHAPTER 24

Mark Polaski's face turned ashen at the news. The message from NRI headquarters had come directly from Stuart Gibbs. Polaski's daughter had been struck by a car while jogging. She'd been taken to the ER with severe head and neck injuries and wasn't expected to regain consciousness. A ticket had been purchased in his name on a direct flight from Manaus to Miami, where a private jet would meet him. The Manaus flight left at 9:43 A.M., if he could get there in time.

He looked at Hawker. "Can we make it there in time?" he asked, quietly.

"If we leave now," Hawker said.

As Polaski climbed aboard the Huey, the others wished him well. Devers handed him his pack and McCarter, suddenly reminded of his own losses back in the real world, promised to look him up on their return to the States.

Polaski barely acknowledged them. He sat in the copilot's seat, staring blankly at the deep, azure sky, fumbling in his backpack for something.

Beside him, Hawker ran through a short version of the checklist, pressing the ignition switch and waiting for the needles to come up. The blades above them wound up slowly. As they began to hum, Hawker pulled back on the collective and the helicopter's weight came off the skids.

Once they became airborne, the helicopter pivoted to the east, lowered its nose and began to move off, gathering speed and altitude as it went.

Before long, they were cruising, droning along at five thousand feet and 120 knots. In three-and–a-half hours they would cover what had taken the group ten days by boat and foot.

Inside the cockpit Polaski had lapsed into a state of silence. Hawker let him be. *What could one say that would matter anyway?* He busied himself with a pilot's routine, checking the instruments and scanning, his eyes settling on one section of the sky, focusing for a moment to make sure it was clear, and then switching to the next in a constantly repeating pattern. Scanning was a process ingrained in pilots from the day they begin flying and Hawker fell into it out of habit, not expecting to encounter any aircraft. But he spotted something just the same.

A tiny black dot appeared in the sky at the Huey's two o'clock position. Like a smudge on the windshield, it was motionless, showing no relative movement—the unmistakable sign of a converging path.

Hawker adjusted his course slightly and put the Huey into a shallow climb.

The other helicopter continued on its path. Before long, Hawker could make out the type, a Hughes 600, commonly called a NOTAR, an acronym that stood for No Tail Rotor, because it used funneled exhaust from its turbine for directional control instead of the standard rear blade. More ominously, this particular NOTAR was black, devoid of any markings and carrying a pair of external pods on either side.

"What's wrong?" Polaski asked, coming out of his trance.

"No markings," Hawker said.

"What does that mean?"

"I don't know," Hawker replied. "But it can't be a good thing."

The NOTAR passed beneath them, off to one side and heading in the opposite direction. Hawker kept his eyes on it, craning his neck around and slewing the Huey to the right in an effort to keep the target in view. Just before it passed from sight, he noticed something else: the NOTAR had banked into a turn. It was coming back around.

Back at the camp, Danielle returned to the satlink to apprise Gibbs of Polaski's departure.

"Confirm they have departed," he said.

"Affirmative," she said. "Five minutes ago."

There was an extended pause and then Gibbs said, "Understood. I'll contact you at nineteen hundred with an update. Gibbs out."

Danielle went to cut the link, reaching for the switch, and then paused as she remembered needing to speak with Gibbs about a bug in the defense system. The latest in a long line of electronic problems they'd been having. She grabbed her notes and pressed *transmit*.

There was no response.

She pressed it again. "Stuart, are you still online?"

She checked the display. *Link terminated*. Apparently, Gibbs had hung up.

She retyped her authorization code, pressed *initiate* and waited. Nothing happened, and then the display read: *Link not established, please retry*.

She tried again, only to receive a more ominous response: *Authorization Invalid—Access Denied*.

A knot began to form in her stomach. She exhaled in frustration and looked around for help, but Polaski was in charge of the beta test on the satlink and he was gone.

Hawker's eyes swung forward. The black NOTAR had continued its turn and would soon be obtaining a position behind them. In an effort to prevent that, Hawker forced the throttle and dropped the nose. As the Huey picked up speed, he looked back for the other helicopter, but he couldn't see it anywhere.

Polaski turned in his seat. "Are we in trouble?"

"We might be."

Seconds later, a burst of tracer fire took away any doubt.

Hawker threw the stick over and dove toward the forest, five thousand feet below. The NOTAR followed, and despite the speed they'd picked up, it was closing in fast.

The NOTAR was two generations younger than the Huey. It was smaller, lighter and faster. Hawker could never hope to outrun it or outmaneuver it over the long run. And without weapons of their own, the situation seemed desperate—like being accosted on the street by an armed man: if they asked for something you gave it up, and if they didn't ask, then you ran like hell and hoped you were lucky. As Hawker yanked the Huey into a hard left turn and dove toward the river; he hoped they were lucky.

"Who are they?" Polaski shouted, trying to be heard above the noise.

Hawker didn't answer. The Huey accelerated rapidly. The needle on the airspeed indicator swung through the yellow arc and past the red line: a marking that pilots call *Vne*, for Velocity—Never Exceed. The speed was labeled that way for a reason. Beyond *Vne* the structural cohesion of the airframe came into question. As if to emphasize the point, the old Huey began shaking violently, rattling and threatening to come apart around them.

They dove to treetops and leveled off with the engine screaming and the craft shuddering under the strain, skimming across the canopy at 150 knots. Shells tore in from the left and Hawker cut toward them, forcing the NOTAR to overshoot. A higher clump of foliage loomed in their path and Hawker pulled up, hearing the skids ripping though its leaves. He dropped down behind and raced on.

"Look out," Polaski shouted.

The NOTAR flashed over the top of them, firing and crossing from the right. A sharp pinging rang out through the helicopter like a metal rod held against a rapidly spinning fan.

Polaski's eyes swung through the cabin, looking for damage. Hawker checked the gauges for the same thing. Polaski saw daylight pouring through a dozen holes in the side. Hawker saw the needles remaining where they belonged, everything functioning as it should. Even though the bullets had hit them, the helicopter was mostly empty space and the shells had passed right through without taking out anything vital.

Hawker watched the NOTAR making a wide arc, setting up for another strafing run. There was only one place left to go.

With the engine roaring and the airframe straining under the load, he cut back toward the river once again. The NOTAR followed, closing in rapidly.

The trees flew by beneath them, falling away, just as the black helicopter fired. Hawker dropped the Huey toward the water and turned to follow the river's course. The NOTAR overshot, swung wide and curved back, moving in behind them and quickly closing the gap once again.

They were on the deck now, thundering along the riverbed. Two helicopters racing across the shimmering water, jinking and turning, with their rotor blades swirling overhead like a pair of massive dragonflies in a territorial dispute.

The twisting course gave the Huey some cover, but the trees lining the banks boxed them in like canyon walls, making their maneuvers more predictable to the other pilot. Hawker cut left but quickly ran out of space against the towering trees. He broke right, crossing in front of the NOTAR's blazing guns and wincing as shrapnel ripped through the cabin.

"What are we going to do?" Polaski shouted. "Why are they attacking us?"

"I have no idea," Hawker shouted back, answering both questions at once, as he whipped the helicopter into another turn.

For a moment the river widened, giving them some space, but up ahead a narrow stretch loomed. With the throttle fire-walled, the Huey raced toward it, aiming for the center of a thin, wooded island around which the river spilt. He turned at the last minute, shooting down the left side of the tall woods, while the NOTAR went right. Two seconds to pass the island, and Hawker broke hard to the right, turning toward the NOTAR and trying to force it into the trees on the bank of the river.

But the NOTAR slowed and Hawker was forced to climb out over the trees or cross right in front of the waiting guns. He pulled back on the collective and the Huey edged the treetops, safe, but only for a moment.

The NOTAR came up behind them with its guns blazing.

Cannon shells ripped into the tail and ran up to the engine housing. A horrible scream of wrenching metal drowned out all other sounds as something in the turbine ripped itself apart. The shuddering helicopter thundered forward, shaking violently and careening out of control.

Hawker tried to stabilize the craft, but with the hydraulics out his efforts achieved nothing. The craft was little more than a projectile now, an object answering only to the laws of physics. It nosed over in a declining ballistic arc, twisting to the right and trailing a dark plume of smoke.

The gap between helicopter and jungle shrank rapidly and the Huey slammed into the forest, shattering tree limbs, rotor blades and Plexiglass. The canopy of trees shuddered from the impact and then closed, swallowing them up like a stone heaved into the ocean.

# CHAPTER 25

B ack at the base camp, most of the group had reluctantly gone to work, spreading out across the clearing to begin various tasks. Danielle and Verhoven remained at the command center, privately discussing the sudden loss of communications.

"Someone jamming us?" Verhoven asked.

Danielle didn't think so. She was receiving a response from the network. And though the response continued to indicate that her authorization code was invalid, it meant the signal was getting through and then being rejected. A software failure seemed more likely, either in her system or the one back in Washington. But software could be fixed, and that meant communications could be restored relatively easily. She saw no reason to break radio silence.

"I've done all I can on our end," she said. "They have a check-in scheduled for nineteen hundred tonight. They should notice the problem then and be able to fix it. If they can't they'll radio us with instructions on the proper frequency, and we won't have to give away our position."

"What did I tell you about this bloody technology," Verhoven said. "No damn good half the . . ."

Verhoven's voice trailed off and he turned to the east. Danielle followed his gaze and heard the sound of a helicopter approaching low across the trees. Hawker had left only an hour before. She wondered why he was coming back.

Verhoven stood up. "Damn!"

An instant later the NOTAR burst out from above the trees and shot across the camp, traveling from east to west.

One look at the armed helicopter was enough. Danielle lunged for the alarm and the air horn went off just as the black, egg-shaped helicopter reached the far side of the clearing and began to pitch up so it could swing back toward the group.

"Hit the smoke!" Verhoven shouted.

Danielle did as he asked and the canisters around them fired in sequence, but as the helicopter finished its turn and came back toward them she realized that smoke wouldn't be enough. She grabbed her own rifle and began to run.

Verhoven caught her. "Wait."

"For what?"

"One second!"

The NOTAR had swung through a half circle, gathering speed as it lined her and Verhoven up. Lowering its nose, it disappeared behind the thickening cloud.

"Now!" Verhoven yelled.

They dashed to the right just as the helicopter fired and a spread of lethal cannon fire tore through the spot they'd just left. The craft followed, sweeping through the gathering smoke, dispersing the cloud in its wake.

Verhoven spun around, dropped to a knee and fired, but the helicopter banked and fired into the tents to the south, shredding the thin nylon before passing by. Danielle watched in horror as one of the porters crawled out and collapsed.

By now the other members of the expedition were running toward the center of camp just as they'd practiced—an act that would bring them into the heart of the danger. As the helicopter circled around for another run, she was certain that they'd all be killed.

In a fury, she fired her own rifle, trying to lead the approaching craft. Verhoven did the same, and as shells from the AK-47s whistled through the air, the helicopter pulled up, crossing the camp and flying out over the jungle without hitting anyone else.

It tracked that way for several seconds before turning and following the curved line of the trees, circling the perimeter like a shark.

Danielle noticed Verhoven looking toward the jungle. "We'll never make it," she said.

He seemed to agree. "The temple, then," he said. "It's our only chance."

They bolted, sprinting for the ancient Mayan temple and its thick stone walls: the only place in sight that could offer them shelter from the helicopter's lethal guns.

As they ran toward the temple, Danielle saw McCarter, Susan and one of the porters running away from it in a panic. "Back," she shouted. "Go back."

They seemed to get the message, stopping in their tracks and turning around.

The helicopter was turning in once again, dropping in behind the remaining two porters and stirring up huge clouds of dust. It closed on them rapidly, a great beast chasing down prey. Its guns flashed and ribbons of dirt flew up around the men. They tumbled to the ground in awkward heaps and the helicopter buzzed over them and then soared up over the trees once again.

By now Danielle and Verhoven had reached the base of the temple. "Up top," Verhoven ordered. "Inside!"

As McCarter's group scrambled up the stairs, Verhoven's men joined them. The three of them had managed to grab their own rifles and a box of ammunition.

"Damn good," Verhoven said. "Now move."

Danielle clambered up the stairs, hearing the NOTAR but not seeing it. She reached the top, took a step forward, then saw the helicopter heading straight for her. She turned and dove back down the stairs just as the pilot fired. Shells skipped off the temple's roof, burning the air. The NOTAR followed, roaring overhead, ten feet above her.

Now was her chance. Bruised and scratched, she hustled across the roof, squeezing through the portal and into the familiar darkness.

Verhoven's men followed, but he remained out of sight, even as the chainsaw buzz of the helicopter closed in once again. Seconds later, he dove through the opening, tumbling down the stairs with gunfire chasing him. Shells caromed off the stone roof and several found the opening, ricocheting wildly off the solid walls.

Danielle looked around. Everyone seemed to be okay.

"What the hell is going on?" McCarter shouted.

Danielle ignored him, listening to the noise above. The NOTAR had turned.

"He's coming back," she said.

Verhoven looked up at the portal atop the stairs. "Probably going to pour a shit storm of lead through this hole when he gets here." He turned to Danielle. "Get to the back room. Keep your heads down."

McCarter led the others into the back room while Verhoven and his men took what cover they could, pressing themselves into the walls that fronted the stairs, crouching and reloading their rifles. Danielle stayed with him.

"What are you going to do?" she asked.

Verhoven looked at his men. "When he passes."

They nodded their understanding.

"What the hell are you going to do?" Danielle demanded.

"We're going to shoot the bugger down," Verhoven replied. "He'll come in slow to try to aim down this slot, but he's got to keep moving in case we're not all down here. When he passes we're going up. It'll be a firestorm in here before that, so get back there with the others."

The noise above grew louder. Danielle looked toward the darker recesses of the temple, where the rest of the group had gone. "Screw that," she said. Six months of weapons training were about to get used.

"Then get behind me," Verhoven ordered.

Danielle ducked in against the wall behind Verhoven and seconds later all hell broke loose. Cannon fire poured down the gullet of the temple, sending shards and sparks and chunks of stone flying through the chamber.

One ricochet smashed the stone in front of Verhoven, blasting chips out of the wall that bit into his face. He spun backward, knocking into Danielle. Another shot tore the rifle out of his lieutenant's hand. Three seconds of terror and noise and the NOTAR had passed. The instant it did, Verhoven and the two men who still held guns scrambled up the stairs.

Danielle followed, bursting out into the light just as Verhoven's group opened fire on the fleeing helicopter. She was surprised at how far away it was and guessed that it had sped up after making its pass.

She brought her own rifle up and then noticed a glowing red dot on the back of the man to her left.

"Get down!" she shouted.

It was too late. The man jerked forward with the impact of the shell, falling face-first into a spray of his own blood.

"Sniper behind us," she yelled, as the others hit the deck.

She turned and scrambled for the edge. Half a dozen men in fatigues were running toward them from the north. She fired into the pack, scattering the group and taking at least one man down. She pulled back as they returned fire. "Five or six on this side," she shouted.

"More on this side," Verhoven yelled back.

Gunfire echoed from both directions and tracers burned the air overhead, crisscrossing above them. In the sky to the east of them the NOTAR had finished its turn and was coming back once again.

Danielle could count only herself, Verhoven and his two remaining men against at least a dozen attackers and a helicopter gunship. It didn't look good.

"Back inside," Verhoven shouted. "Go!"

Danielle crawled across the temple and slid through the opening in the roof. Verhoven and the other mercenaries followed, with Verhoven carrying the blood-stained rifle of his dead subordinate. He tossed it to the man whose weapon had been destroyed in the helicopter's earlier pass.

Crouching in the darkness, Danielle listened as the roar of the approaching helicopter reverberated throughout the temple. "We're trapped in here," she said.

"Would you rather be out there?"

She didn't get a chance to answer as cannon fire poured through the opening again.

Out of frustration, Verhoven fired a burst up the stairs and out into the sky but there was no target in sight.

The NOTAR had passed again, but this time the sound didn't die away, it only dropped slightly, changing in aspect and then maintaining a constant volume.

"Keeping us pinned down," Verhoven said. "That means their men are coming up."

"We're trapped in here!" Danielle repeated.

"They still have to come in to get us," Verhoven said. "And when they do we'll shred them. Get back there with the others," he said to Danielle. "That'll give us two lines." He turned to one of his surviving men. "Go with her."

Danielle moved to the other room and took a position to fire from. Behind her McCarter tried to help a violently coughing Susan Briggs, while Brazos, the only surviving porter, stood by. They looked at her accusingly.

"Get down!" she ordered, then turned back toward the foyer.

She was ready to fight—to the death, if necessary. But despite what Verhoven had said, their attackers didn't *have to* come in to get them. They were trapped like proverbial rats and all their foes had to do now was close the cage. Instead of wading into a withering fire they could simply push the stone back into place and seal the temple. The NRI team would starve, or die of thirst, or probably suffocate long before that. Verhoven knew this of course, but what choice did they have? A charge up the stairs would be suicide. She hoped the enemy would be stupid enough to come in.

The oppressive droning of the helicopter crept closer, like a monstrous swarm of bees. The wind from its downwash poured into the opening as heavy boots began pounding across the stone roof.

"Get ready," Verhoven shouted. In a minute there would be gunfire and flames and death.

Danielle drew back behind the wall and gripped the rifle, gritting her teeth as she waited. For a moment nothing happened.

Above them, the noise of the helicopter lessened a bit and the footsteps ceased as the men crowded around the opening. But still nothing happened.

She began to wonder if there would be a chance of surrender or even the possibility of negotiation. Perhaps these men would be reasonable. Perhaps they could be bluffed or bought. And then she heard it: clunk . . . clunk . . . clunk—a metal object bouncing down the stairs, heavy, solid, relentless. She turned away and shut her eyes.

A blinding flash came through her eyelids, accompanied by an earth-shattering explosion that slammed her into the stone wall and sent her sprawling onto the floor. She lay there dazed and almost unconscious, her ears ringing. She tasted blood in her mouth. She was dimly aware of the others in similar straits—Susan lying prone on the ground, McCarter crawling feebly on his hands and knees. She couldn't see Verhoven or either of his two men.

She looked for her rifle. It lay on the stone, ten feet away. It might as well have been a mile. With great effort she managed a crawling position and began moving toward it. But then she heard the sound again; another metal object tumbling down the stairs. It hit the bottom and rolled across the stone floor.

She closed her eyes tightly and covered her head . . . waiting, waiting, waiting for an explosion. But there was only a soft pop and then a forceful hissing, like air escaping a tire. She looked into the foyer, to see white vapor spraying from a long, cylindrical can. She smelled some type of chemical. And then her eyes lost focus and she crumpled into oblivion.

## CHAPTER 26

Danielle Laidlaw awoke to a soothing voice.

"Can you see me?" the voice asked.

She squinted against a blinding light and her eyes began to focus. She saw a face, with brown eyes framed by dark gray hair. She didn't recognize it.

"Can you see me?"

"Yes," she said. The details of the face sharpened a bit as a jolt of pain ran through her body. The figure backed off, pulling his hand away from the side of her head. It held a rag soaked in blood.

"From your ear," he explained.

Her head was pounding, the sounds around her were muffled, but her field of vision had begun to expand; she saw the blue sky behind the face and realized she was outside. She noticed that the man was wearing a safari jacket and that other men surrounded him, holding rifles and dressed in camouflaged fatigues. The past hour came rushing back to her and she felt a sudden onset of anger. "You're the people who attacked us."

"I'm afraid we are," the man admitted, reaching toward her.

She tensed.

"Relax," he said, reaching out again and grabbing a small black device off her belt. "You won't be needing this."

Her hand went to her belt. He'd grabbed her transponder, a device that each member of the NRI team carried to prevent the sensors of the defense system from alerting of them and their movement. As he tossed it to one of his men, she slid her hand down farther, to the cargo pocket of her khakis. It was empty.

Kaufman caught her. "Yes, I have them too," he said. "Nice of you to return them to the scene of the crime."

Danielle felt a sudden panic and wave of energy flow through her system. She tried to get up, as if she might attack him, but she became instantly light-headed and fell forward to her hands and knees.

"An effect of the drug," he told her. "You seem to have gotten the worst of it. But it should wear off in a minute or two. Don't worry, you'll be tied up before that happens."

She glared up at the man. Try as she might, she didn't recognize him. "What the hell do you people want?"

"I think you know what I want. Care to discuss it with me?"

So these were the players who had been shadowing them, the unseen opponent who'd sent men to attack her at the harbor. "I don't know who the hell you think you are, but I promise you, you do not know who you're screwing with."

"Actually," he said, as calmly as if he were correcting a clerical error, "I know exactly who I'm screwing with.

And though you might think there is a rescue to wait on, I promise you there isn't. I've blocked your communications suite, and your helicopter and pilot were shot down and left burning in the jungle, thirty miles from here."

She looked past the man; the black NOTAR sat on the dry ground a hundred yards away. The gun pods were clearly visible.

Her captor seemed to guess her thoughts. "After what happened at the docks, I couldn't let your friend interfere a second time."

Danielle said nothing; she was stunned. But the bad news continued.

"I tell you this so you'll understand the nature of your situation," he said. "You're beyond the reach of help now. Even from the States."

She glanced up at him, fearing his next words.

"Arnold Moore is dead as well."

Her reaction was instant: a sick, falling feeling and a wave of uncontrollable rage. She swung at him, but he grabbed her arm and held it. She spit at him, trying to pull away.

Still holding her arm, Kaufman calmly wiped the spit from his face, and then he slapped her, sending her back to the ground. Her cheek stung and reddened like it was on fire.

"I can be reasonable if you can," he said sharply, putting away the handkerchief. "Or I can make your life hell. If you want to get out of here alive, along with your people, you'll cooperate. If you're as stubborn as I've been told, well, then I guess you'd rather die."

Her mind was reeling. Hawker dead, Moore dead. What about Gibbs, why hadn't the man mentioned Gibbs? Perhaps there was still hope. She bit her lip and kept quiet.

Taking note of her silence, he waved one of his men over. "You'll change your mind in time."

Across from her the NOTAR began to power up, generators first, and then the engine. Slowly the blades began to turn. She watched it with anger, until two of the armed men helped her up and led her across the clearing to a large tree at the edge of the forest. The tree was burned in places by the Chollokwan fire. A heavy chain, secured by a padlock, encircled it, and the other survivors were there, sitting with their backs to the trunk and their arms pinned behind them.

As the NOTAR lifted off and buzzed out over the forest, Kaufman's men forced her to sit with her back to the tree, laced a pair of handcuffs through the inner side of the chain and then cuffed her wrists. The closed loop of her arms and the cuffs interlocked with the closed loop of the heavy chain like a pair of rings. She could move around freely, even slide along it, but unlike a set of magician's rings, this connection could not be released without breaking one of the chains; a simple but effective prison.

She counted heads; McCarter and Susan were there, along with Verhoven, one of his men and Brazos, the lead porter—everyone who'd been inside the temple, including her, the lucky six. There was no sign of the others. Verhoven's lieutenant, whose name was Roemer, bled from a bandaged wound on one arm, while Susan sobbed quietly and McCarter tried to comfort her.

As the guards walked away, McCarter glared at Danielle, the look of a man who knew he'd been misled.

"Who are these people?" he asked. "What is this all about?"

"I don't know," she said.

"They're mercenaries," Verhoven explained. "Eastern European, from the sounds of their accents. I've heard some Croatian dialect, but mostly German. The leader is older, probably an Ex–Stasi crew chief, who had to flee when the wall came down."

"Stasi?" McCarter asked.

"Old East German secret police. Like the KGB. Only worse."

"What the hell are they doing out here?" McCarter demanded. He turned back to Danielle. "What the hell is going on?"

Danielle stared at him, her worst fears now realized, her mind willing him not to ask her anything else. They didn't need that. "We need to be calm," she told him. "We'll find a way to get out of this."

Whether McCarter believed her or simply sensed that this would be a bad time for a discussion, she didn't know. But he said nothing more.

She looked around at the group. "Anyone else?"

"Only Devers," Verhoven replied.

"Where is he?"

"With them."

Danielle scanned the clearing, suddenly realizing that she hadn't seen Devers during the attack. "Doing what?"

"Getting paid, would be my guess," Verhoven said.

So Devers had sold them out. The why was easy, the how more difficult. Devers was a low-level employee from Research Division. He had little access to the technical side of things and couldn't possibly understand what they were after. In fact, it made little sense at all, until she began to realize that Devers must have been involved with the project from a distance ever since the word go. Gibbs and Moore had consulted with him regarding the Chollokwan and other tribes as soon as they'd decided to come down to Brazil. And he'd had several extensive consultations with Dixon and his team. She doubted that Devers knew what they were after, but it didn't take much to realize it was important. Just as Hawker had said, the presence of her and Moore working the case on the ground level was enough.

"That greedy son of a bitch," she said.

Verhoven nodded. "He is. No doubt. And when I get my hands on him, I'll make him bleed for every penny."

Danielle sat back, trying to figure out a way to give Verhoven that chance, watching as the man who'd slapped her and two of his men walked toward them.

"My name is Kaufman," he said. "I'd like to give you my apologies for what happened here this morning. It wasn't supposed to occur like this. But from here on out, you have my word that you'll be treated well."

"You'd be wise to let us go," Danielle insisted, her cheek still burning from his slap.

"Wise?" he repeated. "No, I don't think that would be the word. But eventually, you'll be released unharmed—as long as you cooperate. In the meantime, I need the freedom to operate unhindered. And some help from Ms. Briggs."

As Kaufman's soldiers moved to release Susan, McCarter became alarmed. "What do you want with her?"

The soldiers unlocked her cuffs and pulled her to her feet.

"What do you want?" she said, meekly echoing McCarter.

"You have nothing to be afraid of," Kaufman insisted. "We just want to borrow your expertise for a moment."

One of the soldiers took Susan by the arm and dragged her off. She looked desperately back toward McCarter, but there was nothing he could do.

Kaufman led Susan to a makeshift table in the form of an overturned crate. He offered her some food, which she refused, and then some water. She hesitated.

"It's okay," he insisted, taking a sip of the water himself. "It's not Pellegrino, but it's drinkable."

Susan pulled back at first but then accepted. Her throat was very dry.

"I'm not here to hurt you," he said, his tone calm and soothing. "The events of this morning were an aberration, a mistake." He pointed to the soldiers. "These men reacted somewhat overzealously and I wasn't here to stop it. But now that I am, I can promise you it won't happen again."

She wasn't sure what to make of this. "They killed people."

"I know," Kaufman acknowledged. "That's what they do. But with the situation secure, they won't have to make that choice again."

"Why are you doing this?" she asked.

"I wish I could tell you," he said. "But that would make things worse for you."

She spoke honestly. "I don't want to help you."

"I can understand that," he replied. "But I need your help. If you cooperate with me, I'll give your friends food and water and a chance to live out the remainder of their lives. If you don't, then I have no choice but to force you. They'll go thirsty and hungry until you change your mind."

She looked down at the table, reeling and dizzy from everything that she'd witnessed and strangely finding comfort in Kaufman's reassuring voice. She was smart enough to realize that he wanted just that, but she couldn't stop the feeling. She didn't want to make him angry, didn't want to hear any more gunfire or see any more blood.

"Ready to listen?" he asked.

She looked up at him and nodded reluctantly.

"Good," he said. "There are some very important items on the grounds here somewhere, probably inside the temple. I want you to help us locate them."

She nodded.

"You've been in the temple?"

"No."

"Your friends, then, they've been in there?"

"Professor McCarter and Danielle."

He nodded. "Did they remove any items from inside? Anything metallic?"

"Metallic?" she said. "No, nothing metallic."

He paused for a moment, as if he wanted her to be sure of her answer. "I want you to go in there with us, show us around."

Now she had a reason to protest. "I can't go in there. I can't breathe in there because of the fumes."

"Yes, I know," he said. "I've heard all about the fumes. A terrible smell, but I think we can remedy that for you." He reached into a box beside them and produced a military-style gas mask. "Will this help?"

Susan stared blankly at the mask. What else could she say—of course it would help.

From his spot at the prison tree, McCarter tried desperately to keep an eye on Susan. "What do you think they want with her?"

"Her mind," Verhoven said. "She knows what you know. But she's smaller and weaker. That's what they're after. You saw them going through our things. They're looking for something, and they want her help to find it."

"I would have rather they take me," McCarter said.

Verhoven agreed. "Well, if she's smart enough to play dumb, maybe they'll come back and ask for your help."

"What about the police, the army?" Brazos asked. "They can't do this here."

"We're so far out," Danielle said, "I doubt anyone will ever know."

"What about Hawker and Polaski?" McCarter said. "They know we're here."

"We can't wait for them," she insisted. "We have to do something ourselves."

"But if they try to reach us," McCarter began, "when Hawker comes back, he'll realize something has gone wrong, then maybe he could—"

"He's dead," she said bluntly, feeling the pain of the words she hadn't wanted to speak aloud. "According to that son of a bitch who took Susan, Hawker and Polaski were shot down long before they could make it to Manaus. That same goddamned helicopter that attacked us."

As she spoke, Danielle felt the chill of her words hit the others, the realization that they were truly on their own. She noticed Verhoven grit his teeth, but otherwise he was nonresponsive. She guessed he had assumed that fact from the start.

As the others fell silent, Danielle tried to get ahold of her reeling mind. It was hard for her to fathom the depths of what had just happened, the speed and severity of the sudden reversal. Twenty-four hours ago she'd been on the verge of success, and now . . .

Now they'd been attacked and made prisoners by some kind of paramilitary group. Mercenaries of some kind watching them, while dead members of her team lay in the clearing covered by tarps. Somewhere in the jungle Hawker and Polaski lay in a mangled, blackened wreck. And Moore . . . his kind face flashed through her mind; a good man, an honest man, who'd been like a father to her. It seemed like some absurd nightmare from which she couldn't wake. She began to seethe with anger, a silent fury building in her, and she vowed to find a way out of this madness, to make these men pay for what they'd done—or die trying.

She turned her attention back to the others.

"Verhoven's right," she said. "We have to use every advantage, no matter how small." She realized that McCarter might be such an asset. "There's a chance they might need you," she said to him. "If they take you, grab anything that might help. Maybe one of your tools or something we could use to work on this chain. That would make our chances better."

"Better?" McCarter said. "Better than what?"

"Better than they are now."

McCarter breathed in heavily. "This is insane," he said, shaking his head. He didn't seem to be handling the situation well. Another reason they should have never brought along civilians.

She turned to Verhoven. "Did you see the soldier who held the keys?" She hadn't thought to look. She'd still been groggy at the time. But as her wits came back to her, she knew that man would have to be a target.

"Yeah," Verhoven said, slyly. "I got a good look as he unlocked the girl. He's got a scar above his left eye, like someone cracked 'im once."

Danielle turned to McCarter again. "You're the only one they're likely to use. If they give you any kind of freedom, you remember him and see what you can do."

Verhoven chimed in. "And if you get a chance, you talk with Susan, tell her to be ready."

"Ready for what?" McCarter asked.

"For anything," Verhoven said. "And when you come back, you look me in the eyes. I'll spit if it's time to try something."

Danielle nodded her agreement.

Beside her, McCarter looked sick. "Spit," he whispered, as if he couldn't believe his ears. "Grab something . . . try something . . . this is insanity."

He breathed heavily, looking hopelessly up at the sky, and Danielle prayed that he would hold it together.

## CHAPTER 27

It took three tries, but Susan Briggs finally found a mask that fit her face. Kaufman then introduced her to Norman Lang, his chief scientist, explaining that she was to help him in whatever way he asked.

Lang seemed nervous. Only a few inches taller than her and probably no more than 140 pounds soaking wet, he certainly wasn't cut from the same cloth as the mercenaries, but there was an edge to him that made her uncomfortable. He was constantly licking his lips and flexing the muscles in his jaw, as if he were clenching and unclenching his teeth. He must have cleaned the lenses on his black-plastic-framed glasses five times in the ten minutes they stood together waiting for Kaufman.

The three of them entered the temple together, along with two of Kaufman's hired guns, all of them breathing heavily through the charcoal-filter masks.

They descended the steps carefully, with Lang videotaping the journey on a digital camcorder. The walls were tinted in places, painted long ago in some reddish hue, but they were also scarred and discolored, with bright yellow stains and splotches. Where the stone was bare it glistened in the light, dripping with condensation.

Lang zoomed in for a close-up on what appeared to be some yellowish form of rust. "Sulfur," he said. "Eating away at the granite."

They walked into the first chamber. Susan stared at the piles of skulls. Professor McCarter's description had not done the sight justice.

Lang ordered all the lights off and switched on a black light in their stead. The UV light illuminated their eyes and teeth and the laces on Lang's tennis shoes, all glowing purple-white as if they were lit from within. It turned the skulls into a ghostly sight and brought out a million speckles hidden within the stone of the floor and walls. But whatever Lang was searching for, he didn't see it. He switched back to normal light and the group continued, through a doorway into a second room.

They examined this room as they had the foyer, regular light first, ultraviolet second. Again nothing of interest was found.

Lang turned to her. "What's next?"

She was navigating from McCarter's descriptions.

"It should be the altar room," she said.

The next room was indeed the altar room, but to enter it they had to pass through the falling beam of light.

Lang held his hand in the stream. It was wide but less then a centimeter thick, a long, narrow slit allowing the sunlight in from somewhere up above. He seemed suspicious.

"Are there any traps here?" Lang asked.

"Traps?"

"Yeah, booby traps, like spears triggered from stepping into the light?"

She blinked though the mask. "You're kidding me, right?"

Lang did not look as if he were.

"You've seen too many movies," she said.

Looking no more comfortable, Lang set himself to go forward and edged through the beam of light. The altar room lay on the other side.

Susan watched as Lang wandered about, probing this section and that, looking through the viewfinder and recording things he saw. Several times he used the black light and occasionally he looked at other instruments he'd brought along. He seemed mostly underwhelmed. Finally, he made his way to the platform, where he switched off the lights once again.

This time something appeared in the presence of the ultraviolet rays: geometric markings hidden within the stone face of the altar.

Susan stared at them.

Kaufman noticed her gaze. "Do you recognize these?"

She didn't. "They don't look like glyphs."

Lang aimed his camera at the top surface of the altar, and another set of marks appeared: two elongated grooves embedded within the stone, running from the front of the altar to the back. Widely spaced at first, the grooves narrowed near the middle, forming parallel lines for several inches before bending outward again. As they neared the back edge, the lines diverged completely, until they ran away from each other, in opposite directions, spreading across the top of the design in flowing, rolling swirls. At various points on the altar there were carved depressions in the stone, all of them within the boundaries created by the two lines.

Susan stood on her tiptoes to peek and Kaufman waved her up. "Does this look familiar to you?"

She studied the pattern. "No, they're not glyphs either."

"No," Kaufman agreed.

She cocked her head. "But it almost looks like . . ."

"Like what?"

She turned to Kaufman. "Like a tree."

Kaufman examined the lines again. He seemed unable to visualize it.

She tried to assist. "Here are the roots," she said, pointing to the closest part of the markings. "The bottom of the tree. And this would be the trunk," she said, as her finger traced the lines to the top. "And these swirls are the branches and the leaves." She turned to Kaufman. "A tree."

Kaufman and Lang stared at the design. The lines were thin, little more than scratches. It was hard to see the pattern as a tree.

Susan realized their hesitance. "I mean it doesn't look like those other marks," she said. "They were angled and straight. These are all curves."

Kaufman looked again. "Why is it you see a tree, when we don't?" He turned to face her. "You're expecting a tree, maybe?"

"No," she said. "Not expecting one. But you do see it repeatedly in Mayan art. It's called the World Tree. It connects the three zones of existence, the underworld at its roots, the middle world that we live in at the trunk and the realm of the gods at the top in the branches. That's what I see here," she said, certain of it now. "This is art. Not writing."

Kaufman took one more look and then tapped Lang, who switched back to normal light. It took their eyes a second to adjust.

"Ms. Briggs, do you know what an electro-graphic ground scan is?"

She nodded. "It checks electrical resistance to determine the mineral makeup of the underground layers. We use them sometimes before we excavate."

"It can be used like an ultrasound," Kaufman said. "We've run several of them this morning, along with a series of ultrasounds, and we think this place is built over the top of a large cavern. Would that surprise you?"

She and McCarter had guessed there was a cave, but she didn't want to give that away. "Not really. The sulfur fumes have to come from somewhere, either volcanic vents or a sulfur cave. We poked around a bit but we couldn't find an entrance."

Kaufman smiled. "That's because the temple was built right on top of it. The water proves it. The temple is the entrance to the cave."

Kaufman pointed to the well and the three of them peered into the darkness of that circular abyss. "Poe would be proud."

Susan gazed into the well again.

Kaufman signaled one of his men. "Take her back to the others," he said. "And make sure they have proper food and water." He looked at Susan. "You see? I keep my promises."

"I suppose you'd be angry if I spoke about what I saw here?" Susan guessed.

"Not at all," Kaufman said. "Feel free to discuss it. Perhaps your Professor McCarter will have some thoughts on what you've seen. If he does, I'd like to hear them."

Susan nodded, confused and surprised, but much calmer than she'd been before.

As she was led out, she glanced back at Kaufman. He was pulling something from his pocket, but before she could see what it was, the guard pushed her forward and she ascended the stairs.

Standing in the altar room, Kaufman turned to Lang. "This is where Dixon found the stones," he said. "And the fifth crystal."

Lang seemed unhappy with that conclusion. "That guy was out of his mind, I don't know about trusting anything he said. If these crystals are what you think they are, then they came from some type of machinery. Not . . ." He waved his hand toward the altar. "This."

"The natives found them," Kaufman said with certainty. "Idolizing what they found, they used the crystals as some type of holy object. Worshipping it for what they knew it could do."

"The NRI's theory," Lang noted.

"It got them—and us—this far," Kaufman reminded him. "It's kind of late to start questioning it."

Lang backed down and turned to the altar, switching the black light back on, illuminating the marks in the stone: the tree that Susan had seen. There were four small depressions in the bottom of the design, one in the central trunk portion and four more at the top. "I'd just like some proof."

Kaufman nodded and opened the small box in his hand. A jeweler's case, it contained the gray metallic stones and the crystal Dixon had found.

He placed them in the depressions, the cubes at the bottom and the crystal at the top. The cubes fit snugly, but the crystal did not. He moved it to the center slot, where it slid into place with a soft click.

From deeper in the same pocket Kaufman pulled a second case, one he'd taken from Danielle after her capture. Lined up inside like darts were the Martin's crystals. He placed the crystals in various spots at the top of the design, moving them around until all three fit snugly. Nothing happened.

One of the mercenaries commented, "No magic," he said, making a whooshing sound as he finished.

"We're not looking for magic," Kaufman said, aggravated.

"Still," Lang noted. "We are one short."

"Yes," Kaufman said, remembering that the NRI had dissected one of the crystals. There were five slots but only four complete crystals. "Although, I don't think it matters here," he said, looking at Lang. "This isn't anything, is it?"

Lang shook his head. "I don't see any way this could generate energy. The girl's right: this is just art. Ancient, primitive art."

Kaufman looked around. "Yes," he said. "Just art. Like any church, the shiny things go up front, but the real truths are kept hidden in a vault somewhere."

Lang nodded. "Why don't we get the ultrasound equipment in here and see what we can uncover?"

Kaufman didn't respond. He was staring at the design on the altar. "Do you see a tree here?" he asked.

Lang studied the markings once again. "Yeah, I guess I can. Like the girl said, 'the path connecting the three zones of existence.'"

"What about a tunnel?" Kaufman asked. "The crystal goes between the lines. That suggests a hollow structure to me. A hollow tree is a tunnel." He looked over the edge and into the pit. "Or perhaps a well."

Lang glanced at Kaufman, then at the design, and the well beyond the altar. "I know what you're thinking," he said. "Let me get the ultrasound done first."


Several minutes later, while Lang readied the equipment for the ultrasound, Kaufman had his other mercenaries begin to move the stone that still blocked half the entrance. He wanted more space to get things in, and was certain they would need the space to bring out what he expected to find. But his men failed to use the caution that the NRI team had shown and the granite slab cracked deeply along a pre-existing fissure. After quick words and a cursory exam, another attempt to move it proved too much and the stone cracked in half, with much of its bulk crashing through the opening and onto the stairs below, where it shattered into rubble.

Kaufman looked at the mess. "Clear it up," he said with disgust.

The mercenaries sprung into action, dropping their equipment and beginning a cleanup job on the stairs.

"That's good work," Lang said, pointing to the mess. "You pay them extra for that?"

Kaufman thought of it philosophically. "Not their finest moment, but if we couldn't move it we would have had to break it anyway."

## CHAPTER 28

The machine was quiet now, still and dark. It had come blasting through the trees like a missile, only to be swallowed up by the rainforest's living depth. But despite the boasts of the NOTAR's pilot, the Huey hadn't exploded or burned. In fact, an hour after the crash, most of its fuel had drained harmlessly into the ground.

After a brief moment of unconsciousness, Hawker had woken and managed to extricate himself and Polaski from the wreckage. He'd carried Polaski's inert form to a fallen tree twenty yards away, where a rag soaked in cold water had helped him come to.

In obvious pain, Polaski mumbled incoherently, his eyes half-open.

"Cold," he said. "So cold . . ."

Hawker covered Polaski with his jacket and the Mylar blanket from the survival kit, but the man continued to shiver.

Polaski was in grave condition. A wound to his head had swollen badly. Several ribs seemed to be broken and small amounts of bloody bubbles were dribbling from his mouth, enough to tell Hawker that he was bleeding internally.

"Help me," he said, looking past Hawker. "Please . . . my daughter."

A surgeon with a sterile operating room might have been able to save Polaski, but there was little Hawker could do except watch him die.

"You're going to be all right," he said, lying. "You're both going to be all right. Just try to be calm."

"It's so cold."

Polaski seemed to look past Hawker for a moment, and then his eyes closed. His chest stopped moving and the bubbles were gone.

"I'm sorry," Hawker whispered. It seemed a foolish, worthless thing to say but the words came anyway.

Feeling drowsy, Hawker rubbed the back of his neck. He guessed that he'd been unconscious for a minute or two. He might have even sustained a concussion. He couldn't let himself go back under without taking a chance on never waking up again.

He forced himself to stand and began to walk in circles. His legs felt heavy and soft, like they were made of wet sand. He shook and stretched and flexed, trying to force some energy into his lifeless muscles.

Pain racked every part of his body. His ribs and neck ached from whiplash and the restraint of the seat belt, his hands were bruised and cut from flailing about the cockpit, half-coagulated blood oozed from a gash across his cheekbone, just beneath his right eye.

At least he was alive.

He looked down at Polaski. There had been a moment when he considered the possibility that Polaski was a mole. The guy was a volunteer who worked the communications system; he was polite and quiet, never drawing attention to himself, exactly the way a mole is supposed to act. But that assessment had been wrong. Polaski was just a kind, mild man who'd wanted to add a little adventure to his life. He'd joined the expedition not knowing the danger he was in, because Danielle and Moore *and* Hawker had kept it hidden. He deserved more than being left for the animals in the jungle.

Hawker pulled a collapsible shovel from his survival pack and assembled it. With a push from his boot, he forced it into the soil, turned it over and raised the shovel up for another strike. As he began to dig, his heartbeat rose and the fog in his mind receded bit by bit. Thoughts began jumping around, jumbled and confused at first, like images trying to find their correct spot.

The attack and its aftermath seemed clearer, but it left him wondering who had done it and why.

It had to be the same people who attacked Danielle and him at the harbor, but no contact of his had been able to dig up any information on them. That meant heavy hands were in the mix somewhere, keeping a lid on the truth.

With no way of determining who had attacked them, he focused on why.

Obviously, they wanted whatever Danielle and the NRI were after, but what that was he still didn't know. It had to be related to the temple. His first thought was the artifacts they'd been uncovering and preserving.

McCarter had warned them that the trade in ancient

artifacts was a fairly profitable enterprise, rife with theft, smuggling and a thriving black market. But how much could such things really be worth? Thousands? Tens of thousands, maybe. Not enough for what he'd seen. A knife in the back, perhaps, or a couple of leg-breakers in a dark alley, but not a purpose-built weapons platform like the NOTAR. The gun pods alone would run a million dollars.

What, then? Diamonds? Gold? Could they really be after something so base? He jammed the shovel down-ward again. It didn't make sense. The NRI was a strate-gic organization. They would only be here after something important on a political or worldly level. And the only thing that still generated that type of need was oil.

While the price of a barrel continued to fluctuate, it escaped no one that the Middle East was just a few bombs from utter chaos. A big strike in a friendly, de-mocratic nation would be welcome. And at times sulfur could be a geologic clue to oil deposits, but for all the criteria that particular guess happened to fit, it was still a square peg in a round hole.

To begin with, the Brazilians didn't need the NRI to find their oil for them, and the NRI certainly couldn't pump it out in secret if they did. For that matter, nor could any adversary. So what would be the point?

No, he decided, this was not a race to stake some kind of claim; it was a burglary, a smash-and-grab job. Two thieves fighting over the jewels in someone else's house. Whatever the two groups were after, it would be portable and a non-commodity, something that had value merely by being possessed.

Hawker stood up straight, wiped the sweat from his

eyes and conceded that the answer was beyond him. He couldn't guess the *who* or the *why* of the incident—but as his eyes fell to the man he was about to bury he suddenly became clear on the *how*.

To Hawker and Polaski and everyone else at the NRI base camp, the flight had been an unscheduled one, a last-minute errand that had become necessary only upon learning of the tragedy in Washington. But to someone somewhere else, the flight had been more than expected. It had been planned with meticulous precision, designed to put Hawker and Polaski in exactly the right place at exactly the wrong time.

There was no other logical explanation. The NOTAR had to have come from a good distance away. To make the intercept, its pilot would need to know precisely when Hawker and Polaski would be transiting the area. A change of ten minutes in either direction would have blown it.

But of course there hadn't been ten minutes to wait. In order to get Polaski to Washington in time they'd had to leave the jungle immediately. That was the setup; the accident involving Polaski's daughter was only the trigger.

There was a chance that the accident involving Polaski's daughter had been a hoax; it made the details of the situation and the message somewhat easier to control. Then again, such a bluff came with its own problems, problems of veracity or confirmation that might expose the truth and rule it out.

If there was one thing he'd learned over the past decade, it was how evil men could be to their fellow man. Not just violent or in conflict but utterly evil in the pursuit of their own goals. Such men might easily destroy a whole family just to move one piece on the chessboard.

Putting the shovel aside, Hawker ground his teeth. Whether the accident was real or not, Polaski had died thinking his only daughter was near death herself. A man destroyed or an entire family. And in ways both direct and indirect, Hawker had played a part.

Racked with guilt, Hawker laid Polaski gently in the shallow grave, folding the man's arms neatly across his chest. As he began to cover Polaski's body with earth, the weight of the man's death pressed down on him. He recalled his gleeful bargain with Danielle. In fact, he remembered it was he who had suggested the deal, offering his silence and loyalty for her assistance, arrogantly believing he could protect those who had come along for the ride without apprising them of the danger. His silence had become part of the chain of events that had gotten Polaski killed, and perhaps Polaski's daughter as well. It had helped convince the others that they were safe.

The others . . .

Hawker began to wonder what had become of them. If their enemy knew Hawker and Polaski's route across the jungle, it meant they had to know where it originated: the closely guarded location of the temple. Surely they would not wait long before moving in on the clearing. In all likelihood the attacks had come simultaneously or nearly so.

"God help us," he whispered, covering Polaski with more of the dark Amazonian soil. "God help us all."

Hawker finished burying Polaski in complete silence,

his mind growing numb as it churned in circles. He tamped the soil down and said a short prayer, concluding with a verse that he thought about often, one that seemed appropriate for both Polaski and himself. "And the Lord sayeth, Come to me all ye who labor and are heavy burdened. I will give you rest."

He smoothed the dark earth of Polaski's grave with his hand. "Rest well, Polaski," he said.

Standing, Hawker was now forced to grapple with a larger decision. He had to get moving, had to try to get help to his friends. *But how?*

The smart bet was to head for the river and take it east. Sooner or later a boat would pick him up and he could make a radio call. He could reach someone in the NRI. Moore or Gibbs or someone who knew of the operation and could coordinate a response, one with sufficient numbers and equipment to deal with whoever had done this thing. But even with the best of luck, it might be a week or so before someone picked him up and another week before help arrived.

*Too much time.*

By then their enemy would be gone and the rest of the NRI team missing or dead. They might be already. He thought of McCarter and Susan and the porters hired for a hundred bucks a day. He thought of Danielle and closed his eyes.

With a fire in his heart stoked by bunkers of anger and guilt, Hawker grabbed his survival pack, checked to be sure his gun was present and heaved the pack over his shoulder. He took a deep breath, set his jaw and turned to the west, heading back toward the clearing instead of away from it.

He would not abandon the others to a callous and murdering enemy, not when his own part in the deception weighed so heavily on his mind. He would make his way back to the clearing on foot, an action that would bring about another war and great shedding of blood— something he'd spent years trying desperately to avoid.

It had become unavoidable now. The darkness had made a home in his soul once again and it drove him on. He would return to the clearing and save his friends or he'd bury their killers, one by one.

## CHAPTER 29

As Kaufman's men turned the clearing into an armed camp, digging foxholes and bunkers, and unloading crates of weapons and ammunition from the helicopter, Norman Lang conducted his ultrasound tests, which confirmed a cavern beneath the temple and a tunnel linking the two. Not the vertical shaft of the well behind the altar, but a steep zigzagging passage that cut through the structure, like a switchback mountain road. It connected to a spot in the altar room, a spot that appeared to lie across the gaping mouth of the well.

Closer investigation revealed a fissure between two of the stones. Kaufman's men forced the stone upward with a pair of crowbars, raising it an inch at a time, until it jammed against something and would budge no farther.

Lang wedged a two-by-four into the exposed space to brace the stone and then supervised the building of a makeshift bridge above the maw of the pit. He crawled across and peered into the tunnel, using a flashlight.

It was a narrow space, perhaps five feet high, but not much wider than a man's shoulders. It fell away steeply, looking more like a slide than a walkway, and he saw evidence of a pulley and counterweight system for the stone, but whatever flaxen rope it might have once used had disintegrated long ago.

Minutes later, Lang was back in the tunnel, this time leading Susan Briggs and four of Kaufman's hired guns. They moved cautiously, with each switchback seeming steeper than the last as the tunnel descended through the temple and into the ground below. Lang began to feel claustrophobic. In truth, he'd been feeling something similar since Kaufman had sucked him into this mess.

For several years he'd been Kaufman's go-to man for risky projects, and in that time he'd come to realize that Kaufman sometimes used questionable methods to gather information, but he had never expected the events that he'd now become part of: shooting and killing and the taking of hostages. Lang was well aware that his own ego, greed and lack of discernable ethics had made him an easy mark, but this was far more than he'd bargained for.

Still, at this point, what choice did he have? No doubt any attempt to back out would result in an unpleasant end. No, he thought, crossing Kaufman outright would be foolish, especially out here in the jungle, surrounded by killers and thugs. Lang was a realist, at least in the sense of knowing what had to be done to survive, and for now that meant doing as he was ordered, trusting in the fact that Kaufman needed him to study and break down whatever items this project recovered. Once he made it back to the States, his approach might change, but for now he would do what was necessary—and if bodies were left behind, that would be okay as long as his wasn't among them.

He turned to Susan. "How much farther?"

She stared at him blankly through the plastic of the gas mask. "How would I know?"

Of course she wouldn't know. It was a stupid question. Why the hell was he even talking to her? He pushed on, sliding and crouching and feeling the burn in his legs—until he stepped out into an open space, a massive chamber where the ceiling pulled up and out of view and the edges ran away from them on either side. It was a deep and echoing place, like a darkened, empty stadium. Words of awe wafted through the air, echoing back at them while their lights skated dimly over distant walls.

They stood far beneath the temple. Directly ahead them lay a wide pool of utterly still, crystal-clear water: a small lake that stretched across the cave for perhaps a five hundred yards. There appeared to be additional land on the far side.

Lang pulled an ELF radio from his belt. ELF stood for Extremely Low Frequency, which was far more adept than standard frequencies at penetrating resistance. The Navy used a similar system to communicate with submarines a thousand feet below the surface. Lang and Kaufman hoped the orange radio with the long antenna would be powerful enough to send a signal through the rock. "We're at the opening of the main cave," Lang said, holding down the talk switch, "a good part of which is filled by water."

Kaufman's reply came back garbled. "Understand you . . . a large . . . filled with . . . -ter."

"Affirmative," Lang replied. There was no answer. He wasn't sure if Kaufman had received or not. It didn't

matter; they would proceed, complete their preliminary
search and then head back out.

As part of that search Lang filmed the area with his
camera, repeating his black-light test and performing a
few tests with a battery of other devices he carried. Finding nothing of interest, he looked across the water. On
the far side of the lake he saw what appeared to be a
raised area. Their lights barely reached it but it looked
flat and level, unlike the rest of the cave. "We've got to
find a way across," he said. "Either that or we're going
to need a boat."

A quick search revealed a pathway running along the
right-hand shore of the lake, and they followed it, sticking to the edge of the water for the first part of the route,
with a detour between a forest of stalactites and a formation of what looked like giant mushrooms made of
wet stone. Past this outcropping, the path turned back
toward the lake and became a narrow strip pinned between the water and the cavern wall. Finally, near the
other side at last, it turned outward and crossed the very
corner of the lake on what appeared to be a man-made
dam. On the right side of the dam lay a group of small
pools, arranged in a honeycomb formation. On the left
side was the lake.

Lang taped the area with the camcorder. "I count
seven of them."

The circular pools measured about ten feet across.
They were divided from one another by retaining walls
of the same height as the dam. The water level was identical in each of the pools, though it was several inches
higher than that of the lake. Lang wasn't sure what that
meant beyond the fact that the water must flow freely

between the group of pools but not between the pools and the lake.

He filmed the formation but the unmoving, black waters gave away little.

"Some kind of construction," Lang said for the video. "The same type of stone as the dam," he noted. "Polished stone. Almost ceramic, or volcanic perhaps. No indication as to what they're for."

One of Kaufman's hired soldiers looked at Lang with a smile, then turned to his friends. "Jacuzzi," he said.

As the others laughed, Lang spotted a more promising site, a recessed area with a wide expanse of flat, smooth stone, a plaza of sorts that had clearly been worked and leveled with tools. "That's where we need to go," he said.

Lang traversed the dam with Susan and the mercenaries trailing out behind.

One of the soldiers stopped. "Wait," he said, training his flashlight more closely on one of the pools. "There is something in there."

"What do you see?" Lang asked, quite sure it would be nothing of consequence.

"A reflection," the man said. "Something shiny."

One of the other mercenaries came up beside the first one. "*Munzen,*" he said. "Gold munzen." German for gold coins.

Lang looked at Susan for an explanation.

"The Maya often dumped things in wells," she told him. "Sacrifices to their spirits. The sinkholes in Mexico are full of offerings. But those are deep, natural structures, not little pools like these."

"What kind of things did they dump?" one of the soldiers asked.

Lang began to answer but Susan spoke first. "Jewelry and pottery, for the most part, sometimes even people."

"What about gold?"

"The Maya didn't have much gold," Susan said.

The two mercenaries chuckled at that. "Gold, for sure," the first one said. "Why else would we be here?"

The other mercenaries gathered around separate pools, as if they were staking their own claims. Lang shrugged. How could he fault these men for gold fever when he and Kaufman were after riches of their own? He decided to take a closer look himself and moved to one of the pools in the rear of the formation, around the curve and farthest from the end of the dam.

The soldiers began talking excitedly among themselves. The one who'd first spotted the reflection was wasting no time. His boots and shirt were already off. "I'm going in," he said.

He undid his belt, and then tore off his pants and underwear without the slightest hint of modesty.

Susan turned away, blushing. Lang wondered if he should be filming. "Europeans," he said, laughing.

The naked German stood at the edge of the pool, bringing his arms up as if he might do a swan dive. At the last minute he seemed to decide against it and his friends howled in disappointment. "Looks cold," he said.

Lang turned his gaze back to the well in front of him. He focused his flashlight on it but didn't see much, certainly nothing metallic. He picked up his camcorder and positioned it on his shoulder. The spotlight was more powerful than his flashlight.

The German was ready to jump now, feet-first.

Lang ignored him, aimed the camera and switched on the floodlight. For a second, the light reflected off of the water and blinded him, but he quickly changed his aim and the glare went away.

On the dam, the others egged their comrade on.

Lang adjusted his lens and the focus cleared, but all he saw was a trail of minuscule bubbles, like the carbonation in a glass of undisturbed soda water. At the sound of a splash, he looked up.

The mercenary had finally jumped in. Holding his nose, he'd plunged in feet-first, to a roar of delight from his friends. He came up seconds later, exhaling a great burst of spray—which quickly became a scream.

For a moment the others laughed, remembering his comment about the water looking cold, but the scream didn't stop and the man thrashed around violently, eyes shut, frantically searching for the side of the well. His friends froze in their tracks, confused. When they finally realized his trouble was real, they ran to help him.

The man had reached the edge of the pool now. He tried to pull himself out, but the dam's polished surface offered nothing to grab on to. The others reached for him, clutching his arms and pulling. But he slipped free, shaking violently and screaming.

"What's happening to him?" Susan yelled.

The soldiers ignored her. One of them stretched out over the water, grabbed the man by the hair and yanked him back to the edge. The others pulled him out of the water and up onto the dam, where he lay, shuddering and convulsing.

His friends stepped back, looks of horror on their faces; the man's skin was dissolving, melting away from his body, bloody foam oozing from his legs and waist as the rest of his skin blistered before their eyes.

They began to shout at one another, wiping their hands on shirts and trousers, anything they could find, their own skin burning. One grabbed a canteen and poured its contents onto his hands. *"Wasser,"* he shouted. The others followed suit, attempting to dilute the corrosive water that had splashed onto them.

As the soldiers frantically washed their hands, they moved away from their comrade, and Susan Briggs caught sight of him for the first time. She fell to her knees and gagged, expecting to be sick. She pulled at her mask, desperate to get it off as she suddenly recalled McCarter talking about a pool of acid. She hadn't seen it. She hadn't remembered or made the connection.

Sixty feet away, Lang stood transfixed. He could see the soldier rocking in spasms on the floor, shaking as if an electrical current was running through his body and choking on his own tongue as it swelled in his mouth from the caustic water he'd swallowed.

His friends moved toward him one moment and then away the next. One of them picked up his rifle and aimed it, apparently intending to put the man out of his misery, but another soldier held up a hand to stop him. The convulsions had begun to lessen.

Lang watched almost to the end before he found the strength to shut his eyes and turn away. He took a deep breath and opened his eyes again, focusing on the placid black pool in front of him. This time he saw something else besides the thin trail of bubbles: not gold as the dying soldier had seen, but green. A small green disk; two actually. They were eyes.

## CHAPTER 30

A dark shape burst from the water. It slammed into Lang and knocked him backward, sending the camera and his body flying in different directions. As the camcorder crashed to the stone floor its floodlight blew out, bathing the cave in a flash of electric blue.

The others turned at the flash, and in the dim illumination of the remaining lights they saw a shape mauling Lang. It pinned him down, clamping its jaws onto his torso and yanking its head from side to side. As Lang struggled, it reared back and, accompanied by Lang's screams, tore him completely in half, slinging the top half of his body toward the shocked mercenaries.

That sight jarred them from their trance and, as the black shape charged toward them, in a panic they grabbed for the weapons they'd just cast aside.

Despite the frantic shots sent its way, the thing hit one of the soldiers in full stride, plunging into the lake with the man in its jaws and disappearing. They watched the light on the man's belt going deeper and then going dark. A trail of bullets followed after it, but to no avail—the beast and the man were gone.

The mercenary who'd been firing backed away from

the water's edge as bloody red foam boiled to the surface. "Is it dead?"

The other soldier looked at the water briefly and then shook his head. It wasn't dead, but their comrade was. He looked at the seven pools and what remained of Lang's body. That was enough.

He took off, sprinting down the pathway in a reckless attempt to get out of there, tripping and stumbling in his haste. His eyes flicked from the path ahead, to the exit on the other side of the lake, then to the water beside him.

His friend shouted to him, but he kept running, dashing for the exit, leaping over piles of rock like a hurdler. He seemed as if he might make it, until a surge in the water's black surface started toward him. The wave closed on him rapidly and the animal burst from the lake, slamming him into the cavern wall and snapping its jaws on his legs like a crocodile taking a water buffalo. Shrieks of agony echoed through the cave, followed only by gurgling sounds as the creature dragged him back into the water and beneath it.

Susan Briggs and the last of the mercenaries remained at the site of the first attack, out on the plaza at the edge of the dam. Susan was on her knees, gasping for air, in the grips of an asthma attack, while the remaining mercenary pulled the blood-covered ELF unit from the lower half of Lang's torso. He shouted into the device. "We are having an emergency!"

He waited for a reply, and then tried again, holding the switch down with all his might, as if that would somehow boost the signal. "Lang is dead, only me and the girl are left. We have been attacked. We need help."

He heard nothing. It was hopeless. They were too deep. The signal could not get through.

The mercenary stopped transmitting and switched off his flashlight, backing deeper into the cave, farther from the dam and the lake and directly across the smooth stone from where Susan was struggling.

From this position he scanned the cave, now eerily lit by the unmoving flashlights of the fallen men. At the lake's edge, a bulky shape was pulling itself free of the water.

Across the plaza, the girl remained on her knees, coughing and wheezing, unaware of the danger. It would go for her and, once it had committed, he would open fire. He placed the radio on the ground beneath his feet and brought both hands to his rifle.

In the shadowy light, the bony, angular thing stalked her. It moved with its belly pressed against the ground, its long limbs folded awkwardly beneath it, its claws quietly clicking with each step. It seemed to move with deliberate caution now, pausing at one point, holding a limb off the floor as if the ground were hot to the touch. It lowered its head to sniff the spot, and then moved around the area for reasons unknown.

A moment later the beast stopped again. The girl had somehow managed to stifle her coughing. The resulting silence seemed to confuse the creature. The head lifted slightly, turning from one direction to another, rotating like a turret.

The mercenary clenched his jaw as the hideous thing crouched; the girl had her back to it, she wouldn't see it coming. He raised his weapon. From this distance he would not miss.

"... re you st ... here? ... ay ... gain ... what ... ppened."

The soldier glanced at his feet. The radio was squawking in a scratchy, electronic tone. He looked up as the animal hit him.

A blur of teeth and claws slashed him, his own blood splattered across his face. It whipped him to the side and his foot kicked the orange radio, sending it flying across the stone. The rifle was gone; he grabbed his knife and swung it upward, but it was jarred from his hand as if it had impacted solid rock. He kicked at the thing and tried to pull free, but the creature's claws dug into his gut and it pulled him closer and then sunk its teeth into his neck. His mouth opened, as if to scream.


Susan watched in horror, backing away as the animal stood above the lifeless body. Strangely, it did not damage him further. It just stood there, eyeing him, its jaws opening and closing, its bony exterior glistening in the dim light. It sniffed the dead man. In the space behind its neck, a row of short, bristly hairs waved back and forth, swaying and parting like reeds in the wind. A gurgling noise resonated from deep within its throat and its segmented tail rose up above its head like a scorpion's stinger. As the tail shot forward, the animal's head tilted back and it released a hideous, inhuman cry.


It would be more than thirty minutes before any help arrived. The leader of Kaufman's mercenaries brought six of his men, half the remaining force. They'd come ready to fight, but encountered nothing that would force them to do so. The only man they found was far beyond help.

One of the soldiers bent close to the body. The smell of sulfur was intense; the acid was still eating away at him. A trail of blood led to the pool next to them.

He picked up the man's discarded shirt and threw it in. The water foamed up and the shirt quickly sprouted holes. "The water. It's acid."

Another soldier suggested a possibility. "Perhaps the girl pushed him."

"Then what happened to the rest of them?" someone else asked.

Their leader looked around, aiming his flashlight into the corners of the cave. He spotted Lang's camcorder and two more great swaths of blood. There was no acid smell at these sites, but there were marks in the blood, two-pronged tracks that led away from each site.

As the soldiers examined them, a piercing call echoed from the depths of the cave. The soldiers froze. It was a haunting sound.

Guns raised in all directions, the leader made a quick decision. "We're going."

"What about the others?" one man asked, remembering that there were still two soldiers unaccounted for. "And the girl."

The leader motioned to the swaths of blood. "You won't find them," he replied, "not alive anyway." He turned around and began heading for the exit.

Kaufman waited on the roof of the temple for his mercenaries to return. As the minutes ticked by, the tension
grew. Devers approached him in the silence.

"I need to talk to you," he said.

"Now is not the time," Kaufman warned him.

"When the hell is the time?" Devers asked. "You said
I'd be out of here as soon as you took the camp. First
flight out, you said. Well, your helicopter is gone but I'm
still here."

"Plans have changed slightly," Kaufman said. "The
natives might come back and I'll need you for that."

"Well, maybe I don't want to be here if they come
back," Devers said, more loudly than he should have.

Kaufman stood up, glaring at Devers, but it was not
enough to stop the complaints.

"It wasn't supposed to be this way," Devers insisted.
"No one was supposed to get hurt."

The temptation to have one of his men beat a lesson
of humility into Devers coursed through Kaufman's
veins, but he decided it would be more important to
straighten Devers out himself, rather than give the man
something else to sulk about.

Kaufman glared at him. "You are embroiled in a web
of self-deception, Mr. Devers. You have no rights here. I
own you. Not just because of the money I paid you but
because you're now an accomplice to multiple homi-
cides. What did you think was going to happen when
two groups of armed men went after the same thing?"

Devers was silent. The first silence Kaufman had
heard out of him since the day they'd met, since the day
Devers and another member of the NRI, a man who had

died with the first team, had volunteered to funnel information to Kaufman on various NRI initiatives, culminating in a project Devers had been asked to interpret for: the Brazil project. Even then, it was not until Kaufman had hacked the NRI's files that he'd realized the importance of what they were looking for.

"This was more than I expected to do," Devers said. "It was just supposed to be information."

Kaufman understood his thinking; it was always the same. As if a little traitorous behavior was somehow less offensive than a lot. "In for a penny," he explained, "in for a pound."

Devers stared at him.

"Now get out of my sight until I need you again."

Devers skulked away just as the mercenaries began to emerge from the temple. "Where's Lang?" Kaufman asked as they reached him. "Where are the others?"

"They were killed," the group's leader told him. "Attacked. The animal you were told about is real. It's down in the cave. I heard it."

Kaufman had made the soldiers aware of Dixon's ranting out of prudence, but he'd been more worried about the natives than anything else. "Are you sure?"

"Tracks in their blood," the mercenary told him. "Two claws."

Just as Dixon had described. "Dixon saw them in the forest," Kaufman said. "Not the temple."

"Then there must be more of them," the head mercenary said, holding up his weapon. "We should get ready."

Kaufman was momentarily shocked. Not only by the

loss of Lang, but by the attack itself. It had happened inside the temple, a place he'd assumed would be safe. It had been safe for Dixon. It had been safe for the NRI group.

"We should seal the tunnel," Vogel said.

Kaufman wasn't listening. He had come to the error in his thinking. *The attack hadn't occurred in the temple, it had occurred in the cave beneath it. Those places were not one and the same; a miscalculation.*

He turned back to the soldiers and spoke to their leader. "The real danger is out here," he said, meaning the forest. "Dixon said there was more than one, even then. He heard them calling to one another, running with the natives. They came after nightfall."

Kaufman looked out over the trees; dusk was almost upon them. "Seal the tunnel," he said. "And get ready for a fight."

## CHAPTER 31

Darkness returned to the Amazon basin. In the Mayan view of things the spirit world had inverted itself, the heavens of the daytime and their powerful lords had fallen beneath the earth, replaced in influence and position by the spiritual forces of the underworld: the Xibalbans and the Nine Lords of the Night.

For the members of the NRI team, however, night arrived with no discernable change from that which preceded it. They remained chained to the tree at the edge of the clearing, watched casually from a distance but mostly unguarded and ignored.

They had struggled and schemed through half a dozen hopeless plans of escape. Verhoven and Danielle had worked the cuffs until their wrists bled, trying desperately to slip their hands free. Whenever one of Kaufman's soldiers approached, their emotions surged with hope and fear, hope that they might be released and fear that they would be shot and left for dead. But neither event occurred, and as the night arrived they fell into various forms of fitful, uncomfortable sleep.

After dozing for an hour or so, Professor McCarter awoke with a cramp in his leg, tight like twisted bands of steel. He shifted his weight and tried to stretch it, grunting in pain and waiting for the pins and needles.

The air around him was cool and still, the clearing quiet and the skies as lucid as any he'd ever seen. The unseasonably dry air meant hotter days and cooler evenings, and it left the night skies brilliantly clear. The camp ahead of him was black. And as he looked around, the others appeared to be asleep, except for Danielle and Verhoven, who were talking quietly.

As he watched them, a sense of anger welled up inside. They'd led Susan and him here under false pretenses, endangering them without their knowledge or consent.

It seemed so obvious now: armed security, guard dogs, coded satellite transmissions. Of course they'd been in jeopardy, right from the very beginning. It wasn't as if he hadn't noticed, but he'd written it off to a general sense of prudence and a healthy fear of the Chollokwan. He stared at Danielle.

"Anything happening?" he asked.

"No," she said.

Verhoven added, "Not yet anyway."

There was something ominous about Verhoven's statement, but before McCarter could say anything he heard voices: the disembodied shouts of hidden soldiers. In the distance, a flashlight came on and then went off again. There was hurried movement, more commands and metallic noises like guns being loaded and readied. In the stillness of the air, it seemed as if he could hear every footfall. "God, it's quiet."

"Too quiet," Verhoven said. "Too quiet, for too long."

McCarter glanced at the South African. "What do you mean?"

There was a sliver of a grin on Verhoven's face. "Trouble's coming."

McCarter's hands tingled. He didn't like the sound of that. "What kind of trouble?"

"Visitors," Verhoven said, nodding toward the trees. "Been around for a while, but these fools are only just figuring it out."

McCarter craned his head around and looked out into the darker void beneath the trees. He sensed something, though he wondered if it was a result of Verhoven's suggestion. "The Chollokwan?"

"They came for us after we went into the temple," Danielle reminded him. "They've left us alone ever since. But these guys have been banging around in there all day long. I fear they may have struck a nerve."

Staying out of the temple hadn't been a conscious decision, but the timing of the two events had escaped no one. McCarter looked back to the forest. The thought of being chained to a tree when an attack came horrified him. He remembered the chanting and the fires.

"Where does that leave us?"

"Stuck at the table," Verhoven said. "With a very bad hand."

McCarter's face wrinkled.

Danielle looked over at him; her eyes suggested defiance. "We're not done yet," she said. "Stay sharp. We might get a chance, somewhere in all the madness."

McCarter understood the situation. He'd questioned their odds before, but now he knew what it meant to cling to even the thinnest ray of hope. They couldn't hold out for a good chance or for even a fair one. It seemed prayers would be wasted on such grand requests. But a hundred-to-one shot, the smallest mistake by their captors, perhaps it was less foolish to ask fate for that, perhaps they'd get that type of chance before it was over.

McCarter tried to stretch his legs. He stared up at the night sky once more. The stars were so ridiculously bright that they seemed to be mocking him.

"The Mayan people cut holes in the jungle like this one," he said. "Just to see the stars. They aligned their temples with the Equinox and the Solstice and even the very center of our galaxy—though no one knows how they determined that. They carved whole sections out of the rainforest, just to study the heavens, the realm of their gods."

McCarter continued to scan the sky above the clearing. "Over time, the jungle crept in and swallowed the other places whole. But the land is still barren here, the stars still shine. A small refuge for the old gods, I guess."

McCarter glanced at Danielle and then Verhoven, waiting for a derogatory comment or some quip about useless philosophy. But despite what McCarter thought, Verhoven actually smiled. "Then let's hope the old gods favor us," he said.

Out in the clearing the activity had stopped.

McCarter let his body grow still. His own quiet seemed to heighten his senses and he soon recognized a soft glow at the center of the camp and the dimly lit outline of a face, bathed in a strange, fluctuating glow. It took a moment before he understood: the soft light came from the perimeter warning system. The screen was flashing.

Verhoven saw it too. "Our friends are here."

His voice was low, but loud enough to wake the only other survivor from his team: Roemer.

McCarter thought to wake Susan, only to remember that she was gone. Another loss he hadn't come to grips with.

"Things could get ugly," Verhoven said. "If you see them, don't move. If they realize that we're prisoners, they might take pity on us. Or they might attack anyway. But if we fight, they'll slaughter us."

"And if they set the trees on fire?" McCarter asked, voicing his earlier fear.

"Then hope they kill you first."

As McCarter tried to block out the possibility, he looked toward the command center. He could make out Devers' face now; he was pointing into the distance.

A flare shot off directly to the west. It carried a half mile into the sky before deploying a small parachute and beginning a gentle float across the camp to the south.

"White flare," Verhoven said. "Trip-wire flare, not from the console. Something's in the forest out there."

The burning flare illuminated the camp. "I see eight soldiers," McCarter said.

"I counted eight as well," Danielle said.

"There are more," Verhoven said. "I know it. They just have their heads down, waiting for the attack.

"Any sign of the Chollokwan?" Danielle asked.

Verhoven twisted around for a better view of the forest behind them. "Not yet."

McCarter's eyes went from the clearing to the forest

and then back again, as another flare shot upward to the north. This time a red one, triggered by the sensors, or manually from the laptop. A rifle cracked, shattering the silence. A second later other weapons joined in, opening up at full tilt.

Things looked bad, and a minute later, when one of the Germans came bounding over to them, McCarter wondered if they were about to get decidedly worse.

The soldier who approached them had been sent at Kaufman's bidding. With an attack from the natives or the animals likely, the prisoners had suddenly become a problem for him. Kaufman didn't want to leave them at the tree, but he had nowhere else to secure them, and he didn't want them causing any problems in the middle of the battle. He'd chosen a compromise: leave them where they were, but send protection. This soldier had drawn the short straw and the unenviable task of guarding them during whatever was about to occur.

He walked up and kicked McCarter's legs.

"I'm awake," McCarter said, pulling his legs back.

"Good," the guard said. "Now be still." He waved the barrel of his rifle at the others. "All of you."

McCarter's eyes tracked the soldier. He was sick of being a prisoner, sick of being afraid. Verhoven had said something earlier about bringing one of them down to the ground, and from that point, a solid kick to the neck or temple would finish him. Maybe now was the time.

In the distance, Kaufman's men began firing again, staccato bursts here and there, probing, searching. The soldier guarding them glanced back toward the center of camp, and as he did, McCarter lunged at him, hoping to tackle him and pin him down.

The move surprised the guard, and also Danielle and Verhoven, but it came with too little thought. The chain and the weight of the others slowed him, and McCarter could only inflict a glancing blow. The soldier fell backward, but got up quickly, angrily.

He turned and cursed at McCarter, bringing the rifle up.

McCarter lowered his head. A shot rang out, but it was the mercenary who fell, collapsing like a rag doll.

The other rifles hammered away in the distance as McCarter opened his eyes and stared at the fallen man.

Danielle and Verhoven glanced around as well, and a second later a shape ran in from the depths of the forest. Verhoven spoke, "Bloody hell," he said.

"Seems like it," Hawker replied, grabbing the dead soldier and dragging him back behind the tree.

"You keep coming back from the dead, mate."

Danielle smiled. "Thank God. Can you get us out of here?"

"I'll try," Hawker said.

McCarter barely heard them. He was silent, virtually catatonic. He stared at the dead soldier: another life taken, in exchange for his own.

As the firing in the distance ceased, Hawker crouched beside the tree and began searching the dead man for keys. "Where are the others?"

"Dead," Danielle said. "Except Devers. He's with them."

"That explains a few things," Hawker said. He rolled the dead man over and dug into his back pockets.

"And Polaski?" Danielle asked.

Hawker paused and looked at her solemnly. "No, he didn't make it."

The radio beside them began to crackle.

"They might have heard the shot," Verhoven said. "They'll be coming. Get me out."

Hawker had finished his search empty-handed. "No keys."

Verhoven looked at the dead man. "Wrong bloke," he said. "Doesn't matter. Get me out."

Hawker weighed the consequences of Verhoven's request, while the demands from the radio increased.

"Come on!" Verhoven shouted. "Get me off this damn chain!"

The others could only guess at the subject of their discussion, but Hawker and Verhoven understood each other. Hawker stood up. "Which hand?"

"Left," Verhoven said, shifting position, resting his left hand sideways against the base of the tree, thumb up and smallest finger against the tree's roots. He pulled his other hand as far away as the cuffs would allow.

The others watched in confusion before turning away as Hawker lifted up a heavily booted foot and brought it crashing down on Verhoven's outstretched hand, crushing the bones and tearing the tendons and ligaments in the process.

Despite his obvious agony Verhoven didn't shout. He clenched his teeth and rolled to the side.

Hawker dropped down on him, pinning him and grabbing the wounded hand, crushing the fingers together in a way that would have been impossible moments before. He forced it through the cuff and out.

Verhoven spun away in agony, writhing in pain,

crawling on his knees and cradling the wounded hand. It would be useless now, but it no longer held him captive. Grunting and gritting his teeth, he turned toward Hawker, his eyes the slits of a mad dog.

"You'll need this," Hawker said, holding out the forty-five caliber gun.

Verhoven could not hold a rifle, but the black pistol fit in one hand. He snatched it from Hawker then watched as Hawker grabbed the dead German's rifle. "Two men armed," Verhoven said. "Better odds than I'd even dared to hope for."

"I've been watching for a little while," Hawker said, "but you'd better explain the situation."

"They've dug some foxholes in a circular pattern," Verhoven told him, pausing to fight off a wave of pain. "Six or seven, two soldiers in each, maybe fifty meters apart, sixty degrees of arc between each one. My bet: this bloke came from the closest one," he pointed. "Which might leave only one man there."

The radio crackled again and Hawker grabbed it. He caught only part of the call, but it was orders, not questions. The man talking wasn't looking for a response.

The clearing remained lit by the red flare up above, but it had drifted lower and southward on the wind, floating out beyond the tree line and over the forest. The angle of light left the prisoners in the shadows, but thirty yards out those shadows ended. There was too much light for a sneak attack and not enough time to wait for the flare to go out. "We'll get only one shot at this," he said. "Wait here."

Hawker put on the dead soldier's coat and the man's

distinctive foreign legion-style cap. He threw the rifle over his shoulder, straightened the coat.

"You must be mad," Verhoven said.

Hawker didn't reply. He'd already started into the clearing.

As he moved, a call came over the radio asking him what he was doing. *Why was he coming back?* Hawker put the radio to his mouth and clicked the switch on and off as he replied in his best German. It was a bad bluff, but he had no choice.

The calls from the other Germans stopped momentarily and Hawker continued toward the foxhole. A figure there waved at him to hurry up and he broke into a jog.

With the flare sinking low behind him, Hawker knew the mercenaries could only see his silhouette. He hoped they'd see their fellow soldier.

Thirty feet from the bunker, Hawker slowed. There were two soldiers in the foxhole, not one as Verhoven had guessed. Both had rifles in hand.

## CHAPTER 32

Surprised, Hawker continued forward. To turn around would be suicide. His eyes went from one soldier to the next and then to the tools they'd used to dig the ditch.

As he approached the edge, Hawker held up the radio, shaking it, hoping to reinforce the thought that it was broken and to draw their eyes away from his face. He tossed it to the closer of the two soldiers and then jumped into the bunker, landing beside a large shovel. He grabbed it with both hands, spinning around and swinging hard. The edged smashed into the bridge of the first man's nose, killing him instantly.

The other soldier jumped back, finding himself in the awkward position of offering a new radio to a man who was trying to kill him. He dropped the radio and tried to bring his rifle to bear, but before he could get off a shot, Hawker landed a blow with the shovel, knocking him down. A strike to the side of the head finished him off.

Hawker dropped down into the bunker and slumped against the crude dirt wall. Seconds later, the flare above burned out and the clearing went dark once again.

———————

Back at the tree Verhoven watched intently. He'd seen part of the struggle in the light of the flare and then nothing, no signal, no shooting, no sign of Hawker.

Beside him, McCarter had begun to escape the trance that he'd fallen into. Danielle fidgeted, trying to see. "What happened?" she asked.

"Don't know," Verhoven said.

"What do you see?"

"Nothing, he's out of sight."

Verhoven kept watching and the longer Hawker stayed down, the more Verhoven feared he might have been killed or badly injured. If that was the case, Verhoven would try to reach him and bring him back, a suicide mission if Kaufman's men spotted him. But Hawker had come back for them and Verhoven wouldn't let him die out there alone.

Finally, a pinprick of light hit his eyes, flashing on and off, tapping out a message in Morse code. *Move your ass!* It had to come from Hawker.

Without the flare, the darkness was complete, but their enemies had night scopes and he'd still make an easy target if he was spotted crossing the field.

Verhoven looked across to the center of camp. He could see the flashing of the defense console but nothing else. He guessed that each foxhole had a zone to cover, a distinct section of forest to watch. Under such conditions, a soldier's eyes were unlikely to stray. He ran, hoping this zone was the responsibility of the foxhole Hawker had taken.

As he jumped into the ditch, Verhoven took a quick look around. "Do they have the keys?"

"No keys," Hawker said. "But plenty of our stuff." Hawker held out a familiar set of night-vision goggles, NRI equipment.

"They ransacked everything when they took over," Verhoven said.

"Looking for something?"

"Seemed that way."

Hawker put the goggles up to his eyes and surveyed the camp. The foxholes were indeed set up in a circular pattern, just as Verhoven had described. He could see most of the soldiers in the other holes, scanning the perimeter and clutching their rifles. Each of them focused on a different zone.

"They don't know we're here," he guessed.

Beside them, the radio came to life, and in the same instant gunfire rang out from several rifles. The two men dove for cover.

"You sure about that?" Verhoven asked, looking up from the floor of the bunker.

The gunfire continued, but the sound wasn't right. The German guns were firing away from them. Verhoven poked his head above the edge of the pit cautiously. "Maybe they're trying to flush you out. I'm guessing that you set those flares, right?"

"I thought it would be helpful if they were looking for a target in the wrong direction."

"How'd you get past the sensors?" Verhoven asked.

"I still have my transponder," Hawker said. "Once I realized they were using our system. I just walked right through."

"Smart," Verhoven said. "And lucky."

Hawker nodded. "We could use a little bit of both right now."

Another order to fire came over the radio and the rifles lit up a section to the north. Hawker and Verhoven took cover again, but less severely this time.

"What the hell are they shooting at now?" Verhoven said.

"I have no idea," Hawker admitted. "But we better do something. Before they kill us by accident."

"We need to go forward," Verhoven said. "Take the command center. From there we can see all of them, and we'll be at their backs."

Hawker looked toward the center of the camp. "That's a long way."

Verhoven glanced at his hand and then across the open space. It was about seventy yards to the command center; he knew he wouldn't be able to fire an accurate shot across such a distance, not with a pistol, not in the dark. "Looks like this is my run."

Hawker nodded.

"When they open fire again," Verhoven said.

Hawker braced the rifle for a shot. "Stay to the right of my line."

Verhoven got in position to run, and the two men waited in silence for the mercenaries to fire again. A full minute ticked by and then another, but the radio and the German guns remained idle.

"Come on," Hawker whispered.

"Maybe they're done," Verhoven said.

That was a possibility Hawker didn't want to consider. He tightened his grip on the rifle, and squinted through the scope. The figures at the defense console were close to the screen, leaning into it, examining it carefully. He could hit them with ease, but in the silence of the night that would have given them away.

The silence lingered and Verhoven shook his head. "We're going to need a new plan."

"Like what?"

"I don't know but this isn't—"

Beside them the radio squawked and Verhoven pushed off, just as the guns began shredding a new section of rainforest.

Hawker braced the rifle, exhaled calmly and squeezed the trigger.

The first bullet hit one target square in the chest, eight inches below his Adam's apple. The man collapsed backward without a sound, just as Hawker fired again.

Running hard, Verhoven heard the second bullet whistle past. He saw the target fall and an instant later he was on them. He recognized Devers rolling on the ground clutching at a shoulder wound and the man who'd called himself Kaufman leaning over the body of one of his mercenaries, desperately trying to pull a rifle out from underneath the dead man.

At Verhoven's approach, Kaufman turned, only to be pistol-whipped across the side of the head. He fell awkwardly, stunned and moaning, only semiconscious.

Beside him, recognition hit Devers like an electric shock. Bullet wound and all, he lunged for the defense console where his own weapon lay, but Verhoven blocked him and shoved him back to the ground. He aimed the .45 at the linguist's head. "That's right, boy," he said. "This is going to be a bad night for you."

The firing in the distance stopped, perhaps saving Devers' life, and Verhoven heard Hawker come running up. He pointed to Kaufman. "You missed one."

"Looks like we both need to work on our counting," Hawker replied.

Verhoven turned to survey the field. From where they stood, a direct line could be drawn to each of Kaufman's foxholes, like spokes emanating from the center of a wheel. Leaving out the bunker they had just come from, there were five manned foxholes, with two mercenaries in four of the five and a solitary soldier in the fifth. The battle was far from over, but he and Hawker now held the advantages of surprise, position and control. Only the numbers were still against them, and that was about to change.

"They're still watching the trees," Verhoven said. "Waiting for the natives to come screaming through the forest like the bloody Zulus."

Verhoven's hand floated over the defense console as he waited for Hawker to get ready. "Too bad for them," Hawker said, steadying his rifle.

With the barrel of the .45, Verhoven casually flicked a switch and the world around them turned to daylight. In the same instant, Hawker drew a line and began to fire.

Kaufman's mercenaries were suddenly exposed, caught against the far walls of their foxholes and looking into the distance, their backs to Hawker and Verhoven. They heard firing but no orders, and they were confused by the sudden use of the floodlights.

They scrambled around, some of them reaching for their radios, others firing in various directions—out into the trees and across the clearing, almost everywhere but toward the center. Those who did turn around saw only the blinding glare of the spotlight. And in the swirling confusion they fell in rapid succession.

Hawker aimed and fired and retrained his rifle, turning rapidly from bunker to bunker. In ten quick seconds, four of the bunkers had gone silent. But before he could draw on the fifth, a spread of shells ripped through the equipment lockers beside him. He and Verhoven scrambled for cover.

"North side," Verhoven shouted. "That's all that's left."

Hawker ducked, turned and fired back.

The men in the bunker popped up and fired again, the bullets kicking up dirt and splintering part of a wooden crate. A stone hit Verhoven, stinging his neck. He put his hand to the spot to make sure he hadn't been hit, then fired back angrily as Hawker changed his position.

"Two at least," Verhoven shouted.

Amid the carnage, Kaufman began to move. "No," he growled, semicoherent and trying to stand. "No. You don't realize what you're doing."

Verhoven kicked him back to the ground as more bullets whipped past, blasting out one of the floodlights in a shower of embers. Hawker's return fire was more accurate and the mercenary who'd taken the shot fell, dead. The other soldier ducked back into the bunker.

"Listen to me," Kaufman begged. "We can stop this."

"Shut up!" Verhoven shouted.

It was too late. The last of Kaufman's men took a chance that he shouldn't have, stepping up for a shot.

Hawker pulled the trigger. The soldier stiffened at the bullet's impact, his rifle tilting skyward and firing straight up into the darkness. A second shot knocked him backward and he fell out of sight. The massacre was over.

## CHAPTER 33

Much like the night of the Chollokwan inferno, this battle ended with a shroud of smoke hanging in the air. In this case, there was also the acrid smell of gunpowder, exhaust from the flares and a growing swarm of moths and other insects flicking around the lights in a maddening, random dance.

In the dark void between the floodlights, Hawker and Verhoven turned from point to point, checking for any sign of life and warning Devers and Kaufman not to move.

Eventually Hawker lowered the rifle, his face a mask of despair. His friends were safe now, but at a terrible cost.

Verhoven seemed to sense the conflict within him. "This is what you are," he said. "Whatever you chose to believe, this is what you were made for."

Behind them Richard Kaufman spoke. "You don't know what you've done. You just don't know."

Hawker stepped toward him, putting the tip of the rifle under his chin and tilting his head up. "But I know what you've done, you son of a bitch. And I'm about to undo it. I'm going to go get my people free, and then I'm going to come back here, and I'm going to kill you."

Kaufman replied coldly, strangely confident for a man in such a position. "Go get your friends, then. You should, they can help. But don't waste your time if you plan on killing me, because without my help, none of you will make it out of here alive."

"We'll see about that," Hawker said. "Where are the keys?"

Kaufman gestured unsteadily toward the dead mercenary. "On him."

Hawker searched the man and pulled a set of keys from his breast pocket, testing the small key on Verhoven's remaining handcuff. It released and fell to the ground.

Hawker turned to go. "Kill the lights," he said.

Verhoven flicked the switch and the metal-halide bulbs faded to a dull orange and then went black. The artificial daylight vanished and the darkness rushed in again, swallowing them whole.

Hawker moved across the clearing quickly, traveling with the distinct impression that he was being watched—a feeling that had come and gone several times in the past few hours. He'd had a similar feeling at the Wall of Skulls. And he now wondered if Kaufman had additional men out there somewhere, if that was the basis for the man's arrogant boast. He stopped, taking cover in one of the foxholes and scanning the area with the night-vision scope. He didn't see anything.

Left behind at the command center, Verhoven moved to a position where he could better see his two prisoners. He waved the gun at Devers, instructing him to move closer to Kaufman.

Devers slid over, his good arm putting pressure on his injury, which was a through-and-through bullet hole in the fleshy part of his shoulder. "You could at least give me something to stop the blood," he said.

Verhoven looked at him with scorn. "I could," he said. "You're right about that."

Kaufman turned to Verhoven and began to plead his case. "Your friend won't listen but maybe you will," he said. "I can help you. But if you let him shoot me you'll never get out of—"

Verhoven bore into the man with his eyes. "Good men you've killed," he said, with a voice like gravel. "Mates of mine for twenty years. So you'd better hope he shoots you, because if he doesn't, I'll stake you to the ground, cut off your hands and leave you for the animals."

"You don't understand," Kaufman replied, slowly. "We're all in danger. Not just me. You, your friends, all of us. If you don't—"

A soft electronic beeping interrupted him. It came from the Perimeter Warning System. Something had set off one of the sensors.

Out in the clearing Hawker's radio squawked. *"Hawk, you listening? There was a target on the west side. It's gone now, but it was confirmed. Cut east before you go down toward the tree, that'll give you some distance from it.*"

Hawker looked through the night-vision scope again, still wondering about Kaufman's men and remembering they had been shooting into the forest long after his charade had ended. Could the Chollokwan really be closing in? He clicked the talk switch on his radio. "What kind of target? How far back?"

"*Target was a single. At the limit of the sensors. About fifty yards into the trees.*"

Hawker acknowledged and, after a quick glance to the west, did as Verhoven suggested, moving east in quick bursts, before stopping cold at a strange sound: the barely audible whine of a crying dog.

Back at the defense console, Kaufman's face seemed to contort. "Your friend's in danger," he said. "You should call him back."

"The screen's clear now," Verhoven replied.

"I don't think it matters," Kaufman said, quickly. "There are animals out there. Animals the natives use to hunt people like us, foreigners, infidels. The same animal that attacked my people in the cave."

Verhoven glared at him. When Kaufman had told them of Susan's death, he'd called it an accident, a collapse in the cave's roof. At the time, all Verhoven really cared about was escape, and he'd been privately pleased that Kaufman had lost five of his people in exchange for the young woman.

"Not a cave-in, then, ay?"

"I know," Kaufman said. "I lied. But you have to listen. They were mauled."

Verhoven recalled the looks on some of the soldiers' faces after the incident. He'd seen fear—not the kind of fear an accident brings but the unease of an ethereal danger, one that cannot be completely controlled. It had struck him as odd at the time, and now Kaufman's words had him wondering. He guessed that was Kaufman's goal. "Shut up," he said. "I'm tired of your mouth."

Hawker's voice came over the radio. Verhoven could hear the dogs whining in the background. They were fearful, pathetic sounds, nothing like the sound the dogs had made when the Chollokwan arrived.

*"I need the lights,"* Hawker said.

Verhoven checked his watch. "Can't do it."

"Call him back," Kaufman said. "Our only chance is to hole up here with the rest of the guns."

"Shut up."

*"Bring up the damn lights."*

"Five minutes," Verhoven said, reminding Hawker of the cool-down period. The lights burned so hot that they needed five minutes to cool off before re-lighting, otherwise the hot filaments would blow out with the power surge.

"Forget the others," Kaufman said. "They're as good as dead."

"Shut your damn mouth!" Verhoven shouted. From seventy yards away, he could hear the dogs' cries drifting through the still night air. And then a sharp call echoed across the clearing, similar to the Chollokwan wail, but more powerful, more resonant.

Inhuman.

"They're coming," Kaufman insisted. "They'll kill him and then us. Call him back!"

Verhoven swung the pistol toward Kaufman. "One more word and I'll blow your goddamned head off."

Staring at the black pistol, Kaufman complied, but even as he did the perimeter alarm began chirping again. A new target had appeared. This one directly across from where Hawker stood.


Hawker had come across the section of camp where the dogs were kept. They called it the kennel, but it was nothing more than a heavy post driven into the ground, to which the animals were tied. The dogs had grown agitated during the battle, barking angrily at the gunfire, but they'd settled down in the minutes after. Something new was bothering them. Something they could sense and smell but not understand.

They sniffed the air with flared nostrils, their eyes darting around. They seemed confused and afraid. Hawker's approach startled them, but they recognized his scent and then turned back toward the trees. One lowered its head, growling and baring its teeth, but the rest of the pack began retreating, backing away from the trees and whatever they smelled. When they reached the limit of the leashes, they began straining against the lines, pulling and stretching them. One of them began to panic, yelping and crying and whipping its head around, trying desperately to slip its lead.

*What the hell is out there?* Hawker wondered. He'd never seen a pack of dogs act like this.

Verhoven's voice came over the radio. "Target straight across from you. Two of them now."

A loud screech echoed from somewhere back in the woods and Hawker put the night-vision goggles to his eyes. He saw nothing.

One of the dogs howled.

"It's right in front of you," Verhoven insisted.

"Shoot it," It was Kaufman's voice, tinny and hollow from somewhere behind Verhoven. "Shoot the damn thi—"

Verhoven cut the line and, to Hawker's right, a twig cracked.

The dogs shot forward, charging at something still hidden within the trees. Hawker spun and fired blindly, shooting into the tree line. Whatever had been there was racing south, away from Hawker and the dogs and directly toward the prisoners, still chained to the tree.

Hawker cut across the camp, sprinting with everything he had. He'd covered only half the distance when the shadow in the forest reached the prison tree.

Hideous screams rang out, the voices of his friends shouting in terror and the sound of a horrendous struggle. Two flares rocketed into the sky behind him, fired by Verhoven. The phosphorous canisters burst into light and something lunged at Hawker's face, stretching out toward him like a cobra trying to strike. Hawker dove to the side and the jaws snapped shut on nothing but air. He rolled and came up firing, blasting the thing as it raced away and disappeared into the trees.

He whipped around toward his screaming friends, just in time to see another shape fleeing from the space. It was bulky and black and dragging something with it.

Hawker aimed and fired, lacing shells into the trees, trying to track the thing by the sounds of its movement, trying to lead it, but it was gone, vanished into the jungle and gone.

Danielle shouted to him. "Hawker!"

He ran over, dropping down beside her and unlocking her cuffs. Handing her the key, he stood guard while she freed the others. He lit a flare of his own and flung it out into the forest, hoping to light up anything that might come their way. The shadows flickered and jumped, but the jungle itself was still.

He glanced at the prisoners. Danielle and McCarter appeared unharmed. Brazos, the last of the porters, was alive but injured and struggling to stand. Roemer, Verhoven's right-hand man, was gone. His cuffs lay on the jungle floor, bands of bloody skin shaved off and clinging to their edges. Something had ripped him from their hold.

In the far distance, they heard him scream.

"It dragged him right out," Brazos said. "It bent my leg, my knee."

McCarter helped Brazos to steady himself, as he could put no weight on the leg.

"What the hell was that?" Hawker asked. "A jaguar?"

"Not a cat," Brazos said. "It stank, dank and rotten."

Danielle agreed. "Whatever the hell it was, we need to get out of here before it comes back,"

Brazos hobbled and leaned on McCarter, his knee swelling where the animal had trampled him as it pulled Roemer from the cuffs.

"Get to the command center," Hawker said. "Verhoven's there."

Without a word the survivors moved off, Brazos leaning on McCarter and Danielle. Hawker stayed behind, backing away from the forest, guarding their retreat. He glanced at the ground. The two-pronged tracks were unmistakable, the same tracks Verhoven had seen near the butchered animals, just before the Chollokwan attack.

The sound of human screaming reached him from deep in the bush. Hawker loosed a few shots in that direction, hoping to hit the animal or even the tortured soul it had taken with it, but he wasn't going out there.

A minute later, at the center of camp, Richard Kaufman saw Hawker coming, saw the purpose in his step and the fury. He wedged himself against one of the light poles to stand. "I tried to tell—"

Hawker slammed him back against the pole before he could finish. "What the hell was that thing?"

Kaufman opened his mouth and blood trickled from the corner. He'd bitten through part of his tongue. "I don't know what they are," he said, turning to spit some blood onto the dirt. "They attacked my people in the cave."

"What cave?" Hawker demanded.

"Beneath the temple," Kaufman said. "They seem to guard this place. We could have killed them, but now that you've interfered there probably aren't enough of us left to do the job. Once they feed on your friend, they'll be back for the rest of us. And if what I've heard is correct, the natives who tried to burn you out will come along with them. Only this time they won't hold back."

Kaufman turned his head and spat out another mixture of blood and saliva. With his hands now taped together, the best he could do was wipe the side of his mouth against his shoulder. He addressed Danielle. "It seems you've brought your people in unprepared."

"I don't know what the hell you're talking about," she said.

"Oh, I think you do," Kaufman replied.

With the point of the rifle, Hawker physically turned Kaufman's face away from Danielle. "You were talking to me," he said.

Kaufman wanted to throw a few more shots at Danielle, enough to start her worrying about the lack of candor shown to her charges, enough to set the groundwork for a deal. And this was the time for it, but as he looked into Hawker's burning eyes, he realized the man was unlikely to let him go on for long. He chose to proceed, hoping that Hawker's response would not be fatal or otherwise permanent.

"Just pawns in the game, Ms. Laidlaw?"

Even before the last syllable had escaped his mouth, Hawker's knee came crashing into his gut. Kaufman crumpled to the ground. As he rolled on the floor, mute and in pain, his eyes focused on Danielle.

She returned his stare, unblinking, and then turned toward the flashing screen of the laptop. The perimeter alarm had begun sounding once again.

## CHAPTER 34

The NRI survivors spent the night crowded around the defense console, watching the perimeter for trouble. They had only two rifles and Hawker's pistol for defense, but no one wanted to go out into the darkness to retrieve the weapons carried by the fallen men.

During the balance of the night the alarm went off a dozen times. Each time, the dogs howled, Verhoven brought the lights up and Hawker fired a handful of shots in the direction of the targets. Sometimes the targets scattered and other times they lingered, drifting slowly backward into the clutter of the forest until they disappeared from the screen; their true nature, as animal or man, went unrevealed.

No one slept and few words were spoken. As the hours wore on, a type of fear began to seep into every heart. Until eventually the sky's black hue began to change. When the sun finally rose it brought with it a palpable sense of relief—as if it had physically banished the danger to some other realm, along with the darkness and the Mayan Lords of the Night. In that moment, McCarter felt an instant kinship with the ancient peoples he had long studied. He understood now, on a primal level, why so many of them had worshipped the sun.

Beside him, Hawker stood. "I need someone's help."

Danielle answered, "For what? Where are you going?"

Hawker pointed to the clearing. "We have to look for survivors."

Danielle narrowed her gaze. "Do you think there are any?"

"We need their guns," he explained. "And we need to be sure that they're dead. And if any of them happen to be alive . . . then we need to help them . . . if we can."

To McCarter, the absurdity of the situation was plain in Hawker's voice. He and Verhoven had spent the night doing all they could to kill these men, to make certain there were no survivors. They had shot most of them in the back in a surprise attack, without the option of mercy or surrender. Now, to the extent they might have failed, they would turn around and do what they could to help anyone who might have survived.

His own heart heavy with the carnage, McCarter volunteered to join the search. He and Hawker moved across the clearing from foxhole to foxhole, recovering eleven German-made Hechler-Koch rifles, a dozen crates of ammunition and their own forfeited Kalashnikovs.

McCarter watched as Hawker checked the fallen men for signs of life, then silently pulled dog tags and ID packets from those who carried them. There was sadness in Hawker's actions, as if the dead had been comrades of his rather than enemies. McCarter wondered what Hawker would do with the items he'd taken. Perhaps he'd send them to some authority or to the governments of the nations that might be listed on their papers.

"I guess even mercenaries have families," he whispered.

If Hawker heard him, he did not respond.

In the last foxhole they found a survivor, a blond-haired man with a reddish beard, who was minimally conscious and highly disoriented. The left side of his face was caked with dried blood, and judging from the gash and the bruising, either a bullet had caught the edge of his face or a ricochet had hit him square with enough force to knock him out and yet leave him alive. He put one hand up weakly, signaling his surrender.

"Do you speak English?" Hawker asked.

The man shook his head. "Deutsch."

*"Wie nennen sie Sie?"* Hawker asked. *What do they call you?*

"Eric," the man replied.

Hawker checked him for weapons and then helped him walk to where the others waited. While Danielle tended to him, Hawker and McCarter dragged the dead men to the bunker farthest downwind and buried the bodies with the soil that had been excavated from it.

When they returned to the group McCarter asked the question on all of their minds. "What do we do now?"

"We get the hell out of here," Hawker said. "Before anything else happens. See if you can find our shortwave or any type of radio that these guys might have brought in." He pointed to Kaufman. "Take him with you, he could probably tell you where to look. If he causes you any trouble, shoot him."

"I'll do that part," Verhoven volunteered.

Kaufman stood, silent and seething. With his hands still taped together, he led McCarter and Verhoven toward another section of the camp.

As they departed, Hawker stepped away, wandering out among the ruins of the camp, looking for room to think. Before long, he came across a loose pile of mud-covered equipment, items that Kaufman's people had picked up on their metal detectors and summarily unearthed. The equipment was modern, untouched by rust and disturbingly familiar.

He crouched to examine one particular piece, scraping at the mud caked on its side. As clumps flaked off, the stamping became visible. *TSC: Texas Sounding Corp.* He shook his head in disgust. TSC was an NRI contracted supplier of equipment. Some of the equipment he'd flown in for Danielle and McCarter bore the same label.

"Of course," he said.

"I wanted to thank you," a voice said from behind him, one he recognized as Danielle's.

"For what?"

"For coming back to get us. For shutting Kaufman up last night."

"Don't thank me," he said, turning. "I already knew what he was going to say."

He noticed her eyes, locked onto the device he held. "How much did they know?" he asked. "As much as we do? Less, maybe?"

"How much did *who* know?"

"The group you sent out before us," he said. "The ones who left this behind."

She was silent.

"This is an ultrasound receiver," he said. "I loaded one just like it the other day. Brought it out for Mc-Carter. It didn't work right, but it's the same exact piece of gear, the same manufacturer. Direct from the NRI equipment list."

He held the receiver up. "This is how you knew to bring an army with you," he explained. "You had another team out here before us. And you lost them."

She folded her arms across her chest. At least she wasn't denying it. That was a step in the right direction. "You should have told me."

"What difference would it have made?" she said.

"You lose a group in the field and it raises the threat level."

She arched her brow. "People shooting at us, dead bodies in the river; that wasn't enough for you?"

She was right, it should have been. He hated everything that had happened, all that had been lost. His heart wanted someone else to blame, but he knew the part he'd played. "What happened to them?"

"I don't know," she said. "They stopped reporting about fifty miles from here. And they weren't headed in this direction at the time." She looked eastward, the direction she'd led the team in from. "They didn't know about the Wall of Skulls, they didn't have the information we had, so how the hell they found this place is beyond me. But apparently they did. After that . . ." She shrugged. "Your guess is as good as mine. The natives . . . those animals . . . I don't know."

Hawker looked around at the carnage, thinking of the men he'd just buried. He hadn't even counted up their own dead yet. "How many have we lost?"

"All the porters except Brazos, all of Verhoven's men," she said. "Polaski, Susan." She shook her head. "They came in firing. A helicopter first, followed by men on the ground. For a while I thought we'd lost you as well."

Hawker looked at her. "When I started back here, I was pretty sure I'd find you all dead," he said. He looked away, thankful that some of them were still alive, but drained by the cost. "We should have never brought these people here. We both knew this was a possibility."

"I know," she said. "And that's on me. But we can't leave yet. Now that we're back in control, we have to find what we came here for. We have to finish this."

He was stunned. "Are you out of your mind?"

"The worst is over, Hawker."

"The worst is not over," he said. "Did you listen to Kaufman, were you even here last night? Do you want to see whatever those things were again? Do you want to be here when the natives come storming in, intent on hacking us to pieces? Those threats are still out there. And don't forget about Kaufman. I don't care what he says, that son of a bitch has other people hiding somewhere. When they don't hear from him for a while, they're going to come looking. You want to wait around for that?"

"Not really, but we still have a job to do."

"Fine," he said. "We can take these people out of here and come back with a new team; you can bring a battalion of Marines if you want to. Then you can get whatever the hell you're after and nobody else has to die."

"Too late for that," she said. "Our cover's blown.

And if Kaufman does have partners out there somewhere, they'll be in and out before we can even get back to Manaus. It's now or never."

He needed her to see reason, to see the danger instead of the goal. When he spoke again his tone was more subdued. "You have to understand: we won last night because Kaufman's people were looking for a different kind of fight. That made them easy targets. We won't be that lucky next time."

She hesitated, glancing across the camp to where Kaufman was walking with McCarter and Brazos. "I'm sorry for everything that's happened here. More than you can know. You probably won't believe me, but I didn't want anything to do with this damn expedition in the first place. But in our business you go where they send you and you do what they tell you. And right now I have orders to bring back what we came here for. Regardless of the cost or consequences, remember? Everything we came for is within our grasp. We just have to get back in there and grab it."

"Grab what?" he asked. He didn't expect an answer, but she gave him one anyway.

"Somewhere down in that cave," she said, "there's a power source. An energy-producing system that we can study and use to create working cold fusion power cells. I'm not at liberty to tell you how it got there, but I promise you it's not a joke. The crystals Martin brought back were slightly radioactive, our tests proved that they had undergone a low-level fusion reaction. They'd either been exposed to it or were part of it."

He stood back, shocked. "Why would such a thing be out here?"

"Somebody put it here," she explained. "That's all I can tell you. That, and that if we find it, we can change the way humanity lives. Global warming, wars for oil, pollution. We can put an end to all of that. Think of it like the Manhattan Project, only the other way around. We can become life, the healers of the world," she said, reversing Oppenheimer's famous quote.

Hawker listened to the words and found his mind reeling. He brought a hand to his temple and rubbed at a stabbing pain.

"Look," she said, "I know you don't trust the system. And why should you? They burned you for something, exiled you. I don't even know what it was; I have a fifty-page file on you and two-thirds of it's blacked out. But from what I've seen, you do what you think is right, even when it costs you."

"Not always," he assured her.

"The point is, that's what I'm trying to do here," she said. "And if you help me, I promise you, it will be worth it. This is your chance, Hawker. It may be the last chance you ever get. You can change your life and if you look at it from the bigger picture, you can change a lot of lives."

The bigger picture. It was something he'd always had a hard time focusing on, especially when the smaller, local picture was so painful to see.

"Hawker," she continued, "I know you want to leave, to take everyone home. But if you go, they will stamp this file closed as a failure and things will be worse for you. Not by my doing," she insisted. "God knows I owe you my life. But those same people who exiled you, they still run things, and they have an interest in this. And they will want someone to blame. This time exile won't be enough. They'll come for you. They'll hound you."

He turned away, angry and confused. *Tell them to bring it on,* he thought, catching the words just before they could escape his mouth. "People are dying out here," he said. "Good people—our people. You lied and I helped you lie and we walked them, smiling, right into hell. If you don't think there's going to be a price to pay for that, then you are sadly in the dark."

"Don't you think I know that?" she said. "People I cared about are dead as well. Leaving won't bring them back. But finishing the job will make their sacrifice have some purpose."

She gazed into his eyes. "I have to go back in there, Hawker. Whether you want to or not, *I* have to. I'll go in alone if you make me. But I'm not leaving here empty-handed."

He could feel the price getting steeper for both of them. "Before this is over," he warned, "I think you're going to wish you had."

She looked at the ground and then briefly back up at him before turning and marching away, off toward the center of camp.

Hawker shook his head, dropping the piece of equipment he'd found and kicking it across the clearing in frustration. It skipped and rolled and then broke into several pieces. For a long moment, he stared at the shattered remnants as if they held some great meaning.

It took the sound of distant shouting to tear him away.

Professor McCarter was running across the camp,

carrying something and waving. McCarter arrived at Danielle first. They spoke briefly before he took her by the hand and led her back toward Hawker. By the time they reached him, McCarter was out of breath.

"We've got to go back inside the temple," he said, panting. "We've got to do it now."

Hawker shook his head in disbelief. "This is like some kind of disease with you guys."

McCarter didn't waste time explaining; instead, he held out a bright orange object he'd been carrying: Kaufman's ELF radio. He turned the volume up.

"Can anybody hea . . . ? Mr . . . aufman . . . please answer . . ." It was Susan Briggs, attempting to reach Kaufman on the low-frequency transmitter.

"She's alive," McCarter said. "We can hear her transmission, but she can't hear ours. She hasn't responded to anything we've sent."

"Where?" Hawker asked. "How?"

"She's in the cave beneath the temple somewhere, and if Kaufman's right, those animals are in there with her. She'll never make it out on her own. We have to go in and get her. We have to go now."

Hawker glanced sideways at Danielle; both of them knew what this meant: she would get her chance to explore the cave after all. "You must have nine lives," he said to her. "Try not to forget which number you're on."

## CHAPTER 35

In the darkness of the cave beneath the temple, Hawker stood back from the edge of the lake and gazed into the clear water ahead of him. The bottom was lined with a smooth layer of whitish calcite, dotted in random places by pea-sized spheres called cave pearls. And in the glare of his flashlight, everything shimmered as if covered in a coat of wet lacquer.

He redirected his light toward the ceiling, forty feet above. Different formations loomed there: huge stalactites hanging in clumps, great daggers of stone pointed toward them, some of them fifteen feet long, three feet thick at the base. Cutting between them was an angled row of smaller, jagged spikes, like an endless row of shark's teeth, a formation known as a welt line, and farther off an array of delicate strands called soda straws dangled from an overhang, their tips glistening with moisture.

"Hell of a cave," he said. The words echoed.

Behind him McCarter, Danielle and Verhoven were reaching the same conclusion. "Sulfur cave," McCarter said, shining his own flashlight around. "Most caves are formed from limestone, but some are carved from the rock by the effects of sulfuric acid. Lechugila in New Mexico for instance. That might explain the acidic water in the bottom of the well. This water too."

Hawker scanned the water with his light. He and Verhoven had viewed Lang's recording several times and they'd heard large splashes. They knew the danger came from the water, but the immediate area seemed to be clear.

"Which way?" Danielle asked.

Hawker pointed. "There's a pathway on the right; it leads to the other side."

He clipped his flashlight to the barrel of his rifle. The others followed suit, except for Verhoven, who carried a different weapon—a pump-action Mossberg shotgun lifted from Kaufman's arsenal. His right hand held the trigger, his swollen left hand duct-taped to the pump, tight enough that he could reload it.

They moved onto the pathway, traveling in a single file and watching the water for any sign of danger. Hawker had the point, with Danielle right behind him. She wore a small backpack stuffed with equipment while a portable Geiger counter strapped to her leg clicked away softly.

"Just a precaution," she'd explained. "The Martin crystals showed traces of radioactive contamination. So does the soil up above."

"Thanks for telling us."

"Don't worry," she said. "It's all low level. We'd have to stay here for years to be affected."

If there was one thing Hawker was sure of it was that they wouldn't be sticking around that long. He continued on, following the rugged pathway to the dam. The seven pools and the smooth stone of the plaza lay just beyond.

Hawker stopped. "The last images on the recording were of this place. You ready?" he asked Verhoven.

Verhoven nodded. "You know those shells won't do much beyond a depth of five or six feet."

"Yeah," Hawker replied. "But it'll be a hell of a wake-up call if anything's down there."

Verhoven nodded. "I'll watch your back."

Hawker moved away, stepping onto the dam, scanning the lake and then turning his back to it. Verhoven took a position at the end of the structure, poised and ready should something come at Hawker from the lake behind.

Hawker stepped up to the first pool, fired two quick bursts into it and then jumped back, waiting for some reaction.

The sound of the gunfire boomed through the cave and echoed back at them from the darkness, vibrating in receding, diminishing waves, but nothing moved in the pool. One down, six to go.

Hawker stepped toward the other pools and repeated the procedure until the entire honeycomb arrangement was clear. It appeared that the pools were empty.

He stepped off the dam and made a quick inspection of the surrounding area. Satisfied, he gave the all-clear.

"Strange formation," McCarter said. "Seven pools. I wonder: Seven Caves, Seven Canyons."

Danielle acknowledged him. "And the Place of Bitter Water," she said.

Hawker aimed his flashlight across the plaza and into the cave beyond. Fronted by the lake, the plaza stretched sideways for at least a hundred feet, with the back edge hard against the cave's stone wall. On the side closest to them lay the dam and the pools and more open cave. On the far side, the broken trail of the pathway seemed to continue into a deeper section of the cavern. Hawker guessed that would be the way to go.

He brought the beam of his light back across the plaza, toward the path they'd just come down. He stopped. Ripples were moving slowly across the surface of the lake, a surface that had been like glass only moments before. His eyes darted back and forth, as he swung the beam of light through the depths of the cave and back out over the water once again.

"What's wrong?" Danielle asked.

"Something disturbed the water," he said. "Went in or came out."

The dried swaths of blood on the stone showed that both victims had been killed in the open part of the plaza. Not a good place to stand. "Come on," he said. "We need cover."

Hawker led them to the back of the plaza, to a spot where the smooth floor butted up against the jagged natural stone of the wall. They pressed themselves against it, with Hawker on the right end and Verhoven on the left and the broad open space of the plaza in front of them. It was a good spot tactically, nothing could come at them from behind, only from the sides and front, and that would leave any attacker open to a withering fire.

"You see anything?" Verhoven asked.

"Just the water."

Verhoven went to speak again but stopped as muted

noise reached their ears, a scraping sound, a raspy scratching, like stone dragged across stone.

Danielle switched off the Geiger counter so they could listen.

"What was that?" McCarter whispered.

No one could say. But their eyes darted around in search of its source, their lights crisscrossing in the dark.

The sound returned. Two long, slow scrapes, preceded by a strangely muted click.

The group fell into utter silence, barely breathing, their eyes straining into the dark.

"What if it's Susan?" McCarter asked. They had tried to reach her on the radio several times since entering the cave, but to no avail. "What if there was a cave-in and she's trapped and trying to signal us? Avalanche victims are found like that sometimes."

Hawker listened as the sounds were heard once again. "It's not her," he said.

"Are you sure?" McCarter asked. "It could—"

"The sounds are overlapping," Hawker said. "There's more than one source."

From out of the darkness the scraping noise whispered to them, soft but unmistakable now: *click, click, scrape, scrape.*

"Where the hell is it coming from?" Danielle asked, her eyes darting back and forth.

It was a fair question. With the strange acoustics of the cave, the noise seemed to be coming from everywhere at once. *Click, click ... scrape, scrape, click, click.*

To Hawker's left, Danielle and McCarter struggled to keep still. He ignored them, grimly sweeping his field of view. He knew Verhoven would be doing the same, and that, armed and waiting with their backs pressed to the wall, they were in a good position. Whatever was out there, stalking them, crawling from the edge of the lake or moving toward them from the farther depths of the cave, it would have to cross the open ground before it could strike.

"Stay against the wall," he whispered. "Whatever happens, stay back against the wall and out of our way."

*Click, click, scrape, scrape.* Louder this time, closer.

Danielle and McCarter pressed into the stone.

Hawker squinted into the darkness, waving the light around. To the right side—his side—the plaza ran for sixty feet before the jagged teeth of the cave took over once again. Beyond that, the cave opened up and a long finger of the lake appeared to stretch into the rocky formations beyond. That area offered the only real cover for anything approaching them, but a near-constant watch had caught nothing. "On your side, Pik."

Verhoven shook his head. "I don't think so."

*Click, click.*

"Has to be."

Verhoven bristled. "I'm telling you, there's nothing over here."

The hollow scraping sound reached them once again, slower and muted. And then there was only silence, more dreaded before long than the sounds that had come before it.

In that lingering quiet they waited, straining for any sign of danger, listening for the faintest sound.

But they saw nothing and heard nothing; there was

no movement, no clicking, only the pounding of their hearts, the rhythmic dripping of water in the distance and the unearthly feeling of time standing on end.

The stone floor glistened with moisture and the heavy sulfur fumes lingered in the air, but nothing in the cave was moving.

Hawker scanned to the left, to make sure Verhoven hadn't missed anything, and then back to the right. *What the hell are we missing?*

As this question ran through his head, a minuscule flash caught the corner of his eye: a speck of dust falling through the beam of Danielle's flashlight, flaring incandescently as it passed, like a microscopic shooting star. Only now did he realize their folly. He looked up.

"Move!"

He grabbed Danielle and slung her out of the way as a shadow dropped from the ceiling fifty feet above. The animal hit the ground where she'd been standing, slashing the back of her calf with the sweep of its claws even as Hawker pulled her away. The group scattered, beams of light swaying wildly in the darkness as claws and teeth flashed and strings of vile saliva swung through the air.

The animal spun and lunged at McCarter.

A slug from Verhoven's shotgun sent it reeling across the floor.

"Look out!" McCarter shouted.

A second beast had dropped in behind Verhoven. As it launched itself toward his back, flashes erupted from the barrel of Hawker's rifle, staccato bursts lighting the cave in a strobelike effect. The bullets tore into the beast as it flew through the air and slammed down on Verhoven.

He tumbled forward as Hawker fired again. The animal shrieked and jumped. And as McCarter's light hit its eyes, the thing hissed, spitting at him and shooting off into the darkness with a trail of bullets chasing it.

The beams of light crisscrossed in the dark. The sounds of the animals scurrying and hissing competed with the heavy footsteps of the men, shouts of warning and the booming sound of gunfire echoing through the chamber.

By now, Danielle had crawled back to the wall. Her leg was cramping, the muscles burning from the pain. She pulled out a flare and threw it across the plaza. The flash of the magnesium blinded at first but as the crimson light filled the cave, it exposed one shape sliding into the lake, another animal pulling its damaged body across the stone of the plaza and a third still on the ceiling, scampering away from the scene of the battle, its claws hooking into the crags in the cave's roof, its back to the lake below.

"Hawker!" Danielle shouted, pointing to the ceiling.

Hawker twisted, sighted the creature and fired. It shrieked in pain—the voice of some tropical bird amplified a thousand times over. Its hind legs lost their grip and it dangled for a second as Hawker fired again. Hit a second time, the animal fell toward the lake, howling in agony. A stream of broken ceiling fragments followed it down as it crashed into the water with a thunderous splash.

Hawker now understood what had happened. The animals had come out of the water, gone up the side walls and stalked the humans from their inverted positions on the ceiling above. The clicking noise was the sound of the animals' claws grabbing and releasing the stone; the scraping, their stiff bodies sliding between the stalactites and other formations.

He scanned the ragged surface above. Stalactites and other projections guarded the pockmarked surface, making it impossible to search quickly or completely from a single location. His slid sideways, craning his neck around. Twenty feet away McCarter did the same, while Danielle threw out another flare.

As the others searched the ceiling, Verhoven got back on his feet. He'd landed on his wounded hand and it throbbed with a pain beyond anything he could have imagined. The tape holding it to the shotgun had been partially torn, but Verhoven managed to load one more shell before ripping the hand angrily from the pump. He scanned the plaza around him and then glanced briefly at the ceiling above. With no sign of danger, he turned his attention to the cause of his pain; the injured animal wriggling spastically on its side, desperately trying to drag itself to the lake.

Verhoven walked toward it, cursing as he struggled to shake loose the remaining tape. When he reached the creature, he aimed carefully and then blasted a slug through its skull. The thing slumped instantly to the floor.

With great satisfaction, Verhoven lowered the Mossberg. The others were still searching the ceiling. He made another quick scan himself and then a smirk came out. "They're gone," he shouted, the buoyancy of a conqueror in his voice. "Dead or gone, take your pick."

Verhoven had been in more firefights than he could count. Each one had its own unique pace; this battle was no different. With one animal dead, and the others gone, wounded and bleeding back into the lake, he could feel the energy of the fight dissipating already, blowing past like a storm on the wind. He took a final look around, ground level and roof above. They were in the clear. He walked back to Danielle.

"You all right?"

Danielle was sitting, first-aid kit by her side, pouring hydrogen peroxide on the slash across her calf. "I'll live," she said, as the peroxide bubbled and foamed.

Verhoven turned to where McCarter and Hawker were systematically checking the ceiling. "Give it up," Verhoven shouted. "You're liable to get hurt swinging your necks around like a bunch of bloody pelicans."

McCarter paused in his search, took a few more peeks, then lowered his rifle and started back toward the others. But beyond his position, Hawker continued checking the deeper part of the cave, systematically scanning the shadows between the chandeliers of hanging stone.

Verhoven laughed. "Paranoid," he said.

He turned back to Danielle, examining her injury. "A good war wound, that. Make you a nice scar." Danielle glared at him and Verhoven laughed again, more animated than any of them had seen.

On his way back to the others, McCarter stopped for a closer look at the animal that Verhoven had killed. It lay on its side, very much dead, but still twitching in places. Dark fluids oozed from its wounds and an oddly pungent odor wafted from its body. The smell reminded McCarter of rotting vegetables. At close range the scent was strong enough to compete with the sulfur of the cave.

This animal was smaller than the one that had attacked them on the chain the night before. Maybe half the size. It looked sort of gangly and long in the limbs, almost like a juvenile. He guessed its weight at two hundred pounds, though it had seemed much larger as it dropped toward them.

He examined what was left of its head, damaged badly by the shotgun blast that had killed it, a blast that would have disintegrated a human skull. The head was large in proportion to the animal's size, and very angular, almost wedge-shaped, narrowing sharply at the front. Its remaining eye was unlidded, glistening beneath a viscous gel, like a polished, wet stone. It was black from head to toe, with stripes of a slightly lighter shade that were mostly visible as differently textured skin. The surface of the skin itself was slick with some type of dark secretion, which it seemed to be oozing from millions of tiny pores.

Whatever it was, it was unlike anything McCarter had ever seen or heard of. Even the shape was foreign. The body was all angles, like overlapping plates. The arms and legs were thick, but the joints were simple and exposed, like hinges on a door, one slot for the lower half and one slot for the upper. Muscular sinew could be seen where they bent, like bundled wires in a conduit. The severely pinched neck seemed almost insectlike and behind it stood distinct rows of stiff, bristlelike hairs that grew in a converging V-shaped pattern.

An evil-looking thing, McCarter thought, with all the tools of a predator: stereoscopic vision, a sleek, strong body, claws that resembled angled steel blades. Its mouth hung open on a set of powerfully muscled jaws and was filled with teeth like sharpened railroad spikes.

McCarter looked up toward the ceiling, upon which the animals had been crawling. The image of that ancient Mayan painting came to him, humans standing erect on the ground, blithely unaware of the Xibalbans directly beneath them, walking inverted with their feet on the underside of the earth's surface. *If I knew something like this lived down here,* he thought, *I'd consider this the underworld too.*

As he shook off a chill, Danielle and Verhoven came up beside him, gawking at the thing, just as he had. Danielle seemed especially interested in the entry wounds from Verhoven's shot. The damage resembled a pane of glass punctured by an errant baseball, with long fissures radiating from the wounds.

With the barrel of her rifle, Danielle reached out and pushed on the body. It was stiff. She tapped on it. It almost sounded hollow. "An exoskeleton," she said. "Bones on the outside. Large animals don't grow like this. Only insects and crustaceans."

"It's a damn gogga, then," Verhoven said, using the Afrikaner slang for crawling bugs.

McCarter nudged Verhoven and pointed out a broad purple smear on his jacket, where the animal had hit him. The fibers of the coat were fraying and discolored, as if the smear was corrosive.

"Some kind of secretion," Danielle said. "It's all over the body of this one."

As Verhoven pulled off the field jacket and tossed it

aside, Danielle leaned closer to the animal. "Do you smell that?"

McCarter nodded. "Almost like ammonia," he said. "I smelled it when the other one attacked us last night. But this is a lot stronger, even though this one is smaller."

Danielle nodded, looking back toward the pools by the dam. "I was thinking the same thing," she said. "And I think I know why. Ammonia is a base, an acid neutralizer. I think that's what this thing is secreting—only, from the way it's destroying that fabric, I'm guessing it's a lot stronger than ammonia."

"What good would that do them?" Verhoven asked.

Danielle nodded toward the pools. "That's how they survive. They secrete this stuff to counteract the acid."

McCarter remembered trying to help his son learn chemistry and repeated trips to the science department to ask fellow professors questions he could not answer. Bases were just as dangerous as acids. When the two were combined they would neutralize each other, but individually acids were corrosive and bases were caustic. Both were horrendously destructive to organic tissue and to materials far stronger than human skin. He turned to Danielle. Her calf was exposed where she'd cut off the torn section of the pant leg. Her skin was red but not blistering. "What about your leg?"

Danielle looked down; she guessed the torn section of her pant leg was fraying like Verhoven's jacket, although she'd discarded it into the darkness somewhere. "I put peroxide on it," she said. "I was thinking about infection, using it as an antiseptic, but peroxide is an acid, to some extent, it must have counteracted any of the base that got on my skin. It does feel strange though, almost like it were burning with a cold fire, like peppermint on the tongue."

"Might want to use some more peroxide," McCarter said.

As Danielle pulled out the plastic bottle, Verhoven held his hand out over the dead creature. "Notice anything else?" he said, looking at Danielle.

She shook her head.

"Dead animals radiate heat," he said. "When you take one down, you can feel it pouring from the wounds. But not this thing."

"What does that mean?" she asked.

"Cold-blooded maybe, or colder-blooded than we're used to."

"Might explain why the heat sensors have trouble picking them up," Danielle said.

Verhoven pointed to the tail, where the tip split into a pair of spikes, like dual stingers. "Remind you of anything?"

Danielle nodded and McCarter thought of the body in the water with the two great holes in its chest, wounds from something that went in and came back out. It was terrible, a killing machine—but part of McCarter could not help but be in awe. "What the hell are these things?" he asked.

He exchanged glances with Danielle and Verhoven, but it was clear that neither of them had a clue.

A moment later Hawker joined them. He took a brief look at the animal. "Nice," he said, sarcastically. "This trip is so much fun. Remind me to bring the whole family next time." He turned to McCarter. "Let's not forget why we're down here."

Despite an unshakable sense of awe they moved on, following the path that led beyond the plaza as it took them back into the deeper part of the cave. Soon, the craggy walls narrowed, closing in on them before becoming smooth with tool marks once again. They continued in a narrow valley that soon became a tunnel as the ceiling sloped down on them. The carved tunnel led to an even narrower rectangular doorway less than four feet high and perhaps eighteen inches wide at the most. They had to squeeze and duck to force themselves through. As soon as they reached the other side, a weak, raspy voice called out to them.

"Mr. Kaufman?"

McCarter responded. "It's us, Susan. Not Kaufman."

She stepped from the shadows. "Professor McCarter?"

"Are you all right?" he said.

She ran to them. Right into McCarter's arms, who grabbed her in a bear hug, only slightly embarrassed. He could hear her wheezing and pulled out her inhaler, which he'd found and remembered to bring with him.

She used it immediately. "I heard the guns," she said, her eyes welling up with tears. "I didn't know if—"

She broke off her sentence, scanning the faces and stopping on Hawker's. She seemed confused. "What are you doing here? What happened to Kaufman's men?"

"Most of them are gone." McCarter said. "Kaufman's up on the surface. Brazos is guarding him. We heard you on the radio," he added. "Apparently you couldn't hear us."

"I didn't get any response," she said. "Not sure I was using it right, and I think I killed the battery trying to call out."

She went on to explain the attack, and details of her survival. "When it killed the other man, the radio came sliding across the floor and hit me. I grabbed it and I just ran," she said. "I came down here and I found this door. It turned out to be a dead end in there, but by the time I tried to get out those things were trying to get in. They scratched and dug at the entrance for hours, but I guess they couldn't fit through. So I stayed put."

"That's somewhat comforting," Hawker said. "But we still have to go back that way to get out. And the sooner we go the better."

Susan took McCarter by the hand. "Yes," she said, very seriously. "But there are some things you have to see first."

She led them deeper into the chamber, down a long, narrow passageway, past one empty room after another, rooms that had been cut from the rock itself, rooms with smooth, vertical walls and flat, even floors. It was a level of workmanship more advanced than that of the plaza outside. In fact, where Susan's footprints had cleared the dust, the ground shone like expensive marble. McCarter bent to examine it, but Susan beckoned him to follow.

She pointed out a wall, covered with strange geometric symbols and, beside them, carved Mayan glyphs. And then she led them to a pile of debris where part of one wall and the ceiling had collapsed. She knelt down beside it.

McCarter paused, stunned. A figure lay there, half-buried in the rubble, partially hidden by the piles of rock. In the gray darkness it appeared to be the body of a child, but as the lights converged on the remains it became clear that it was something else.

The body was perhaps four feet tall. The legs and pelvis had been separated from the torso and whatever meat or flesh it once carried had long ago succumbed to decay. The skull was shaped like a man's but deformed and bulbous. A pair of great empty holes that must have once contained eyes sat in the upper half of the face, with bony ridges above and a forehead that sloped radically backward.

Instead of a rib cage, the body had two broad plates that curved out from its backbone, wrapping the body and fusing together in the front, completely covering the chest cavity. Somewhat like the exoskeleton of the animal outside, with thousands of pinprick holes in the bone.

McCarter touched the fragile skull, running his finger across its smooth surface. It reminded him of a horseshoe crab he'd found washed up on the beach when he was a child.

"It was almost completely buried," Susan told them. "I cleared most of this away. It helped me pass the time."

"What is this?" McCarter asked.

Susan shook her head.

Danielle didn't seem to hear. She was staring, eyes and mouth wide open. "My God," she whispered. "I never expected . . . I don't believe it. I just don't believe it."

## CHAPTER 36

Danielle Laidlaw gazed at the malformed body lying among the rubble. She had an idea of what it might be, though it was a conclusion she still found hard to accept.

McCarter seemed to sense her feelings. "This means something to you," he said. "Something more than it means to the rest of us."

Words flashed into her mind—deceptions. She could tell them it was just what it appeared to be, a deformed skeleton that had been entombed in the temple for a thousand years or more, a birth defect gone horribly to the extreme. But she guessed it was more than that. And she was sick of lying.

She looked back at the skull, studying the smooth curve of the forehead. She noticed a thin line embedded within the bone, a strand of golden fiber, not much thicker than a spider's thread. Similar strands led from each eye socket back across the top of the skull, a third strand from where the ear would have been. The bone had grown over them in places, like a tree might engulf a wire tied around it.

She was certain now, as certain as she could be, and

when McCarter noticed the metallic strand and looked toward her, she knew the time for the truth had arrived.

"It does mean something more to me," she said, finally answering McCarter.

He was staring at her, his jaw clenched. "It's been pretty damn obvious since Kaufman and his people showed up that we were here for more than Mayan artifacts," he said. "So is this what we came here for? Is this what everyone is so willing to kill for?"

"Take it easy, Doc," Hawker said calmly.

"No," Danielle said, waving him off. "It's all right." She put a hand to her forehead. She felt sick.

Across from her McCarter took a deep breath. "I would like an explanation," he said.

She nodded and spoke plainly. "I needed your help to find this place," she said, "because we—the NRI—believed we could find a power source here, a device or piece of machinery that would be capable of creating energy through the process of cold fusion."

McCarter's face softened, but more, she thought, from surprise than anything else. He asked almost the exact same question Hawker had asked an hour before. "Why would you possibly expect to find something like that here?"

"Because that person," she pointed toward the body, "whoever he or she was, brought it here."

McCarter looked back toward the body, blinking and shaking his head as if his mind were in a fog. "I don't mean to be deliberately thick," he said, finally. "We're all exhausted and not thinking clearly, but I honestly have no idea what you're trying to tell us."

Danielle took a deep breath. "I'm saying that if the

NRI's theory is correct, the body you're looking at, which has been entombed here for a couple thousand years or so, was born in a different time frame, somewhere in *our* distant future."

They stared at her, searching her face for the slightest hint that this was a lie, just another cover story or even some cruel joke. She offered nothing to suggest that, and McCarter turned back to the body. She could see his eyes focused on the gold filaments, probably wondering, as she was, just exactly what they were.

"You're serious?" Susan asked.

Danielle nodded.

"Can you explain this to us?" McCarter asked, less aggressively but still clearly upset.

"I'll try," she said. "It'll probably be easier to understand if I start at the beginning, two years ago, when an assistant curator at the Museum of Natural History brought the Martin's crystals to our attention. He'd seen something in them, something he couldn't identify, a strange haze that formed in the stone when viewed under polarized light. He insisted that the crystals were unimportant in general, hadn't been out of the back room in as long as he could remember, but he was curious, and he was a friend of Arnold Moore, my old partner.

"So we had some people look at them and what we discovered was hard to fathom. The crystals themselves were basically quartz but they were doped with a complex substance, glowing with low-level radiation and harboring a residue of gaseous tritium in certain places."

She looked around at the faces. "I don't know how much any of you know about tritium, but it's a gas that can only form in a nuclear reaction of one type or another. This suggested that the crystals had been used or exposed to a low-level nuclear reaction, one that our people could only reconcile as a form of cold fusion."

"How did you know that it wasn't some type of natural occurrence?" McCarter asked.

Danielle remembered asking the same question herself. "At first, we considered that a likely possibility," she said, "though it would have required a type of phenomenon never seen before. But as we studied the crystals more closely, it became obvious that they were the result of something even harder to explain: a human factor.

"By using a scanning electron microscope and other highly precise instruments, we determined that the crystals had been purposefully grown, manufactured and designed with precise geometric lines and a series of tunnels hidden within the quartz lattice. In a sense, the tunnels were a pattern of fiber-optic channels operating on an almost molecular scale, smaller than the smallest of today's nano-sized creations, and something we could not duplicate with today's technology. It was honestly mind-boggling," she added, "and because the pattern showed an intelligent, non-random design, we had to conclude that it had been created by human hands."

She studied McCarter's face, she could see that he was following.

"We even considered the possibility that it was a hoax," she added, "but our investigation ruled it out. The photographs, the chain of custody, the measurements. All of it matched up. The crystals we had in our possession were the same crystals that Martin had found, photographed and brought back from the Amazon in 1926. Which begged the question: what was a primitive tribe of indigenous natives doing with such things in the middle of the Amazon, twenty years before the dawn of the nuclear age, fifty years before microelectronics and fiber optics?"

Now McCarter nodded. It seemed he could understand their curiosity.

"Without an answer, we turned our attention to the rest of Martin's haul. We made a breakthrough when we studied the golden cradle."

As she spoke, Danielle recalled McCarter's sharp eyes studying the photograph of the cradle weeks before. She remembered thinking that he was instinctively looking for more.

"Do you recall the photo I showed you?" she asked.

He nodded.

"That photo covered one quarter of the underside. One panel out of four," she said. "I have to tell you, from a normal viewing distance the artwork on the panels looks like nothing more than random decoration: dots and scratches and curving lines. But as you saw on the photo, the panel proved to be a distinct star chart. The other three panels, which I didn't show you, were also star charts. By comparing them with astronomical data we were able to come up with possible explanations as to what location each panel represented."

"How?" Susan asked.

"The same way sailors navigate at night," she replied. "You can tell where you are on the globe by where the stars are above you, using their angles above the horizon and in relation to one another. In this case we had data from the planets and where each was positioned in its orbit. The data was like a time code—because each planet moves at a different rate, their positioning relative to one another gives you an approximate date. It is a little more complex than that," she admitted, "but there are other objects on each panel that helped us narrow down not only location, but time frame."

They were looking at her skeptically. She wanted them to understand. Now that she was explaining she wanted them to comprehend and to believe. That way they might understand the choices she'd made.

"At its simplest, it's like this: you look up at the sky and see the sun directly above, you know it is sometime near high noon. If you can see the sun and the moon, and you know the day of the year, you can tell where you are in a longitude and latitude. The same thing with the stars at night. Now, if you look up and you also see Halley's comet, you know that it is either 1910, 1986 or 2061 or any other year on the 76-year interval in which Halley's comet returns.

"Add enough objects like that to your map, and include some information on orbital position of the planets, and you can pinpoint exactly when and where you are. That's what we found on the panels of the cradle.

"In this case the first panel was the southern hemisphere sky chart I showed you, which gave us a winter solstice date, and a latitude of approximately two degrees south of the equator."

"Right where we are now," McCarter noted.

"Exactly," she said. "Only we couldn't get longitude off this panel, so we had to start searching."

"What about the other panels?" he asked.

"They were more complex. But based on the positioning of the stars, planets and comets marked on them, we determined the second and third panels to be similar southern hemisphere views, but with two widely disparate dates. The first was August 3114 B.C.; the second dated to December 2012 A.D."

"The start and end of the Mayan Long Count," McCarter noted. "The Mayan calendar."

Danielle nodded. "You know better than I how obsessed the Maya were with the concept of time."

"With those two dates in particular," McCarter said. She noticed that his voice had returned to its academic tone, his intellectual curiosity fully engaged.

"Still," he said. "Many Mayan writings and works of art contain astronomical observations. In most cases depictions of extreme accuracy. It's not too surprising that you would find something like that on a Mayan artifact. It doesn't mean it traveled here from the future."

She understood his skepticism. There was something unbalancing about the idea, which created an almost automatic prejudice against it.

"Of course," she said. "By themselves, simple star charts don't prove the theory any more than having a calendar for next year proves that you've been there already, but we found objects on those panels that could not be seen with the naked eye, not even with a powerful optical telescope. I'm talking about comets in the cold depths of space at the apogee of thousand-year orbits, neutron stars that emit no light, just radio waves and X-rays: The Maya could not have seen these things, Galileo couldn't see these things. Some of them can only be studied with massive radio telescopes like the dish in Arecibo. Something the native tribes and the Maya obviously did not have.

"One example that made me believe was on the third panel. It displayed the remnants of an exploded star, a supernova in its correct position and magnitude, the light from which did not reach earth until 1959. Don't forget the cradle had been recovered in the 1920s, and presumably created long before that. If it had been a simple description of where some astronomer of that era had calculated the star would be, then this supernova object would be depicted like all the other stars, but it wasn't. The icon clearly depicted a star that had exploded. In other words, the design wasn't based on what someone could predict; it was based on what someone *knew* as history."

"And the fourth panel?" Hawker asked.

"A northern hemisphere view," she said. "The year 3197. We don't know the significance but one guess is obvious: the time frame from which the expedition was launched."

The room fell silent, the group awed by the moment. If they were anything like her, their minds were fighting a back-and-forth battle between what the facts told them and what they found believable. It had taken her a long time to accept the possibility. Even as Stuart Gibbs had sent them here, they came with the knowledge that they would most likely find nothing. In fact, a chart of probabilities had been worked out, one that operated something like the Richter scale, with each additional level a full order of magnitude less likely to occur than the one below it. A level 1 result was finding nothing at all, level 2 would be the recovery of relics unrelated to the Martin's crystals. Levels 3 and 4 described their chances of finding true Mayan artifacts. Level 5 would have meant additional recovery of items like the Martin's crystals; level 6 would mean they'd found enough additional material to begin reverse engineering a cold-fusion device. And level 7, considered to have a likelihood of one chance in ten million, was that they would find the remains of a human who had made the journey back in time.

"I know it sounds crazy," she said, "but most physicists believe that some form of time displacement is possible. They disagree on how and on how much and whether it would be something that a human could physically survive."

She looked at the deformed body, wondering if the journey had caused the damage or if that mutated shape was truly what humankind was destined for. "We came to believe that it had been done at least once. We assumed it would be some type of unmanned vehicle, one that would come with a power source, perhaps even something to power a beacon, one that would signal for thousands of years, so the senders could find it in their own era. We assumed the crystals were part of its power source, a cold-fusion device, similar to the nuclear materials we send on deep space probes like Voyager and Pioneer. Like the self-contained solar cell on a cell tower in the desert or a lighted beacon out at sea."

She looked at their faces, McCarter's in particular. "We decided that at least it was something worth searching for, operating under the theory that it had crashed, or appeared among the natives, who tore it apart, using the incredible things they found as ritual objects."

"And the cradle and its depictions?" McCarter asked.

"I realize it's a sort of anthropomorphism to assume others are acting as you would, but every probe we've sent into deep space carries a disk of gold, with various information, including greetings and music and a visual description of where earth lies in the solar system. Our guess about the cradle was that these natives found a similar object on whatever had been sent back here—perhaps even something the people who sent it could look for in the ruins of the past to prove that their experiment had worked—and they copied it meticulously."

"Manhattan Project," Hawker said.

She nodded. There was nothing more to say. Either they believed or they didn't. She would let them consider the facts, while she looked for more proof.

She turned and her flashlight picked through the piles of crumbled rock before settling on the far wall. She stepped toward it and the Geiger counter began rattling again. "Are there any other passageways down here?"

"None that I've found," Susan said.

Danielle looked around. She saw nothing to refute that. She took off her backpack and slid out a notebook computer that held the data from Kaufman's ultra-sounds and electro-magnetic ground analysis. She brought up a three-dimensional representation of the cave.

The resolution was quite good, but because the screen was flat, the three dimensions were hard to determine at points. Manipulating the image on the screen, she was eventually able to fix their location in relation to that of the lake. She rolled the image around to look at it from the reverse angle, then increased the magnification and zoomed in on their current location. It indicated nothing out of the ordinary, just water, open space like the room they were in and more stone. There were other chambers to the cave, both beyond the wall and behind them, but they were irregular, jagged and natural in shape. She didn't think they would find anything there.

She scanned the room once again. It was expansive, despite the caved-in portion, but it was utterly empty except for the body they had found. It almost seemed to have been looted. Not looted, that was a messy job; more like purposefully cleared—cleaned out and sanitized, just as she would have done, given the chance. She wondered if someone had beaten them to the site, but then discounted that possibility. The body would not have been left behind.

She searched the four corners of the room, going from one to the other, checking her instruments. She walked back into the narrow tunnel and examined the other room they'd passed. Nothing there, just cavernous, vacant space, half a warehouse in size, but completely empty, exactly like the room they were in.

She raised her head, desperately hoping for a sign that there might be machinery or equipment or conduits of some type, but not even the remnants of anything like that could be seen. There was nothing around her but the smooth, polished stone. She put her hand out, touched the wall. There was nothing to bring home, no victory left to be won.

With a deep breath she folded the screen down, closing the laptop with a click.

She stood up slowly. The group was watching her. She turned to them. "We have to think about getting out of here," she said, softly. "The sooner, the better."

## CHAPTER 37

One by one they stood, gathering themselves and beginning the long walk down the hallway through which they'd come.

McCarter lingered, his attention held by the body they'd found. For a moment he contemplated taking it, or at least part of it. He'd removed bones and artifacts from sites all around the world, but this felt different, as if he'd seen something never meant for his eyes. In a moment of unscientific emotion, he decided against it. He stood slowly and joined the group.

Thirty minutes later they had reached the top of the zigzagging tunnel. Once they had crawled across the narrow planks, Hawker knocked the brace from beneath the stone and the massive block of granite came down like a hammer, crushing the wooden planks and sending their splintered remains plummeting into the well down below.

They hoped that would keep whatever animals were still living in the cave trapped down there, but one look into the well told them that more needed to be done. It seemed likely that the acidic lake in the cave flowed into the acidic water at the bottom of the well, and having seen how the animals could climb, no one doubted that they could make their way up the chimney of stone. They made plans to put a motion sensor over the pit and to set up a trip wire with explosives as well. Whether it would be enough to secure the structure they didn't know, but they didn't want anything coming out unannounced.

A moment later they were out in the pungent jungle air, breathing freely and squinting against the blinding midday light. Brazos waited for them, guarding the prisoners with a rifle.

"Can we go now?" he asked.

Danielle looked at Hawker, then nodded. "We're leaving."

Devers and Eric stood up, but Kaufman remained on the ground, apparently uninterested in moving.

"We're not going to carry you," Hawker said. "So unless you want to get shot and left behind, get on your damn feet."

Kaufman didn't move. "If you walk out into that jungle, you'll never see the other side; in fact, you'll probably never see tomorrow. The animals from last night, they'll hunt us in the forest. They're already out there. You know that. The natives are as well. And in that place they have all the advantages."

"Do you have a better option?" Danielle asked.

"I have help coming," Kaufman replied, proudly.

"Of course," Danielle said. "Your helicopter."

"I was wondering when I'd see that bastard again," Hawker said.

"Yes, the bastard who shot you down." Kaufman said, smugly.

Hawker smiled at the veiled insult. "Wasn't really a fair fight. But if we can fly out of here instead of walk, I'll kiss the son of a bitch."

"I'll bring him in," Kaufman said, "but I want something in return."

"You'll get your life in return," Danielle responded. "That ought to be enough."

Hawker smiled. "She's the boss."

Kaufman pursed his lips. He was in no position to bargain.

Hawker pointed to the shortwave radio. "Let's get out of here before nightfall."

"Yes," Kaufman said, strangely. "That would be preferable. I only wish we could."

"And why can't we?"

"Try the radio," the CEO said. "See what you get."

Hawker switched the radio on and received a sharp squeal and then a painful burst of static. He switched frequencies, to no avail, and then shut it off. "What's wrong with it?"

"Almost every electronic device we've brought in has malfunctioned," Kaufman said. "Or is on the verge of doing so. Both shortwaves are down—ours and yours."

"From what?" Hawker asked.

"The radiation in this area has an electromagnetic component to it," Kaufman explained, "one that destroys transistors and other micro-electric circuitry. It's similar to what the military calls EMP—Electro-Magnetic Pulse. The more compact the device is, or the more power that runs through it, the quicker it fails. That's why the shortwaves went first. If we had an old-fashioned radio with vacuum tubes in it, it might still be working. But printed circuit boards die quickly out here."

Danielle spoke up. "He's right. Things were going down before they came. Including the satlink."

"Well, some of the equipment is working," Hawker said. "The defense grid, the walkie-talkies."

Kaufman nodded. "Those items have a military pedigree. They're hardened against this type of thing, because you find a giant electro-magnetic burst in any atomic explosion, and the military doesn't want everything going down when the big war begins. But all the equipment will fail eventually, it's just a matter of time. So, if you want me to make a call, you need to find a mil-spec radio, and soon."

"Can we use this one?" McCarter asked, holding up the ELF radio.

"Sure," Kaufman said, sarcastically. "If you want to be rescued by a submarine."

"Normal radios won't pick it up," Hawker explained to McCarter, then turned back to Kaufman. "You have some type of contingency, I assume."

"I do," he said. "Since I've been here, my people have been operating silently, just like you. No calls in, no calls out. Without an early request to expedite the process, my pilot will return with supplies at a pre-arranged time, approximately seventy-two hours from now. He'll fly into the area and wait for a signal. He'll be expecting a specific flare pattern. Once he gets it, he'll make a final approach and land. Then we can fly out of here, avoiding what I can only characterize as a most unpleasant walk."

"What do you think?" Danielle asked Hawker. "Can it carry all of us?"

"Maybe," Hawker said. "Weight might be a problem, but we should be able to off-load some fuel." He turned back to Kaufman. "How far is your staging area?"

"I have a barge in the river about a hundred miles from here."

"That sounds like a good idea," Brazos said.

"I agree," McCarter added. "I was too quick to judge the merits of helicopter travel before, I should like to try it again."

Hawker watched them grasping at the hope that the helicopter represented. It seemed a rational choice, far preferable to fighting their way through the jungle, but it would come with other dangers, not the least of which was trusting Kaufman. Still, hope was a powerful motivator and Hawker saw no reason to dash that spark. He looked at Danielle, who nodded.

"All right," he said, "we'll wait for your extraction. But if something goes wrong, if your bird comes back and tries to take us out, or if some friends of yours come crawling out of the jungle to challenge us, I promise you, you'll be the one who regrets it. In other words: don't fuck with us. It'll end badly for you."

At his most basic, Kaufman was a man of business, not given to emotion or sentiment. What he cared about was the bottom line, the end result. In this case, that was survival. Given the choice of dying in the jungle or going back to the States in chains, he'd gladly face justice, with his Armani-clad lawyers at his side and all the NRI's abuses to bring to light. In truth, he doubted it would get that far. Deals had a way of being struck.

"I'm sure it would," he said finally, then turned away from Hawker and studied Danielle. It was hard not to notice the disappointment etched on her face. He knew what the NRI was after. Mainly because he'd had access to their early data, and his people—Lang, primarily—had reached the same conclusions. They were all after the same thing: the cold-fusion machinery, which they believed had been left here. To go through all they had been through and end up with nothing . . . In his own way, he felt a sense of sympathy for Danielle.

"Is there nothing down there?" he asked.

"Nothing," she replied. "Nothing but empty space and stone and death."

Kaufman's disappointment ran as deeply as hers, his regret just as real. "A great pity," he said. "After all that's happened, a greater shame."

## CHAPTER 38

So they would wait. They would wait in the clearing for Kaufman's helicopter, until it came or until it failed to come. They would turn the camp into a stronghold and take cover in it, avoiding the dark labyrinth of the jungle with its vaporous shadows and infinite blinds. They would dig trenches and build obstacles and horde the weapons and ammunition that both parties had brought. And if their attackers came back for blood, they would have to brave a storm of overlapping fire to get it.

This had been Kaufman's plan from the beginning, since his very first conversation with the scarred and wounded Jack Dixon. Right away he'd recognized the mistake of entering the jungle, even before he'd listened to the harrowing tale of his trek to the river. But then, Dixon needed to leave and it had always been Kaufman's intention to stay, to deal with the problem and then find what he was looking for, unhindered by either the animals or the Chollokwan. Now, in the aftermath of the plan's initial, failed version, the survivors of both camps would attempt a second act, one they hoped would fare better.

It fell to Verhoven to build the new fortress, and he began by throwing out most of what had already been done. He realized that if he and Hawker hadn't breached Kaufman's battlements, the animals or the natives soon would have. The network of foxholes was spread too thin, too far from one another to do much good. The arrangement belonged in the world Kaufman's Eastern European mercenaries had trained for in the past decades: a modern battlefield with its mechanized terror and high explosives, a place where the distance prevented multiple positions from being wiped out by a single missile, bomb or shell.

Verhoven, on the other hand, had spent his life in close combat, in small arms battles on grassy savannahs, in jungles and on tribal lands, fighting against enemies who possessed lesser technology but usually greater numbers. That situation, like the one they were in now, required defenders to be bunched closer together, where a concentration of firepower was the best protection against being overrun.

In his plan, Verhoven would dig a new set of bunkers, shallower out of the necessity of haste, but packed tightly together, like circled wagons in the old American west. With each bunker able to add its weapons to that of its neighbor, they effectively doubled and tripled the available firepower, no matter what direction the threat approached from. It would make their small force seem like a platoon of armed men.

Kaufman's surviving mercenary, Eric, and the traitor, Devers, were forced to do much of the digging, while Verhoven watched and critiqued. Despite their injuries, they dug for all they were worth.

A short distance away, Danielle conducted an impromptu clinic on firearms with Susan. The young woman had never fired a gun before, and showed little desire to do so now, but Verhoven's plan and the group's small numbers required her to at least know how to load. Over the course of an hour she learned to handle a Kalashnikov. Loading, aiming, firing, practicing the removal of jammed cartridges. Through two full clips of ammunition her shots were never accurate, but it almost didn't matter; she would only fire if the Chollokwan were storming them, and in that case there would be too many targets to miss.

While Susan practiced, Brazos and McCarter used the expedition's tools to enhance their situation as best they could, augmenting electronic sensors with the most primitive of defenses, cutting the steel pry bars into pieces and wedging them into the ground, with the sharpened ends pointing up and out. They added a phalanx of sticks and piles of loose rock as obstacles, forcing anything that charged them to negotiate a weaving path or to come straight down the line of fire.

While the rest of the group built their defenses, Hawker dragged Kaufman across the camp, retrieving what remained of the weapons cache. They went through crates of neatly stacked equipment and box after box of weapons and ammunition, all carried in from Kaufman's barge downriver. As he'd boasted to Gibbs, Kaufman's men were far better equipped than the NRI group had been, and the two battles for control had ended so quickly that much of the equipment had never made it out of storage.

Hawker inventoried the supplies, separating the useful from the merely burdensome, and they began to carry boxes back to the center of the camp. About an hour before dusk, he pulled a tarp off something, and a smile came to his face. Lying before them, nose-up on a tripod, was a massive, heavy caliber rifle with a laser scope attached to the barrel. A Barrett M107: a fifty-caliber monster, accurate at over a thousand yards, firing huge shells that traveled at two thousand miles per hour and could punch through several inches of hardened steel. Against this weapon, the bony armor of the animals would be useless.

Hawker grinned. "This is what I call a problem-solver."

He turned to Kaufman. "How much ammunition do you have for this thing?"

"I don't know weapons," Kaufman replied. "That's what I hired them for. You'd better check with Eric."

Hawker brought the radio up to transmit the question, but a sound like paper ripping interrupted him. Behind them, a flare snaked into the sky.

The sound startled Hawker, but he knew what it meant and he spun around, firing, even before he could get his weapon on line. The rifle chattered as a shape launched itself toward him. Shells ripped into the charging beast, but the animal hit him full bore and both of them went tumbling across the ground.

A second creature followed, charging Kaufman, who bolted in the wrong direction, away from the center of camp instead of toward it.

Recognizing his mistake, Kaufman tried to bend his

course back toward the heart of the clearing, but the animal cut him off, tripping him with a flick of its front claw. Kaufman went down in a cloud of dust. Before he could recover, a stabbing pain fired through his shoulder and he felt himself being yanked and swung around. He screamed.

Fifty yards away, on his hands and knees, Hawker gasped for air. He was coughing so hard that he thought he might throw up. The force of the blow had been taken on his bruised ribs, and every breath was fire. He looked around in a daze, shocked even to be alive. The animal lay a few feet away in an awkward heap. Several shots to the creature's head had been fatal, but as it crumbled to the ground its momentum had carried into Hawker like a runaway train.

Seeing only the lanyard of his rifle, Hawker grabbed it and pulled. The weapon came snaking through the dry grass toward him. He snatched it up, racking the slide twice to make sure it wasn't jammed, and stood. In the distance he could hear Kaufman's agony.

Out in the trees, Kaufman's face banged against the rugged ground as the animal dragged him. His shoulder burned and strained as if his arm was being ripped off, and then just as suddenly, he was in the forest and free.

Moving on pure adrenaline, Kaufman scrambled to his feet, only to be slammed back to the ground, dragged another dozen feet and then flipped over onto his back.

"Help me!" he screamed.

The hideous thing pinned him down, crushing the wind out of him. As he struggled to breathe, Kaufman reached for the animal's throat. But there was no soft windpipe to crush, just bone and a thin joint where the plates slid over one another. He grabbed for its bulbous eye but the head pulled back and the weight on his chest increased.

Unable to move beneath the five-hundred-pound bulk, Kaufman squirmed in horror as the segmented tail rose up above its head and pointed toward him. He watched the spiked tips extend slowly from their sheaths and drops of some clear liquid bead up on the sharpened points.

"No!" he shouted. "No!"

The tail shook slightly, went utterly still and then shot forward.

Hawker arrived seconds later, but he found no trace of either Kaufman or the animal. He saw trampled brush and blood and then freshly cut gouges in the bark of the tree. Up above, the higher branches swayed in the breezeless air and some of the leaves were wet with smears of the animal's oily secretions. It had taken Kaufman into the trees, like a leopard carrying off its kill.

*They'd been vertical in the cave,* he thought. *Of course they'd be vertical in the forest.*

As he scanned the foliage, the sound of gunfire reached him from across the camp. He waited for it to cease, but it continued unabated. Reluctantly, he broke into another run.

By the time he reached the center of camp, the guns

had gone silent. He counted heads; everybody was present.

The others looked at him curiously. Bright red blood poured down one side of his face, flowing from the reopened gash below his eye.

"Where's Kaufman?" Danielle asked.

"Gone," Hawker said.

"Escaped?"

"I wouldn't call it that."

Danielle winced, realizing what that meant.

Hawker popped the clip out of his rifle. "Shells?"

She pointed to one of the storage boxes that he'd brought over earlier and Hawker sat down next to it and began reloading. He gazed out toward the perimeter as he shoved the cartridges into the clip. He wanted to go back for the big sniper's rifle, but the trees were swallowing the sun whole and the weapon sat too close to the forest to chance it in the failing light. It would have to wait until morning.

If they lived that long.

That night the camp came under siege. The motion trackers picked up movement along the perimeter thirty-nine separate times. At first, the men and women from the NRI took carefully aimed shots, hoping to hit or at least scare off the intruders and conserve ammunition. But as the creatures became more aggressive, the response from the camp's defenders grew less controlled. Before long, the night was filled with gunfire. Tracers and flares lit up the darkness while the floodlights blazed along with the guns.

"Why are they attacking now?" Susan wondered. "We've been here for a week. Why now?"

No one knew. Maybe it had been the continued incursions into the temple or perhaps the blood they'd shed in their own battles and the scent of the dead bodies had drawn the beasts in, but whatever the case, it was clear early on that this night would be far worse than the last. And as the animals grew accustomed to the light and noise, they began charging through the camp in ones and twos, ripping down the tents and smashing equipment, flying past the small stronghold of circled bunkers.

One of them got close enough to slash McCarter's arm, only to be driven back by a blast from Verhoven's shotgun. Another, tripped up by the obstacles, tumbled and landed right in front of Brazos. He fired into it from point-blank range but the thing stumbled away, still alive, at least for the moment.

The smaller creatures made faster charges; one of them leaped in the midst of its attack, landing in between the bunkers, right in the center of the circle. No one could fire at it for fear of shooting the others, but the dogs attacked, and in the melee of a vicious animal brawl, the dogs took the worst of it, especially with their nylon leashes hindering them.

Verhoven grabbed a machete, and in one great swing at the stake to which their ropes were tied, he cut them free, but the animal they fought was invulnerable to teeth and claws and the canines were dying all around it.

"Everybody down!" Hawker shouted. A quick burst from his rifle drew a piercing shriek from the beast and it leapt away, tore off into the distance and disappeared into the trees.

In between them, three of the dogs were dead, the other two bleeding and injured. With a look of pain on his face, Verhoven spoke, "We need to clean their wounds when we get a chance."

Danielle grabbed the medi-kit, but before she could begin, the perimeter alarm went off again, announcing yet another attack.

Two hours past midnight things took a turn for the worse. It was a random occurrence, but to the overtired minds of the NRI team, it didn't seem that way. In two separate attacks, over a span of five minutes, the animals destroyed the entire lighting system that had so aided the humans' defense.

In the first attack, one animal crashed headlong into the post that held two of the spotlights. The pole came crashing down and the lights exploded, showering the group with incandescent sparks. Minutes later, a much larger animal got hopelessly tangled in the power cords. The beast twisted frantically, jerking and spinning like a shark caught in a net. In doing so, it yanked down another floodlight and then pulled the entire generator off its blocks, shorting out the system and plunging the clearing into sudden darkness.

With quick hands, Danielle fired off a flare. But the animal had escaped its entanglement and disappeared.

For the next three hours they had only flares to light up the night. They launched dozens of them, some triggered from the control panel, some from flare guns and still others thrown by hand into the clearing.

At some point a drum of kerosene took a hit from

one of the rifles. It exploded in a burst of orange light, and the flames soon ignited the drum next to it. The fires crackled and popped as tongues of flame leapt toward the sky half hidden by the oily, black smoke.

By now the survivors were approaching the breaking point. They were exhausted beyond measure, under siege from things they could not have imagined existing just days before, bizarre animals that showed no fear of humans and their guns, nor any real reason to fear them.

In all of the night's attacks not one of the animals had been definitively killed; they'd been driven off, and many were surely wounded, but not one had fallen in the expanse of the clearing.

Various reasons were guessed at. For one thing, most of these animals were larger than the ones they'd seen in the cave. Danielle guessed that the ones from the cave were juveniles and these had been out feeding and growing. That would make their skeletons proportionately thicker and stronger. Verhoven noted their strange shapes, guessing that the oddly slanting exteriors acted like the armor on a tank, deflecting any projectile that came in at a flat angle, like a stone skipping across the water. Still, no one could be sure.

Worst off were Devers and Eric, the surviving German mercenary. They sat in a foxhole, unarmed, with their hands and feet tied, knowing that their fate depended on the very people who had been their prisoners. A soldier who understood his situation, Eric shouted warnings when he thought it appropriate. Devers, on the other hand, spent the quiet moments between attacks either complaining or protesting his innocence. At least until Verhoven kicked him in the ribs, putting a stop to his whining for the night.

For the others, time and stress began to take their toll. Their minds were soon playing tricks on them, seeing and hearing things that weren't there. Emotions swung wildly from one extreme to another. McCarter found himself drifting into utter despair at one moment, wishing it would just be over one way or another, then laughing at the absurdity of it all a few minutes later. The others struggled through similar states.

And then, in the last hour before dawn, things got worse.

Another sound began to make its presence known, the hollow, rhythmic voice of chanting men, hidden somewhere within the trees. The Chollokwan had returned.

Soon they could see glimpses of fire through the tangled mesh of the trees, and gray smoke began to fill the clearing. But this time the Chollokwan did not build the inferno they'd created before. They set fires only sporadically, gathering in groups, chanting and shouting in waves once again.

Their voices were coarse and threatening. Haunting the survivors, mocking them and, above all else, reminding them of something no one wanted to recall: they had been warned.

## CHAPTER 39

As dawn approached the Chollokwan voices faded, receding into the forest along with the morning mists. But this time, the rising sun brought no feeling of safety or redemption, no false sense of relief, only the stark realization of how bad things really were.

Shell casings littered the ground by the hundreds, scattered like cigarette butts from some mad smokers' convention. Burned-out flares lay in small heaps of ash amid circles of blackened earth while the piles of stone loomed like rubble between ugly eruptions of sharpened steel. The tents they'd once slept in were little more than shredded lengths of nylon, jagged strips hanging limply from mangled frames. Farther out, the drums of kerosene crackled and burned, belching thick, oily smoke and fouling the air with acrid fumes.

In this harsh morning light, the clearing showed itself for what it was, for what it had always been, a wasteland, a graveyard, a malignant spot in the middle of paradise, where nothing lived and nothing grew. As the Nuree had insisted, it was a place that had been rejected by life itself.

Still, with a respite from the attacks, the survivors

took the chance to recover and sleep, dozing in shifts, with their loaded weapons beside them, waiting for the next phase to begin and hoping somehow that it would not. They'd barely survived through twelve hours; most wondered how the hell they would last through sixty more.

At noon the shift changed and Hawker took the lead watch from Verhoven.

"Break time," Hawker said.

"Uh-hm," Verhoven replied, as he set the safety on his weapon.

Verhoven wasn't a man given to deep reflection, things were what they were in his world, but Hawker sensed a thorn in the man's side somewhere.

"Something wrong?" Hawker asked.

"Been counting ammo," Verhoven said. "Another night like the last one and we'll run dry before the sun comes up."

Hawker hadn't taken the time to inventory things, but he sensed the same thing. If the animals continued their onslaught unabated, it would be a war of attrition that the humans could not win. "We'll have to be more sparing in what we use," Hawker replied.

"They're wild, Hawk," Verhoven said. "Even Danielle, who's a hell of a shot, uses too much ammo. And the others are all over the place."

"They're afraid," Hawker said. "They'll be a little better tonight."

Verhoven looked at the ground for a second and then back at Hawker. "If they're not, I'm taking the guns out of their hands. I don't care what they say. If it comes to that, you and I will do the firing. No one else. Better they be pissed off and alive than empowered and dead."

Hawker hesitated a second. He doubted Danielle would give up her gun, but the others would not fight the logic. He nodded, and Verhoven turned and walked off.

A few minutes later Danielle approached him with the medi-kit in her hand.

"I can only hope you're going to examine me," he said.

"Much as you'd like me to," she said. "There's a lot more wrong with you than I could fix."

He smiled.

"We do have a problem, though."

"Really," he said, looking around, "because I hadn't noticed."

"Kaufman," she explained.

He stared at her for a second. It was like she'd read his mind. "Yeah, Kaufman."

She explained. "Without that son of a bitch to send up his flare pattern, who knows if his helicopter will land. That means no extraction, no free ride home."

"I thought about that," he admitted, "although I wasn't sure he was telling the truth with that story to begin with. You use flares to draw attention to yourself when someone's looking for you. Kind of odd to use them for a party that already knows where you are. More likely you'd use smoke. That would keep any distant observers from locking in on the position and it would give the pilot localized info and wind direction as well."

She nodded. "Seemed a little odd to me as well. My

guess is: Kaufman was either lying or he didn't know, and he made up that story to give himself some type of residual value and reduce the chances of being shot at sunrise. He was a bastard but he was smart."

"Yeah," he said. "But now what? If we pop the wrong color smoke, or shoot the wrong flare it could scare off the pilot. It might be better to do nothing, let his curiosity bring him in closer. We can dig up Kaufman's people and put on their uniforms." Hawker looked out to where he and McCarter had buried the dead mercenaries. "If the pilot sees us like that, he might land . . . or he might just strafe us as he flies past and then head off into the distance."

"I'm not real interested in going through that again," she said. "But the only alternative is five days in the jungle. Choose your poison."

After the night they'd just lived through, Hawker had no desire to face even one of those things in the tangled darkness of the rain forest. He guessed that the helicopter would come back, but it was a coin flip as to whether they'd last that long and another question altogether as to what would happen after that. Still, two days in the well-defended clearing and a fifty-fifty shot seemed like better odds than four or five days trudging through the jungle.

Either Danielle sensed this or had come to the same conclusion. "Let's wait," she said. "And let's keep this from the others."

Hawker nodded, and noticed McCarter walking toward them. The professor had bled through the dressing on his arm. "Looks like you've got another patient."

Danielle turned around. "Sit down," she said, looking at McCarter. "Let me rewrap that."

McCarter took a seat and tried to hold still as Danielle cut the gauze from his arm. He seemed distraught to Hawker, almost despondent.

"Rough night?" Hawker asked, trying to lighten his mood.

McCarter did not respond directly. "When my wife was sick," he said finally, "there were nights, during the chemo, that I would hear her throwing up violently in the bathroom down the hall. Dry heaves for what seemed like hours, and then she'd rest against the closed door, and it would rattle as she shivered."

He closed his eyes for a second and choked back a lump in his throat. "But she didn't want my help or my pity," he said at last. "She just wanted to be well again. And in her mind, as long as I didn't hear, she could pretend it was working, she could pretend that she was getting better. So I would lie there, hour after hour, fighting every urge in my body to run to her, so we could both pretend she wasn't dying.

"That's what last night felt like to me," he explained. "Like a message being delivered over and over again and we're all pretending not to hear it, all pretending like we're not going to die."

As McCarter finished, he and Danielle exchanged looks and they seemed to make some kind of connection. Hawker didn't know what it was, but as much death as he'd seen in his life, most of it had been mercifully quick. He was thankful for that.

He looked McCarter in the eye. They needed him to

hang on, they needed everyone to hang on. "We're not dead yet," Hawker said.

"But tonight will be more of the same," McCarter replied.

"Maybe," Hawker said. "Maybe not. In any fight, things always look worse from your perspective. All you see are your own losses but none of your enemies'. Your mind tells you he's still at full strength, when undoubtedly he's weakened."

Hawker pointed out into the jungle. "We didn't do so bad last night. We're alive. And we lit those things up pretty good. Some of them are going to die off, others will lick their wounds and stay away, and that means less of them around to bother us tonight."

That thought seemed to bolster McCarter. "That makes sense," he said. "But they will be coming back."

"Yeah," Hawker said. "I'm guessing they will. We just have to make sure we're ready for them this time. More ready than we were yesterday."

"And how do we do that?" McCarter asked.

"First off, we need to do some research," Hawker said.

McCarter's face brightened. "Research," he said. "I like research. What are you thinking?"

"Yeah," Danielle said suspiciously as she wrapped McCarter's arm in new gauze. "What *are* you thinking?"

Hawker pointed toward the forest again. "We have to go out there and poke around in the trees for a bit. Take a look at a few things."

McCarter's face showed a negative opinion of that

BLACK RAIN383

plan. "Did I tell you how much I hate research? Can't stand the stuff."

Danielle laughed as she finished taping off his new bandage.

"No, seriously," he said. "I always have the assistants do it for me."

"Nice try," she told him. "But he suckered you on that one."

A minute later Hawker and McCarter were grabbing two radios. The first one sounded intermittent and weak.

Hawker grabbed a second one and clicked the mike; it seemed to be working. "This one's good."

"Try to make it last," Danielle said. "The charger's down."

Hawker clipped the radio to his belt. "Great," he said. "We'll be living like the Amish soon."

Danielle watched as Hawker grabbed his rifle and led a reluctant, but far more positive Professor McCarter across the clearing. Despite his humor she sensed a great weight on Hawker's shoulders, the weight of expectations put upon him by the others. They looked to him for hope, trusting him to get them home. As long as he believed they could survive, then they believed it too, but if he faltered or hedged his words, they would sense it and their own hearts would fall.

As he walked toward the trees, she found herself thinking about him on a deeper level and wondering how he'd become who he was. And she found herself

sitting next to the one person in the world who probably knew the answer.

She turned to Verhoven, who sat on the edge of his
foxhole, awkwardly loading clips with his one good
hand. "Tell me about Hawker," she said.

Verhoven looked up briefly and then went back to the
task at hand. He didn't seem interested.

She produced a tin of tobacco, one Kaufman's people
had taken from him. "I'll make it worth your while."

Verhoven cut his eyes at her, a sly grin on his face suggesting he appreciated her style of bargaining. "What do
you want to know?"

She handed him the container. "You worked together
before, right?"

"A long time back."

"So what happened? How'd you become enemies?"

Verhoven's leathery face wrinkled as he pulled a wad
of dark tobacco from the container and shoved it into
the side of his mouth. "I tried to kill him," he said
plainly.

Danielle was shocked. She'd guessed at some type of
pride-filled argument, a strategic disagreement, a fight
over money or action or even a girl.

"Or so he thinks," Verhoven elaborated.

"Why would he think that?" she asked.

Verhoven exhaled grumpily before continuing. "At
one time Hawker and I were friends," he said. "Good
friends, despite our differences. We were working in Angola, Hawker with the CIA, me with South African Special Forces. Our job was to stir up resistance to the
regime that had been oppressing the place for thirty

years. It was a hell of a job, it always is out there. Eventually Hawker made some choices that put him in opposition to everyone he knew, including me."

"I know a little bit of it," she said. "I know he violated some orders."

Verhoven spat the first shot of tobacco juice onto the ground. The act seemed to bring him great joy. "There are orders," he said, "and then there are orders. Some are even given with the expectation that they'll be disregarded, especially in that world. But others are the law."

"Hawker disobeyed the wrong kind."

Verhoven put the can of tobacco into his breast pocket, picked up a new clip to load.

"Yes," he said. "But it's not that simple really. To understand what happened, to really understand, you have to first understand Africa."

He shoved another cartridge into place. "Aside from my country, most of the continent exists in a state of intractable, cyclical anarchy. Show me a nation, I'll show you a war. Show me another, I'll show you a genocide or two. Angola was no different. The CIA had been there for decades, most of it spent supporting a lunatic named Jonas Savimbi. By the time Hawker got there they'd realized that the man was no better than a mad killer. So they began to diversify. Hawker and I worked with the smaller groups, the ones not linked to Savimbi. In any other place they would have been allies, united against a common enemy, but reason and logic mean precious little in Africa, and Savimbi saw that as a threat. And so a deal was struck, the kind that leaves certain parties out in the cold."

"Your parties," she guessed.

Verhoven nodded. "The money was to stop, the guns were to stop and the tribes Hawker and I had been working with were to be left on their own, to fend for themselves with an entire division of the Angolan army bearing down on them, smelling blood and looking for someone to make an example out of."

So that was the order Hawker had disobeyed. Of course it wasn't in the file; it would never be officially written in the first place. "And Hawker kept arming them," she guessed.

"As best he could," Verhoven said. "He'd made fast friends with them. Given his word. So he went outside the ropes, buying guns and weapons on the Agency's account, and stealing them after the Agency cut him off."

Verhoven paused in the narrative to load a few more shells. "Your government didn't like that much and they asked us to stop him and bring him in. Well, we did, eventually. And while Hawker sat rotting in one of my camps, the Angolans massacred those people."

Danielle looked away, feeling ill.

Verhoven continued. "While the CIA tried to figure out what to do with him, a man named Roche walked into Hawker's cell and shot him in the chest. Hawker thinks I ordered it."

"Why would he think that?" she asked.

"Officially, Roche was under my command," Verhoven said. "In reality, he took orders from someone in Pretoria. It seems my people and I had been involved with Hawker for too long to be trusted with the real job of catching him. So Roche and his special team came out to do the job, but for the better part of a year Hawker made them look like fools, hiding, moving, even getting

away from a sting Roche had set up with the weapons
and the money. As it looked, Roche was about to be replaced when he finally succeeded."

Verhoven sucked at his teeth and his voice turned.
"The first time I saw Hawker after Roche caught him, I
barely recognized him. They'd beat him to a bloody
mess."

"You couldn't stop it?" she asked.

Verhoven glared at her coldly. "I told you, Roche
didn't answer to me."

Danielle leaned back, taking a deep breath and scuff-
ing the dirt at the bottom of the foxhole with her boot.

On Verhoven's side another shell went into the clip,
another shot of tobacco juice into the dirt.

"How did it go down?" she asked.

"I don't know exactly," he said. "I heard a shot and
when I came in I found Hawker on the ground bleeding from the chest. Roche was standing there with his
pistol, babbling something about Hawker escaping, but
Hawker was still chained to the bloody rail. I almost
killed Roche right there and then. As it was, I beat him
half-senseless with his own gun—and I would have finished the job too, but one of his people came in and
stopped me. Apparently there was a more pressing
issue—the CIA had someone on the way out to collect
Hawker that very afternoon. I think Roche expected
them to let Hawker off and he couldn't stand the
thought. So he snapped."

Verhoven shook his head recalling the events. "I
checked Hawker myself and he was dead. I mean, he
was blue and without a pulse. You know? We couldn't
turn him over to the Americans like that, so we put him

in the back of a jeep, drove him out a couple of miles into the scrub and dumped him there. We told the American counsel he'd escaped."

A smile crept onto Verhoven's craggy face. "The irony was, Roche couldn't tell anyone he'd shot Hawker or they'd have hung him. So he had to pretend that Hawker had beaten him to a pulp and escaped once again. It drove him mad."

"How did Hawker survive?"

Verhoven shrugged. "Don't know. Didn't know he had for a while. A couple months later I started hearing rumors of an American working the arms trade on the West African coast. Not too many whites out there, even fewer Americans. A few months after that, the CIA sent me a surveillance photo to examine. It had been taken the week before in Liberia. It was Hawker, clear as day."

Danielle grinned. "What did you do?"

"What the hell could I do?" he said. "I smiled actually, and then I cringed. By that time I was on my way out anyhow. My country had gone through its change a few years before and things were different. The truth squad was coming my way, you know?"

Danielle nodded, remembering the history of post-apartheid South Africa. "What happened to Roche?"

"A few years later, he took a walk off the top of a sky-scraper in downtown Johannesburg." Verhoven raised his eyebrows. "Twenty-story kiss to the concrete."

"Hawker?"

Verhoven shrugged. "Roche had a lot of enemies," he said. "By then, he'd joined the trade himself, but he was known as a skimmer; always looking to leave a few men behind just to up his share of the take. So maybe it wasn't Hawker—or maybe it was, doing the rest of us a favor."

Verhoven looked out toward Hawker in the distance. "All I know for sure is that everyone involved in that mess has died in one bloody way or another—shot and killed or blown to hell. Every one of those sons of bitches that Roche used, they're all dead now."

Verhoven turned back toward Danielle. "So, thinking what Hawk thinks, and knowing that I dumped him in the desert, I'd expect he's got a bullet in that gun for me, somewhere." He shoved one last cartridge into the clip he was loading. "And who knows, maybe I've got one for him too."

Silence hung in the air, with Danielle and Verhoven staring at each other, until the radio squawked beside them. "Anyone awake back there?"

Danielle grabbed it. "Go ahead, Hawker. What have you got?"

"Missing bodies. Looks like those things dug up the men we buried. So much for putting on their uniforms."

Danielle made a sour face. "Wasn't really looking forward to that anyway."

"Yeah, me neither. Looks like they took the animal I killed too."

"Scavengers as well as predators."

"Seems that way. Listen, we're almost to the trees. Before we get in there I want to make sure the area's clear."

Danielle checked the laptop screen one more time; some of the pixels were beginning to drop out. "There's nothing on the screen," she said. "For whatever that's worth."

A double click let her know he copied and she turned back to Verhoven. She now understood Hawker's anger with the system, with orders and those who gave them. "When this is over, let me talk to him," she said. "Let me try to explain it. I owe both of you at least that much."

## CHAPTER 40

Across the clearing, Hawker and McCarter entered the rainforest, passing through the scorched zone, where the Chollokwan fires had blackened everything bare, and reaching the lush green section just beyond it.

Wondering about his own sanity, McCarter turned to Hawker. "Tell me why we're doing this again?"

"Those things kept coming from this direction," Hawker said. "It became predictable. And some of them lingered here after they left the clearing. I want to know why."

"What makes me think you already know why?"

"I don't know anything," Hawker insisted, examining the trunks of several trees and then moving deeper into the jungle. "But I have a theory. Their bodies are somewhat like insects, they have exoskeletons, incredibly strong but with simple joints. They took the body of the one I killed yesterday, presumably to eat it. Most predatory animals don't do that. A lion will kill its rival but it won't eat the body. Neither will hyenas or tigers. Sharks will—in a frenzy, when they're biting anything that moves—but they're also known to swim away from dead sharks found floating on the surface, as if the bodies are cursed. They even make a type of shark repellent from an enzyme found in dead sharks, because it contains a compound that triggers the flight response."

Hawker's eyes went from tree to tree and then to the ground looking for tracks. "But ants will eat their own," he said. "So will roaches and all the other bugs of this world. They'll carry the dead back to the nest and tear them apart like an old car for spare parts. So maybe these things are like insects. And if that's the case, then maybe they follow pheromone trails. Maybe they came in and out on this path because one of them laid down a trail and the others just followed without even thinking. In and out on the same line as if it's the only road home, like ants who've found their way to the sugar bowl."

As he listened to the theory McCarter had to smile, "It takes imagination to think of it that way."

"I suppose," Hawker said, moving to the base of another massive tree. "But if it's the case, then maybe we can set a trap for them—rig up some of Kaufman's explosives and set them off when the bastards show up for their midnight snack. And if we can do that, enough of that, then maybe they'll go off looking for easier prey."

"There are a lot of *ifs* in that theory."

"Yeah, I know," Hawker said, examining the gray bark of yet another trunk. "The main problem is, they only show up intermittently on the scanners, but they're not invisible, they're just cold-blooded . . ." He stopped, having found what he was looking for. "And vertical."

McCarter's eyes took in the tree in front of Hawker. The massive Brazil nut tree had to be ten feet thick at the base. It soared upward for two hundred feet or more, its branches spreading through three layers of canopy, supporting nests and orchids and different species of animals at various levels, though nothing appeared to be living in it now. Its branches blotted out the sky in a pattern of overlapping shadows and multiple hues of chlorophyllic green.

"Vertical," McCarter said, looking up.

Hawker nodded. "When we saw them in the cave, they were climbing around on the ceiling. And the one that took Kaufman went straight up into the canopy. Vertical. But our defenses are set up to look for the horizontal, the man on the ground. The heat sensors can't see these things at all and the motion trackers only see them when they drop down. That's why they seem to appear and disappear. But if we can recalibrate the motion sensors and point them up in the trees at the proper angle, then we can spot them earlier, and do something about it. But to do that we're going to have to know how high they climb."

McCarter examined what Hawker had found, deep gouges running up and down the trunk. The grooves began at a point five feet off the ground and tracked straight up, deep claw marks in the living wood.

"They must scurry right up," McCarter said. "Like a repair man on a telephone pole."

"Yeah," Hawker agreed, "and we have to get up there and see how high. Give me a boost."

Reluctantly, McCarter laid down his rifle and put his hands together, interlocking his fingers. As Hawker stepped into the hold, McCarter boosted him up and

Hawker stretched and grabbed the lowest branch, then pulled himself up.

As soon as Hawker was in the tree, McCarter snatched up his rifle and checked the area around him. "How high are you planning to go?"

"As high as they went," Hawker said.

McCarter glanced up as Hawker ascended through the branches. "How long do you think it's going to take?"

"I'm not sure," Hawker said. "Do you have an appointment or something to get to?"

"No it's just . . . Never mind," McCarter said, studying the jungle around him. He wasn't too sure he liked the idea of being alone on the forest floor, but if the creatures used the trees to get around he certainly didn't want to be up there either. "I knew this was a bad idea," he mumbled to himself. "I can't believe we're out here."

"We should be okay," Hawker said. "I think they're mostly nocturnal."

"It's the mostly part that worries me," McCarter replied. "But that's not what I'm getting at," he added. "When I say out here, I don't mean out here in the trees, with you, right now—although this certainly qualifies— I mean out here at all. We should have left when the Chollokwan threatened us. We should have left after the fire."

"It would have avoided a lot of trouble," Hawker agreed.

"Hell yes, it would've," McCarter said. "I mean, what on earth were we thinking?" He shook his head. "Check that. I know exactly what we were thinking:

*We're the big men, we have the guns, no one tells us what to do."*

Up in the tree Hawker laughed.

"You think I'm kidding," McCarter said, looking up. "Well, I'm not. I'm dead serious."

McCarter was acutely aware of the sudden wave of energy that had come over him. He felt hyper and agitated, intoxicated on a second wind like a child who'd eaten five chocolate bars.

"I'm telling you," he continued, "we should have left that very day. We should have gone right back to that hotel, ordered up a nice bottle of scotch and hit the spa."

Hawker chuckled. "You don't really strike me as a spa guy."

"You're right," McCarter said, realizing the flaw in his logic. "To hell with the spa—I'll go right for the scotch. The point is, we should have left this place to the Chollokwan just like they wanted us to."

"They did seem upset about our being here," Hawker said. "Kind of makes me wonder why."

McCarter was puzzled. "What do you mean?"

Hawker stopped and looked down, shrugging as if it were obvious. "I mean, why are they so pissed off at us? I get it: we shouldn't be here, we're desecrating the land with our presence—the plague, or whatever we are to them. But so what? This place isn't theirs to begin with, right? It's a Mayan temple. One that's been abandoned for a few thousand years. So why the hell do they even care?"

"Well," McCarter began, "it's probably because . . ." He paused, rubbing his forehead and refocusing his thoughts. "I would guess that it's based on . . ."

This time he stopped completely. It didn't make any sense. There was no reason for the Chollokwan to show interest in the temple, or to care about the NRI's trespass. The temple was a Mayan structure, that was without question, and there was no indication the Chollokwan had adopted it as something of their own, no sign within the clearing of their presence or their use of the place. They even left it for months at a time during their nomadic wanderings, something usually not done with holy sites that required violent protection from interlopers.

In fact, the more McCarter thought about it the less sense it made. The two groups were virtual opposites. The Maya were a civilization, structured and rigid— even here, in what was presumably one of their earliest incarnations. They built things and changed things. They changed the face of nature around them. They cut down the forest and *civilized* it.

Like all builders, the Maya painted themselves in the foreground, their temples, their cities and the stelae they carved; all of which was meant to remind the world of who they were and what they'd done. They were keenly aware of the passing of time and very intent on preserving their own place within it.

But the Chollokwan were diametrically opposite. They remained in the background, part of the fabric of nature itself, like the jaguar and the trees and the ants. They lived only in the moment, unchanged and isolated. Though they touched nature in some small ways, they did little to change it. As the saying goes, they left nothing but footprints.

McCarter looked up to Hawker. "They shouldn't care," he said.

"No," Hawker said. "But they do."

"Yes," McCarter agreed. "They most certainly do."

While McCarter considered the thought, he watched Hawker resume his climb, struggling to reach the point at which the animals stopped their own ascent. Hawker was at least fifty feet above and almost completely obscured by the foliage when he paused. "Nice," he said, using a tone that clearly meant the opposite.

Try as he might, McCarter couldn't see the object of Hawker's concern. "What's wrong?"

"There's something up here," Hawker announced, a certain flavor of distaste in his voice.

"What kind of something? A creature something?"

"No," Hawker said. "It looks like a nest. It's mostly dried mud and leaves."

"Well, shouldn't there be nests up there?" McCarter asked. "I mean, a lot of animals—"

"There's a hand sticking out of it."

McCarter's face scrunched up. "Ah, yes," he said. "That's not good."

"Watch out," Hawker said. "I'm going to see if I can knock it down."

McCarter stepped away from the base of the tree, to a spot where he could see better. Hawker was fifty feet above, kicking at an oval-shaped formation of dried mud. The nest was attached to the tree in the Y angle between the main trunk and a large branch. McCarter couldn't see the hand, but the cocoon was large enough that it might have encased a man.

As Hawker kicked at it, mud began to flake off and

crack. McCarter stepped back farther to avoid the debris that was raining down. After a half-dozen shots, the entire thing broke free and went tumbling earthward, hitting the ground with a loud crunch.

While Hawker continued his investigation in the tree, McCarter moved to the fallen cocoon. With a stick, he began to pry away the caked mud, and before long he could see the man's face and his upper torso. He recognized the clothing as the same fatigues Kaufman's men had worn. He pried another large chunk from the man's chest and then stopped. He thought he'd seen the man's arm move.

He blinked and stared, careful not to interfere. And then it moved again. A slight move, like the man was signaling.

## CHAPTER 41

Grabbing his radio, McCarter signaled for help. "Danielle," he said. "We have a problem. Bring the medical kit. Hurry!"

McCarter's call brought a near-panic-stricken reply from Danielle. *"Why? What's wrong? What's happened?"*

"Um . . . ah . . . nothing has happened," McCarter mumbled, realizing how his message must have sounded back at the ranch. "Nothing bad anyway. Well, not too bad. Well, actually kind of bad." He stopped and gathered his thoughts. "Hawker and I are both okay," he clarified. "But we've found someone else who might need your help."

There was a brief delay and then Danielle replied that she was on her way.

As Hawker began his descent, McCarter examined the man more closely. He prodded and poked for a minute, but saw no more movement. He touched the man's skin. It was cold, and McCarter realized that the man was, in fact, quite dead.

When Danielle arrived a moment later, a quick inspection told her the same thing. "This man is pretty much beyond hope, Professor."

"I know," McCarter said, sheepishly. "I was confused. His arm moved. It moved twice, actually. I thought he was . . . you know . . . alive."

From the lowest branch Hawker jumped down. "Good thing he was dead," Hawker noted. "Because that fall would have hurt like hell."

Together, Danielle and McCarter cleared away the rest of the encasing mud, revealing two large holes bored in the man's chest. Cutting his shirt away revealed a group of blackened bulges under his skin. They'd seen those wounds before, on the body of the Nuree man found floating in the water.

This time, however, there appeared to be movement in the swollen bulges, little displacements running like quicksilver, back and forth under the skin.

"Gas bubbles," Danielle guessed. "I bet the movement of these bubbles tugged on the skin and caused his arm to flinch."

McCarter was relieved. "At least I'm not crazy," he said.

Danielle put on a pair of latex gloves and pulled out a scalpel blade.

"What are you going to do?" Hawker asked, sounding slightly nervous.

She looked up at him. "You wanted information, right?"

"Are you a surgeon or something?"

"No, but one of my degrees was in microbiology. We dissected all kinds of things." Without waiting she sliced into one of the bubbles. It split open with a pop and a small amount of blood squirted out. Hawker stepped back.

Danielle looked up. "Are you all right?"

"Just trying to stay out of your way."

As Hawker stepped back, Danielle repositioned the man's arm; it moved freely. "That's strange," she said. "Rigor mortis hasn't set in yet." She looked the body over. Like the man in the river, there appeared to have been little decomposition at all.

With a hypodermic needle she drew blood and deposited it in a test tube. Next she examined the damage done by the punctures; they went through a rib and deep into the chest but not out the other side. A controlled punch. Again, just like the man they'd found in the river. She began to think that Verhoven's guess might have been correct; perhaps the Chollokwan had tied the Nuree man up as a sacrifice to the animals. But then why hadn't he struggled against the rope? And why, after throwing him in the river, did they tie stones to his feet and a floating log to keep him from sinking? Had the Chollokwan really dragged him there and sent him down river as a warning to the Nuree?

She went in for another sample, and spotted something moving in the remnants of the blister she'd just lanced. She pulled back, watching. "That's strange," she said.

"There's not a lot here that isn't strange," Hawker said, "so maybe you could be more specific."

She smiled but didn't reply; instead she used a pair of tongs to extract a slimy, gray object from the man's chest cavity. It resembled a leech, but with two long tendrils trailing that remained attached to something in his chest.

She put the parasite down without cutting the tendrils and went for the connection point, a major blood vessel just above the man's heart. Cutting out a section of the artery, she pulled the bloodsucker free.

The leechlike parasite wriggled impatiently against the grip of the tongs. The tendrils released the section of artery and began snaking back and forth, curling in on themselves like a pair of miniature fire hoses that had broken loose. They seemed to be searching for something.

"What is that?" McCarter asked.

"I'm guessing it's the reproductive form of those animals," she said.

Hawker looked even less enthusiastic than before. "A larva?"

She nodded. "Deposited as a parasite."

Hawker's face wrinkled in disgust. "Are you sure?"

"No," she said. "But it seems likely. Many species reproduce through parasitic means, insects especially. Wasps in particular. They sting other insects, paralyze them and deposit their eggs. In such cases the host lives while it is consumed from the inside."

"More insectlike traits," McCarter noted.

Danielle pointed out the thin, veinlike tendrils, which were longer than the larva itself. "I'd bet it's been feeding off the nutrients in his bloodstream. Its own waste gasses probably caused those bubbles."

She held it toward Hawker for a better look.

He stepped back again. "Take it easy with that thing."

Laughing, she turned to McCarter, who seemed more interested.

"What about the other welts?" he asked.

She placed the grub in a container and went back to the body. Sure enough, each dark bruiselike blister contained another larva.

"I'm going to study this thing," Danielle said. "It might tell us something."

Hawker looked unhappy. "I knew you were going to say that. Just don't lose track of it, all right? I'd hate to wake up with that thing in my foxhole."

As she placed the last of the larvae in a jar, Hawker used his radio to call Verhoven. "Bring out some of Kaufman's C-4, a handful of fuses and some wire," he said.

"What are you going to do with that?" Danielle asked.

"I'm going to booby-trap it," Hawker said.

"What?" Danielle and McCarter asked the question simultaneously, shock and disgust in their voices.

"Look," he said. "They took the bodies we buried. They're going to get this poor son of a bitch anyway. Going to get him again, apparently. I'm going to use it to our advantage."

There was something vile in the thought of using a dead human body as bait for a trap, but at this point survival was all that mattered, and neither Danielle or McCarter questioned him further.

While Danielle finished taking samples, Verhoven arrived with the explosives. Hawker rigged the body and then climbed the trees to do the same here. The others waited for him to come down and then they walked back to camp together.

McCarter turned to Hawker. "Did we learn what we needed to know?"

"More than we even wanted to," Hawker said.

McCarter nodded, thinking Hawker meant the body and the larva, and indirectly, he was right, but Hawker was concerned with more than the body of one dead soldier and the grubs that had come from it. At the top of the trees he'd seen cocoons of all sizes spread out among the branches, dozens of them, like an orchard of rotting fruit. Some appeared to be new, with dark mud and smooth sides, while others were older and dried out and still others were only broken husks, the larvae—and whatever else had been inside—long since gone.

He now understood why they'd seen no wildlife to speak of. The animals had been clearing the forest of every living thing. The proof hung rotting in the trees.

## CHAPTER 42

As soon as he made it back to the camp, McCarter began searching for the things that had been taken from them, his notebook and drawings in particular. He dug through piles of Kaufman's supplies and equipment, violently slinging aside anything that wasn't what he was looking for. And feeling triumphantly empowered as he did so.

A cough from behind him put a stop to it. "Professor?"

He turned to see Susan, dirty-faced, her rifle slung over her shoulder.

"Shouldn't you be resting?" he asked.

"I can't sleep," she said. "Every sound makes me jump, and I'd rather not sleep than keep waking up like that."

He could understand that, he'd found sleep hard to come by himself.

"What are you doing?" she asked. "I mean, it looks like fun but—"

"Ah yes, I'm looking for something," he said. "Trying to take back what's ours, actually."

She held up his old leather-bound notebooks. "I

didn't want you to forget them when we got out of here," she said.

McCarter could almost feel his eyes welling up with tears. She was just a kid. He couldn't imagine how she was dealing with what she'd been through. What they were all going through. "And your family didn't think you could hack it out here," he said.

"Can you believe it?" she said, tears welling up in her eyes just a bit. "I turned down Paris for this."

McCarter took the notebooks from her and sat down. "We'll get you there," he said. "In the meantime, you want to help me with what's basically a pointless academic question?"

She unshouldered her rifle. "Sure, maybe it'll help me feel normal again." She sat down next to him. "What are we trying to figure out?"

"Hawker asked me a question about this place," he said.

"Hawker?"

"He's quite smart," McCarter said. "Despite what he'd have us think. He notices things. And of all people, he noticed that the Chollokwan have an unexplainably strong interest in an abandoned temple that has nothing to do with them. Any thoughts?"

She took a moment, looking around at their surroundings. "Only that he's right," she said.

They discussed the question for a while, talking the subject around and bouncing thoughts off of each other, but no real progress was made, until they considered a different question, one that had been with them from the beginning: Was this temple or city Tulan Zuyua?

"It all starts there," McCarter noted.

"We can't prove it either way," Susan said.

"No," he agreed. "But it does seem possible. Seven Caves, the Place of Bitter Water, glyphs that reference things that occurred before the original Maya left Tulan Zuyua." He scratched his head. "If we were to assume it to be true, would that help us? I mean, what do we know about Tulan Zuyua that might tell us something?"

"Humans were given their gods there," she said. "And they left in an exodus, of sorts."

"Right," McCarter said. "And from what we've found—or rather, what we haven't found—it doesn't seem like this place was occupied for very long." He was referring to the lack of everyday items that formed the bulk of any excavation: the pottery for cooking and carrying water, the tools, the bones of animals consumed for food, all of which piled up in ancient garbage dumps. Nor had they found extensive writing.

"We saw glyphs on and inside the temple, as well as one of the smaller structures—the beginning of something, but not a body of work like the gardens of stone at the classical Mayan cities. And in certain places, the work seems to have been cut short, like half-finished sentences. All of which suggests a sudden exodus to me."

"You think they fled," she guessed.

"Abandoned the place," McCarter said. "A little different than the orderly departure described in the *Popul Vuh*, but even there the imagery of them trudging through the darkness and rain evokes the look of refugees."

She seemed to agree. "What else do we know?"

McCarter rubbed the sandpaper stubble on the side

of his face and then reached for his notes. He began to flip through the pages once again, going backward this time, starting from the most recent and moving toward the beginning of the expedition. It was a trick he'd learned long ago, one that forced him to review the written pages, to study the words, instead of just scanning what he knew to be coming next.

Page after page moved through his hands—drawings he'd made, notes he'd scribbled that seemed almost indecipherable now. He squinted at the chicken scratch and racked his brain and then continued to backtrack. The pages flew by one at a time, until finally he stopped and held his place.

His fingers rubbed at the paper, the tactile sense of its fiber familiar to him, the half-circle stain from a coffee mug reminding him of the day he'd written on that particular page.

He stared at his own writing and the glyph he'd transcribed, one that he'd copied not in the clearing or at the temple but back at the Wall of Skulls. His eyes scanned it repeatedly as his mind made a leap it would not have been capable of just days before. He'd found his key.

He marked the spot in his notes, and began to riffle through the rest of them in search of a drawing he'd made at the base of the altar inside the temple.

He told Susan what he was searching for. She produced a printout of a photo she had taken with her digital camera, before it and the printer had succumbed to the electro-magnetic degradation.

McCarter thanked her and took the photo. He scrutinized the image for a moment and then referred back to his bookmark. Firmly convinced, he turned the picture in Susan's direction.

"This set of glyphs," he said, pointing to the left side of a photo that had been taken inside the temple. "Do you remember what we decided about them?"

Susan examined the picture briefly, mumbling to herself as she translated. "The offering to the one for whom the temple was built. Which would be the Ahau: the king."

"Correct. And this is the point of all that deference," he said, moving his finger to the right side of the photo and pointing out another more opulent, yet unreadable glyph—unreadable because it was damaged, smashed as if by a hammer or a stone. It wasn't the only glyph that appeared to have been damaged in that way but it was the only one on that particular section. It had left McCarter with the distinct impression of vandalism. The fact that it was probably the Ahau's name only made the feeling stronger. He thought of the Pharaohs erasing the name of Moses from all the obelisks in Egypt.

Susan examined the photo again and sighed.

"Unknown," she said. "The glyph clearly represents a name, but being damaged and this far from the rest of Mayan civilization, we might never find a matching symbol, in which case we would have to assign it a name ourselves."

As always, McCarter thought, a textbook explanation. "That's what we assumed at the time. But in fact, we already know who this is, though the answer will surprise you."

She looked at him with suspicion.

McCarter folded the page of his notebook over and

handed it to her. On the page in front of her was the drawing he'd made at the Wall of Skulls. The undamaged portions in the photo were identical to his markings. Next to it McCarter had scribbled a name, an English translation: Seven Macaw.

"That's impossible," she said. "Seven Macaw was one of the wooden people. Part of their pre-history, their pre-human mythology."

He arched his brows. "Think about the description of the wooden people," he said. "With no muscle development in their arms or their legs. No fat to speak of. With masklike faces and deformed bodies."

"The body in the temple," she said.

"Exactly," he replied. "At the time of the wooden people, we have Seven Macaw holding himself out as a god, right? The leader, at the very least. But the authors of the *Popul Vuh* have him painted more as a usurper. He's repugnant to the gods, something just wrong, foreign and unnatural."

"Subhuman," she said.

He nodded. "But in a place of power he becomes something more. Instead of a pitiable creature, he becomes an abomination: Seven Macaw."

She glanced at the photo of the vandalized glyphs as he went on.

"Here's the thing," he said. "Seven Macaw was described as having a nest made of metal, and possessions that could create light. In fact, he claimed to be the Sun and the Moon and that he could light up the whole of the world, but even the writers of the *Popul Vuh* knew this claim was false. They knew the light he created could only reach a short distance out into the night."

He nodded toward the temple. "If Danielle is right and that body down there is indeed the remains of a person who traveled here from the future, I'm guessing they would have come in some type of vessel; something ancient people might have described as a nest made of metal. I mean, what would they say if a plane crashed here, or a space capsule like Mercury or Apollo? Even our spotlights illuminated a large swath of ground before they were destroyed, who knows what type of lighting someone from the future might have."

"But not enough to light up the world," Susan noted.

"No," McCarter agreed, "whatever they might boast."

"That would fit," she said, excitedly. "I mean, if they did have such things, primitive people would have a hard time describing them."

McCarter nodded, but remained quiet for the moment. He was thinking of the skull in the cave and the golden filaments that ran from the eye sockets back across the top of it. He thought about his uncle, who had a titanium knee, a pacemaker in his chest and an artificial lens in his eye where a cataract had been removed. He guessed that the filaments they'd seen were something similar, a prosthetic or part of one, designed to aid sight in some way.

"Remember when Seven Macaw was shot with the blow dart," he said. "The heroes took the metal from his eyes."

She nodded.

"It's probably a stretch," he said, "but I suppose it's even possible that the body you found down there, that actual body, could have made it into legend as Seven Macaw."

Suddenly, Susan was the voice of reason. "Or," she said, "perhaps the name and the term came into use later, to describe this malicious force that held the people down."

More likely she was right—legends had a way of being embellished and expanded in the aftermath, and almost all tales of woe tended to derive their pain from a specific villain as opposed to a group, even if that had not been the case.

"Either way," he said. "I have to believe there is some connection here. And if that's the case, then I think perhaps it can help us understand these animals we've been fighting a little bit better."

He watched as she worked it out, coming around to the same conclusion he'd now reached. "You think those animals are the Zipacna," she said, guessing his thoughts. "The son, or apparently sons of Seven Macaw."

"That'd be my guess," he said. "Sons of his, but not in the biological sense. After all, George Washington is the father of our country and Ben Franklin is called the father of electricity, but they didn't give birth to those things."

"'Father' could mean *patron* or *protector* . . . or *creator*," she said.

He looked toward the temple. "So if that body in the cave is Seven Macaw, either in fact or in general, then he could be Zipacna's creator, his father in that sense. Growing the Zipacna in those pools, cloning them perhaps."

"But whoever that is down there, he's dead," she noted. "Why are the animals still here?"

He'd thought about that. "Danielle was looking for machinery. Perhaps our presence here triggered some kind of alarm. Maybe when Kaufman placed the crystals back on the altar."

"Or when we walked through the curtain of light," she said.

"Booby traps do have a habit of sticking around," he said. "Just look at all the minefields strewn across the world, littering the ground long after the wars have moved on. And if that's the case here, then perhaps these wooden people or deformed humans—or whatever we're calling them—set up a system like that here. It's all guesswork, but . . ."

"Maybe not," she said. "I didn't remember to show you this when we were down in the cave. We were talking about the body and everything, and I just wanted to get out of there. But before you came down I had nothing to do but try to reach Kaufman on that radio and pray that those things wouldn't reach me first. To take my mind off it, I studied those glyphs and the other marks as well. Among the geometric drawings, I'm quite sure there was a double-helix design. It could mean anything, it could be the infinity sign turned on its side, but it looked like a stylized drawing of DNA. Kind of like what you might see on a drug company's logo."

He nodded.

"And among the Maya writing," she added, "I recognized glyphs referencing the children, unlearned, or they will not learn, and then violence. The last glyphs indicate retribution or destruction."

McCarter took a breath, thinking. "In that order?"

She nodded. "I took it to mean the children would not learn," she said, "and so were punished. I'm guessing the children were the locals, and they were punished by releasing the animals, the Zipacna."

He looked over at the bandaged dogs, resting near the foxholes. "We have our loyal friends. Perhaps they have their own service animals."

"But why?" she asked. "What's the point? Why build the pyramid at all? Why would anyone want to live down in that cave?"

"Ahh," McCarter said. He'd been waiting for that. "An important question. And I think a most important answer. That temple seems to be a deliberate cap on the cave, keeping the sulfur and the acid on the inside, increasing the concentration in the air. The environment down there is completely different. After we brought you out, you had to wash off with fresh water because your skin was burning, remember?"

"Of course," she said, rubbing a hand over her forearm. "It still itches."

"The water was extremely acidic. It killed the soldier you saw jump in and yet the animals lived in it without any problem. Danielle thinks it's because they secrete an oily base substance to counteract the acid. From that alone I'm guessing they're used to it, designed for it even. On the body you found, we saw similar pores in the bony plates. That leads me to believe an acidic environment was their natural habitat."

"Acid rain in our future after all," she said, sadly.

He nodded. "A ruined environment for which man and animal have evolved or been genetically engineered to survive in. And when they came here they needed a similar place to call home."

"So they capped the cave deliberately," she said. "Trying their best to create an artificial environment down there, one that would keep them comfortable, or at least alive."

"Their version of a bubble on the moon," he said.

She seemed to be thinking it over, confirming it in her own mind, only to realize that they still hadn't answered the original question. "Okay," she said, "based on what we've seen, I can buy into what you're saying. The wooden people and the Zipacna as real. I can even see them forcing these early Maya to build the temple as a cap to the cave because they need the acidic environment to survive in, but I still don't see what that has to do with the Chollokwan."

McCarter answered her question with one of his own, ready at last to link the two ideas together. "What happened to the wooden people when they ignored the call of the gods, when they exalted themselves and failed to keep the days?"

"They were killed off," she said. "Hurricane and the other gods destroyed them. Turning their own animals against them."

"Right," McCarter said. "Their own animals, including beasts that attacked and ripped them apart, something that quite accurately describes what the Zipacna do. *They raced for the trees and they raced for the caves,*" he added, quoting the *Popul Vuh* again. "*But the trees could not bear them and the caves were sealed shut.*"

"You think the inhabitants of this place tricked

them," she said. "Sealed the temple just as a storm came."

He nodded. "If I was to take it all the way, and try to match it up with the legend, I would suppose that the Mayan people rebelled, injured Seven Macaw and sent him fleeing to that temple. And then they sealed him in. With a storm coming, and nowhere to hide, any Zipacna that may have been out here went crazy, attacking everyone and everything, including the other wooden people—if there were any. And then the storm hit, drowning one and all with burning rain."

*"It rained all day and all through the night,"* she said.

"And the earth was blackened beneath it," he added, quoting the ancient Mayan text one last time. As he finished, McCarter watched Susan's face light up. He was certain that she'd made the connection, certain that she knew his next question and the answer to it as well. He asked it anyway.

"And what were the Chollokwan doing with those crystals when our friend Blackjack Martin so casually took them away?"

"They were praying," she said. "Praying for rain."

"Damn right," McCarter said, slamming his notebook shut. "The Chollokwan care about this place, because they're descendants of the Mayan tribe who built it. And they were praying for the rain, not to make the crops grow or the river flood or for any of the other reasons normally associated with such a request, but because their salvation, or at least that of their ancestors, once depended on it."

## CHAPTER 43

Across the camp Hawker stood beside Danielle, staring into an empty ammunition box, now covered with a makeshift grate. Scampering around in the box was the larva they'd retrieved from the body in the forest. It had been just two hours, but the thing barely seemed like the same creature. It had grown little arms and legs and the beginnings of the lethal tail. Viewed from above, it was beginning to resemble the animals from inside the temple.

Hawker could hardly believe the change. "How long did all that take?"

Danielle glanced at her watch. "Ten minutes after we got it back here, its skin hardened into the bony shell we saw on the adult animals. Then the tendrils separated and it ingested them."

The little thing disgusted Hawker and this latest revelation did nothing to change that. "It ate its own arms?"

"Uh-huh," she said, smiling at his discomfort. "You should have seen it."

"No thanks," he said, looking around. There was

only one grub in the box, a fact that concerned him. "Where are the rest of them?"

Danielle frowned. "This one killed them before I could stop it. As soon as its shell had hardened, it became very aggressive."

"All of them?" Hawker said.

She nodded. "For the most part. I pulled one of the half-eaten things out before it could finish, but it would have gulped it down if I'd let it."

"Hungry little bastard," Hawker noted.

"It is," she said. "And I think I know why. I took a sample from the dead one and looked at it under a microscope. Its cells are packed with mitochondria, maybe three to four times what a human cell has. That gives it a tremendous metabolic rate. To maintain such a metabolism it would likely have to eat its body weight in food every four or five days. I would guess the need at half of that for the adults. Maybe less, but still very accelerated."

"That might explain why they're so aggressive," Hawker said.

"I think it explains something else too, something that might help us to fight them," she said.

Hawker leaned toward her, interested in any detail about the creatures that might make them easier to kill. "Tell me," he said.

"Let me put it this way," she said, "there are many different rates of life in the natural world. A hummingbird has an extraordinarily high metabolic rate; its wings beat so rapidly that they're a blur to the naked eye. To keep that rate up they have to consume their body weight in nectar every twenty-four hours or so.

"In comparison, a species like the tortoise or the starfish has a glacial metabolism. To the naked eye a starfish looks immobile. Yet they are moving, not just wafting around in the current but traveling—there are even great migrations of them roaming unnoticed across the ocean floor. You can see it with time-lapse photography."

Hawker smiled at her excitement. "Let me guess, oceanography was another major."

She shook her head. "A summer hobby really. I liked the sun and the surf, and I looked pretty good in a wetsuit."

He laughed. "I bet you did."

"The point is," she said, "if a starfish could see us, we would be nothing more than a fleeting blur to it. Yet, to the hummingbird we move like molasses in winter. Almost as if we're in slow motion."

She pointed to the grub now scratching around in one corner of the box. "These animals live somewhere between the hummingbirds' scale and our own. They move rapidly, they react with incredible quickness." She held up a pair of tongs. "Go ahead, try to grab it."

"I'll pass," Hawker said. "Otherwise I'll never be able to eat Chinese food again."

"Chopsticks or tongs," she said, "you'd be hard-pressed to catch this thing. It jumps out of the way; no matter how fast you go for it, it scampers around. I think it—and by extrapolation they—see our movements as ponderous and slow."

So they would have to be quicker, he thought. It now made sense how he'd killed the one that charged him when Kaufman had been taken. He fired blind, acting on instinct. Not taking the time to think or even aim. It was a good point, a good lesson. "Any other cheery news?" he asked.

"Two things actually. First, the man we took this from had an enzyme in his blood that kept it from coagulating, allowing the larvae to feed off of it. It's likely that the enzyme was injected at the time of death, like the mosquito does when it bites and draws blood. I think it is the same enzyme that retarded the biological decay."

"And the second thing?"

She looked toward the tree line. "If these animals need as much food as I think they do, they face a problem. The more life they destroy, the less remains behind to feed them or to lay eggs in. Most likely they've killed or eaten everything in this area and then moved outward in search of better prey. I'm guessing that's why we didn't encounter them when we first got here. Because we basically entered a vacant space, like a burned-out spot in a forest fire; you're safe among the charred timber because the fire has already moved on."

Hawker thought about what he'd seen in the trees; all of it suggested that Danielle was right. "A break for us," Hawker said. "But why are they coming back, then?"

"Maybe they picked up our scent," she said.

Before he could ask her anything else, Professor McCarter and Susan Briggs came running over.

"We're making a big mistake," McCarter said loudly.

"What are you talking about?" Danielle asked.

"Sitting here, it's a mistake. We should be out there." He pointed toward the trees. "With the Chollokwan."

Hawker raised his eyebrows. "The ones who put the curse of a thousand deaths on us?"

"I know," McCarter said, holding up a hand to hold off the questions. "I remember what was said. But I think it was a warning as much as a threat. I think they made it because they knew what would happen if we entered the temple."

"How could they know?" Danielle asked.

"Because it's happened before," McCarter said. "When we were looking for a radio Kaufman told me you had another team here before us, a team that got wiped out. I'm sure he was trying to con me into helping him at the time, but even then I didn't think he was lying."

"He wasn't," Danielle said blankly. "We didn't know they'd come here, but we found some of their equipment."

McCarter nodded, seeming to appreciate her honesty. "Kaufman told me that a man named Dixon survived. He crawled out of here with a broken leg, which was lost to gangrene—but Dixon held on to what he found, a crystal that came from inside the temple, one that matched the Martin's crystals.

"Okay," she said. "I'd believe that. What does it mean?"

"It means your earlier party did more than just find this place," McCarter explained. "It means they opened the temple and went inside. Yet when we arrived, the temple was sealed shut. So who closed it up? Someone had to do it, and certainly not the men who were running headlong into the jungle, trying to escape. So who? The only possible answer is the Chollokwan. They came here and put the stone back in place to keep those animals inside."

"What about the fire?" she asked. "The first one and then last night?"

"Same thing," McCarter replied. "Bad conclusions based on false assumptions. *Fire for fire,* they said, remember. *Fire for the plague.* We assumed that we were the plague. But the fire was for the trees, where we found that thing." He pointed to the grub. "I'm guessing it was to burn them out, to destroy the nests before the larvae hatched. And then last night we heard their voices and drums again. We assumed they were building a war party or something. But they didn't attack, and if you remember the sequence, the animals disappeared just as the drums came. I'll bet the Chollokwan were hunting them then too."

"With spears and clubs?" Danielle said.

"And pits filled with water," McCarter replied, reminding them of the strange trap at the wall of skulls.

"But why would they even try?" Danielle asked. "It's almost suicide."

"Because they're not just primitive nomads who live in the rain forest," he said. "They're the descendents of the Mayan people who once lived here. The Chollokwan are the ones who stayed behind."

"In the Tulan Zuyua story?" Danielle asked.

"Yes," McCarter said. "And in reality as well. In fact, I'm pretty certain that there's not much of a difference. At least as it concerns this place."

He turned to Hawker. "Don't you see," he said, "it's the answer to your question. You asked me why they cared about this place. The only response I could come up with was that they shouldn't. They should pass it by as if it were just another spot in the forest, ignoring it or at most regarding it as some type of curiosity. But they don't ignore it, they come here every year, they burn the trees back and keep this place clear of foliage, just like Blackjack Martin said they'd done at the Wall of Skulls. They tend to this place and keep outsiders away, year after year, century after century, because it's theirs. Blessing or curse, it belongs to them."

"But you said the city was abandoned," Danielle reminded him.

"It was," McCarter told them. "The inhabitants deserted this place. They sealed those animals inside—just like the story of Zipacna being sealed under the mountain of stone—but it's not a rock-strewn mountain, it's a structure shaped like a mountain, a pyramid made out of stone blocks." He turned around. The pyramid of the temple stood behind him.

Hawker stared at it. He understood what McCarter was getting at. "So the legend is real."

"It's a version of reality," McCarter replied, "distorted through time and retelling but essentially true."

Danielle looked at the temple. "In the legend the Maya left Tulan Zuyua like refugees," she noted, "while others—unidentified others—stayed behind. You think those remnants were the Chollokwan."

McCarter nodded. "You paid me to tell you if this place was Tulan Zuyua and in my opinion it is, at least it's one source of that legend, and the pyramid temple over there is likely to be a form of the Mountain of Stone. In the legend itself the two are not that closely connected, but legends have a way of morphing. A few thousand years and few thousand miles can wreak a lot of changes. But there are always touchstones of truth that remain, and in our case, we've found enough to convince me.

"I think this place was or is Tulan Zuyua," he reiterated. "And I think those who built it were being tormented by a group of people who seemed only vaguely human to them—the body we found in the temple being one of them. They called those people the wooden people. If you're right we might know them as our descendents, but to these people they were despots, and if we follow the legend, the people who lived under their tyranny eventually threw off their chains with the help of a thunderous storm. Finally free, but probably fearing it wouldn't last, they took their possessions and left this place, leaving a band of warriors behind to keep this temple sealed forever. Perhaps they even continued to communicate with the ones who remained behind, but over time and distance it eventually became impossible, actions that are mirrored in the *Popul Vuh* as the departure from Tulan Zuyua, the receiving of different gods and the inability of those who left to communicate with the tribes who stayed behind. Over time the people who left became the Maya, while the warriors who stayed became the Chollokwan, and their one task became a religion of its own."

"But they don't write, or keep time, or build anything," Hawker said.

"If our civilization was wiped out today, no one would be building skyscrapers or jet planes tomorrow. We'd be lucky if we could put up a house without a leaky roof. All civilizations build up a body of what we call societal knowledge, knowledge that's only useful as long as the body stays intact; specialization leads to interdependence, interdependence leads to vulnerability. Break up any civilization and the specialized skills are the first to go as the people struggle just to cover the basics.

"In the Mayan world only the priests wrote and understood the calendars. Only the artisans could carve the glyphs and build. That's how the elite controlled the masses. A legion of warriors wouldn't have any of those skills. All they would know how to do is fight."

McCarter's gaze moved from Hawker to Danielle. "Here's the proof: eighty-odd years ago Blackjack Martin stole those crystals from the Chollokwan after they were used in a rain-calling ceremony. Now ask yourself why the Chollokwan would even want it to rain. Agricultural societies want the rain, not hunting societies. The Chollokwan aren't farmers—they're hunters and gatherers, nomadic and migratory wanderers. The rain makes their lives exponentially more difficult. It turns the ground to mud and keeps the animals hidden in their dens and nests. It allows what game there is to spread far and wide instead of gathering at the edge of the rivers. If the Chollokwan were just simple nomads they would abhor the rains, but they don't, they pray for them to come, just like the early Maya did."

"Why?" Danielle asked.

"Partially because of their heritage," McCarter admitted. "A learned and ingrained behavior. But there's another reason as well, a more important reason."

He paused for a moment, and seemed to decide that

actions would speak louder than words. He took the canteen from his belt, unscrewed the top and began to pour the contents over the torpedo-shaped grub in the box.

As water hit the thing, it jumped, shrieking as if it had been zapped with a thousand volts. It banged into the grate covering the box and fell back again, writhing around violently, flipping itself onto its feet and darting from corner to corner in search of safety.

As McCarter kept pouring, the parasite hissed and spat, scratching at the smooth metal walls, trying to climb. It jumped and clung to the grate, falling back as he finished dumping the canteen over it.

By now, the water sloshed an inch deep in the metal box and there was no way for the creature to escape it. It shot to the front corner and tried in vain to climb the wall. It jumped and fell and jumped again. Springing repeatedly, doing all it could to stay out of the water, until it landed on its back and began convulsing in a series of violent spasms. The box shook with its movement as the convulsions became more pronounced. In thirty seconds it was writing in a death spiral of agony.

Eventually the intensity of the reaction began to wane and the angles of the grub's body began to soften, deforming into a thick, black ooze. The chemical bonds of its structure were breaking down and separating. It was melting, like a slug coated in a thick layer of salt. The water in the box was turning murky and dark with the residue.

"What the hell happened to it?" Hawker asked.

Danielle answered. "It's secreting that chemical base I told you about: the dark oil that was destroying Verhoven's jacket. A substance like that can be as destructive as sulfuric acid, only in the opposite way. It's caustic instead of corrosive, but the results are similar."

McCarter nodded his agreement. "In the temple their secretions were used to counteract the acidic water. But the canteen was filled with distilled water. No acid content. So the animal's own secretions are destroying it."

"*It rained all day and all through the night,*" he added, quoting the ancient Mayan text. "*And the earth was blackened beneath it.* This is how the wooden people were destroyed, and these are the Zipacna, the sons or creations of the wooden people."

"From the legend," Danielle said, and before he could correct her, she added, "and in reality."

Hawker stared at the animal dissolving in its own fluids. At first it struck him as odd that the creature's own reaction could destroy it, but even in humans the body's overreactions were sometimes self-destructive and deadly. Autoimmune disease and allergies were a prime example. Anaphylactic shock could cause a sudden massive drop in blood pressure from a small quantity of otherwise harmless allergen. He could think of other examples, including a friend who'd died when his plane skidded off the runway into shallow but frigidly cold water. Undamaged as the plane was, all Hawker's friend had to do was pop the canopy and release his seat belt. But the water was so cold that his body instantly restricted the blood flow to his extremities, a natural defense mechanism designed to maintain the body's core heat. In this case, it caused the pilot's hands to clench into unusable fists, and Hawker's friend drowned in ten feet of water, otherwise unharmed by the crash.

As he stared at the dead grub, Hawker guessed that

the thing had met a similar fate. As soon as McCarter had dumped the canteen over it, the grub began releasing the base secretions, manufacturing them as a defense mechanism possibly in proportion to the amount of water hitting it. Only, without the water being acidic, the animal's secretions had nothing to counteract, and its own defense mechanism destroyed it.

He looked at Danielle, who nodded her agreement as McCarter began to summarize.

"I believe the body in the temple entered Mayan mythology as Seven Macaw. And these animals, as the Zipacna. In the legend, only the wooden people were present for the deluge, but they both came from the same place—or time." He glanced at Danielle. "And the rain—our rain—will do the same thing to these Zipacna that it did to the wooden people three thousand years ago."

Danielle had one more question. "And the natives?" she asked. "You think they know this."

"They know," McCarter insisted. "They've always known." He jutted his chin toward the forest. "For three thousand years they've been coming here in their wanderings. Always to this place, always in the dry season, guarding it, waiting for the rains to come and grant them absolution for the rest of the year. Eighty years ago, when Blackjack Martin took those crystals from them, they were waiting for the rain to come, praying for it out of spiritual dogma, out of sheer habit. Now, somewhere out there, they're doing the same thing, only this time out of a desperate need. If we want to survive, we have to find them, we have to show them that we know, and beg for their help."

## CHAPTER 44

McCarter's explanation struck a cord with Danielle. And twenty minutes later, she found herself in the rainforest, hiking with Hawker, McCarter and Devers, following a trail to the Chollokwan camp.

Verhoven had volunteered to go in her place, both because the Chollokwan were a strict patriarchy and because her leg was injured, but Danielle had overruled him. To begin with, Verhoven's hand was worse than her leg, and the jungle hike required almost as much hand work as walking. But more importantly, she had a feeling that this might be their best and possibly last chance to get out of the jungle alive. She wasn't about to leave a moment like that to anyone else.

McCarter would have preferred it otherwise, and said so. But with little choice in the matter, he could only beg her not to talk unless spoken to. The male-dominated Chollokwan society would not respond to it, he insisted. She'd agreed to let him do the talking, but this was still her show and there was no way was she staying behind.

As they traveled along, the jungle thickened around

them. They hiked through the rainforest proper now, not the edge of the clearing, where McCarter and Hawker had been before. Massive trees with overarching branches created the feeling of walking through a tunnel, while the tangled undergrowth hid scurrying things. It all seemed foreign to her now, as dark and sinister as the cave beneath the temple, and similar in many respects. And it created in her a low-level anxiety that seemed to grow stronger the farther they traveled from the clearing and its relative measure of safety, like the old sailor's fear of losing touch with the shoreline.

With great effort she forced the thought aside. The animals, McCarter's Zipacna, were out there somewhere. And while Hawker had guessed them to be nocturnal, they knew from the attack on Kaufman, which had occurred just before sunset, that such was not entirely the case.

After observing the grub in the ammunition box, Danielle concluded that it was not the daytime that the Zipacna avoided, but the daylight itself. The grub had cowered in the one corner that offered shade and when she'd covered half of the box with a rag, the thing had chosen the shadowed side no matter how many times she switched it. If she was right, then the animals could hunt in the forest twenty-four hours a day, for beneath the triple canopy, where the group now trod, less than ten percent of the sunlight made it through to the ground.

Knowing this, Danielle kept her eyes on the move. She walked beside McCarter in a loose formation, her eyes flicking between the jungle, McCarter and the traitorous William Devers, who traveled a few yards ahead, unencumbered but unarmed. She half expected him to try something, but he seemed to know it would be suicide for him to run off into the jungle alone.

A few yards in front of Devers, Hawker strode with a purpose. There was a strange rhythm to the pace he kept, moving briskly for many minutes, then stopping suddenly, before resuming the rapid walk. At each stop he scanned the jungle ahead and behind, sometimes pausing for agonizing minutes in complete silence and stillness, as if waiting for some spirit to pass over. At other times, he pointed out the marks that enabled him to track the natives—crushed plants, disturbed moss, churned ground. "A hundred *white faces* leave quite a path," he said.

Two hours of tracking and hiking brought them to an area where Danielle noticed a slight smell of smoke. As they continued, the leaves around them began to appear white, carrying a thin layer of fine ash, like dust on the furniture in an empty house.

And then the natives were there.

She grabbed McCarter and stopped him. There were two darkly tanned men directly ahead and three more off to one side. She guessed there were others still hidden in the brush, but she couldn't see any. The stone axes in their hands were held high and their faces appeared harsh, their eyes seething with anger.

One of them shouted something, which Devers did not translate, though perhaps he didn't need to—it was spoken so violently it had to be a threat or a curse. Several others appeared from the forest and in a moment they were surrounded by a dozen Chollokwan men.

It was now or never. "Talk to them, Devers," she said. "Tell them we come in peace."

Devers took a deep breath and then managed a few words. But there was no reaction from the natives. Beside her McCarter began to lower his rifle in a gesture of benevolence.

Hawker shook his head.

"Not yet," Danielle said. "They'll rush us."

Devers tried again, explaining that the people from the NRI only wanted to help the Chollokwan, not to fight with them. That they were waiting for the rains to return just as the Chollokwan were, and to help the rains along, they'd brought the crystals that had been taken from the Chollokwan so long ago. They would return them in exchange for help.

Initially, the Chollokwan said nothing, staring blankly at the foreigners as if confused. Finally, the one who'd shouted began to speak. His words had an acerbic tone, and Danielle felt quite sure that the offer was being declined.

Finally Devers translated. "His name is Putock," Devers said. "He insists that he is not afraid of us, or of Western men. He says he has killed many before."

"That's comforting," Danielle said.

"He says this question is not for him to answer and that—"

Putock interrupted Devers with another shout, and then he and the other Chollokwan turned back into the forest.

"He says the others will decide."

"What others?" Danielle asked.

"The elders," Devers explained. "The council."

She looked at Hawker and then at McCarter. This was what they wanted. They moved off, heading deeper into Chollokwan territory.

## CHAPTER 45

Professor McCarter had been caught off guard by the native's sudden disappearance into the bush. He rushed to catch up, reaching the others just as they arrived at the outskirts of the native encampment.

The village itself sat beside the long curve of a broad stream, one wide enough to part the jungle and let the sun shine down over its waters. McCarter guessed the location to be a deliberate one. Not only did it put the Chollokwan in close proximity to a source of fresh-water and fish, but it protected them from attack on two-thirds of their perimeter. The remaining section was guarded by sentries, groups of them on the forest floor and others perched in the trees. Seeing this, McCarter began to wonder if the Chollokwan had indeed stood guard on the ramparts at the Wall of Skulls.

Between the sentries burned a long line of small fires, fifty or more spaced evenly in a long, curving arc that stretched to the water's edge on both sides of the village, a barrier on the land, forming the front line of defense.

The fires burned hot and filled the air with white smoke and the fine ash that they'd seen on the leaves some distance away. Stacks of wood lay behind them, which the younger members of the tribe were continuously adding to.

The Chollokwan sentries acknowledged Putock as he approached and then sprang to their feet at the sight of the Westerners. Putock waved them back, said a few words and then the group of foreigners passed by, walking between the fires and into the village.

McCarter strained to take it all in. The land itself was almost bare, stripped of anything that could be used as fuel for the fires. Only the larger trees remained. It was more of a camp than a village, the only structures being rickety shelters of animal skins and bundled wood. But then, the Chollokwan were nomads and when the time came, they would tear the place down and disappear, carrying their shelters away with them. McCarter wondered how long they would stay. Until the rains came, he guessed, or until the first wave of rains passed.

As they followed Putock, they passed additional blazes. Around these fires lay the wounded and the dying, and around those victims gathered loved ones who mourned them.

A pair of distraught women hovered over a recent, bloodied arrival, wailing in anguish at the sight. Other men with similar gashes were tended by more stoic guardians—mothers, sisters and wives long since cried out.

All of the victims had been slashed and torn open, skin and muscle cut cleanly to the bone, or torn away in great chunks. Smaller wounds had been cauterized with the scalding heat of stone tools from the fires, while larger injuries were covered with dressings of mud and leaves. McCarter counted twenty badly wounded men and a dozen more that must be dead already. He wondered how many hadn't come home from their sorties, how many had been taken by the Zipacna and hung in distant trees.

Beside one of the dying, a woman and an older child sobbed. Not far from them, a three-year-old played. Too young to understand, the little boy danced around, chirping like a small bird, throwing a stone at the fire. It reminded McCarter of his wife's funeral and their grandchild dressed for church, who just wanted to run and laugh. As he thought about the universality of life and death, it grieved him to consider the pain his group had helped cause.

Putock led them past the wounded and brought the foreigners to the largest blaze yet, a huge bonfire near the center of the village, beside which sat a mountainous pile of wood.

The envoys from the NRI stood beside it, enduring waves of heat and murmurs and stares from the Chollokwan crowd. As the number of onlookers grew, they pressed closer together, and McCarter soon felt claustrophobic, encircled by a human wall.

After several minutes a stir went through the crowd, and the Chollokwan bystanders parted. The council of elders had arrived, as promised.

The council numbered five, but of primary importance was the leader, a tiny man, slight of build to begin with and shrunken further with his great age. He moved with a grace born of caution and a frame twisted and bent like an ancient tree. Scaly, mottled skin covered his hands and face, and his eyes lay half-hidden behind folds of wrinkled flesh. He was called the Ualon, the Old One: the Great Father and leader of the tribe. The Chollokwan honored this frail man above all others. His decision would bind them.

Before he would talk, the Old One inspected his guests. He stepped close to them, touching their faces in spots and some of their hands, judging them against a lifetime's priceless knowledge.

He looked at the bandage around Danielle's leg, touched the wound on McCarter's shoulder, the bloody gash etched on Hawker's cheek. "Warriors," he said in the Chollokwan language.

The Old One and his fellow council members took a position across from them. Both groups sat down and the crowd closed ranks around them.

A cracking whisper came from the ancient man's throat, his words forming slowly in the strangely labored Chollokwan tongue.

Devers translated. "He says that the seers have foretold the arrival of the 'West Men' and that there would be a struggle between the ancient and the new. He says his father told him this when he was a boy, and now it has come to pass."

Devers had used the term "West Men," but McCarter suspected it was one of his own invention, as there was likely no English translation for the Chollokwan word that described outsiders. He was patently aware that to the Chollokwan the NRI team had in fact come from the East, from Manaus, downriver.

He looked at Danielle. She nodded.

"Tell him we've not come here to struggle against them," McCarter began. "Tell him we've come here to ask for their help and . . ." McCarter bobbed his head slightly, "to return what was stolen from them, probably in the time of his father."

"You'll have to show him the crystals," Devers said. "The warriors didn't seem to understand me, and I think they may have a proper term instead of a description."

Devers turned to speak and Danielle pulled out the box she had reacquired from Kaufman before his demise. From it she produced the Martin's crystals. She handed them to McCarter as a murmur of surprise surged through the crowd.

The Old One leaned closer to inspect the crystals. *"Ta anik Zipacna,"* he said, which Devers translated as: The eyes of Zipacna.

McCarter reeled from the statement. It told him he was right, these simple nomads were the descendants of the Maya.

"Zipacna are the Stealers of Life," the Old One explained. "They are the Takers of Men; the Plague, the Zipacna are the Many Deaths Who Walk the Night. All these names are for the Zipacna."

No further explanation was needed.

The Old One raised his hands outward to indicate the entire tribe. "The People come to watch for the Zipacna, to see if they rise from the pit—from the depths of the stone mount. It has been more than the time of many great fathers since they were seen. Yes, always they have slept until now. Until the West Men set them free. Because of this, the Great Sky Heart is angry, the rains will not fall."

*Sky Heart.* McCarter thought the Mayan term was

"Heart of the Sky," a term that described the gods, the chief god in particular, Hurricane.

McCarter addressed the Old One directly. "The rains would kill the Zipacna," he said. "If the Black Rain fell it would save the People."

Now the Old One stared at McCarter, perhaps reeling in the same way McCarter had only moments before. His eyes were open wide, their luminescent brilliance no longer hidden by the curtains of skin. McCarter had used the words "Black Rain" because they were an integral part of the ancient legend—what he didn't know was that the Chollokwan used the same words to describe the first heavy rain of the season.

*Here they would wait, until the falling of the Black Rain.* The heavy rains would tell them it was safe to leave the clearing and the stone temple behind. In most years there was so much rain, even in the dry season, that they had to arbitrarily choose which particular storm would be counted as the Black Rain, but in certain years, especially El Niño years like this one, the choice would be clear.

McCarter could see the essence of this on the Old One's face and he felt an opening. He watched as the frail body turned and conferred with his council before speaking again.

"He wants to know what kind of help we request," Devers said. "And what kind of help we believe they could give us."

"Tell him we want to leave the jungle. We were asked to leave before and now we will, but we need their help to make the journey. We offer the crystals, the Eyes of Zipacna in exchange for this help." McCarter held up the box again. "Tell him we wish to return to our homes, to a place beneath our own sky."

The other elders whispered among themselves but the Old One did not consult them. He looked at McCarter and spoke, his words flowing through Devers.

"Many who journey do not return to their homes." He pointed to the river. "The water flows strongly." He made a fist. "The current takes men away. To return home one must fight against the power of the stream. For some this is too much. For you," he said, waving a hand over the NRI group, "it will be too much, it seems."

"But the current flows to our home; the river will take us." McCarter replied this way, though he guessed that the statement had not been meant literally. "It was the journey to this place that was most difficult for us."

"Then you must go," the Old One said. "With or without help, you must leave."

As the Old One spoke, McCarter's heart sank. He had assumed that the crystals held a high place in the Chollokwan beliefs, and from the way the elders stared at them, he believed he was right. But it seemed practicality forbade them from rendering assistance. As McCarter guessed, the able-bodied would not be wasted on escort duty for strangers and foreigners, and that, McCarter feared, meant doom for their small and dwindling party.

As McCarter fell into silence, Hawker whispered to Danielle, "This isn't exactly going well."

She leaned over to McCarter. "Don't give up," she said, quietly. "We'll never get another chance at this."

"I don't know what else to say," McCarter replied.

"Make something up."

"Like what?"

"Offer them guns," she said. "We'll give them rifles and bullets if they'll help us."

McCarter shook his head. "What good would that do? It would just be a trick."

"We'll teach them how to use them."

"No," he said. "It's beads for Manhattan all over again."

Before Danielle could say anything more, the Old One spoke. "The time for talking is over," Devers explained.

"Professor," Danielle urged.

McCarter's mind was spinning.

"We cannot help you," the Old One added.

Danielle nudged him. "Say something," she pleaded.

He couldn't think of anything. And the Old One stood and turned to go.

"Wait," she shouted. She stood. A wave of shock ran through the Chollokwan gathering.

"Oh no," McCarter said. He'd warned Danielle not to speak, explained to her that the Chollokwan would take it as an insult if she addressed them directly, that her presence would seem odd to begin with and counter-productive if she projected herself as their leader. She'd pretty much scoffed at that when he'd explained it the first time, but so far at least she'd kept to the plan. Now, he guessed, that plan was going off the rails.

For Danielle it was an innate reaction. And even as accusing glances flew her way, she found herself speaking boldly. "We will come here," she said, launching into a new offer, one she hadn't discussed with anyone.

"We will come here and help the People fight." She turned to Devers. "Tell him we've been fighting the Zipacna as well, we've killed several of them already. We can join forces with the tribe, if they'll let us.

"Quickly," she said.

Looking surprised, but no doubt realizing that the village with a hundred warriors would be far safer than the desolate clearing at this point, Devers stood and voiced her new offer. "We will join our small tribe to yours. We have weapons of great power." He pointed to the rifles. "And warriors, if only a few." He pointed to Danielle, McCarter and Hawker, all of whom were now standing. "Our help would be of great value to the People. It would be of great help against the Zipacna."

Across the fire from them, the wizened old man chewed on the edge of his lip, his eyes going from Devers to McCarter to Danielle. He remained silent, apparently considering the offer, gazing at Danielle for a long moment before speaking. "The tribe of the West Men have fought the Zipacna, but it also fights with itself," he said, finally. He pointed to Hawker. "White Faces bring death to their own in the night."

Apparently they'd been watching the clearing, with mixed results. Try as she might, Danielle could think of no way to explain the strife and combat between her people and Kaufman's, fighting that must have appeared to the Chollokwan as a civil war.

The Old One continued. "These ways cannot help the People. For one part to attack the other brings more anger to the Sky Heart."

"But we can help you," she insisted.

The Old One turned his face to the fire, putting his

hands together in front of his lips, fingers touching like a yoga master.

For a prolonged moment, Danielle watched the reflection of the flames dance in his eyes. She guessed at the old man's thoughts. A great internal struggle, weighing the benefits of such an alliance with what she assumed would be resounding spiritual ramifications. She didn't know these people the way McCarter and Devers did, but she could read the conflict on the Old One's face.

"The Sky Heart is angry," he said, still gazing at the fire. "He is angry with those who have stood upon the poisoned ground and opened the mountain. He is angry, because the maw of the great pit gazes at him, day and night. And for this he withholds the rain. To please the Sky Heart, the tribe of the West Men must seal the pit. Close the Mountain and the Black Rain will fall once again."

As Devers spoke the words in English, Danielle's heart sank. "We can't," she mumbled. "The stone's been destroyed."

Devers translated her words—though she hadn't specifically intended that he do so—and a wave of fear swept through the Chollokwan crowd.

This news was the most grievous yet.

The Old One turned to his fellow council members, and now they spoke rapidly, words of fear and blame and panic, if she guessed right. They shook their heads and wrinkled their brows, their statements too compressed and overlapping for Devers to follow.

Finally, the Old One cut off the discussion. His voice was abrupt. "If the pit cannot be sealed, the Zipacna will return, they will nest until the rains depart. They will come forth again and the plague will have no end."

Danielle tried to suggest an alternative but their host had grown too angry to listen, shouting her down with a voice unbelievably strong for such a frail man.

He turned to go, and Danielle felt sick. Without the rains to drive the Zipacna back underground, they would continue to clear the jungle of life. Many Chollokwan would surely die, perhaps all of them. And the strangers whose help he'd just refused would fare no better. She could not accept this end. She could not believe they would turn down help under such horrendous circumstances.

"You can't fight them alone," she shouted, grabbing Devers by the arm and chasing after the departing elders.

It was a dangerous move. One of the warriors blocked her and pushed her back, while another stepped closer with an axe in hand. Hawker jumped in between, shoving the guard backward and bringing his rifle up—and the powder keg needed only a spark for the bloodbath to begin.

With all the strength she had, Danielle turned her eyes away, lowering them meekly, bowing her head subserviently and focusing on the ground, her hands shaking uncontrollably as the seconds passed.

Slowly the tension faded, but by now the Old One was gone, having passed beyond reach. There would be no more talk, no more speech for the tribe of the West Men.

McCarter put a hand on her shoulder. As she looked into his eyes, she sensed the same frustration; like her, his heart was sick with thoughts of failure, dizzy with the impact of what had just occurred. He tried to smile, but it was a sad look and she did not respond in kind.

Beside them Putock shouted a command and the Chollokwan crowd parted to let the group out. Devers went first, but both McCarter and Danielle hesitated and Hawker would not leave their side.

Finally, Hawker spoke. "Come on," he said. "You did what you could. We'll have to find another way."

Danielle took a deep breath and stepped forward. She turned to see McCarter hesitating. He still held the case with the Martin's crystals in it. He crouched and placed the box on a flat stone beside the fire: the Eyes of Zipacna had found their way home.

## CHAPTER 46

Two hours later, the group had made it back to the clearing. Verhoven greeted them as they arrived, but from his tone it was clear what he assumed.

"What the hell happened?"

"We found them," Danielle said, dejectedly. "And they don't really care what we do. As long as we die alone and let them do the same."

Susan and Brazos looked stricken as Danielle explained what had happened.

Hawker stepped away; he didn't want to hear the details again. He stared into the western sky at the rapidly falling sun. There was an hour before dusk, maybe a little less. Enough time to put some distance between them and the clearing, if they dared.

He interrupted Danielle's report. "Come on," he said. "We're getting the hell out of here."

Brazos stood up, leaning heavily on a walking stick, but the others didn't move.

"Grab your things," Hawker said. "We have a lot of ground to cover, and we have to move while we still have some light." He threw his own pack over his shoulder and reached for an extra canteen.

Danielle put a hand out, stopping him. "Where are we going?"

"To find a stream like the one that protected the Chollokwan village. We'll follow it or build a raft and float on it or wade in the damn thing if we have to. But once we reach the water, we'll be safe. And from there—all roads lead to Rome."

He could see their confusion, their tired minds trying to make sense of his plan.

"The water is poison to these things," he said. "And the sun burns their skin. An open stream with blue sky above would be sanctuary for us, but the water itself should be enough."

He turned to McCarter. "You said it without realizing it; the river will take us home. And it will, but we've got to move now, while we still have a chance."

"What about the helicopter?" someone asked.

Hawker shook his head. "Without Kaufman here to signal it, who knows if it'll land? And even if it does, we might not be here to see it. We used up more than half our ammunition last night, and at that rate, three days of waiting will be at least one day too long."

The group looked around at one another, beginning to understand his argument, beginning to believe in it.

"I passed over a couple of streams on my way back from the crash," he told them. "If we hustle, we can reach the closest in an hour or so, before it gets completely dark. But we have to leave now."

One by one, the others began to move, shaking off the sluggishness that despair had brought on. Brazos grabbed his pack and pointed to the water he'd collected, Susan began gathering the belongings that lay around them.

"Okay, let's go," Danielle said.

"About damn time," Verhoven added.

Their pace quickened as a sense of hope began to spread through the gathering. They were excited again, energized by the possibility of survival, thrilled, at the very least, to be leaving the accursed clearing behind.

In the midst of the activity Professor McCarter remained still. He'd spent the entire hike back from the Chollokwan village dwelling on the subject of survival, pondering both life and death and trying desperately to shake the image of the playful three-year-old from his head.

And though he'd considered surviving the night an unlikely possibility—at least until the advent of Hawker's new plan—he'd begun to realize that there was more at stake here than just their lives. Finally he spoke. "I think we should stay."

The movement around him stopped.

"What?" someone asked.

"I think we should stay," he repeated.

Devers dropped his pack. "You've got to be kidding me."

"We won't last here," Hawker said, speaking in a more kindly tone. "If you want to see home again, this is the only way."

"This is our responsibility," McCarter replied. "Those things are free because we set them free. We opened the temple, just like Dixon's group did before us. We ignored the warning. Now the stone is destroyed and the temple can't be sealed again, and we're just going to walk away? Leave it to the Chollokwan to fight these things . . . or die trying?"

The others were quiet.

"We're not the only ones in danger here," McCarter continued. "The whole place is in danger, the Chollokwan, the other tribes out here, the Nuree downriver. These things are a plague, like a swarm of locusts with no natural enemies, but it's not crops they're stripping, it's every living thing in the area."

He looked from face to face. "Aside from the Chollokwan, and the rain, there's nothing to keep them in check. Well, the Chollokwan won't last much longer, and with the temple open, even the rains will be powerless to do any harm to those things. They'll crawl back inside like roaches hiding from the light and when the storms pass they'll come out again and they'll continue clearing the forest of life and moving on to new hunting grounds. They'll burn their way through the jungle like a fire in search of fuel, until eventually they'll reach other places where they can hide from the rains, places with windows and cellars and doors.

"The Chollokwan have taken it upon themselves to fight these things," he added. "They're honoring an oath made three thousand years ago, and they're paying with their lives."

Of all people, Devers spoke. "Who the hell cares?"

Verhoven shoved him to the ground. "You don't get a vote," he said, then looked at McCarter. "You're bloody crazy if you want to stay here."

McCarter was undeterred. "If we leave now, we may live. And then again we may not." He turned to Hawker. "I admit, from everything I've seen, your plan should work, if we can make it to the water. But that's not a certainty. Not with an hour of light left and the pace we're likely to keep." He looked at Brazos, who could hardly walk; he'd been hobbling around the flat ground of the clearing with great difficulty. How much he would slow their pace in the jungle was anybody's guess, but it would be substantial. And Brazos wasn't the only problem. Susan's asthma made it impossible to run or walk quickly over long periods. Danielle had been limping since her leg had been slashed in the cave; she'd struggled to make the hike they'd just completed, her calf repeatedly cramping for the last hour back.

Hawker's march of just more than an hour would take three or four, or maybe five—and most of that in the dark. As McCarter spoke, the others followed his gaze, and he hoped his thoughts as well.

"If we walk out of here now," he said, "we leave knowing we've killed off an entire race of people, brought this curse down on them and then just left them here to die. Men, women and children—an entire village. But if we stay, we can hold the high ground, morally and physically. We can fight those things on our own terms and maybe keep them away from this place long enough for the Chollokwan to recover, long enough for them to get the upper hand.

"We can't reseal the temple," he said. "But we can keep those things from getting back inside, at least for a while. Who knows how much that could help?"

McCarter truly didn't believe they would make it through the jungle if they left and he wasn't sure they had the right to leave anyway. "Maybe it's not about living and dying anymore. But what we live for and, if necessary, what we die for."

When McCarter finished a heavy silence lingered. Some of them looked off into the distance, others at the dusty ground, anywhere but right at him.

Danielle had listened to McCarter closely, her own thoughts heavy with all that had occurred. She remembered Hawker's words, his prediction that she would regret staying, that there would be a price to pay for what they'd done. Now she felt it with all her heart.

To her it seemed unlikely that any of them would make it out alive, but as she stared at Brazos, the only survivor from the group of porters she'd hired, she knew it would be almost impossible for him.

In fact, as she saw it, there was probably no way out. If they stayed, the animals would soon overwhelm them and retake the temple. And if they left, then the animals would reclaim their nest with ease and then branch back out into the jungle, foraging for food once again. They would find the NRI group quickly, long before the stumbling humans reached the nearest stream, and that would be the end of them.

*Good people,* she thought. *Her people. And in a few hours they would all be dead.*

Unless there was another way.

She'd come here and stayed because she finished things, that's who she was. But for all her efforts, there had been nothing there to find. The only thing left to do now, the only job left to finish, was to get her team home. She guessed it would take everything she had.

She turned back to McCarter. "I brought you all

here," she said. "I lied about the reasons and the danger. The explanations don't really matter, but you have to believe me when I tell you I'm sorry."

She looked at McCarter. "More than that, I understand why you want to stay . . . but you can't. You have to leave," she looked around, "all of you. This is my responsibility. I'll stay and I'll hold those things off as long as I can. If you can help Brazos while Hawker and Verhoven cover the flanks, you'll be able to move faster. I'll stay behind and make life difficult for those animals while you make your way. Perhaps they'll be distracted long enough for you to reach the stream. You never know, a couple of hours might make all the difference."

McCarter smiled at the gesture. "That's brave," he said. "But it doesn't change things for me. I'm not going anywhere. Not this time."

Susan said. "I'll stay too, if that's what we all decide."

Brazos nodded as if he knew he would not make it through the forest. "Maybe the helicopter will come?"

Devers cursed and complained, careful to stay out of Verhoven's reach. And then all eyes turned toward Hawker.

All Hawker wanted to do—all he'd wanted to do since everything blew up—was get them the hell out of there. Take Susan, Brazos and McCarter back to Manaus, where they'd be safe, where their blood wouldn't be on his hands. Apparently McCarter felt the same way, only in his mind, the arc of responsibility cut a wider swath. And Danielle . . . Hawker turned to her, gazing at her face, her sweaty, dirty, beautiful face. Apparently she agreed with McCarter. He hadn't expected that.

"You know we can't win this," he told them. "You understand that, right?"

McCarter shrugged.

Danielle allowed a smile. "Sounds like your kind of fight."

Hawker looked around him, and then out at the approach of dusk. He would have chosen to leave, out of his own survival instinct as much as anything else, but he understood better than the others just exactly what McCarter and Danielle felt, exactly why they would make this choice. To McCarter it meant living for something that mattered, dying for it if necessary, an act that gave life meaning in the process. For Danielle it was penance, a chance to make amends for past choices and mistakes. For Hawker, it might be both.

He looked at the two of them, almost thanked them. "We're going to need fire," he said, thinking about the Chollokwan village. "As much as we can build."

Across from them, Pik Verhoven shook his head in disgust. He didn't give a damn about the Chollokwan or the ecosystem or anything else on McCarter's long, drawn-out list, but he believed in the soldier's code: you never let your brothers down. Hawker had come back for them and even though Verhoven might have made it to the river by himself, he would not leave now. He glared at Hawker. "So that's it, then. Another damn crusade?"

The two stared at each other for a long moment and then Verhoven turned to the others. "Well, you heard the man," he said. "Let's get him some damned fire."

Over the next hour they built a small network of fires

using splashes of fuel on bundles of cloth, dry brush and wood. Soon, thirty small blazes were burning around the perimeter, with others surrounding their cluster of foxholes. Bathed in the flickering glow, they waited as the shadows deepened and night fell.

## CHAPTER 47

That night, Danielle Laidlaw saw herself in a dream. She lay asleep and unmoving, even as three great birds dove toward her from the midnight sky. Two owls and a falcon locked in combat, slashing and tearing at one another, falling headlong toward the jungle floor.

At the last moment they separated, peeling off in different directions and racing across the grass, before soaring back up into the gloom above the temple to renew the battle once again.

As they fell a second time, the trees began to shake and the Zipacna charged from the forest. In the dream, she could not run, or move, or even shout a warning to the others as they slumbered.

She woke with a start, her heart pounding, her shirt soaked with sweat. But as she looked around, the night was quiet and calm. A soft, humid breeze gently caressed her face.

Despite the dream and its unresolved battle, Danielle awoke feeling surprisingly refreshed. Perhaps a few hours of rest had done more good than she would have believed, or perhaps it was the feeling that she'd finally made the right decision in all the waves of madness.

Exhaling slowly, she eased back against the sloping wall of her foxhole and noticed Hawker on watch a few feet away. She couldn't be sure but in the flickering firelight he seemed to be smiling.

"What are you up to?" she asked.

"Just watching you sleep," he said.

"Don't you have better things to do?"

"Yeah," he said. "But none as entertaining."

She looked at him suspiciously.

"You talk in your sleep," he said.

She had always been a restless sleeper. "I was dreaming," she explained. "McCarter has been telling me about these birds. Messengers of the gods: a falcon and a one-legged owl. In my dream they were fighting, ripping each other apart in some kind of death struggle."

"A one-legged owl?"

"The messenger of Xibalba. We found the symbol on one of the stones I bought."

"And the falcon?"

"The messenger of Hurricane," she said. "The Sky God: the one who sends the rain. They were fighting over this place."

She looked around. The clearing was quiet, the small fires burned in the distance.

"Who won?" he asked.

She rubbed the back of her neck. "I don't know. But then the Zipacna charged and I...I..." Her voice trailed off. She wondered if the dream meant she'd killed them, her inability to speak and warn them standing in for bringing them here under false pretenses to begin with. She looked around the clearing for movement—

looking for anything out of place. The absolute peace and quiet stunned her.

"It was just a dream," she said finally, as if certain of it for the first time.

Hawker smiled at her, staring into her eyes long enough to make her nervous. "Maybe," he said, and then he looked away.

Danielle studied his face. She recognized the smile now. It was the same cheater's grin she'd seen on his face in Manaus.

"What are you hiding?"

He nodded toward the sky and she turned her eyes in that direction. The full moon shone like a beacon, luminous enough to cast shadows across the ground, something she never saw in the glare of the city lights. She studied it like she'd done as a child, when her father had brought home a telescope and her interest in science first blossomed. She tried to remember the names of the craters and the vast gray seas, searching for the Sea of Tranquility, where humans had first set foot on another heavenly body.

It was a calming sight, but not all that interesting, at least until her eyes drew back, relaxing their focus. Suddenly, she saw what Hawker wanted her to see: a ghostly white halo surrounding the moon.

"In Marejo, they call it the Lua de Agua," Hawker said. "The water moon. Moisture in the air, diffusing the moonlight. It means the rains are coming."

A pang of hope shot through her, accompanied by the fear that it might be false hope.

"The winds have shifted too," Hawker said. "Coming

from the north now, down from the Caribbean. You can feel the humidity on your skin."

She did feel it; the air was soft, the moisture heavy in the type of omnipresent way one normally felt in the tropics, a feeling that had been strangely lacking since they'd left Manaus.

"The rains are coming," he said again. "Maybe to-morrow, maybe the next day, but they're coming."

Danielle turned her attention back to the heavens, staring at the ghostly moon. For the first time since the chaos had begun, she felt they might somehow actually survive.

## CHAPTER 48

The first half of the night passed quietly, perhaps due to the fires or the number of animals wounded the night before. But during the latter stages, the Zipacna began to prowl around the clearing once again. They set off the perimeter alarms at least ten times, drawing small bursts of fire in each instance, but only twice did any of them attempt to enter the clearing, and neither foray got very far.

Hawker killed both creatures with lethal shots from the Barrett rifle. The first Zipacna simply fell, unmoving. The second was blown apart, shattered, like a clay target on the firing range. A short while later, an explosion erupted in the tree line, as one of the animals attempted to reclaim the body the team had rigged with explosives.

After that the animals became more cautious, lingering farther back in the tree line, away from the flickering firelight and piercing red beam of the laser. By morning they were gone, and the NRI team went back to work.

As day broke, the team began moving their weapons and ammunition to the temple's summit, a spot they would defend to the last.

The plan was simple: keep the Zipacna away until the

rains came. From the temple's roof they would occupy the high ground with a perfect field of view; the Zipacna would literally have to storm the castle to get back inside.

Initially, they guessed that a charge might come from all directions, but as McCarter examined the sides of the temple, he grew suddenly thankful for the level of Mayan workmanship. The three faces without the stairs were steep, a seventy-degree angle or more, the fit of the stones tight and unyielding, the surfaces smooth and slick. Even with the creatures' incredible ability to climb, he doubted they would be able to scale those walls. That left a frontal assault and the stairs as their main concern.

To defend against this they excavated a shallow trench ten feet out from the bottom of the stairway. It stretched across the front and a quarter of the way around either side. They lined it with plastic sheets and trash bags, items that had been brought in to protect artifacts and other treasures. They filled it with kerosene, placing one of the two surviving barrels next to it. The remaining explosives were set at various points along it, and as a further defense, they relocated the metal spikes and other obstacles to its inner side.

They worked the day with their heads down as the color bled slowly from the sky. By midafternoon the horizon was sickly white and the air was thick with haze. The hills that had once been visible from the top of the temple were no longer in view, and the sun was a perfect orange disk, robbed of its glare and floating in a murky, white sea.

By now every member of the camp knew what

Hawker had discerned the night before: the rains were coming and the rain would save them—if they could hold on long enough. But they also suspected that the impending storms would bring the Zipacna home, calling them like a siren to the one place they could find shelter for ten thousand square miles. And they raced to finish their preparations in time.

Out in the rainforest, Hawker and Danielle worked on the sensors, trying to recalibrate them so they would search the trees as well as the ground. Hawker stood by with the healthiest of the surviving dogs, while Danielle fiddled with the controls on the motion detectors. They moved from sensor to sensor, calling back to Brazos to shut the grid down momentarily and then having him bring it up again once the sensor had been reset.

The first few changes went off without a hitch, but on the fourth try a static burst snapped the air between Danielle's finger and the sensor.

Brazos radioed them instantly. *"What did you do? The whole screen's gone crazy."*

Danielle backed off and Hawker asked Brazos, "How's it look now?"

There was a delay, presumably while Brazos cycled the screen. *"It's okay,"* he said, in obvious relief.

"The humidity is making the static worse," Hawker said. "You might want to hurry."

She cut her eyes at him and he spoke into the radio once again. "Shut it down."

Back in the clearing, Brazos threw a switch and the screen faded to black. For the next minute they would

462                              GRAHAM BROWN

live without eyes, and Brazos had found he could not stare at the blank screen for such a length of time.

He surveyed the camp. McCarter stood on the temple's roof by the Barrett rifle, while Eric, the lone survivor from Kaufman's team, carried two heavy boxes of shells to the roof. Out near the original center of camp Susan rooted around in the remaining supply lockers for anything else of value, while nearby Verhoven worked Devers mercilessly, forcing him to pile heavy stones upon an improvised sled, which he would then have to drag toward the trench and unload. A dozen trips had left the linguist drenched in sweat and his shoulder wound bleeding through its gauze.

Next to them the other surviving canine sat calmly, licking at its bandaged wound and panting softly.

Brazos picked up his radio. "Can I switch on now?"

In the forest, Hawker looked at Danielle. "I don't mean to rush you, but . . ."

Danielle ignored him as she struggled with the tiny dials. Finally she stepped back from the sensor. "That should do it."

Hawker pressed his talk switch. "Go."

As they waited for Brazos' response, Danielle bit her lip softly.

"How's it look?" Hawker asked.

The reply came with some uncertainty. *"More static. I think in sector two this time."*

Sector two was halfway around the circle. "Doesn't make sense, we haven't gotten there yet. He's probably looking at the wrong thing."

Hawker brought the radio up to call Brazos again, but before he could the German shepherd beside them stiffened. A second later distant barking reached them from the canine in the clearing and the dog beside Hawker bolted for its companion.

The air-horn alarm sounded across the clearing as one of the creatures burst from the forest and raced across the open ground, heading for the temple.

Caught in the space between, Susan panicked, dropping what she was doing and dashing toward McCarter, unwittingly putting herself right in the animal's path.

Verhoven shouted to her, but she was gone. He grabbed his shotgun, stepped into the line and pulled the trigger.

The solid lead slug hit the beast and cracked its shell, but it caromed off the angled shape and failed to bring the creature down. Without his hand taped to the barrel, Verhoven could not reload.

The animal leapt.

Verhoven swung the shotgun like a club, but the Zipacna crashed through the blow, knocking him to the dirt and savaging him.

Brazos was the closest. He fired and the Zipacna spun back for an instant.

In the brief moment that the animal was off him, a bloodied Verhoven pushed himself backward with his legs and pulled Hawker's pistol from his belt.

The animal turned and lunged for him, the open jaws coming down just as Verhoven swung the pistol upward, into the mouth. He pulled the trigger.

The top of the animal's head blew outward and the head swung laterally, tearing the gun and huge chunks of flesh from Verhoven's arm. It staggered back half a step and then fell to the side.

Hawker reached him a few seconds later, shocked at the damage the thing had done. Verhoven had managed to protect his face and neck, but blood was spreading rapidly from a wound in his side and squirting in pulses from a torn artery in his forearm.

Hawker ripped a section off Verhoven's shirt for a tourniquet and shouted for Danielle.

Verhoven looked at his arm, his eyes drooping. "Where's the girl?"

"She made it to the temple," Hawker said, threading the fabric around Verhoven's arm.

Verhoven nodded weakly. "Stop," he said.

Hawker cinched the tourniquet, and started another.

"It's too late for that," Verhoven said, his voice dropping to a raspy whisper. "Better to go like this . . . than in a home somewhere."

Hawker paused and Verhoven looked at him, coughing up blood.

"All sins forgiven?" Verhoven asked

Hawker stared at his old friend, his old enemy. The man was a ghost already. Hawker shook his head. "None to forgive."

Almost imperceptibly Verhoven nodded. "Damn right," he managed. Then, as Danielle came over, he reached out and grabbed Hawker's shirt. "You finish this," he said. "Finish this, and get these people home."

Verhoven shook him once, as if to emphasize the order. But his grip had already begun to fail. He held on for a moment, gazing at Hawker, and then his hand fell, dropping to the dry earth. With his eyes still open, Pik Verhoven died.

Danielle crouched beside Hawker, a hand on his shoulder. Hawker stared at Verhoven, finding it impossible to look away.

Brazos' voice reached them, breaking the silence. "My God," he said.

Both Hawker and Danielle looked toward him. Brazos was staring at the defense console with a grim expression on his face.

Hawker put a hand out and closed Verhoven's eyes. The black pistol Hawker had given him lay on the ground. He grabbed it, stood and walked with Danielle to the console.

Targets were showing up, at least a dozen already, gathering on the western edge once again. Their numbers were growing rapidly, as if they were massing for a charge.

Hawker looked up. The haze above them had thickened into a solid layer of darkening gray and the sun had all but vanished.

On the brink of the storm, all of them, animal and human, had run out of time.

## CHAPTER 49

Hawker glanced at the computer screen; the electromagnetic radiation had almost destroyed it by now, but from what he could see the gathering at the western edge was still growing. "Get to the temple," he said to Danielle.

She looked at the screen. "I'm not leaving."

Hawker pointed to Brazos. "He won't make it without you."

She nodded reluctantly.

"Fill the trench and light it," he added. "And do it quickly. You don't have much time."

Danielle grabbed Brazos' arm and helped him stand. "Come on," she said. They began walking and the two dogs followed.

Hawker gazed out at the tree line. The trees had begun bending from the wind, branches swaying, leaves turned inside out. In the spaces between he saw movement if not shapes. The animals were there, jostling for position, grunting and calling to one another. They seemed nervous, hesitant; perhaps it was the fires or the remaining daylight, or the death of the first animal, but something seemed to be holding them back.

Whatever it was, it wouldn't last. The sky was growing darker by the moment and the wind had turned cold; downdrafts in the looming thunderstorm. Leaves and chaff were blowing across the clearing in a haphazard fashion. Before long there would be a tipping point, when neither the sun nor the rain was present. The charge would come then.

"Let's see if we can give you something else to think about," Hawker said, as he fired a quick burst into the pack and then turned and loosed a few shells at the remaining drum of kerosene, halfway between him and the western forest.

The container blew apart in a baritone explosion and the animals scattered, but they quickly re-formed, and a minute later one of them stepped through the trees.

Hawker stared at the animal in awe. The animal was a beast; the size of a Roman war horse, nine feet tall at the shoulder, broad and angled. Its jaw opened slightly with its breathing, exposing daggerlike teeth. It perched for a moment on its hind legs, sniffing the air, a hideous gargoyle chiseled from some black volcanic stone.

Down the row, a slightly smaller copy stepped through the tree line, grunting softly, the rows of bristles behind its neck moving back and forth like reeds in the wind. Its eyes went from Hawker to the raging kerosene fire, to the temple looming beyond.

Hawker put his hand on a concussion grenade, slipped it loose and pulled the ring. With his eyes on the largest beast, he hurled it toward the trees, watching as the animals tracked it against the dark sky. It exploded beside them, just as he opened fire.

Dark blood and chunks of bone flew in all directions

as the jacketed rounds from Hawker's rifle tore into the larger beast. It fell where it stood, as if its legs had been cut out from under it. The second animal turned back toward the trees, but collapsed under a hail of bullets as it entered the forest.

Startled by the sudden attack, some of the Zipacna retreated but several charged. The first group fared better. Hawker took down the charging beasts in quick succession, his aim as cold and accurate as any machine.

When the last of the charging beasts fell dead, Hawker jammed another clip in the rifle and drew his fire across the tree line on full automatic. The bullets cut into the forest like a blade, tearing into the Zipacna hidden there even as the first sound of thunder rolled in the distance like the great tumbling boulders.

Lightning flickered across a canvas of heavy slate as Hawker continued the assault, raking the trees from left to right and back again. He fired and loaded and fired again, spent shells flying around him, the gun smoking, the barrel hot, the first hints of rain splattering in the dirt.

He felt it on his shoulders and the back of his neck, a few sporadic drops, heavy and cold, followed by a sickening pause.

And then, the torrent finally came down.

Thunder shook the ground again as lightning flashed across the sky and the rain began to fall. In seconds, the storm grew louder than the gunfire, an overwhelming downpour hammering the clearing and the forest with a sound like a rushing train. The creatures were hiding now, cowering in the tree line, backing away from the gunfire and the wind-whipped rain.

Unleashing his own anger and guilt in the assault, Hawker stepped forward, pressing the attack. Loading, firing and loading again, relentless and oblivious until the bolt of the rifle slammed itself open and refused to move. He'd burned through fourteen clips—over four hundred shells. But it didn't matter now. The rain was pouring from the sky, flooding the ground and sweeping across the clearing in great lashing sheets.

Thunder shook the air as he peered through the darkness. Everything in sight was moving, tree limbs and bushes swinging back and forth with the wind; leaves were torn loose and whipped around like confetti. It was a hurricane in all but name and Hawker stood in the middle of it, balancing with difficulty, squinting through the storm and the stinging rain, getting brief glimpses of the animals in the trees. The dead and injured littered the ground.

One of the beasts crawled from the forest, wounded, dragging its leg. It fell in a heap, its body convulsing rhythmically. Another dropped behind it, its angular head just visible.

Watching the devastation, his chest heaving with adrenaline, Hawker unconsciously lowered his weapon. He heard the high-pitched cries of the Zipacna, anguished and wretched calls cutting through the wind and rain. The animals were suffering from the rain and the gunfire, dying in the storm.

And yet, even as it poured, one of the Zipacna poked its head through the trees, locking its eyes on Hawker. It snarled, looked up through the rain and then ducked back into the relative shelter of the forest.

A few seconds later another one appeared. It began to

pull back like the first one had, but it stopped, whipping its head from side to side, like a horse trying to shake away flies. Sheets of water flung off in all directions and the animal growled menacingly. Instead of retreating, the beast stepped forward, moving free of the trees completely. It tilted its triangular head skyward and released a defiant, bellowing howl.

Next to it, another one stepped through, growling and scratching at the ground. Farther down, a third one joined the group.

Hawker stared at them in disbelief. They were standing in the rain now. *Standing in it!* Even as it poured and swept across the clearing in great lashing sheets. And though it was bothering them, stinging and burning perhaps, by no means was it killing them.

As the full dread of this realization dawned on Hawker, he mumbled an extended curse and took a cautious step back. And when the largest of the beasts looked right at him, Hawker turned and ran.

The Zipacna charged.

## CHAPTER 50

Hawker sprinted for the temple, tossing the rifle aside for speed.

Two of the Zipacna chased him. The leader closed in on him rapidly, reaching striking distance and lunging toward him before crumpling to the ground at a full run, its right leg ripped off by a massive shell fired from the Barrett rifle, high atop the roof of the temple. The second animal leapt over the first and continued the pursuit.

Hawker never looked back, never saw it. He raced to the edge of the trench with the second animal following him. He leapt just as someone hit the detonator for the explosives. The charges blew simultaneously and the length of the trench flashed. The blast knocked Hawker off course in midair and he hurtled toward the phalanx of sharpened pry bars. He twisted to avoid being skewered and hit one with a glancing blow. It punched through his shirt and scraped his ribs, but didn't stab him.

It did, however, hold him, like an insect pinned to a board. As he tried to rip free, he heard the echoing howl of the Zipacna. He turned back to the wall of flame to see the second Zipacna hurtling over it, aimed right for him.

He flattened out and the beast impaled itself on the bars around him. It retched in agony and ripped the spikes out of the ground, stumbling away and releasing a cry that Hawker thought would burst his eardrums.

Even as it screeched, Hawker could see it was not dead, and he quickly realized the danger he was in. There would be no cover fire here. He was too close to the steep face of the temple. The tripod-mounted Barrett rifle could not depress that sharply.

The animal turned toward him, a four-foot length of metal still lodged in its chest. Hawker ripped free of the bar that held him, but it was too late; the creature was raising its claws and baring its teeth to strike. It lunged for him, but its head jerked sideways and its skull exploded, shattering from a stream of bullets.

Hawker turned to see Danielle, down at the base of the stairs, jamming another clip into her rifle.

"Tired of seeing my people die," she shouted. "Now let's get the hell out of here."

She fired across the clearing, as more of the Zipacna began their desperate charge.

Hawker yanked the bar from the dead animal's chest, and then he and Danielle raced up the stairs to the temple's roof.

By the time they reached the top, the battle was raging; equal parts gunfire, thunder, lightning and rain. The Zipacna were spread out before them, trapped in a killing field without cover, caught between the forest, to which they did not want to return, and the rapidly fading wall of flame. At least thirty living animals had made

it into the clearing, many of them wounded and limping, but their numbers were dropping rapidly as the
automatic-weapons fire rained down on them from
above. Still, the mass of the group continued to push
forward, and other Zipacna could be seen sprinting
from the trees.

Eric handled the Barrett rifle, firing at the creatures
with brutal accuracy, picking his target, pulling the trigger, then retraining the rifle on another animal. Spread
out around him, Danielle, McCarter and Brazos strafed
the field with the assault rifles, while behind them Susan
loaded new clips and Devers stood by, unarmed and
panicked, shouting what he thought were helpful instructions.

A group of the animals breached the trench, jumping
the fading barrier and rushing onto the stairs. Danielle
fired down the stairway, blasting the attackers to pieces
before they got halfway up. At the same time, McCarter
took aim over the side at a pair of animals ascending the
wall he had been certain could not be climbed.

Susan pointed out another on the south side and Brazos shot it until it fell away, writhing and unable to
stand.

Out in the clearing more of the creatures were slogging through the mud, slower now, a trudging herd,
pressing forward even as the humans continued to rake
the field.

Hawker grabbed a rifle and found it empty. He
grabbed another, but that one was also empty. He
looked at Susan. She shook her head, there were no
more cartridges. He turned to shout a warning, but it
was too late.

First one weapon and then another went silent, until only hammer blows of the fifty-caliber continued to sound. And when the echo of its last report faded in the distance, the voice of modern man disappeared from the clearing.

With the rain spitting and hissing on the near-molten barrel, Eric stood up and stepped back to join the group.

Hawker asked again to be sure, but there was nothing left. He stepped to the edge of the temple as a fork of lightning ripped across the dark sky. In that flickering instant of purple light, he saw the mud-soaked field clearly. Dead creatures lay strewn about everywhere, while dozens more struggled and twitched, mortally wounded and lying in the mud, their oily secretions destroying their own bodies and blackening the earth around them.

But others still moved toward the temple, latecomers perhaps, beasts that had avoided the slaughter by mere chance. These survivors moved across the field at a much slower pace, as if dragging heavy weights.

The rain *was* harming them. Even if it wasn't killing them in the dramatic fashion they'd seen with the grub, it was doing substantial damage. It might still destroy them given enough time, but Hawker doubted anyone on the temple would live to see it.

As the lightning flashed again, he counted six Zipacna approaching. Try as he might, he couldn't think of a way to kill even one. He checked his pistol: it had only three shells left, and in all likelihood the soft lead bullets would splatter on the creatures' bony armor like so many paintballs.

As the first of the remaining Zipacna drew near the

temple's base, Hawker clenched his teeth and tightened his grip on the pry bar. He shouted through the wind and rain, "Get ready!"

Behind him the others picked up various weapons to use as clubs, metal bars like Hawker's or the rifles they'd exhausted.

One of the Zipacna had reached the stairs now, followed a moment later by a second one—but a few steps up, the two animals stopped. The Zipacna in the clearing halted as well, their heads turned back toward the forest.

Danielle moved up beside Hawker. "What are they waiting for?"

The animals remained still, gazing warily at the forest, their raised tails snaking back and forth, their heads tilting oddly.

One of the German shepherds began howling, and soon the humans heard it too, barely audible above the storm, a resonance closing in from the forest.

Seconds later, the Chollokwan burst from the tree line, howling and raging, pouring into the clearing from all directions, charging with spears and axes hoisted up above their heads.

They swarmed over the Zipacna that remained in the clearing, drowning them with sheer numbers, covering them like ants on fallen fruit.

The two animals on the stairway turned and pressed their attack.

One of them was injured and could not take the stairs with any speed, and the natives caught it halfway up. But the other beast raced forward, charging up the stairs, rushing toward the safety that lay inside the temple.

As it reached the top, Hawker aimed at its head, firing the last shots from his pistol and swinging the pry bar with his other arm.

The animal jumped to the left at the sting of the pistol shells; as the metal bar clanged off of its back, it swung its head sideways and up like a bull, sending Hawker flying over the front of the temple and tumbling down the stairs.

Farther back on the temple's roof, the other NRI survivors were trapped against the gaping hole of the open stairway. Danielle flung her rifle at the beast and it bounced off the animal's head, distracting it long enough for one of the Chollokwan warriors to jump up on its back, swinging his stone axe.

The Zipacna flipped the tribesman off and lunged for him, grabbing the man in its jaws and whipping him aside, but other natives rushed in undaunted.

One of them went for the beast's legs with an axe, only to be crushed under a bloody claw. Another jabbed toward its eye, but the animal swung its head away and its flying tail whipped around, decapitating the man. A third swung his axe in a great arc, smashed it into the plating, cracking both the shell and the stone of the man's weapon.

The Zipacna lurched to the side, then spun and snapped its jaws on the warrior's neck, flinging him over the edge of the temple.

It was free for a second, but then a new surge of Chollokwan warriors threw themselves at it. One native drew blood, jamming a spear into the beast's side, finding the notch between the shoulder and the breastplate.

The pain sent the creature into a howling rage, which seemed to restore all the strength and speed that the rain had taken away. It slashed the man lethally across the throat and face. It snapped its jaws on a second man and plunged its claws into the ribs of a third. The tail whipped around like a flying blade, slashing yet another man, who fell backward, clutching at his abdomen, trying desperately to hold his intestines in.

In its frenzy the animal was fearsome, howling as it lashed out. But the Chollokwan matched its intensity, and though they were dying on all sides, they pressed the attack.

Putock, the warrior who'd led them to the Chollokwan council, was with the attacking force. Covered in blood from head to toe, he somehow managed to survive the hail of teeth and claws. He lunged forward just as the animal turned, the joint between its neck and body exposed for a second. He drove his spear downward and into it with all the strength and weight he had. The surface erupted in a geyser of black blood; the Zipacna's head tilted back and upward with the blow, and it released a hideous, inhuman scream, a sound that echoed across the forest.

As the creature came back down it lashed out at Putock, and he stumbled back with a vertical gash from his shoulder to his waist. But even as he fell and his life poured out onto the stone of the temple roof, Putock saw the damage he'd done.

The animal grabbed frantically at the embedded spear, splintering the shaft into kindling in an attempt to pull it free. And then, as it realized it couldn't overcome the wave of attackers, the beast turned toward the dark hole in the temple's roof.

It stumbled forward, no longer interested in the fight. But the main body of the Chollokwan force had reached it now and they overran the beast, bringing it down with heavy blows and the weight of their own bodies.

It tried to throw them off, rearing up one more time and howling thunderously, as if the titanic sound of its own voice might somehow set it free, but as the last spear was driven home, the Zipacna buckled and collapsed under the weight. Its head hit the stone with a heavy thud.

For a minute or two longer, the Chollokwan continued to hack at it. But as they exhausted the fury in their hearts, they began to step away. One by one they turned from the hideous creature, moving to their wounded and cleansing themselves in the falling rain.

At first, no one in the NRI group stirred. They looked on in disbelief, unsure of what to do. Danielle gazed through the storm, but not a single beast could be seen alive. The only things moving in the clearing were the native warriors and the wind-driven sheets of rain. It was hard for her to believe, but the madness had finally come to an end.

As her sense of balance returned, she asked McCarter and Devers to speak with the Chollokwan, and then began to pick her way across the temple's roof, looking for Hawker. As she approached the stairs, he reappeared.

He struggled to the top, looked over the carnage and then glanced at her and the others. Seeing that they were safe, he turned around and sat down on the top step, looking out over the rain-soaked clearing.

Danielle made her way to where he was and sat down beside him just as the thunder crashed again. "You okay?" she asked, half shouting to be heard above the storm.

He looked at her and nodded, appearing too exhausted to speak.

She looked across the clearing at another flash of lightning and then pulled her wet hair back from her face. The rain was still pouring, but the wind was at their backs. "I can hardly believe it's over," she said. "I can hardly believe we're still alive."

As he managed another exhausted nod, she turned her eyes skyward, squinting as she looked up through the rain, laughing at the sudden joy that it brought to her. "It's a beautiful feeling, being alive."

He turned to her and smiled, a satisfied look creeping onto his face. "They have a saying in Africa: the rain is life." He looked around and then back into her eyes, staring at her for a long moment. "The rain is life," he repeated. "The rain *is* life."

The thunder crashed above them and he closed his eyes and leaned back against the temple's wet stone roof.

She smiled and then reached out to touch his face. Without a word, she lay down beside him, both of them alive and reveling in the glorious, pouring rain.

## CHAPTER 51

The weather pattern had changed across Brazil. The feared El Niño and the high-pressure ridge that had been funneling dry air into the Amazon were gone, replaced by a steady flow from the north, which pumped massive quantities of moisture from the Caribbean out over the heart of the rainforest, bringing clouds and rain that stretched unbroken from central Brazil to the coast. At the clearing where the temple stood, it would rain without end for nine solid days.

Amid the sheets of pouring rain, the Chollokwan began the somber after-tasks of war. As they swept their dead from the field, they came upon the body of Pik Verhoven and carried it off without a word. In time they would place his body beside the other warriors, and the cremation ceremony would begin. Around the great fires there would be sorrow, but also chanting and singing as the smoke carried brave spirits to the sky.

The NRI team's survivors would not witness the ceremony, as they remained in the clearing with a group of Chollokwan warriors.

Under partially reconstructed tents they waited out

the rains. On the second day the Chollokwan brought them food. With game in short supply, it was a powerful gesture.

As he finished a small bite of some type of fish, Hawker turned to Danielle and McCarter. "How long do you think it will take them to cut a new stone for the temple's roof?"

"They said it would be done," McCarter replied. "But I didn't see any stonework at their village. Truthfully, I doubt they have the skills."

"That's what I thought," Hawker said. He put down his plate, slipped out of the makeshift tent and hiked toward the temple through the misty rain. McCarter and Danielle followed him, crossing the clearing, climbing up the stairs of the temple and then down into its interior.

Cautiously, Hawker disconnected the trip-wired explosives and removed them. A moment later he was raising a sledgehammer and smashing it into the curved wall around the well. The rock cracked and split and shards flew in all directions. Another blow sent huge chunks over the edge, crashing down into the water below.

Alerted by the noise, several of the Chollokwan came into the temple. At first, they appeared surprised by the commotion, but they quickly realized what was being done. They grouped together to assist, turning their attention to the massive chunks of rock lying about, pieces of the stone that had once sealed the building. They slid the jagged sections toward the well, lifting them up and dumping them into the pit one by one.

As they worked Hawker continued his assault on the

well's surrounding wall, and when that was finished, he turned his attention to the altar. The natives shouted to their brethren up the stairs, and soon a daisy chain of sorts had begun, with the Chollokwan bringing in baskets full of rock and wood and even small boulders, all to be poured into the well.

Exhausted, Hawker relinquished the hammer to McCarter, and after a few minutes he turned it over to Danielle, as they took turns destroying the altar. In thirty minutes the job was all but finished, the bulk of the Mayan altar broken up and shoved over the edge, a massive pile of stone jamming up the hollow well.

The Chollokwan continued to add to the pile, promising to fill the well right up to the top. The plug of rubble would weigh ten tons or more, making it impossible for any more Zipacna to escape from the underworld.

As the Chollokwan men left to get more stone, Danielle rested against the wall, the sledgehammer heavy in her hands. Her gaze drifted around the room and then back to the ruined altar, where a trace of light caught her eye.

"What is that?" she said, gazing at a soft glow amid the debris.

As Hawker and McCarter looked on, she leaned the sledgehammer against the wall and stepped toward the object. Crouching amid the dust and pulverized rock, she cleared some of debris aside and the glow brightened marginally. She reached down and pulled a glowing object from the mess. It was a triangular-shaped stone, the size of a large dictionary.

She gazed at it, wiping the dirt and dust from its surface, running her fingers over its smoothed corners and beveled edges. It seemed to be made of a clear substance, and it felt like some type of heavy acrylic.

"It's warm," she said, carefully feeling the object.

"What is it?" Hawker asked.

She shook her head. "I have no idea. Unless it's from . . ." She considered the fact that the Martin's crystals and the small radioactive cubes had sat in revered positions on the altar. It made her wonder if she might have found what she was looking for after all.

Upon rescuing Susan and finding the cave to be barren, she'd concluded there was nothing there to be found. But after Kaufman's explanation of the electromagnetic radiation, she'd begun to doubt that assessment. The electro-magnetic pulse had to come from somewhere.

"Remember the Tulan Zuyua story," McCarter said. "The parsing out of the gods, their essence given in special stones."

Danielle nodded and as she stared at the stone once again, a presence appeared in the foyer to the altar room. She turned to see the Old One standing there, another native supporting him. He looked as frail as ever, but his eyes were bright. He walked slowly toward Danielle, regarding the glowing stone as he went. He did not seem to be surprised.

*"Garon Zipacna,"* he said.

Without Devers there to translate, they did not understand him.

*"Garon Zipacna,"* he repeated, thumping lightly on the center of his chest.

"I think he says it's the heart of Zipacna," McCarter guessed.

She looked down at the stone and then tried to hand it to the Old One, but he refused, holding a hand out and pushing it gently back toward her. He looked into the pit, logjammed by the growing pile of rubble. Seeming pleased, he turned and walked over to McCarter. He opened the palm of his hand and displayed a small object.

McCarter looked closely. It was a compass, one that looked to be a hundred years old. It had to have been Blackjack Martin's.

McCarter took it almost reverently.

"For the journey," the Old One said, with words McCarter recalled from the meeting in the village.

Next, he went to Hawker, presenting him with an obsidian spear tip, before touching the latest of Hawker's wounds and speaking the Chollokwan word for warrior.

Hawker bowed in thanks and the Old One turned back to Danielle, placing his hands together like a yoga master once again. Looking her in the eyes, he spoke the word *"Ualon,"* nodding at her.

McCarter recognized that word too. "He's calling you the Old One," McCarter explained. "But it doesn't mean old, it means *Chief.*"

Danielle nodded, surprised by the compliment. She mimicked the Old One's actions with her hands and smiled at him. He smiled back, then turned and, with the help of his assistant, began to walk away.

The next day, with several Chollokwan warriors as escorts, the NRI group left the clearing, in the midst of what had become a variable but near-constant rain. What had been a four-day hike in dry weather became two weeks of slogging through the mud. And even as they reached the river beside the Wall of Skulls, the skies darkened and the rain poured down upon them once again.

Danielle shivered in the cold, but her eyes caught sight of things she hadn't noticed before: fine mist spread on a fern like beads of liquid silver, fuchsia-colored orchids among the trees and a brilliant yellow flower closing up suddenly just as the downpour began.

She'd been in the rainforest for over a month and, until now, hadn't noticed any of it. She almost wished they would encounter another line of industrious ants for McCarter to point out and marvel over.

From the Wall of Skulls they turned south and hiked back toward the Negro. Five days later they hailed a passing vessel—a diesel-powered barge loaded down with mahogany and trailing a second bundle of logs in the river behind it. As they clambered aboard, Danielle looked back for their Chollokwan escort, but the natives had already gone.

Aboard the vessel, the NRI team thanked their new hosts, politely deflecting questions about their battered and grungy appearance, until eventually they were left alone to ponder their own unanswered thoughts.

McCarter found himself spending a great deal of energy thinking about the temple they had left behind. Despite what they'd learned, it remained in the greater sense a mystery. One that left him to guess, mostly, with big gaps in what they could prove or even grasp—much like the study of archaeology itself. Still, in a private discussion, he offered a theory of the temple they'd found. He looked at Danielle. "I admit to having a hard time accepting what you suggested, about the cave and the body. But like you, I can't explain it any other way. Especially considering what we found," he said, referring to the stone in her pack.

"If you're right, the deformed body we found was probably one member of a group. A team of people or perhaps even test subjects in an experiment who came back in time. When they got here they found a world that did not agree with them, sun and rain that burned their skin. With few other options to choose from, they forced the natives who lived here to build that temple as a cap over the cave, training the natives to use rope and tackle and stone. Imposing themselves as demigods in the process, perhaps even over the nascent beliefs these people had begun to develop. In the *Popul Vuh* we see this as the ascent and self-magnification of Seven Macaw."

Susan sat next to McCarter. "I've been thinking about the heroes who vanquished Zipacna," she said. "They were shown to have trapped him. But he's never described as being killed, just subdued beneath the mountain of stone. I wonder if that was supposed to be some kind of warning, if the original tellers of the story knew the Zipacna could get out again if the temple was opened."

"A warning, hidden in plain sight," Danielle said. She looked at the water gliding past. "Like the floating body we found."

McCarter nodded, guessing the Chollokwan had dumped the man in the river as a warning to the Nuree tribe, but also, knowing what the water did to the Zipacna, they could be sure the larva growing inside him would not survive.

"Honestly," McCarter said, "I could see this place influencing many of the Mayan legends. The evil beings of the underworld: the Xibalbans, the wooden people, Seven Macaw and Zipacna. We tend to think linearly in the Western world, one answer for one question. But in many older cultures, things were not as black and white. Oral tradition meant constant changes to the story. Groups intermingled, often borrowing from one another and repeating themselves with different variations. From the same base come different versions of the truth."

Danielle looked his way. "I can understand that. I came here looking for the source of those crystals, thinking they were part of some machine, a creation from a more advanced time. They were parts to us, really—like spark plugs or fuel injectors—and we wanted the whole engine. But to the Chollokwan they were sacred objects that could help bring the rain. Relics from the original Black Rain. And who's to say they're wrong? We returned them to the tribe and the rains came. Two versions of the truth, both correct in the eyes of the respective beholders."

McCarter listened and nodded, then looked over to Hawker, who had been quiet since they had left the clearing. McCarter wondered what Hawker was thinking. While his own mind tended to concentrate on what they could figure out, he'd noticed that Hawker tended to focus on things more remote than the question at hand.

"Any thoughts?"

Hawker smiled, as if he'd been caught at something. "It just makes me wonder," he said. "I've been on a few journeys in my life. Seven days across unpaved desert in a truck, two months on a freighter that seemed to find one storm after another. I wouldn't have made those without something important to do on the other end. But this, traveling through time. It had to be horrendous. Why even try it? And why go back to such a primitive era when you did? It didn't seem to work out all that great for them."

Susan offered an answer. "Maybe the process is not very precise. Maybe they didn't mean to go that far back."

Danielle seemed to agree. "An experiment of some kind," she said. "Like Columbus trying to find a new route to India. Sometimes you get lost and bump into things, places you never meant to go."

"Maybe," Hawker said, looking away, "but it feels like there should be something more."

McCarter found himself silently agreeing, though what that something might have been he couldn't guess. In some ways, what they'd found was enough for him. It seemed as if they'd discovered one source of what would go on to become the Mayan religion, a religion that eventually took root on another continent, growing into the greatest civilization of the preindustrial Americas, flourishing for a thousand years before collapsing back into a less ostentatious but more personal set of beliefs. All unbeknownst to its earliest members, who still existed: the Chollokwan tribe of the Amazon.

The journey downriver continued slowly, the dark waters of the Negro bringing them back to Manaus. As they grew closer, the lush banks of the river widened, and they began to notice huge plumes of smoke at various points on the horizon.

The smoke came from the plantations lining the river. With the rainy season finally at hand, the plantation keepers were burning off the standing foliage to prepare the ground for crops: the slash and burn that marked the beginning of each planting season. Seeing this, McCarter had one more thought.

"We expected the rains to kill the Zipacna, like the canteen water did to the grub. But the air of today is filled with pollution, including sulfur from coal and other sources. It may not be like acid that can strip paint, but it's far more acidic than the rain of three thousand years ago."

"You think that's why the Zipacna didn't die from it so quickly," Hawker guessed.

McCarter nodded, then turned back toward the smoke. "These fires create a little pollution," he said. "But all across America, Europe and Asia, coal-fired power plants are pumping billions of tons of sulfur into the air. Not to mention carbon and other poisons." He looked at Danielle; in some ways he now understood her quest. "Seems like we're making a world more fit for other life than for our own."

Several hours later, they reached the outskirts of Manaus, a sight most of them never thought they would see again.

During this last leg of the journey, Danielle found

herself drawn to the prow of the barge. They were almost home, and she'd begun to wonder what awaited them there. An hour from their arrival, the captain of the vessel came to find her. "You are Americans?"

Danielle nodded.

"Yes, well, someone is looking for you," the captain told her. "They fear you are lost."

"Who?" she asked, suspiciously.

"On the docks," the captain said. "Another American. He radioed us. Looking for a lost group, with a pretty, dark-haired woman named Danielle. That's you, no?"

"Yes," she admitted. "I guess that's me. Do you know who this other American is?"

The captain shook his head. "A friend of yours," he said, excited, as the bearer of good news should be. "He say they look for you everywhere, checking every boat that comes back from upriver. That's an amigo, then. For sure."

Hawker came up as the captain walked away. "What was that all about?"

She looked at him unenthusiastically. "We have an *amigo* waiting for us on the docks."

Hawker's brow wrinkled. "I thought we were all out of amigos."

She nodded. "We are."

An hour later they approached a crowded wooden dock, quite near the spot where Hawker and Danielle had been shot at. After some deft maneuvering around smaller boats, the barge had come close enough for

Danielle to see three men standing among the locals who crowded the dock. Two wore dark sunglasses and seemed to be armed; the third wore an open-collared linen shirt, with his arm in a sling. She recognized him instantly. "Arnold!"

He smiled at her from the dock. "You're a sight for sore eyes," he told her.

The boat touched the dock and Danielle jumped off. She hugged him carefully. "I was told you'd been killed."

"Yes, well. As I've said before: never confuse the official version of reality with the truth."

"What happened?" she asked, looking at his arm.

"Fractured it when I fell, the only thing twenty-four layers of Kevlar couldn't prevent."

Moore explained how Gibbs had betrayed him and how he'd survived the bullet and the fall, only to shatter his arm on the bridge's caisson and nearly freeze to death clinging to the pylon underneath it. He hadn't suspected Gibbs' actions, but believing he was meeting the men who'd killed Blundin, he wasn't taking any chances.

Danielle relayed the short version of events while the others began to come ashore.

Susan Briggs came first, with the two surviving German shepherds on their leashes at her side. Behind them McCarter helped Brazos hobble onto the dock, and finally Hawker emerged, dragging a disoriented William Devers, whom Danielle had sedated as they approached Manaus to prevent him from escape. Last out was Eric.

Moore's guards moved toward him, but Hawker stopped them. "This man goes free."

"He's coming with us," Moore said. "He has information."

Hawker pointed to Devers. "You'll have to get it from him."

"He won't have what I'm looking for," Moore said.

Hawker stood his ground. "Then you'll have to guess at it."

Moore exhaled loudly and the two men stared at each other. But Hawker would not move aside; if not for the man's accuracy with the Barrett rifle, Hawker would have been dead.

"Let him go," Danielle said, firmly. "It wouldn't be right. Not after everything that went down out there."

Moore huffed in exasperation. "Very well," he said, smiling and seeming to approve of the change he sensed in her. He turned to the mercenary. "You're free to go, young man. You've been given a gift today—your life back—use it wisely."

The blond-haired man looked at Moore and Danielle and then Hawker. He seemed unsure. "Get out of here," Hawker said. "Go back home, if you can."

With halting steps, the former mercenary began to walk down the dock, glancing backward several times, before disappearing into the crowd.

Moore turned to Hawker again. "Speaking of going home," he said, "I understand that a deal has been made. And though the expedition has failed, you seem to have held up your end of the bargain. This is not unappreciated. However, in our current situation, we appear to have lost any ability to reciprocate. Our director of operations has disappeared and is under investigation for a wide range of crimes, including embezzlement, forgery and murder. Young Ms. Laidlaw here is listed as missing and is considered to be a suspect as well. And I . . . well, officially I'm dead."

Moore shook his head softly. "Be that as it may, we are in your debt, and if we don't end up in prison ourselves, we will do what we can for you."

Hawker knew the situation. He turned to Danielle. "You could always stay here," he said. "I know a certain nightclub owner who might be willing to hire you on."

She smiled at him; it was tempting. "Maybe next time," she said. "I have some things I have to straighten out first."

## CHAPTER 52

Three months after leaving the Amazon, Professor Michael McCarter waited in the warmly lit corridors of the Harry Hopkins Federal Building. The hallway exuded a quiet charm, its walls covered with cherry-stained wood, its railing and handles made of polished brass from the glamorous, stylistic decade of the 1920s. Surrounded by that ambience, McCarter lingered, having just finished giving some testimony in front of a hastily convened Senate committee.

The senators on the panel had questioned him politely and directly for the better part of four hours. But in a style that he found welcome at first—and strange later on—they avoided pressing him for any type of significant detail. Only in the later stages of the hearing did it occur to him that they were being deliberate: they didn't want complete disclosure.

At the hearing's conclusion McCarter was sworn to secrecy under the Espionage Prevention Act of 1949, thanked deeply for his service and dismissed. Since then he'd remained in the foyer, reading his newspaper and waiting patiently for another of the participants to finish testifying.

As the five o'clock hour approached, the doors to the conference room opened, spilling bright light into the hall. The participants came walking out. Among them he spotted Danielle.

Danielle had been the last to testify and had gained her own unique perspective on the events. To her great surprise the senators did not consider the actions of the NRI to be all that egregious, even though they violated American, international and Brazilian laws in at least fifteen different ways.

One senator even commended Danielle for being so bold in the name of her country. As it turned out, the only real problem for the committee was Stuart Gibbs and his private pursuit of the technology. That had quickly become the focus of debate, and in his absence the blame fell heavily upon him—as it should have. As both she and Arnold Moore had been unaware of Gibbs' illegal actions, they were exculpated—even lauded, in part.

Now, with the hearings winding down and the transcripts in the midst of being sealed, the rumors had begun to fly. It appeared that the NRI would survive, and it was privately expected that Arnold Moore would be promoted to the director's position, though nothing had been put in writing just yet.

Danielle shook her head. *Only in Washington.*

A voice called out to her and she looked over to see McCarter. She smiled. "What's a nice guy like you doing in a place like this?"

"Who says I'm a nice guy?" he asked, laughing at the private joke.

"I do," she insisted.

"They told me I could speak with you after you got out, as long as we didn't discuss the specifics of our testimony." He glanced toward the hearing room, its doors being closed. "Are you finished in there? Or do you have to come back?"

"We're done," she said. "This is the last of the hearings. And from the look of things, we seem to have held our own."

McCarter looked around nervously, appearing uncomfortable speaking in the halls of power. "Can I walk you out?"

He offered his arm in the fashion of a gentleman and she accepted. Together they walked across the polished floor to the large foyer. A uniformed guard opened the outside door to the muted sound of softly falling rain. In late April, a mild spring storm had settled over the northeast, the third front to move through since they'd arrived home.

As they stepped under the well-lit porte cochere, a taxi came swishing down the curved driveway, lights blazing, wipers flipping back and forth. It stopped and a passenger got out and dashed inside the building.

"More rain," she noted, gazing at the drizzle and fog.

"I don't think I'll ever complain about it again," he said.

She smiled. "Neither will I."

McCarter looked at her in a kindly way. "I was wondering if you'd heard from Hawker."

Her smile faded. She hadn't. "Not a word, I'm afraid. No one has."

"Any chance they'll let him come home?"

"I'm not done fighting with them yet," she said. "But

they're attempting to save the organization by the looks of things, and they seem unwilling to make it harder on themselves by trying to deal with Hawker's reputation."

McCarter seemed greatly disappointed. They'd all grown to care deeply for Hawker.

"Don't worry about him," she insisted. "If my guess is right, he's down there in the sun, tipping back a beer at some riverside café, with an absurdly pretty woman or three to help soothe his aches and pains."

McCarter smiled at her and she wondered if he detected the jealousy in her voice. Either way, he changed the subject.

"Are they going to leave it alone?" McCarter asked.

"As far as I know," she said. "We brought back what they were looking for. The body . . ." her voice trailed off. "No one's all that interested in the effort it would take to retrieve it. It's a long way from here, in a friendly country whose sovereignty we've already violated once. To go back would mean another clandestine mission or opening up a giant can of worms with the Brazilians about what we did there the first time."

"It's just . . ." he began, "I wonder if we could learn something from it. Maybe things we need to know."

She'd thought that herself. There were clues to the future of humanity in the cells of that body. Clues that might paint a horrendous picture. Was that really mankind's destiny? Perhaps it was better not to know. "It's buried," she said. "Maybe it should stay that way."

McCarter pursed his lips and nodded. "Maybe it should."

He smiled at her like a proud father. "You're a good person," he said. "I can only imagine the pressure they put on you. I'm guessing you did the best you could with the position you were in."

She would've liked to think so. "No, I didn't," she insisted. "But I'm working on it."

Another taxi curved down the circular drop-off in front of the building. It pulled to a stop, brakes squealing slightly, the rain falling in thin pencil lines through the beams of its headlights.

"Share a cab?" he asked. "I'm down at the Omni."

Danielle shook her head. "I'm the other way, I'm afraid."

"Right," he said. "Well then, this one's for you." He opened the door.

She stepped forward and kissed him on the cheek. "Give my best to Susan," she said. "And please, take care of yourself."

"You as well."

Danielle climbed in and McCarter shut the door behind her, just as the taxi began to pull away. She watched through the rain-streaked window as another cab pulled in for him and then she swung her eyes forward and pressed herself into the seat.

With the taxi moving cautiously into the traffic, Danielle pulled a folded sheet of paper from her purse. It was the promotion letter that Gibbs had sent to her before she went into the Amazon. One of the senators had asked her to bring it, but when given the chance they'd chosen not to put it in the record. Their explanation was simple: they now considered it irrelevant to the investigation. One senator even suggested the promotion was probably still valid, if she wanted it.

Danielle read the letter over again, cringing in disgust

at the words and the ego boost they'd once brought her. With deliberate force she crumpled it up, dropping it in the small bin between the seats, right beside an empty soda can and the wrappers from someone's fast-food lunch.

She sighed, leaning back once again and listening to the sound of the windshield wipers, the tires on the wet road and the static-filled news on the radio. For the first time in as long as she could remember, she had absolutely nothing to do, no deadline to meet, no superior to answer to, no goal to chase with every waking moment. To her great surprise, she found it a supremely agreeable feeling.

Twenty miles away, in the basement of Building Five at the VIC, Arnold Moore stood in a darkened, lead-lined room with the NRI's head research scientist and another specialist, who worked with fusion theory. They'd been studying the glowing, triangular stone that Danielle had brought back from the Amazon.

"It's definitely generating power," the head scientist told Moore. "Massive amounts of it, in fact. But how, I don't know."

"Not from cold fusion?" Moore asked.

The scientist shook his head. It seemed they'd been looking for one thing and found something else.

"It's more advanced than that," the scientist told him.

"Is it hot?" Moore asked.

"Warm," the man said, "but the heat is the least of its manifestations."

Moore wanted answers. "So where is the power going?"

"Most of it is being channeled into an electromagnetic pulse," the scientist said, then pointed to the walls around them. "That's why we had to bring it down here and line this room with lead."

The glowing stone sat in front of them. Clean and polished now; it was almost invisible from the right angle. Unlike the Martin's crystals, it contained no inclusions or scratches. To the naked eye, at least, it appeared devoid of any internal structures at all. And yet, the white glow had to come from somewhere, as did the heat and the power.

At this point, the researchers had only just begun to study it, but Moore expected they'd find similar properties to the Martin's crystals, including the microscopic lines, nano-tubes and other, even more exotic designs.

It was machinery, Moore knew, but it looked like art. There was something mesmerizing about it, almost hypnotic. The longer he stared, the more certain he became that he could actually see the fluctuating pulse the men were talking about. It was rhythmic, harmonic.

"Does it always do that?" Moore asked.

The scientist nodded. "That's the pulse," he said. "The pattern is extremely complex with rapid fluctuations. But it *is* a pattern and it repeats itself over and over."

Moore stared. He could see it, sense it.

The researcher gazed at him, studying his face. "You know what it is," he guessed.

The data had not yet been disclosed to him, but

Moore had a feeling about it. "Yes," he said gravely. "I think I do."

The two men exchanged glances. "Well, you should know," the scientist said, "that we believe you're right."

"A signal of some kind," Moore said. "A message."

The man nodded. "As I told you, it repeats itself, over and over, identical and unchanging," he said. "Except for . . ."

Moore looked into the man's eyes. "Except for what?"

"For one minor change," the man explained reluctantly, "one we didn't notice until we separated out the various phases of the signal."

"What kind of change?"

The man flicked on a computer screen that displayed what looked like a sound chart, a digital representation of this complex signal, with thousands of peaks and valleys. With a click of the mouse, the chart began scrolling to the left. It moved that way for seventeen seconds and then froze. A second color began to overlay it. The peaks and valleys were identical, matching exactly as the screen scrolled along. Except for the very last one, which, in the new color, was of a slightly lesser magnitude. Moore watched as the third iteration of the signal reduced the last bar once again.

"It's counting down to something," Moore said, guessing at the significance of what he was seeing.

"Each new version of the pulse is fractionally shorter than the one previous to it," the scientist said.

"Have you calculated the duration?"

The scientist nodded. "If we're right, the signal will reach a zero state sometime on December 21, 2012."

Moore knew that date. *The end of the Mayan calendar.*

"We don't know what it means," the researcher added. "But considering the power this thing is generating, we are concerned."

The man offered nothing further, except a grim face and a tightly clenched jaw. Moore felt his own concern beginning to build.

He turned his attention back to the softly pulsing stone. Try as he might, he could not take his eyes off it, or strike down the sense of awe it filled him with, or shake away the feeling that the destinies of a great many people would be affected by what was found in that stone.

## AUTHOR'S NOTE

As a writer, reaching the end of a novel is something of a goal in itself. As a reader, I find that same point to be only the beginning of a journey. Whether it's the Knights Templar, quantum mechanics or the cloning of dinosaur DNA, the best works of fiction have always made me want to know more.

In case this book has had that effect, I offer the following.

### The Mayan Civilization

The main premise of the book, that a branch of the Mayan race existed in the Amazon, is of course fiction. There is no evidence of any Mayan presence that far south. As Professor McCarter comments early in the book: "The Maya in the Amazon? I don't think so." The choice to set the story there was a literary one, done for the purpose of separation, both to separate the Chollokwan as far as possible from the classic Mayan civilization and to separate the NRI team as far as possible from the modern civilization we all live in.

On the other hand, the legends quoted in the book

are based on the Mayan manuscript *Popul Vuh*. This incredible work tells the Mayan creation story, the manner in which the world and humankind were constructed and the efforts of two heroes to make that world safe. It contains incredible imagery, fascinating adventures and a worldview both widely divergent from and surprisingly similar to our own.

There were probably many written versions of the *Popul Vuh* in the days prior to the conquistadors. Unfortunately, the mass burning of Mayan books stole from history not only any hieroglyphic copy of the *Popul Vuh*, but presumably thousands of other texts, charts and works of brilliance.

It's a tremendous shame that we know so little about this once sprawling and multifaceted civilization, and a greater shame that members of the clergy were responsible for much of the destruction. And yet it was a clergyman who gave us the *Popul Vuh* as we know it today. Father Francisco Ximénez transcribed the text between 1701 and 1703, either from an earlier document or from listening to an oral recitation. Father Ximénez wrote his version in both the Quiché language and Spanish. The document he wrote still exists and resides at the Newberry Library in Chicago.

In the years since, there have been many translations of the *Popol Vuh*. Three that I found interesting were *Book of the People: Popul Vuh*, the 1954 translation by Delia Goetz and Sylvanus Griswold Morley, which is a clear, concise read; *Popol Vuh: The Sacred Book of the Maya*, a 2003 translation by Allen J. Christenson that includes a wealth of background information and even explanations of how specific terms and concepts were derived; and Dennis Tedlock's translation in book form, *The Popol Vuh: The Mayan Book of the Dawn of Life and the Glories of Gods and Kings,* which is less like reading than like having the story told to you by someone who watched it all unfold. I urge anyone interested in this part of history to pick up a copy.

## Fusion Power

As we begin to move through the new century, we remain heavily dependent on fuels discovered during the prior two, a situation not so different from being stuck using an abacus and a quill pen. But what will replace them? Can fusion actually become a legitimate power source? I guess we will have to wait and see. The big project, as described in this book, is the ITER, which is being funded jointly by most of the G-20 nations. While ITER has been translated as "the way," the acronym actually stands for International Thermonuclear Experimental Reactor. It's a truly massive experiment, weighing 23,000 tons and standing a hundred feet tall. You can learn more at the official ITER website: http://www.iter.org.

As for cold fusion, it remains a mystery. In some ways the concept has become a scientific vampire, continuously rising from the dead. After being written off as a hoax in 1989, it made a comeback in the 1990s as venture capitalists and other scientists took a chance on the technology. When nothing panned out, it fell away once again.

But it may still be alive. Respected labs are now looking at it and once again reporting excess energy, neutrons and even traces levels of tritium, effects that can only come from a type of nuclear reaction. Even those who consider it a wasted effort seem willing to at least look at the data before pronouncing judgment. Who knows, some entrepreneur might yet find a way to light up the world.

And perhaps it will come none too soon. According to a recent U.N. study, by 2050 at least nine billion souls will inhabit Earth. Without new sources of energy and a massive effort to reduce, recycle and reuse, what will become of our atmosphere, of places like the Amazon? What will become of the seas, fished to near extinction and filled with plastic leftovers? The current path is unsustainable. If we do not turn, we will eventually go off the cliff. And if it is adaptation that ensures human survival at that point, then who can say what the people of the thirty-first century will look like? As Professor McCarter states near the end of this book, in some ways we're creating a world more suited for life other than our own.

Thank you for spending the time with me.

Sincerely,
Graham Brown

READ ON FOR A SNEAK PREVIEW OF
GRAHAM BROWN'S NEW NOVEL

COMING SOON FROM
BANTAM BOOKS

*Southern Mexico, November 2012*

Danielle Laidlaw scrambled up the side of Mount Pulimundo, sliding on the loose shale and grabbing for purchase with her hands as much as her feet.

Passing through nine thousand feet, her legs ached from the effort and her lungs burned as they tried to cope with the decreased level of oxygen in the thin air. But with everything that was at stake, she had no time for rest.

She glanced back at the two men who accompanied her: a twenty-year-old Chiapas Indian named Oco, who was acting as their guide, and an old friend and colleague, Professor Michael McCarter. McCarter was struggling, and she needed him to move.

"Come on, Professor," she urged. "They're getting closer. We have to keep going."

Breathing heavily, McCarter glanced behind them. Imminent exhaustion seemed to prevent a reply, but he pushed forward with renewed determination.

A few minutes later, they crested the summit. As McCarter fell to his hands and knees, Danielle pulled a set of binoculars from her pack. A mountain lake filled the broken volcanic crater of Mount Pulimundo a thousand feet below. At the center, a cone-shaped island burst upward, its steep sides thickly wooded but unable to disguise its volcanic nature. Yellowish fog clung to it, drifting downwind from vents and cracks concealed by the trees and the water.

"Is this it?" Danielle asked.

Oco nodded. *"Isla cubierta,"* he said. Island of the Shroud.

"Are you sure?"

"The statue is there," he insisted. "I saw it once. When I came with the shaman. He said the time was coming, the time when all things would change."

Danielle scanned the terrain. The lake sat a thousand feet below them, down a steep embankment of loose and crumbling shale on the caldera's inner cone. It would be a hazardous descent, but much easier physically than the climb they'd just completed.

She retied her hair and looked to McCarter. He'd made it to a sitting position, though his chest was still heaving.

"We're almost there," she said. "And it's all downhill from here."

"I've been hearing that load of tripe," he said between breaths, "ever since I turned forty. And so far nothing has gotten any easier."

He waved her on. "Go. I'll try to catch up."

"We stick together," she said. "Besides, you're the expert. You're the one who needs to see this."

"And what happens when they catch us?"

"They want the statue. We'll learn what we need to

know and head downstream. They're not going to follow us."

She extended a hand, which McCarter eyed suspiciously before reaching out and grasping it.

She helped him to his feet and the three of them went over the side together, skidding and sliding and running where they could.

As reached the bottom, she could hear shouting far up above. Their pursuers had come to the crest.

"Come on," she said, racing across the last ten meters of solid ground and diving into the cold mountain lake.

McCarter and Oco plunged in behind her. The three of them raced toward the wooded island at its center.

Halfway across, gunfire began cracking from the ridge. Shots clipped the water to her right, and she dove under the surface and kept kicking until she could no longer hold her breath.

She came up shrouded in the sulfurous mist. McCarter and Oco surfaced beside her.

The gunfire had ceased, but another sound caught her attention, a distant rhythmic thumping reaching out across the mountains: the staccato clatter of helicopter blades, somewhere to the east. Apparently, their enemies had a new trick in store.

"Where is it?" she asked.

Oco pointed toward the summit. "At the top," he said. "Hidden in the trees."

They climbed the steep angle of the island's slope, using the trees as handholds. They found the statue at dead center—a great block of stone with the outline of a man carved into it, a Mayan king in full regalia. In his right hand, he carried what looked like a net holding four stones. In his left, he held a shield. Hieroglyphic writing scrawled across the bottom and a great snake twisted across the top, with its large open mouth stretching down as if to devour the king with a single bite.

"Ahau Balam," McCarter said, reading the title glyphs. "The Jaguar King. Spirit guide of the Brotherhood."

Oco, who like many of the people in the Chiapas area was of Mayan descent, fell silent in awe. McCarter did likewise.

Danielle was more concerned with the danger closing in on them. The helicopter was growing closer, the men behind them no doubt scrambling down the cliff. They needed to get the information and disappear.

"What does it tell us?" she asked.

McCarter studied the writing, eyes darting here and there. He touched one glyph, and then another. He seemed confused.

"Professor?" she asked.

"I'm not sure," he said.

The sound of the helicopter lumbered towards them, growing into a baritone roar.

"We have a minute," she said. "Maybe less."

He shook his head in disbelief. "There's no story here. No explanation. It's just numbers."

"Dates?"

"No. Just random numbers."

Her mind reeled. She couldn't believe what he was saying.

"Maybe if I—"

She cut him off. "No time."

She pulled out her camera, snapped off a shot, and then checked the screen. The stone was so weathered that the glyphs didn't come out clearly. She took another from a different angle, with a similar result. There just wasn't enough definition.

The helicopter was closing in. She could hear the men on foot shouting as they came down the caldera's embankment.

"It's not clear enough," she said.

McCarter stared at her for a second and then tore off his shirt, dropped to the base of the statue, and pressed it up against the raised hieroglyphs. Holding it there with one hand, he began rubbing fists full of the volcanic soil against the surface of the shirt. Oco helped him.

The helicopter thundered by overhead. Slowing and turning. Looking for a place to land.

She dropped down beside him to help. The shapes of the carving began to emerge, the edges and the details. It looked like a blurry, charcoal drawing, but it was working.

Pine needles, leaves and chaff began to swirl around them. The helicopter was moving in above them, its downwash blasting everything about.

"That's it," Danielle said. "No more time."

McCarter rolled up the shirt and tucked it into his backpack as she pulled her gun.

Weighted ropes dropped through the trees, unfurling like snakes.

"Run!" she shouted.

Men clad in midnight blue came sliding down the ropes, crashing through the trees, aiming and firing strange weapons.

McCarter and Oco took off. Danielle wheeled around to fire. Before she could pull the trigger, she was hit in the back. Two prongs penetrated her shirt and a shock racked her body. She fell forward, unable to move or even shout, crashing like a sack of flour, convulsing from the Taser.

Lying on her side, she saw McCarter and Oco running. Wires stretched out toward them as flights of Taser darts were fired their way. Oco went over the side safely and McCarter dodged the metal darts, only to fall suddenly at the hammering of a submachine gun. A thin spatter of blood flew as he tumbled over the steep embankment.

The next moments were a blur. Another jolt from the Taser; men surrounding her and zip-tying her wrists behind her back, while the trees bent and whipped beneath the helicopter's thunderous symphony.

She glanced up. The dark shape of the helicopter filled a gap in the trees. A Sikorsky Skycrane, a huge beast shaped like a hovering claw, with an empty space for a belly where it could secure incredible payloads. Tractor trailers and small tanks could be suspended beneath it. The thing would have no trouble with the stone monument.

Heavy chains dropped from the monster, and moments later, the whirling blades roaring even louder, the chains pulled taut and the statue that had topped this volcanic rock for three thousand years was pulled free and hauled away.

A radio cackled on the lead man's hip.

He grabbed it. "Tell Kang we have one of them," he said. "And better than that, at long last we've found the key."